The Forest

By

Michaelbrent Collings

Written Insomnia Press
WrittenInsomnia.com
"Stories That Keep You Up All Night"

DEDICATION

To...

Chad Henkel, who is a good friend and always knows it's me on the phone because I tell him it is,

And Robert Mortenson, who keeps buying my stuff even though I tell him he doesn't have to,

And to Laura, FTAAE.

"The dead don't stay dead in the forest.
Remember that."

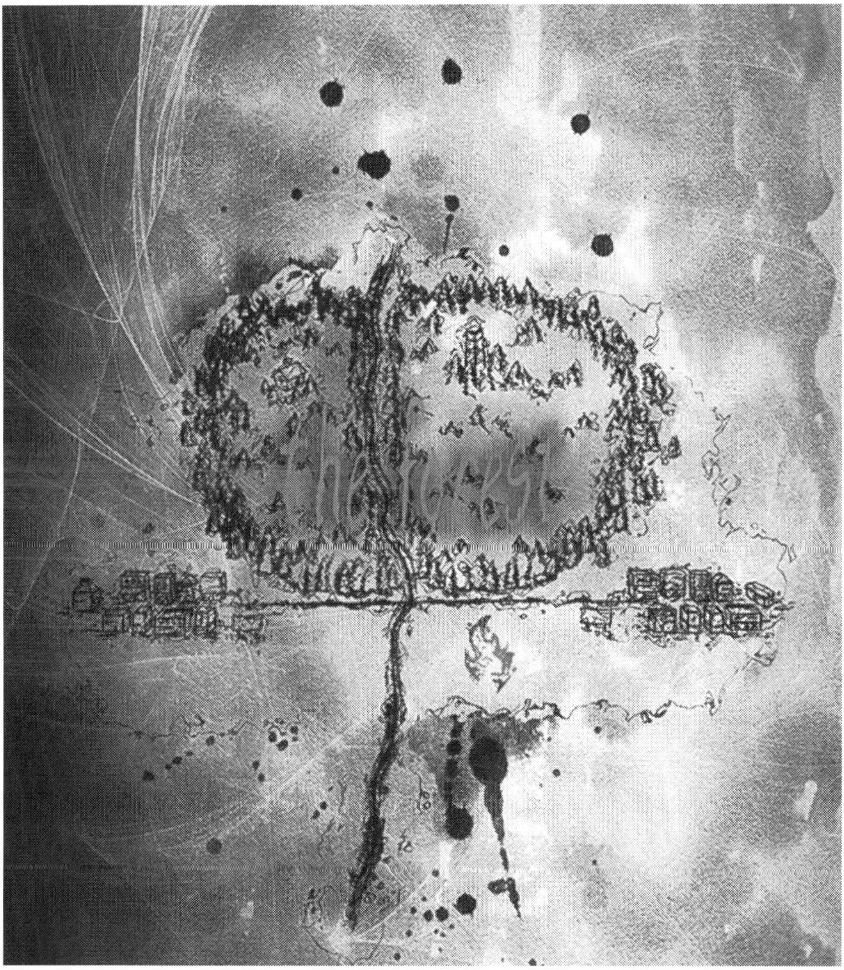

1
Revelation
(When All Has Become)

It is said by "those who know" that telepathy does not exist. That it belongs in the same category as spoon-bending on old late night television shows, faith healers, and real romance in Las Vegas chapels.

Of course, a great many things once thought by the knowledgeable to be impossible have *always* existed, and are being discovered anew every day.

Failure to see a thing isn't proof of the absence of that thing.

Regardless, what is certain is that the two young people – barely more than children, really, though both mature and *much* brighter than their years should have permitted – were thinking the same thoughts as they ran through a place full of ghosts and fog and blood and pain: "I can't die here. Not today. Not here, in this forest."

But of course, that was because they couldn't see their own deaths. So they didn't believe, on some level, that their deaths were real, or even a possibility.

The forest through which they ran, however, had seen many deaths, and *would* see many more.

That is fact.

That is the forest.

ONE:
GHOSTS

2
When Tricia Was Young

The branches of the forest jutted upward through the mist, and Tricia wondered – fleetingly, flittingly – if they looked like fingers from above. Like hands jabbing wildly through the surface of some green ocean: the last sign of someone drowning, dying… then nothing at all. Just darkness.

Or, worse, the silvery light of the mist.

Tricia was drowning right now. So was Alex. Drowning in terror, in fear. Drowning in whatever strangeness had exploded around them soon after they came looking for Sam.

Tricia looked around, realizing suddenly that the person they had come here for was nowhere to be seen.

But he was here. Just a minute ago. Where did Sam –

(You know where he went.)

She pushed away that thought; that reality. "Where's Sam?" she shouted.

"I don't know!" shouted Alex behind her, gasping for breath as he ran. "I don't –"

The rest of his answer was lost in his labored breathing. Just like they were both lost in the forest, and would likely remain lost for the rest of their lives.

However… long… that is…

Even in her mind, she was gasping. Even in her mind, Tricia was almost out of strength.

How long could someone run before she had a heart attack and died? she thought.

She didn't know. So *many* things she didn't know. Like where Sam had disappeared to. Like where the ghosts had come from, or…

The man in the tree.

None of it made sense. At least she knew there was someone actually following them – not the whispering ghosts, but a real person. Even that was no comfort, because there is no comfort in knowing you're being chased by a maniac.

Tricia dared a look over her shoulder. The forest was silent, save Alex's panting. She suspected he could have kept up with her, pace for pace. They were so alike in so many ways it would have been no surprise. But there was no room to run side by side here. He had fallen back, that much closer to the person –

(And the things.*)*

– that followed them.

Tricia only glanced back for a moment – she had no desire to be one of those idiot "heroines" in a horror movie, who stumbled over a root at just the right time to get massacred. But a moment was enough – enough to *see.* Even through the mist that had swallowed her and Alex along with most of the forest, she could still see and hear the shadows all around them.

One shadow belonged to a madwoman, real and terrible. The others were unknowns. Wraiths in the mist. Unreal, impossible – but undeniable, just the same, and far *more* terrible for that.

She and Alex stopped running – just for a moment. Alex bent over, air heaving in and out of him.

"We have to find him," Tricia said. "We have to find Sam."

Alex didn't answer, but she saw him grit his teeth and dig deep for the strength to run more and run faster.

Tricia turned around as she caught something out of the corner of her eye – almost fell, how stupid stupid *stupid* – and saw…

"Sam!" She spun again. Looking for Alex, to make sure he had seen, too. She found Alex in the mist –

(So thick I can barely see him even this close, and besides that he seems farther *somehow. The forest again, always playing games with the what and when and where of it all.)*

– and then shouted, "Alex, I see him!"

Alex nodded curtly, even as Tricia turned toward the boy they had come to find.

Sam was their age, about the same height as Alex and Tricia. But he was thinner, and the bright red backpack he wore seemed somehow to make him even smaller. To diminish him in a way that Tricia wouldn't have thought possible.

Though what of any of this *was* possible?

Sam stood still. Maybe twenty feet away, barely visible through the fog all around. Tricia ran as hard as she could, trying to ignore the fact that she didn't know if it was day or night, or how long they had been in this place. The forest, it seemed, was a place out of time. Eternal, and unforgiving.

"Sam!" she shrieked. The mist boiled around them.

Sam's face twisted in relief. "You came for me," he said, his voice breaking as tears threatened.

Almost at the same time, Tricia heard the whispers.

"Sam, *run!*" Alex shouted behind her.

Tricia glanced at Alex: her best friend for so long she couldn't remember a time without him. So long that "we" came easier to both their lips than "I."

She found Alex in the mist. He wasn't looking at her *or* Sam. He was looking *beyond* Sam. And at the same time, the mist flashed, as it had so many times to signal that things were about to get even worse.

Something is coming.

Tricia looked forward again, expecting to see Sam close ahead. She had been running forever, and surely she must have reached him by now.

But he seemed not closer, but *farther* away. The forest had played another trick and bent time and space and existence itself to keep Tricia and Alex from saving their friend.

She saw something in the mist behind Sam.

It's her. It's his mother!

The whispers around them grew, even as the shapes and shadows that surrounded them darkened. The wraiths – the whisperers – closed in. The whispers became sibilant hisses, then murmured sounds not-quite-heard. Then words. Snatches.

"... get out of this place..."

"... hear anything..."

"... see anything..."

"... just fog..."

"... turn around..."

"... this rotting place..."

Sam was shouting, "Where's my mom? *WHERE'S MY MOTHER?*"

From anyone else in this situation, the scream would be one of pleading. Asking the heavens to send the one person required to save a child. But Tricia knew Sam meant exactly the opposite. The whispers and shadows were bad, but in a photo finish for absolute worst was Sam's mother. She had brought her son here to kill him, and now wanted Tricia and Alex dead as well. The woman ran at Sam from behind, the knife she held flashing brightly in the strange glow of the mist.

"Where is she?" Sam shouted. Still far away, and seeming to draw farther from Tricia with every step she took. "Where is*aaaaugh*!"

His scream turned to a wordless shriek as he looked over his shoulder and saw his mother. Saw what Tricia did: that he was far closer to the madwoman than to either of his friends, his "rescuers."

Some rescuers we turned out to be.

"Don't!" Sam shrieked, holding up his hands as though to ward off the knife, and at the same time Tricia heard the same word burst out of her own throat, and from Alex's as well.

In answer, Sam's mother bared her teeth and slashed the air. She slashed again, then screamed as she ran toward her son, "Just *die*. Just *die and let everything never begin again."*

The glowing mist pulsed, and pulsed, and became a continuously flashing thing, the lights that had appeared at random through this nightmare now continuously surging on-off-on-off-on-off with the regularity of a metronome.

Or a heart. A breath. The mist is alive, the forest *is alive.*

The light pulsed, and each brightness felt like a cut against Tricia's mind. She winced away from the lights and from whatever madness had caused them.

"You have to die!" Sam's mother shrieked, and Tricia realized the woman wasn't just shouting, she was *sobbing*. Whatever had shattered her mind, some grief lay at the base of it.

Tricia fell.

Just like the idiots in the movies, like the ones she was so determined *not* to be. But could anything else have happened, here in a place so strewn with roots, and where the trees themselves seemed to be her enemies?

She fell, and screamed, then screamed louder when she felt pain shoot a white-hot bolt through her shoulder.

"Trish!" Alex shouted behind her. He had spoken – or screamed – only in shades of terror for the last few hours. Even so, his voice took on a newer, more deeply felt fear. She knew it was for her, and loved him a bit more for that even as she saw why her shoulder hurt and shrieked yet again.

She had fallen against some stick that nature had prepared for this moment.

Not nature. The forest.

The branch was only an inch in diameter. It should have snapped in pieces when she fell against it, instead of impaling her through the shoulder. But in this place where nothing was right…

She gasped, then screamed again, as Alex called her name, then called out Sam's, then shouted for her again.

And then a final scream raked the air, so jagged with terror it momentarily overpowered even the pain in Tricia's shoulder.

She looked up. Looked over.

Saw Sam.

Sam's mother stood only inches away from her son. Sam wasn't running; wasn't even moving. Horror and anguish had rooted him to the spot where he would be captured, cut, killed.

"It can't start!" his mother shouted, and slashed down again.

Sam finally broke free of his terror. He dodged to the side, and even as his mother jumped to cut him off he was running the other way. He spun as he twisted away from her, a jittery dance move that somehow took him just outside the range of her knife swing.

He dodged around her and ran toward his friends. "Alex! Tricia!" he shrieked, reaching for them.

Tricia couldn't answer, and couldn't reach back. The agony in her shoulder flared into being, along with the dismal thought that the branch that had thrust through her body was still attached to a tree.

She was pinned like a bug. Couldn't escape. Couldn't even try. Even if Sam and Alex got away, she was as good as dead when Sam's mother caught her. That woman wanted to kill her son more than anything, that was sure. But Tricia knew that she would settle for eviscerating Tricia and/or Alex as a consolation prize.

Alex had reached her, and apparently did the same math Tricia did – that she would die for sure if she stayed here – because he said, "Hold on," and Tricia had barely enough time to wonder what she was supposed to hold onto before Alex put his strong arms around her and *yanked*.

Tricia screamed as he pulled her free. Alex screamed, too, like he could feel the same pain she did. Maybe that was true – he had his own wounds. But she knew even in the depths of her agony as Alex pulled-yanked-twisted her away from the branch that he was feeling only for her in that moment.

That was what love was, wasn't it? Feeling another person's pain as your own, even when you were in pain yourself?

The branch pulled free from her flesh. It made a sucking sound that she thought must be a punctured lung, and she knew there was no way she could get away from the maniac woman in the mist... or from whatever else was there.

The whispers surged, as though in response to her thought.

"... Alex..."

"... get out of here..."

"... Tricia..."

"... get out..."

"... Sam..."

"... in this Hell..."

"... people don't stay dead..."

The whispers coalesced and grew. The forms in the mist grew closer... and that was when she heard Alex, his arms still around her, go insane.

3
(When Alex Was Young)

Can't lose her. I love her.

The thoughts were a clock ticking in Alex's mind, though whether to some far-future moment or to an impending, terrible end he couldn't say.

Only the forest knew. Only the forest would decide.

He and Trish had come here to find their first real friend. Because the two of them had always been so close, "outside" friends had been hard to come by. Neither of them eschewed the company of others, but even if he and Trish hadn't been smarter than everyone else at the high school, *including* the teachers, it would have been hard for any third party to break into the network of inside jokes and shared experiences that bonded him and Trish so tightly.

Sam, though – he was different. For the first time Alex could remember, he and Trish clicked with someone *not* themselves. And so the three of them spent every waking moment together – at school, at least, when Trish and Alex weren't in the periodic lockdowns imposed by their parents, and Sam wasn't with his own mother.

Then Sam disappeared. Alex and Trish went to find him, and found so many other things first. Terrible things, things Alex didn't want to think about – and couldn't think about, actually. Not now, with a branch shoved right through Trish's shoulder; not now, with Sam running full-tilt through the forest toward Alex and Trish, his insane mother shrieking and spitting as she tore after him.

Sam oozed blood from a million cuts where a million branches had whipped across his skin during the nightmare run the three of them had shared. Behind him, his mother was closing in, ready to open fresher and wider wounds that would not merely dot him with blood, but *bathe* him in it. Sam's eyes got wider as he ran, and Alex knew that his friend could feel how close his mother was.

Trish went silent. Just for an instant. Alex felt her warm blood washing over his hands and arms, and for a moment wondered if she had died – if he had killed her by pulling her away from the branch. Maybe severed an artery or something.

Then she screamed. Alex felt relief – she was alive.

Horror returned as he realized that Trish wasn't screaming in pain. She was looking at Sam. Alex followed her gaze and saw Sam's mother swing her knife at her son. There was no way Sam could make it to safety. Only a few feet away from his friends, but too far for all that.

The forest had played many tricks on them, but this was the worst. So close to their friend, to the person he and Trish had come to the forest to save.

The mist that had fallen all around them – that strange, glowing fog that had appeared slowly and silently and gone unnoticed until it was their entire world – surged forward as Sam's mother sliced at her son's back, angling her blade to bury it up to the hilt.

She swung the knife. Mist surged, and swallowed both her and Sam the instant before the knife made contact.

But even though he didn't see it, Alex knew she had done it. She had killed her boy. There was a single scream from that part of the fog. A ghost-shriek of pain and terror. Then nothing but the strange, glowing mist that flashed and flashed in faster and faster surges of light-dark-light-dark-light.

Alex realized suddenly that his friend's dying scream had momentarily drowned out the other scream that was still going on: Trish. She was in agony, mind, heart, and body.

Alex had to get her out of this place. Sam was gone, but his mother was not. The insane, murderous woman was waiting in the mist. Maybe even circling around to get behind Alex and Trish – though Alex sincerely doubted she had the presence of mind to do anything so coherent. No. She would come from the front. A straight assault. A rush with the knife still covered in the warm blood of her own son.

"I have to get you out of here," he told Trish, his arms starting to pull her up, though he knew it would be agony. "Can you run? She's out there, she's coming, I know it, but I don't know where or what she'll do." He felt like he was babbling, losing direction mentally like –

(Like a stream that goes all the wrong ways.)

– he was about to lose it. And he couldn't do that. He had to get Trish out of here. He couldn't, *wouldn't,* lose her. Not to the whisperers, or to the madwoman who had just killed his friend.

And where is *that delightful lady, Alex? You think she might be around, hmmmm?*

The lights –mist-lights, fog-lights, *ghost*-lights – had stopped as he lifted Trish. Now they flashed again, brightening the already-glowing mist, illuminating the shapes and shadows within the fog.

Some of the shadows, he knew, were trees.

Others, he knew, were not.

He suddenly felt like Sam's mother was right behind him, about to pounce. She would cut Alex's throat, then kill Trish. His world would end here.

He spun around. Nothing. He looked toward the place where he had seen the madwoman; the place where he had lost his friend.

And the mist parted. For the first time, it allowed Alex to see they were in a spot where the trees of the forest were taller than anywhere else they had been. The trunks continued in unblemished lines for thirty feet or more before the first branches appeared, bony fingers clawing their way out through the bark and into the forest's gloom.

The heart of the forest?

He thought so, just as the mist fled for a moment, and he saw what it had hidden as they ran – perhaps the one thing that had waited for them all this time. Not the shadows, not the whisperers, not even Sam's mom, but the monster at the center of it all.

Alex felt sanity falling away, felt madness take its place.

He screamed.

Sam was nowhere to be seen. Neither was his mother, and as soon as Alex saw what *was* in the fog he would have given anything to have nothing worse to worry about than a knife-wielding madwoman and a forest full of ghosts.

The thinning fog revealed a *thing*, about as tall as a person, but with far too many legs, too many arms. A head – misshapen and dented – jutted out of one scarred "shoulder." The thing's torso twisted strangely, its ribs and spine a fused mass of bones that pressed so hard at its mottled skin that Alex could see their outlines in painful detail. Several of the ribs appeared to be *outside* the thing's trunk, gray-white-red arcs, some of them broken into two or three sections, protruding from the thing's flesh. Parts of the bones shone in the mist, too, reflecting the light with the glint of polished metal.

Cloth draped the thing in a mockery of clothing – a hodgepodge of fabrics and weaves that looked like the final work of a deranged garment maker.

The creature keened an almost woeful scream. Two of its hands reached forward, and the receding part of Alex's mind still capable of rational thought realized that the hands each had part of a face embedded in their palms: an eye on one, spinning wildly about as though trying to take in the whole world at once; a partial jaw in the other, complete with teeth and a tongue that lolled forward out of the strange hole that went right through the creature's hand to reveal what was behind.

Alex screamed again, and realized that he had clapped his hand over Trish's eyes at some point. He had to spare Trish this sight. If she ever saw what he was seeing, she would lose herself to the madness that now swept Alex along on a current of darkness. It was too much to bear, and he could not let her share this sight.

He couldn't save her. They were going to die, he knew that now.

But Trish could at least die without knowing the true face of the nightmare. He could give her that, at least.

The mouth on the thing's hand was moving – it was the source of the sound, it was *screaming from its hand* – but then an even greater horror came. The thing stopped screaming, and a whispering, reedy *voice* started issuing from both its "mouths." The word-sounds were garbled to the point of incomprehensibility, but Alex knew they *were* words. Or at least, as close to words as a thing of pure madness could hope to make.

Alex was still screaming. Trish was still screaming, one hand scrabbling at her wounded shoulder, the other scratching at Alex's hand and arm, trying to get him to uncover her eyes.

The thing kept making sounds from its hand-face. Then the other face – mottled, with tufts of hair sprouting not just from the top of its head, but from its cheeks and even one of the three eyeballs set in its forehead – opened its mouth and screamed as well. Two wails from one creature. A chorus that should never have been, and which rose louder and louder, until…

… they cut off, as though they never existed in the first place.

The mist surged again, swallowing the thing in its depths at the same moment that Trish yanked Alex's hand away from her face.

Alex kept screaming for a while. What had he seen? Not a nightmare, but a nightmare of a nightmare. The thing that made terror itself sit up in fright.

Eventually, Alex's screams waned. He looked around. The mist was still there, but the shadows were nowhere to be seen. The wraith-things that had dogged his and Trish's steps had disappeared, as fully and completely as the *thing* had just done.

"Help me," said Trish.

The smallness of her voice jerked him back to the moment, and back to something resembling sanity. He looked at the girl he had loved as long as he could remember, and saw that her face was as pale and translucent as the glowing mist that still enveloped them. He looked at her shoulder. The blood that had soaked her shirt appeared to have slowed from a gush to a trickle. But she still wasn't out of the woods, figuratively or literally. He pulled her to her feet. She groaned, but didn't scream.

She had always been the strongest of them.

"We have to get out of here," said Alex.

She actually chuckled, though the sound turned into a groan before it was fully formed. "Really?" she said. She turned her head, looking at the spot where Sam, his mother, and –

(The thing what was it don't think about it it wasn't real how could a thing like that be REAL?)

– the monster in the mist had been.

"Where's Sam?" she asked.

Alex could tell from her tone she already knew the worst had happened. Though to her, the "worst" was Sam's death and disappearance, not the *real* worst. The thing Alex had seen had to be the zenith of evil, the nadir of hope.

If it even happened.

Did *it happen? Or was this all just a dream?*

Is any of this real? Am I *the lunatic?*

"I don't know where Sam is," Alex managed. Then he added the word that had to come next, the only word that fit in this insane place. "Gone."

Trish looked like she was going to say something. Probably protest that Sam couldn't be gone; that he was still out there. *"We have to find him,"* she would say. *"We have to save him."*

But she said neither. Alex *hoped* she hadn't seen what he saw – not just the monster, but the moment the fog took Sam and his mother away just as the point of her knife was finding his back – but he could tell that she felt the same thing he suddenly felt himself.

Something was different. Something had ended, perhaps. Maybe the forest would finally let them escape.

He hoped so.

"How are we going to find our way out of here?" he asked. He was mostly speaking to himself, but Trish answered.

"Pick a direction."

He nodded. She was right: one way was as good as any other in this place. He remembered a passage from *Alice in Wonderland:*

> *"But I don't want to go among mad people," Alice remarked.*
>
> *"Oh, you can't help that," said the Cat: "we're all mad here. I'm mad. You're mad."*
>
> *"How do you know I'm mad?" said Alice.*
>
> *"You must be," said the Cat, "or you wouldn't have come here."*

Alex remembered it perfectly. He remembered most things perfectly, but *Alice in Wonderland* was, along with *Peter Pan,* one of his two favorite books.

He wondered if he would ever read it again. Even if he made it out of here, could he ever willingly visit fiction that had him traipsing through madness as though it were a thing to be enjoyed?

(We're all mad here.)

He shoved the thought away and forced himself to take a step, then another, Trish's good arm over his shoulder. They walked a few paces.

He looked at her. "Okay?" he said. She nodded. He gave her a quick smile, then stepped forward again. Only this time Trish didn't come with him. She pulled him back, and toward her, and he had an instant of confusion, then an instant of delight before she touched her lips to his.

It lasted forever. It lasted no time at all.

It was the worst time, the worst place for this to happen.

But it was also the best time and place for this moment. It was an island of sanity in the madness, a shelter of pleasure against the pain.

They parted. She smiled. "I'm okay," she said, and for a moment, before he realized she was just answering his previous question, he worried he had hurt her somehow.

He turned back to face the forest and took another step forward as a grin spread across his face.

Maybe we'll get out of th –

A root reached up and grabbed him. The forest was doing it again. It extended hope, then stole it away at the worst moment, because even a thing as pure as hope could be twisted to corruption by this place.

Trish moved as he fell, and Alex realized that she was actually trying to hold him up. But all she did was get herself pinned below him. Her eyes widened as his weight tore the wound in her shoulder. She screamed and finally, mercifully, passed out.

Alex rolled off her as fast as he could. Had he just killed her? Killing her would be the same as killing himself. He couldn't live without her.

And even if I could, I wouldn't want to.

He sat up too fast. Dizziness gripped him and he pitched to the side, barely stopping himself before falling on Trish *again*. His hands flattened against the thick, rich dirt on each side of Trish's head, and his breath came in shallow gasps against her face.

The whispering started again. The whisperers still lived in the mist, and still spoke to those who dared the forest.

The wraith-lights came again, too. The soft glow of the mist grew bright and then snuffed out in rapid successions that turned the world into a storm of darks and lights.

Alex looked around, panic welling up as he realized they were right back among the tall trees where Trish had been wounded and the monster appeared. He saw the smooth trunks, the finger-branches clawing out of them.

He thought they had left the monster, but that wasn't true. The monster *was* the forest.

And the forest wasn't ready to let them go.

"Alex?"

He turned. He didn't want to, but he *had* to. The voice was Sam's.

Only Sam's dead. Stabbed to death by his mother, his body stolen by the mist.

Dead.

But the forest was lying then, or lying now, because the mist parted, and Sam was still there, still alive, standing right where he had been in the moment the blade had come down.

"How?" Alex managed.

Sam smiled. In that moment, bloody and torn and weary from heaven-only-knew how many years of terror, he was beautiful.

He reached toward Alex. "I think I –"

A twig snapped. Sam froze.

The mist flashed and swirled. It enveloped Sam again. A twisting eddy twirled it apart long enough for Alex to see his friend one last time.

Two hands reached out of the mist. Alex could not have said whether they belonged to a man or a woman, only that they came from the mist, from a place where nothing had been only a moment before. One hand lay on each of Sam's shoulders.

Alex did something he would have thought utterly impossible only minutes ago: he forgot about Trish. He stood and ran toward his friend so quickly and fluidly it was almost a single motion, shrieking, "Sam! Watch ou –"

The hands tightened on Sam's shoulders. Sam's mouth curled in something strangely akin to a smile.

The hands yanked him into the mist.

Alex ran after Sam and whoever had done this.

His mother. Has to be.

But it wasn't. The mists curled and flashed, but not enough to completely hide what had pulled Sam away. Alex saw a face that didn't belong to anyone he had ever seen, staring quietly. Waiting.

Man? Woman? He couldn't tell. It all happened too fast. The eyes turned toward Alex and said nine words. The mist swirled and…

Sam was gone.

The face and hands that had taken him away were gone.

The whispers with their shadow-wraiths were gone.

Alex screamed. Not about what had just happened, but about *everything*: the kidnapping, the arcane symbols they had seen, the madhouse in the forest, the man in the tree, Sam's death… and then Sam's second death and disappearance as the mist consumed him once more.

Everything went dark. He heard the words that had been spoken, and they were the last and only thing in his world for a long time. Just nine words that made no sense in this destructive place, and which bore him to oblivion.

4
(When Alex Had Grown)

"But you don't remember those words?"

Alex blinked. "What?"

Dr. Coleman sighed, shuffled some papers as though referring to his notes – though he was doing no such thing, Alex could tell – and said, "You heard words in the forest, the day you went looking for your friend?"

Alex blanched, just as he had when speaking a moment ago. "I… yes."

(I heard words yes I did a hundred years ago or was it only twenty I don't know I can't tell I remember the face the faces covered in blood and worse, so much worse –)

"I think so." Alex sighed. "I don't know. Everything's… muddled. I dream of it sometimes, but it's like everything's in a fog. I can only see hints of it, and only hear these whispers that make no sense. But in the dreams I know if I can understand it, then I can have him back."

The psychiatrist cocked an eyebrow. "You can have Sam back? Or Sam*my*?"

Beside him, Alex felt his wife move. He glanced at her. She was shifting her wedding ring, turning it around and around on her finger. An eternal circle, the same thing over and over again. It was a great symbol for marriage, *if* that marriage was working. But if it wasn't… well, eternity could be quite the horrible prospect.

Trish shrugged, almost hunching over. She scratched at the shoulder where a star-shaped scar marred her skin. She wore turtlenecks, rain or shine, day in and day out, to keep anyone from seeing the scar there, or the matching one on her back. As though she had gotten it doing something shameful.

He didn't remember how she'd gotten the wound – neither of them did, which was part of the problem between them – but he knew she hadn't done anything to be ashamed of. In spite of the trouble they'd been having in their marriage, Alex knew –

(Temporal lobe to tips of toes, brain to balls, right?)

– that his wife was a good person. However she got the scar, it was not something that demanded guilt or embarrassment.

Trish stiffened, obviously aware he was looking at her. Not long past, his attention had made her happy. In that past she would have looked back, and winked, and maybe they would have cut out of work a bit early so they could go home and make love or play a game or even just sit and talk while holding hands.

Now, she shied away from him.

Alex looked back at Dr. Coleman. Dr. Scott Ray Coleman's office was a uniform beige, with a few muted tones here and there to remind visitors they weren't actually *dead,* just very calm. At least, Alex surmised that was the intent. In reality the color scheme just muffled everything. Everything seemed a bit out of focus, like he was looking at the world through a smudged window.

Coleman himself was just as beige as his office, and seemed just as smudged and far away.

Even his voice sounded distant. "Whatever happened out there, that day, we know that you lost someone important to you. No one begrudges you forgetting some no doubt painful details." He smiled, somehow managing to convey perfectly that he did in fact fault Alex for missing those details.

Within the first ten minutes of meeting the shrink – ten minutes which cost, by Alex's calculation, seventy five bucks – Alex had come to the conclusion that he kind of hated the man. But Trish seemed to talk more here, so he kept coming back. The marriage was on the rocks, but Alex had no intention of letting it sink. He would do whatever it took. Anything. Even skipping work or dealing with someone who was the human equivalent of tapwater.

"It must have been a lot to deal with," Coleman was saying. He turned to Trish. "Getting hurt like that, then losing your friend."

He waited. Neither Alex nor Trish said anything, though Alex sensed his wife reaching self-consciously for the neck of her turtleneck, tugging it up a half inch more.

Coleman sighed. Looking at his notes again, he said, "You named your son Sam, too, didn't you? After your friend? What were you trying to say with that gesture?"

Trish said nothing. Alex opened his mouth, realized that if he spoke it would be nothing but a string of curses and maybe a straight-up temper tantrum, and closed it again. "Sammy," he finally managed. "We called our son Sammy."

"Because he was different," Trish whispered. She sounded like a ghost. "He wasn't Sam, we knew that. But we also wanted Sam to be alive, so…" She shrugged. She never looked away from her ring once, twist twist twist, turn turn turn.

Coleman made a notation on his pad. Without looking up, he said, "Do you remember how you got out of the forest?"

"We called for help," Trish whispered.

"What was that, Tricia?" asked Coleman.

Alex repeated it. "We called for help."

"How?"

Trish whispered something – this time so low that not even Alex could hear it. It sounded like something he had heard before. Not the words, but the *tones*. It sounded like…

(The whispers. The whisperers.)

"What was that?" Coleman leaned forward in his chair. It squeaked.

Trish whispered it again. This time Alex heard her well enough to translate what he should have simply guessed. "I don't know."

Trish looked up. "But we must have called for help, right? I mean, we didn't walk out, wounded and with me the way –"

She tugged at her turtleneck.

Coleman glanced at his notes, then leaned back – another squeak, and Alex was starting to think he hated the chair as much as the man on it – and said, "What about – what did you call it?" He looked at his notes again. "'*The man in the tree*'?"

The tone of his voice, disbelieving, patronizing, and even a little amused – the worst of the three – made Alex tense. Before he could say anything, Trish spoke up. "He was *real*."

Coleman smiled. "I'm sure he is. But you don't remember who he was, or what he was doing in the tree? Or why that detail keeps coming into your dreams?" His brow furrowed. "Is it just a man climbing a tree in the forest? Was it someone who hurt you? Was he the one who hurt you both and took Sammy – sorry, *Sam*, away from you?"

His voice had that caring, patronizing quality one reserved for children. Exceptionally *stupid* children who ran around chewing on bars of lead and inhaling glue. But Alex couldn't fault him for it, really. What was he seeing? A man and a woman, marriage in the process of slowly dying. Both of them with genius IQs, able to recite pi to a hundred decimal places, able to recall every word they read in last week's reports at the labs where they worked…

… yet unable to remember anything during that single day in the forest.

Sam was real, they knew that. They knew, too, that they had gone to school that day. They remembered they had gone to the forest looking for him for some reason.

But beyond that, nothing. It was just a blank space, in which their friend had disappeared.

Trish had picked up on the man's tone. Unlike Alex, she was apparently willing to vocalize her disapproval. "I'm sure none of it's real, actually. We just made it all up because we wanted to hang out with a guy as *interesting* as you and thought this would be the best way to do it. We made up the dreams, and the big ol' black hole of a day no one could understand." Shifting gears, she said, "We have presented a construction that ensures the existence of numerous globally consistent string compactifications with the chiral spectrum of the Standard Model within the framework of F-theory. This is the largest ensemble of which we are aware, outnumbering other quantifiable results published under peer review by approximately ten orders of magnitude, which arise due to variance of the base of a universal class of elliptical fibrations introduced previously."

Coleman blinked. "I'm sorry?" he asked.

"It's from a paper a grad student wrote –"

"I'm not sure how that –"

Trish spoke right over him, as though he didn't exist. "– in my grad course. He wrote it over a year ago, and that's word for word. Bottom of page four, and it has two footnotes which I can also recite. But I just thought it would be cool to pretend to forget *some* things, so I came up with this strategy. What do you think?"

In that moment, Alex remembered – all at once – what he loved so much about her. She had always said the things he was thinking. When he didn't have the strength or the will or the desire to say a thing, she was there. If it needed to be said, and he didn't… then she did.

Coleman looked at his notes, and this time Alex didn't mind. Because this time he could tell that the man was embarrassed. Just like everyone was. Whenever Alex or Trish told the story, everyone was incredulous. Anytime they finally trusted someone to hear about the forest, they always ended up gazing on eyes filled with disbelief. Even now. Even someone paid – by *them* – to listen, could not hide the anger or the embarrassment or the laughter or whatever awful thing greeted them whenever they talked about what had happened. Or rather, what they didn't remember happening.

Sam was gone. They all knew that. But everyone they talked to after that agreed that he had just *left*. His mother transferred him out of the school, and left no forwarding information – which was strange, but hardly unknown.

Alex and Trish knew different. They knew he wasn't at another school. They knew he was *dead*. But they didn't know how they knew that, or if that had prompted the empty day. They assumed it did, because on one side of that void was their new friend, Sam, and on the other side he was notably absent.

Trish, her outburst of ire spent, went back to twirling her ring. The ring Alex gave her, along with the promise that they would love each other forever. That he would have her and hold her and possess her as his own, and she would have and hold and possess him as well. They would own each other, and so would take the greatest care with their greatest possessions.

Then it went south. Not just because of that one dead day, but because of what happened after that.

First Sam, then Sammy.

Silence. When it stretched out so long there was no bearing it anymore, Alex looked up. Coleman was staring at him. The look on the man's face – blank, neutral, so carefully vacant it spoke volumes – crashed into him so hard he almost gasped. He looked away, looked for Trish. She would help. She always helped. She –

She was looking at her ring. Twist, twist, twist. It started to slide down her finger, like she wasn't just twisting it, but trying to take it off.

And watching her ring coming slowly off her finger, he realized that they had spent decades believing what they said. That, he suspected, was the only reason they hadn't been put in a nuthouse for kids – they *both* said the same things. They went into the forest. They came out again. No idea what happened in between those hours.

But they had stood together. They repeated the story as one, they married and *were* one in so many ways. They made a child.

Now the child was gone. And so was the unity that had brought them through their first, forgotten ordeal and into one another's arms.

So what if none of it *was* real? If the thing he knew better than anything – Trish – had turned away… what else could be counted on?

"There was a lot going on that day," he said. It came out almost as a sigh of relief. A whisper that said, *"Please, let it all have been a dream."*

Trish finally looked up; looked at him. "No," she said. Then she shouted it: *"No!* Don't start denying what you know. We saw something, we *did* something, and Sammy was *gone,* he –"

Her eyes widened as she realized she had said the wrong name. She had meant to say "Sam," but instead named their child. She fell silent and pulled at her turtleneck.

Coleman's blandly smug expression returned. "Look, you two are obviously meant to be together. I mean that. You have so much in common – born in the same town, went to school all the way through *grad* school together, working together to this date. More than that, you married and had a child, which is a blessing for some, a curse for others, and a stressful event for everyone. And then….

Trish stiffened at that. She never wanted to talk about the "and then" that was their lost boy.

Alex automatically reached for her. He wanted to hold her hand again, the way they always had. He wanted *everything* back to the way it was before they lost their child.

She pulled away from him. It made Alex feel like a leper. Coleman noticed, too. He opened his mouth to say something, then shut it for a moment as Trish's hand darted out. She held Alex's hand – clutched it so tightly it hurt. But the gasp that came from his throat wasn't one of pain. It was relief. It was joy.

He put his free hand over hers. She did the same, all four of their hands knotted so closely it was hard to tell where one stopped and the other began.

Coleman smiled. A genuinely kind smile this time, and Alex suddenly wondered how much of the man's sanctimonious disbelief was actually there, and how much of it was just Alex. Just projection.

Most of it?

No.

All *of it.*

The room shifted a bit. The maddening pastels and beiges seemed to brighten. The room seemed to come closer, to seem more real. Trish's hands in and on his own made the world come alive.

Oh, I've missed that.

Coleman sat back and steepled his fingers again, and now Alex saw the movement for what it was: not a patronizing motion, but a nervous tic. Just a habit picked up from a professor or a parent, and carried on throughout Coleman's life.

We're all products of what has gone before. That's certainly true of me, so why not of him?

The world sharpened. It became real for the first time in ages.

Then that reality spun away so quickly it left Alex dizzy as Coleman said, "Have you ever gone back there? To the forest, I mean?"

Trish said something. At least, Alex thought she did. Everything was far away again. Trish was drawing away, and would soon be lost to him.

All Alex could see in that moment was Coleman's eyes, watching him carefully. All he could hear with any clarity was Coleman's voice. "I didn't think so." The psychiatrist took off his glasses, sighed, then put them back on again. "I think you should. You have an anniversary coming up. You lost a friend in that forest, and a child while passing by it years later. But not since. If you look at the place where you were so afraid, and see that it's…"

Silence again. The world ricocheted from *here* to *there,* from *clear* to *confused* in Alex's mind.

"What?" said Trish. "If we see it's what?"

"Just trees," said Coleman. And now Alex saw both real kindness and that smug superiority. He saw them superimposed over one another like film negatives that had melted together, and he couldn't tell which was real and which was only happening in his mind. "Maybe if you see it's just a forest, then you'll be able to move on. Or at least begin to heal."

He was right. Alex knew that. He was making perfect sense.

So why was Trish twisting her ring so fast he could see the skin start to bleed? And why was Alex himself so very, very afraid?

Because if I remember, it's like it's happening again. What happened to Sam will happen again, and we'll live it over, and we don't remember it but whatever it was we know it was a –

(monster)

– bitch to get through.

And besides… going back means we'll have to see where we lost Sammy.

5
Interlude
(When Sammy Was Young)

He sits in the back of the car. Daddy and Mommy sit up front, laughing. Then the laughing stops. A silence grows – but even so young, the little boy in the back of the car knows that it is an odd silence. A wrong *silence.*

He knows this, just as he knows many things that most children his age do not.

The silence grows heavy. Like another seatbelt across his shoulder, crossing his heart and hoping to die to die to die die die.

He holds his unicorn tightly. Its name is Silly Corny, which he thinks is hilarious, because Mommy tells Daddy his jokes are Silly and Corny. It is red and soft and he loves to put his cheek against it when he's scared.

He puts his cheek against it now.

"You think Erika will liked my present, Daddy?" says the child.

Daddy answers absently. "'Liked,' not 'will liked,' Sammy."

Mommy reaches for Daddy. Sammy can see that her hand is clenched so tight on Daddy's that both are turning white.

Daddy seems to shiver a bit in his seat.

He looks out the window.

Sammy looks out, too, though he has to scooch forward in his carseat to do so. He sees nothing but a forest. Buncha trees. Trees are interesting, but not terrifically so. Not like Star Wars *or the cool stuff where Daddy and Mommy work.*

Daddy looks forward again. Mommy, Sammy notes, never moves. She does not even glance at the trees that stand so tall as the car whips past them.

The boy has a strange thought: What if the car *isn't* moving? What if the *trees* are? What if the whole *universe* is spinning, and the car is the only thing not moving in everywhere?

The thought is both strangely comforting and bizarrely funny. Sammy pictures a universe spinning around and around with the car at the center, like a tiny black hole (black holes are something he learned about recently, too – though from Mommy this time).

He laughs.

The laugh does something magical. It makes Daddy smile, too. And a moment later, Mommy smiles as well.

Daddy looks at Sammy in the mirror. His eyes crinkle. "I think Erika will liked her present great."

Sammy laughs louder. He looks out the window again. He sees not only trees this time, but fog. It looks puffy and cloudy, but as he watches, it seems to come together and turn from cotton candy to a thick blanket. He can see shadows inside it, which he figures are the trees in the forest.

Only… some of the shadows seem to move.

He doesn't like it.

Sammy scooches up in his seat again, this time not to see out the side. He has discovered he can see out of the front window if he turns his head just so. *He can see between Mommy's neck and the outside wall of the car, and he would like that now. He doesn't want to see the fog or the weird shadows.*

So he scooches, he leans, he sees. The fog is already laying across the road, like it distracted him with bits of cloudy white, almost silver, on the side, while its main body went in front. Like it was trying to stop them. Or maybe eat *them.*

Sammy suddenly feels like, if they drive into the fog, it will turn out to be solid. The car will crunch like an aluminum can did when Daddy crunched it before tossing it in the recycle bin.

And worse, there are shadows there, too. But Mommy and Daddy don't see them, because Daddy is glancing back at him as Mommy turns in her seat so she can look at Sammy, too.

"You okay, champ?" she says, and Daddy says, "You all right, bud?"

Mommy and Daddy do that sometimes. They talk along with each other, and sometimes say just about the same things. Sammy usually likes that. Now it seems creepy. They are looking at him, *which means they aren't –*

"Watch out!" shouts Sammy as he sees one of the shadows move right into the path of the car. He thinks it is a man. Maybe a woman.

Either way, he/she is right in front of them.

Daddy's eyes had been watching him. Now they snap forward, and Daddy says a Bad Word. He spins the wheel and the car jerks sideways so hard that Sammy's head, still tilted and craned just so, *slams into his window. He hears the sharp crack of glass breaking, and everything inside his head spins around.*

An instant later, everything outside *his head spins, too. His thoughts jumble and tumble the same as everything else:* The car isn't the center after all. The center is *me,* and the universe is spinning around but please Daddy please Mommy I don't want it to spin please make it st –

The prayer works. Everything goes black.

*A moment later – or maybe longer; Sammy feels like he was asleep forever, and will wake up Way Old like maybe thirty or even thirty-*five *– Sammy feels heat. He sees flickering. At first he thinks, in a jumbly-confused way, that the fog must be flickering.*

He opens his eyes to flame.

"Daddy? Mommy? MOMMY!" he screams. But no sound comes to his ears. His screaming was inside his head.

Even my sounds are spinning.

Then a good sound, a real *sound comes to him. "You okay?" screams Daddy.*

"I think so," Sammy manages. He realizes his hands are hanging above his head.

No. *Below.* I'm upside-down.

Sammy tries to turn his head. It hurts. He looks up/down and sees a thick pool of blood below him, still growing from the drip, drip of blood coming off his own fingers.

Bleeding! Bleeding! I'm not okay, I'm –

He tries to look away. He sees Daddy, also upside-down. Daddy's trying to turn to look at Sammy, and Sammy screams when he sees all the blood on Daddy's face.

Mommy isn't moving.

"I'll get you out of this," Daddy murmurs. "Get you out…" His eyes flutter. He shivers, harder than when he looked at the trees. The shivers turn into a strange jerking – a comvulshon, Sammy thinks. Mommy and Daddy didn't teach him about comvulshons, but he saw about them on one of their late-night shows after he snuck onto the stairs.

Daddy stops comvulsing.

Is Daddy *dead?* DON'T LET DADDY BE DEAD!

There is a strange sound. A tearing, ripping, banging. Daddy's door opens. Hands – they must belong to the person who was in the road – reach in. Something clicks and Daddy suddenly falls to the floor/roof of the car. The hands drag him out.

Sammy is happy. It is getting hot. The car is on fire. On fire, but Daddy is safe.

"Mommy," he whispers. His voice is low. He feels spinny. Has he finally started moving himself? Is he no longer the center of the universe? No matter. "Get Mommy."

He cannot tell anymore if the voice he makes is inside his head or outside. But the stranger's hands clunk-thunk-tunk the door open on Mommy's side as well. They reach in. They make her fall to the roof/floor. They drag her out.

During it all, dark foggy things gather at Sammy's eyes. They float at the sides of what he sees, then they reach into the center of what he sees. Everything gets darker. But at the same time, everything gets brighter. Hotter.

Is the car going to blow up?

Before he can answer himself, he hears someone – Daddy? Mommy? – shrieking. "No, no, NOOOOOOO!"

6
(When Tricia Had Grown)

Tricia knew she had been selfish. She knew they *both* had. That was one of the worst parts of grief: it shrank your world. It took people that had once thought of themselves as part of everyone around them, and made them hurt so bad that they couldn't think of anyone else.

Grief isolated you. It cut you off, then cut you apart, and if you weren't careful, the most important parts of you just died.

She didn't know if that had happened yet. Certainly it had started. It started when Sammy died.

Maybe even before that. Maybe in the forest. Yes. That was it. The grief started with the forest. It ebbed and flowed, and for a while it was so small and silent she thought it was gone. Then Sammy…

Tricia looked at Alex. He was holding the steering wheel of the car, but hadn't moved since he got in. The keys weren't even in the ignition, but she wondered if he was driving just the same. Driving down that road beside the forest, the last place they ever saw

No. Don't.

She wanted to do something. Her world was so small. How could she do anything in a place so tiny she felt like she couldn't even move a finger?

But she *did*. Somehow she moved her hand, and her arm. Somehow she laid her hand on Alex's shoulder, and her world got a little bigger. Somehow she spoke. She said, "It wasn't your fault," and the world got bigger still. Hardly *large*, but at least she felt like she could take a breath.

That was the secret: to include someone else. Not to cut them off in your grief, but to hold them close. To let them share the grief with you, and make a small, isolated world of sorrow into something bigger and less lonely.

Easy to think. Harder to do.

Alex blinked. He didn't look away from the invisible road Tricia was sure he still traveled even a decade after he was last there.

Why did Sammy's little friend have to have a birthday party? Why did we have to go? Why did we have to drive past the forest to get there?

She thought all of these things, and her world contracted again. Her jaw tightened, then she forced herself to relax as she said again, "It wasn't your fault."

Alex shook his head. The movement was slow, taking forever to move from side to side and back again while his eyes remained fixed ever forward. Forward, but looking back just the same.

"He just appeared," Alex said. "There wasn't anything, I swear, and then there was this fog and…" His breath hitched. "He wasn't there, Trish."

Trish.

Alex was the only one who had ever called her by that diminutive. To everyone else she was *Tricia*. She realized this was an exclusive club to which only her husband belonged – *The Official Trish Fan Club. No whiners allowed.*

Her world got a bit bigger again.

"I couldn't get to him, Trish. I couldn't stop what happened."

She suddenly felt tired. Her hand dropped from his shoulder. Her world was small again. "Are we over?" she said. Strange words. Most people would have asked about a *divorce*. But *over* was the only way to describe what was happening to her world. How could that world – a world that had *always* been "we" and "us" – have disappeared?

"I don't want us to be over," Alex said. Tears glinted at the corners of his eyes.

After a moment, Tricia sensed he would say no more and said, "We should get moving."

"Home?" Alex asked. "Or do you want me to take you back to your apartment?"

She blanched. The separation was new, and though her world was so small breathing was near impossible, she had discovered that grief had a strange power over time and space. No one had told her about it in grad school, when she was learning about the individual bits of matter floating in a void. Fermions, bosons, gluons. Charginos, neutralinos. Tachyons and mirror particles.

No one ever talked about "grief." But that was perhaps the strongest power she had ever encountered, and it could compress space and rend time with the best of them.

"Trish?" said Alex. He was looking at her now.

"It will all be all right in the end." She didn't know where the words came from. Some movie, perhaps, or one of the dumb songs the grad students blasted at tailgate parties. She laughed a bit. The world got a bit bigger.

Laughter did that, even when it was the painful kind of laughter. The pain remained, but it wasn't *all* that existed.

She shook her head. "Do you think it could be true? Can this – can *we* – be all right in the end?"

Alex's eyes went forward again. Grief had the power to shift time, space, even vision – basic photonic paths. She knew, because the light particles hitting his eyes weren't reflected off the parking lot outside Coleman's office. He was seeing the road in the past. The day they lost their child.

"I want to," he finally said. "I want to go back there."

She didn't have to ask where "there" was. Cold dread twisted its way up her spine.

But also, perhaps, something warmer. Something that wasn't hope… but might grow to be hope someday. A hope for hope, if nothing else.

"Do you want to try it?" Alex asked.

She shrugged. "I don't know. We won't find Sam, and we'll probably come back with nothing new to remember. Just the same gap, around the same forest. The same place –" She cut off what she would have said.

But grief, which could bend time and space, had no trouble at all twisting sound and minds. So she heard the words unsaid, and knew Alex did, too.

"We won't find Sammy there, either."

7
Revelation
(When All Has Become)

They drove. Neither had a plan, really. Just to drive, and maybe – *maybe* – to see.

Both of them were smart. They had both learned about things so difficult and profound that they left the average person openmouthed and incredulous. Most people they talked to about their jobs said, "Are those words even *real*? Or are you making stuff up?"

So yes, those two people driving that one road were very smart.

But smart people can be incredibly stupid, you see. Smart people think they are smart enough to know and to understand a great deal of their world. But it is only the *extraordinarily* smart, the rarest of geniuses, who grow smart enough to know how unalterably *stupid* they still are.

The man and the woman who drove to the place they had been counseled to go were very smart. So they were very stupid. They thought they knew much, and so were blind not only to what they didn't know, but all the things they didn't even know that they didn't know.

(If you're smart enough, you'll understand that last. Temporal lobe to tips of toes, brain to balls. If not, nothing I can do will help you get it. Just leave it alone and hope you wise up someday.)

They drove into the town. They drove past the sign they had seen thousands or tens of thousands of times. It still said, "Welcome to Sunrise: Where Every Day Begins!" And below it, in smaller letters: "Pop. 2067."

The man in the car wondered, as he always did, how they could put the population count in there, given that it had to change constantly. Especially since the paint had read "Pop. 2067" every day of his life. According to the sign, not only did Every Day Begin in Sunrise, but every day would have to be exactly the same, and in that event it should have said, "Welcome to Sunrise: No Births No Deaths No Nothing."

(Maybe the sign was stupid. Which would make the sign very smart, wouldn't it?)

The woman didn't notice the number. She just noticed the bits of dust on the dashboard of the car, which she had been staring at since they left Coleman's office. It wasn't too far a drive – just a few hours – but they hadn't been back to this spot since they lost Sammy. They stayed in the general area, because neither of them wanted to leave this place where they had lost so much of themselves. But they didn't want to *see* it, either.

They hoped for healing. They hoped for a long time. Then hope died, in bits and pieces. And now Dr. Coleman (even *saying* that name confuses me sometimes, for reasons I may choose to explain later, or maybe not, or maybe I'll choose to do it after I *don't* choose to do it because so much is changeable) had found an ember of hope. He fanned it just a bit, even if it was still so small that neither the man nor the woman could see or sense it in their hearts.

But it was there. It made Alex (if that's the right name; sometimes it's hard to remember) drive to Sunrise. It made Tricia (if that's her name; memory can be a funny thing) not object, even though most of her wished they were anywhere *but* here.

Hope: a powerful, invisible force. Enough to fight off ghosts and wraiths and monsters and even (worst of all!) people?

Perhaps.

So hope pushed them through their hometown of Sunrise ("Where Every Day Begins!") and made them continue on to the strange sister town of Sundown, which had its own sign, its own unchanging number, and its own stupid-smart slogan.

Thinking about it, I revise my earlier statement. They may have driven past that sign *more* than tens of thousands of times.

Perhaps it was millions or even *billions* of times. Maybe more – memory twists numbers as easily as anything else.

And there's another reason I can't be sure of the number: because I *am* that smart. I have learned so much that I am no longer sure of anything at all, which means I can learn everything I wish and it will all be new.

I'm bragging, I know. And rambling to boot. But as the storyteller, I can tell the story how I wish. And here are the most important things to remember from here on in.

First: I am very smart.

Maybe the smartest ever.

Second: the story is mine.

I will tell it how I wish, even though it spins out of my control whenever *it* wishes.

Third: neither of the people in the car believed in ghosts.

Because they were just smart enough to be stupid.

TWO:
WELCOME TO SUNDOWN

8
(When Tricia Was Young)

Tricia used to pretend to pay attention to the teacher. She'd prop up the class textbook in front of whatever other textbook she was *actually* reading and pretend to follow along.

The teacher knew, of course. But after calling on Tricia for a solid week – when he wasn't calling on Alex for the same reasons – and hearing nothing but correct answers given in the offhanded way that both she and Alex used when they thought their time was being wasted, the teacher gave up.

After awhile, Tricia abandoned even the fiction of following along. She would sit down, get whatever book she was devouring that day out of her bag, and tune out the world. She did continue to listen with about two percent of her brain, of course. She had learned early that every so often an uppity teacher would try to catch her with her guard down. Those who didn't hear the right answer immediately after whatever random question they asked were the most likely to take her book away.

She always got it back, eventually, and went right back to reading. But losing the book – and inevitably dealing with angry looks from students who were already pissed about what she and Alex did to the grading curve – was a pain.

Alex was nicer. He kept up the pretense. Even now, he was nodding every once in a while even though his tatty copy of *Peter Pan* was occupying twenty times more of his brain than the teacher's ramblings.

Alex was never caught off guard, any more than Tricia was. He knew the answers, and was the only one who understood her when she complained about how dumb the teachers could be.

They never complained about how dumb the other *students* were. That was an unwritten rule. Sometimes the best way to get things done was to speak up and speak loud. Other times, the best way to get what you wanted, more or less, was to shut up and pretend as best you could that you were just like everyone else.

High school belonged firmly in the latter category.

High school itself was a strange thing into which she and Alex had been shoved. Neither belonged here – they should have been taking classes at the local community college, at the very least – but their parents had both come independently to the conclusion that high school was a necessary experience. It was one of the only things Tricia could think that they had ever agreed on, other than that their children should have as little contact with each other as possible.

Tricia lived with her father, Alex with his mother. Something had happened between their parents years ago, so even though she and Alex lived next door to each other, their parents never spoke; couldn't stand each other.

She asked her dad about it once and got a look that was set to -274 degrees Celsius and falling fast.

When Tricia asked her dad why she (and, implicitly, Alex) had to go to high school rather than just do stuff that would actually teach them something, she had been favored with a look that was only -273 degrees Celsius. Positively balmy compared to that other question about why Dad and Alex's mom refused to even look at each other when they crossed paths at the corner store.

But no answer other than that.

Once, on one of the nights he screamed in his sleep, Dad got drunk. He slurred, "I wish I'd never done what I did," and that was the closest she ever got to an answer to any of the Big Questions. Alex reported the same results when they compared notes periodically.

So… the state of enforced ignorance known as "high school." Talking about the teachers' stupidity. *Not* talking about the stupidity of the other students. Always knowing the right answers, and never being taken by surprise.

"… what do you think, Alex?"

The math teacher – whose name, uproariously, was Mr. Angle – looked at Alex, who dutifully looked up, unfazed, and said, "Depends."

Mr. Angle smirked. "*Caught ya!*" that look said. Tricia paid closer attention now, because the guy was kind of a tool and his pants were far too small to house such an epic butt, so seeing him fall on that butt might be amusing.

"Are you talking about rotational speed, or linear?" said Alex.

"Well, of course –"

"Because the rotational speed is easy to figure out based on the circumference of the wheel, but the linear speed ranges from the speed of the car at the topmost point to zero at the point it touches the ground. At least in theory. Though the way some people drive, the linear speed on the bottom –"

A hand shot up and another student yelled, "How can the wheel be going zero when the car is going a hundred miles per hour?"

A bunch of other students started talking. None of them liked math, but apparently they all liked being confused and then arguing about it.

Mr. Angle turned to address what had become the bigger problem – a class suddenly *too* interested in his lesson, or at least in the weeds around the edges of it – and so left Alex alone. Tricia had to respect what Alex had done. It was elegant, fairly kind (all things considered), and had certainly livened up a class where the most exciting thing most of the kids did was count the Gummi Bears some enterprising student had cut in half and managed to stick to the ceiling panels.

"Good for you," said a voice. "Though it doesn't account for the linear speed of the land masses, the earth's rotation, the turning of the universe, or even whether those things can actually be calculated in reference to singularity points."

All voices halted. All eyes turned. Even Tricia looked, and saw Alex looking, too. Something interesting had just been said, which meant something interesting might actually be happening.

Nope. Not in Sunrise. Pop. 2067 and never counting. "Interesting" has never lived here.

But she *did* look, and something interesting *did* happen.

The kid who had opened the door was nothing special to look at. He had the color hair that could be either light brown or dark blonde depending on the sunlight, and even at a distance she could tell his physique was similarly blah. A bit shorter than Alex and her, a bit skinnier; but nothing really noteworthy. The embodiment of average.

Only his eyes were arresting. The color was just as any-color-every-color-no-color boring as the rest of him, but there was no hiding how quick they moved around, searching faces, then corners, then shadows, and then back to the faces. They were the eyes of an animal that was often hunted, but had learned confidence as much as fear. They were the eyes of a survivor, and Tricia knew it, temporal lobe to tips of toes as her dad always said. (Alex said "brain to balls," which she pretended to be horrified at but secretly thought was hysterical.)

Either way, the thought behind it was the same, and she knew that Alex would be taking in the details of the new kid, and coming to the same conclusions she had.

Mr. Angle was walking over to the guy. "Are you –"

"Sam," interrupted the newcomer.

"All right, Mr. Jones," said Mr. Angle. He gestured for the new kid to follow him, then started walking across the classroom. He was headed toward Tricia and Alex – situated in the back corner so that hopefully (for Mr. Angle) no one would ever notice they were there or how easily they flouted his authority.

Mr. Angle had a look on his face that Tricia did not like. He was smiling, and not in the smug way he got right before he inevitably got knocked on his huge butt/tiny pants. He was smiling like he actually knew something that Tricia did *not* know.

"Uh-oh," said Alex, so low that no one but she could hear it.

Mr. Angle stopped right between their two desks. Jerking his thumb at the newcomer, he said, "Meet Sam Jones."

Alex nodded. Tricia shrugged and said, "Charmed, you're sure."

Mr. Angle bristled a bit, but the irritation disappeared quickly, swallowed by that supremely disconcerting smile. He turned to Sam. "There is a bench just outside the door. Why don't you take the books you showed the receptionist outside and show them off for a bit?"

Sam shrugged. He glanced around the class, as did Tricia and Alex. Again, she knew what Alex was seeing on all the faces, because she saw it herself: confusion, curiosity; a mixture of irritation that none of the other students had been singled out to go outside, and relief for the very same reason.

She didn't know what Sam thought when he looked around. Probably something dumb.

Even after what he said at the door? Dumb?

Sure. Even a parrot can mimic something smart if it hangs around the right people.

By the time she had gotten up and followed Sam out of the room, Alex right behind, Mr. Angle was already droning about the *actual* speed of the tire that had started all this nonsense, and Tricia had convinced herself that the new guy was probably dumb. It would be just like Mr. Angle: *can't keep up with Tricia and Alex, so let's give them a handicap to keep them at our level.*

But those handicaps never worked out in favor of anyone but her and Alex.

Alex, as always, appeared to have come to the same conclusions that Tricia had, because as soon as the door closed behind them he said to Sam, "That was a cute sentence in there, it was nonsense."

Sam grinned, and the smile was a familiar one: Tricia had seen it on Alex's face from time to time, and she knew she herself made that expression. It was an "ain't I funny?" grin with a bit of a "screw you" twist at the corner.

"I know that," said Sam. "But no one *else* in there knew that." He winked.

Tricia felt a bit off-balance. This was new, and it was interesting, and only five minutes ago she would have given a lot for new and interesting to walk through the door. Now, she wondered if she had been right to wish for such a thing. "But do you know *what* about what you said was nonsense..." she began.

Alex picked up the thread of her sentence, "... or did you just learn... to... say..."

His voice drifted to silence. That was fine; Tricia wouldn't have heard anything he said past that anyway.

9
(When Alex Had Grown)

Something touched his skin, and Alex jumped.

"Just me," said Trish. Her hand traveled down his arm, and he felt an electric thrill, so like the time before. The time they entered the trees and held hands and kissed for the first time.

Now where did that *come from? We didn't kiss in the forest. Did we?*

No. It happened here.

Alex looked out the front windshield. He had stopped the car here on purpose. The point of the trip was to go to the forest, to "face their fears" or whatever psychobabble Coleman had been pushing, but Alex knew it was really for him and Trish to come together again. And where better than in Sundown? In their place of Firsts?

So he had stopped outside Tina Louise's Diner. He was kind of amazed that it was still there. It had been there his whole life, and assuming that the eponymous Tina Louise opened it in her thirties or forties, she had to be in her seventies or eighties by now.

Still, the neon sign was on just like always, blinking day and night. The only thing that had changed was that the paint was a bit more faded, and the "e" in "Diner" flickered off a bit faster than the rest of the letters.

"Why'd you stop here?" said Trish.

"You know why," he said.

"Firsts," she said. She even smiled a bit, and he thought he could have lit a fire with the warmth that smile brought.

She had smiled less and less since they lost Sammy. More recently, she smiled not at all.

"Firsts," he said. He smiled, too. It felt good, and for a minute he figured if he could bottle that feeling and sprinkle it on them, they'd both fly away to Neverland.

But Neverland is a horror. It's where the little boy never grows up.

The thought sobered him, and he might not have gotten out at all if Trish hadn't done so. But she did, so he followed her out and together they entered the diner. Another change: instead of a bell over the door, an electronic tone sounded to announce their entrance.

"Take a seat," someone shouted from the kitchen. "Be right there!" Then the person – a woman – said, in quieter tones obviously meant for someone else, "No, you *won't*." A voice responded, too low to be heard, but Alex thought it sounded angry. "Because the timing has to be just right or it'll happen too early or too late, and then what happens, huh?" Tina Louise barked back at whoever she shared the kitchen with.

Trish cocked an eyebrow. Alex did, too, wondering what *that* was about. It sounded serious, and more than a little strange. He was about to say something about it, but something crashed in the kitchen area, followed by the angry murmurs of a muffled back-and-forth argument.

Alex flinched at the crash, as did Trish, and both did the same thing everyone does in a diner when there's a loud noise: they looked around to see who did it, who had noticed, and how people would react.

They couldn't see who did it. Tina Louise's was a fifties-style diner. White tile floors, red-vinyl-coated seats. A long bar where you could eat dinner or just have a shake. Whatever had fallen had done so in the back of the diner, behind the bar and the small wall beyond it. Alex saw a flash of movement through the window cut-out that allowed cooks to slide orders through to the waitress, but nothing more than that.

As to who noticed, and how everyone would react, that was easy to see since Alex and Trish were the only patrons. The place could probably seat fifty in a pinch, but there was no one else in here now.

Alex hummed the theme from *The Twilight Zone*. Again, Trish almost laughed. Again, the moment was lost as someone slammed through the swinging door that led to the kitchen.

It was Tina Louise. No doubt about it, and no one else it could be. Not only did she have her hair done in the same beehive getup she always wore, not only was she wearing the same skirt that was far too short for a woman her age, but she had the same odd-colored hair. It had to be dyed at this point in her life – maybe it always *had* been dyed – but the hair that curled in sweaty ringlets around her temples and at her neck was an impossible shade of bright red that Alex had never seen on anyone else's head, before or since.

"Don't wait to be seated, folks, this isn't that kind of place," she said.

Alex and Trish made their way to the same place they had sat every time they came here. The booth in the back corner.

"Firsts," he murmured again. He turned to see his wife blush a bit.

Tina Louise trailed them. Alex wondered if he should say her name. Would that be weird? She wouldn't remember them, surely, among all the tens of thousands of people she had served.

Or maybe it was only us. Not very crowded in here now, that's for sure.

Whether she remembered them or not, Alex *definitely* remembered her and this place. He and Trish had only come here twice – both wonderful events: the Firsts.

Then they had come here a third time – or at least driven past it – on the day they lost Sammy. A First of a different, horrible kind.

Thinking of that almost made Alex leave right then. What were they *doing* here?

But Trish was already sitting down. And she looked, not happy, exactly, but *better.*

Of course, that might be easier for her. She hadn't seen what happened to Sammy. She was out cold.

But was that really a mercy? At least he could hear me screaming his name, maybe knowing how much I loved him when he went.

Either way, Trish was sitting, she was staying. So he would sit, he would stay. Staying together was their only chance, something inside him whisper-screamed.

As he sat down across from Trish, Tina Louise pulled a white pad from the apron she wore – longer than her skirt, which always cracked Alex up. "What can I getcha folks?" she asked. Her eyes widened. "Aren't you…" She coughed, as though a huge load of spit had just slid down her windpipe. Turning her head, she got herself under control. With a lopsided grin, she said, "Sorry." Then she shook her head. "You two those kids I found back here once?"

Now it was Alex's turn to blush.

Tina Louise saw the look, and grinned. It was a strange grin: full of nostalgia and a bit of happiness, sure… but there was also something hiding under the surface. Something dark, rippling, *crawling,* and more than a little terrifying.

The look disappeared as fast as it came. Just the smile remained, sincere and happy enough that Alex was sure he'd imagined that other look. "Not many kids have the guts to make out as hard as you two, right out here in front of God and everybody," she said.

"Well…" Trish began.

Her hand snaked across the table to take his. For a moment he was in the past. The moment she took his hand for the first time. Told him she wanted *more.* The moment he slid off his bench and onto hers. Kissed her.

It hadn't been planned, but it happened. And when it did, the floodgates opened wide and he knew they would be together, always and forever, and maybe for longer.

He lost himself in that young kiss, as did she, and the next thing he knew, a *slightly* younger-seeming Tina Louise was looming over them so close he was worried he might see up her skirt, telling them if they didn't cut it out she'd turn a hose on them to cool them both down. "We do the cooking in *back*, kids," she'd said. But she winked and brought them a single milkshake with two straws, whispering as she set them down, "You melted this ice cream into liquid, so you might as well drink what you made."

It was the day of Firsts. First hand held, first kiss (followed quickly by first very excellent make-out session), first realization she loved him in the same particular, total way that he loved her.

It was a year to the day after Sam disappeared. The closest they dared to come to the forest since it all happened, and neither of them really knew *why* they came. They just did, and Alex often wondered if, had they not, they would have ended up together. He had no doubt they would have been friends, but would they have been husband and wife? Would they have made Sammy, and then lost what they had made?

No answers there.

Now, the Tina Louise of this place and this time was nodding. "I can see you are." She put a mock-stern look on her face. "Am I going to have to get the hose?"

"We'll be good," said Trish. "Promise."

"Cross my heart," added Alex.

"Oh, don't do that. No need to swear upon death," said Tina Louise. "Just, a 'no, we aren't going to try out for a Playboy photo shoot' will suffice."

Alex and Trish both raised their free hands as though swearing a solemn oath, which made Alex chuckle. Trish did, too, and that made him full-on laugh.

Tina Louise had been smiling. Now her eyes shifted to look over Alex's shoulder. "Tim-get-back-in-the-kitchen!" she shouted, the words belted out so fast they melted together like the rat-ta-tat of a machine gun.

Alex swiveled to see what was happening and caught a glimpse of a young face and bright red hair.

Tina Louise shook her head as she turned back to them. "Sorry. He's new in Sundown," she said, as though this was some explanation that should make sense to anyone who walked in.

"I was here before you!" came a voice from the back, surprisingly angry.

Tina Louise spun toward the back of the diner. "That's not the way I remember it, Tim!" she shouted in a voice every bit as incensed. She turned back around, sighed, and said, "He's still acclimating."

That struck Alex as odd. "Acclimating to what?"

The smile that flew to Tina Louise's lips was so rigid it turned her kind face to a mask, a poor parody of confusion. "Sorry, what?" she said.

"You said he was 'acclimating,'" said Trish. Her hand, still holding Alex's, squeezed a bit, silently communicating,*"This is weird,"* before she said: "Is he your son?"

"No, my brother," Tina Louise said automatically.

"He's young," said Alex, then realized – too late – how offensive that statement might be to her.

"Oh. Um..." Tina Louise visibly struggled to figure out what to say next. "He arrived late. Much later than *I* would have expected." She laughed, a bit too boisterously, then said in a lower tone, "Him showing up was a bit of an accident."

Trish laughed at that – hesitantly. Alex did the same. Under most circumstances the statement could be construed as sibling rivalry. But the way Tina Louise said it...

"But enough about him," she continued. "I'm sure you're not interested in my weird family history – though I must say it's an interesting one! Not even sure *I* could explain it sometimes." Her index finger drew circles around her ear. "Hard for me to keep it all straight some days, let alone what it all means. That's one of the blessings of age: I get to be stupid and not have it affect my dance card."

She laughed. The laugh was strange and stilted, and again she flicked her eyes toward the kitchen. Then she recovered and her smile grew less stiff, more sincere as she looked back at Alex and Trish and finally answered the original question: "I probably meant *I* haven't acclimated. I wasn't expecting him to show up here when he did. And we don't get many new folks in Sundown." She nodded, this time out the window.

Alex and Trish both looked out, and saw something they remembered well. Sundown had its own sign, just like Sunrise. It even looked like the same designer had been hired for both, because the colors and sizes were the same, even though the mottos and populations were different. Sundown's sign could be easily seen from the diner:

Welcome to Sundown:
Where You Find Yourself At Home!
Pop. 1985 (And Counting!)

Like Sunrise's "Pop. 2067," Alex knew Sundown's "Pop. 1985" was a lie. Had to be, statistically.

"Anywho," said Tina Louise, "I remember you two certainly… um… *found* each other." Before either Trish or Alex could respond to that, she squinted and added, "You came back again once more, didn't you?"

"You must have a mind like a steel trap," said Alex, and meant it. He was aware of how smart he and Trish were – he rarely met anyone smarter, even in a field populated by people who scored off the charts – but he was still surprised from time to time by a person who could outshine him –

(Like Sam did; like we always hoped Sammy someday would.)

– in one way or another. For the owner of a diner to remember two people coming in, specifically and with detail, over a period of decades…

Trish whistled. "That's impressive," she said. "For you to remember us both times."

A shadow fell across her face, and Alex felt like hitting Tina Louise. Just for an instant. For realizing what Trish had, and for knowing what the proprietor of the diner was likely going to say. She had remembered them making out decades ago. She had remembered them coming in again ten years later. It stood to reason that she remembered why they were there that second time, too: their second major First.

It's okay. She won't remember everything. Just –

"You were pregnant," she said quietly. "You showed the ultrasound picture to everyone."

Trish mouthed a word: *"First."*

Alex thought another: *Last.*

"I was sorry to hear about what happened to that boy," she said. "To Sammy."

Tears welled in Trish's eyes, which Alex barely saw because the same thing was happening to him.

"How did you…" He couldn't finish the sentence.

"It was front page on the Sundown News Gazette, but even if it hadn't been, we would have known. It happened in our town, so what happened to you happened to all of us." The smile she gave them wasn't fake, but wasn't happy, either. Sadness made the lines in Tina Louise's face grow deep enough to fracture anything bright. "You two order whatever you want. Birthdays are on the house here."

"It's not our birthday," said Trish.

"Hush," answered Tina Louise. "If you're back in Sundown, it's either a birthday or a deathday, and I'd rather think it's the first."

She hurried away, dabbing at her eyes a bit. When she came back, she took their orders. Alex didn't know what he ordered. He ate it, though it didn't taste like anything but ash and lost yesterdays.

Trish held his hand, though. She ate a burger and fries one-handed, and her other clutched his so hard it felt painful. But the pain was good, because it was a pain she had given him. It was a pain that she shared with him, and he would take it gladly.

Sharing was something they hadn't done lately.

Maybe it was good they had come.

"Are we really going to that place?" Trish said suddenly.

He didn't know if she meant to the place where the car rolled, then caught fire, then exploded: or if she meant into the forest, where the first Sam had been lost, a blank spot in their memories given to them in return.

Either way, the answer was the same: "I don't know."

Trish nodded. She wasn't crying anymore, but the glimmers of brightness he had seen in her mood were gone, snuffed out by the well-intentioned Tina Louise.

And that particular well hadn't run dry, either. Tina Louise came out with a red bundle in her arms. Alex saw that color, and felt Trish's hand clench so hard that he was certain he would have bruises.

That color was one they knew well. As bright as Tina Louise's hair, and seeing it Alex was rocketed into another First. A good First. The day he and Trish found a friend, and also met the first person who was smarter than them.

10
(When Alex Was Young)

Alex stared at the new guy's bag. "That's quite the shade of red," he said.

It was actually the first thing he noticed about the new guy – the backpack that was about the brightest shade of red Alex had ever seen. It looked like a neon fire engine driving over a pair of jeans and a button-up shirt fastened all the way up, so close to the guy's neck it pinched the skin.

Then Alex noticed the guy's eyes. A color that washed right past you without being noticed. A *way* of looking at you that could not be missed by anyone with half a brain.

Alex prided himself on having a whole brain – or at least three-quarters of one, since that last twenty-five percent was devoted more and more to thinking about Trish. The way she smiled, the shine of her eyes. And that was saying nothing of the way she was filling out in all kinds of interesting ways.

Not now. Get your mind out of your pants, man. She's your best friend. She's like your sister. So –

New Guy spoke. He had a voice as arresting as his eyes, and Alex cursed his dumb teenage testosterone for taking so much of his attention. What had everyone been talking about?

"Yeah, the backpack is cool, ain't it?" said the new kid.

Alex barely heard the words. He was too busy backtracking through the hormone weeds that had momentarily choked out the usually well-ordered garden of thoughts he cultivated. So he fell back on what he had been thinking a few minutes ago – the thing he thought *before* seeing the backpack, when he was pretending to read while thinking about Trish, then pretending to think about Mr. Angle's dumb question while thinking about Trish, then pretending –

DUDE! Easy!

Too late. He was totally short-circuited. So he did what teens – and, he would someday discover, adults – almost always did when confused: he went on the offensive.

"Yeah. The stuff you said was nonsense. If you're going to account for variables like planetary rotation and orbit in order to compile an answer to a 'how fast' question then the end answer approaches infinite variables and null and is pointless for the question. Facts are only useful for thought games at a point where comprehension is possible."

"Oh, I know that," said New Guy. "But sometimes spouting purposeful nonsense is the best way to shut someone up, don't you think?"

"What kind of –" Alex cut off, not really sure how to respond to that one; not sure if his failure to speak was because New Guy was wrong or because he was right.

It's what we do, isn't it? We spout "purposeful nonsense" all the time to get people to shut up, or to ignore us.

Who is *this kid? Do you think Trish will like him? Like,* like *him?*

Alex realized that Trish wasn't joining in the discussion. Probably because she was a girl and so, unlike him, didn't struggle with sex thoughts that derailed him seven or eight times a second.

But she *had* been derailed by something, Alex noted. Specifically, the books that this Sam kid was pulling out of his blindingly red backpack. She started reading titles.

"*Fundamentals of Quantum Physics; Heavy Quark Physics; Non Trivial Integrals and Perturbative Renorm* –" She looked up. "I've never even heard of that one. How did you…" She frowned as Sam brought out yet another book from his seemingless endless stack. "What's *that* one?"

Sam said something Alex didn't understand. Not comprehensively, but linguistically – it was literally a different language.

"What's *that* supposed to mean?" said Alex. He was a little confused and more than a little irritated. He didn't understand what was going on, though a glimmer of comprehension had started to form, and he wasn't sure how he felt about the possibilities being suggested here.

"*Die altägyptischen Pyramidentexte,*" Sam repeated. "It's the gold standard for understanding the Pyramid Texts, in my opinion." Sam smirked. "Which makes it kinda the German bible of ancient Egyptian religious rituals describing transformation into Akh." He laughed as though what he had just said was terribly funny.

The glimmer exploded into a bonfire. Alex sighed. "Sonny, pretending like this ain't cool."

"Uh, Alex," said Trish. She was flipping through one of the texts that Sam had produced. "You –"

Alex barely heard her. For once he wasn't thinking of Trish and –

(The way she's started to look and act and things like her eyes and smile and also the way her t-shirt keeps stretching and –

DUDE! Respect! Sister-thoughts!)

– he was thrilled to be able to fixate on something else. "Pretending like this just proves you –"

"Alex, he –" Trish broke in again.

And again, Alex rode over her words: "– are a bigger fool than you would be if you just came into class admitting you were a moron."

"Alex, you should –"

"I mean, maybe you're ahead of the curve, but you aren't –"

"Al-*lex*."

Alex spun to look at Trish, surprised to see that in spite of her strident tones, she was still looking at the books she held in her lap and several she had tossed open on the bench beside her. "*What*?" he barked.

He was ashamed almost instantly. He never talked to Trish like this. Not even before –

(She turned into a babe.

DUUUUUUDE! Keep it in your PANTS!)

– they started high school and settled into the most annoyingly boring phase of life in the already-annoyingly boring world of Sunrise.

"Sorry, Trish," he said.

She didn't seem to notice the apology. She looked up and said, "Alex, there are *notes.* Good ones."

Alex felt like the world took a big step forward under him while he stayed rooted to some cementlike singularity in space-time. He looked at Sam, who had stayed silent during Alex's aborted tongue-lashing.

Alex knew what Trish was saying with her comment. Of course he did – they always understood each other, even when Alex's gonads *were* screaming for attention. "There are *notes,*" she had said. Then added the clincher: *"Good ones."*

Alex knew that it was easy to own the trappings of anything: you could *look* rich, you could *look* important, you could *look* popular. Heck, high school itself was basically a cult that worshipped at the altar of False Pretense. And looking clever was easy, too. Talk about your future plans to go to the right schools, mention your past test scores (real or imagined), or even just… have the right books in your cringey red backpack.

Pretense was easy.

But actually *being* rich meant you had to have money. Actually *being* popular meant you had to be crowned Homecoming Royalty. Actually *being* clever meant not just having the right books but a) understanding and b) being able to coherently comment on and discuss the subject matter.

Trish revised her earlier comment. "At least, I think they're good notes."

Alex spared her a quick glance before returning to Sam's laser-gaze. "What do you mean?"

"I mean he *understands* this stuff. At a level I don't." She looked up, and Alex would have sworn that joyful tears were in her eyes. "Someone finally came to Sunrise who is actually *smart*."

That was really all it took. Trish believed the new guy was smart, so Alex immediately believed it himself. He had yet to disagree with Trish about *anything* of import.

He looked at Sam with new eyes. Less hostile, more honestly appraising – though he had to admit he was feeling a pinch of jealousy at Trish's response to the guy's apparent brilliance. He managed to quash it, though, with the help of more than a little curiosity. He shuffled closer to Trish, craning his neck to look over her shoulder while standing in front of her. He craned his neck less as he sat down beside her on the bench, his eyes never straying from the book she held.

Then he craned his neck not at all, because he had pulled yet another book out of Sam's bulging red backpack, put it on his lap, and begun skimming both the text and the copious notes the new guy had made in the margins.

He looked at Sam. The dude was still standing there, hands now shoved deep into his pockets, looking at Alex and Trish with a strangely blank expression.

Alex opened his mouth to say something. Maybe "What does this mean?" maybe "Who are you, man?" or perhaps, "What test tube did you say they made you in?" But nothing came. He said nothing at all, and reflected that this was the first time he could ever remember being at a loss for words. And he remembered *everything*, pretty much from potty-training on.

He realized Trish was looking at the new guy, too, and knew without looking that she was going through the same strange wash of emotions. The same questions were on her lips, but just like Alex, her brain couldn't manage the leap to actual word-sounds.

Sam looked a bit embarrassed. No, that was wrong. Not embarrassed, just shy. He looked down at his feet, then – apparently only through an act of sheer will – looked up again. He pointed to a page on the book Trish was holding, which was covered by equations and text, with notes occupying every other available millimeter, and said, "You want me to tell you what I meant when I wrote that?"

Alex experienced something strange. He knew, suddenly and completely, what the new guy meant. He had never felt this way with anyone but Trish, and he knew that was, at least in part, because he had never met anyone as smart as him before. Not the other students, not the teachers. Occasionally he felt like his mother might be that smart – she never acted like it, but in between chain-smoking and biting her fingernails to nubs, glaring at Trish's dad whenever she saw him, she occasionally made some observation that led Alex to believe she knew a *lot* more about history, math, science, and a bunch of other subjects than she ever let on.

But that was it. Just him, Trish. Maybe his mother (and, Trish said, maybe her father as well, though she was as unsure as Alex was of his own parent).

They had never before met anyone else like them. Anyone else truly *smart.*

Until now.

So Alex knew what Sam was really asking. It wasn't "Want me to tell you what I wrote here about the value of chromodynamics as applied to the Pyramid Texts?" or even just "Want me to discuss the curve ball I tossed Mr. Angle?"

It was *everything.* It was, "Do you want me to explain anything you don't know about in those books?" It was, "Do you want me to tell you my own personal conclusions?"

It was, simply, "Do you want me to tell you everything I know?"

"Yes," said Trish, and Alex echoed, "Hell yes."

That was all it took.

Sam went to the bench. He shimmied between Alex and Trish – something no one had ever dared before – and then grabbed the book Alex was looking at. He flipped through the pages. Frowned. "There's a better one in my bag."

"I'll get it," said Alex. He pulled the bag open, surprised at the number of books the bright red eyesore still held. He also noticed something he hadn't seen before.

"Why do you have pants and a shirt in here?"

Sam shrugged. "Just in case." He shrugged again. "You never know."

"In case what?"

Sam shrugged. "In case my mom turns out to be right."

That was all he said on the subject. He reached across Alex and pulled out another book. Flipping through it, he said, "Okay, let's start here."

Alex listened to Sam. A moment later, Trish asked a question. Alex followed up with an observation. Trish challenged it, posited an opposing conclusion – one Alex admitted had more merit, but which he also knew Trish would not have come up with had she not first heard his idea. They bounced ideas off each other like this all the time, neither of them quite sure *whose* idea they settled on, because there was no making a decision or coming to a conclusion before both had contributed, crafted, refined.

Sam frowned. "I think you're both right, but in a way that brings us to a third position." He frowned, then rummaged through his bag, drawing out a book. "Here, Schwarz makes a decent point of it when he says…"

He was reciting the passage before he even opened the book – another thing that Alex had never seen anyone but him and Trish doing.

They talked, on and on. The bell rang for class to be over, and when the following bell marking the beginning of the next period came, they were still sitting at the bench. No teacher came to fetch them, and Alex knew in the back of his mind that no teacher would bother.

The bench became school. The three became teachers and students to one another.

By the end of the second day, Alex was worried that he might have a rival to his burgeoning affection for Trish. By the end of the third day he knew it was a non-issue, because the three of them had moved beyond questions like that. By the middle of the fourth day he realized that Sam was bonded to them, and they to him. He had started thinking of Sam in the same terms as he did Trish. Not the beauty, of course – Trish was still the one thing Alex's body ran to whenever it could convince his brain to turn away from friendship and turn to other, more basic appreciations – but Alex had started to include Sam in the "*we*" that shaped his universe.

Alex.

Trish.

Sam.

Friends, he knew, forever.

But of course, Alex was a teenager. He could not know that "forever" was quite a different thing to experience than it was to think about. He could not know, either, that "forever" would take a dark turn the next day – the day Tricia found her home violated and her pets killed; the day they met Sam's mother.

The day they followed Sam into the trees, and fell into the only true "forever" – the dark eternity that could be found only in the forest.

11
(When Tricia Had Grown)

Tricia stared at the bright red thing in Tina Louise's hand. Brighter than the brightest parts of the diner-owner's hair. Brighter than an apple, new from the tree and polished to a sheen. A shade of red she knew she should hate, but which she could only love.

Or at least, a shade she *had* loved. She didn't know if she loved anything anymore. Love, she had discovered, was more than a feeling – more than a noun with abstract, vague qualities. It was a verb. It was *actions*.

But she hadn't been able to do much of anything since losing Sammy. She had pushed through the pain at first, but soon she found that just showing up to her job and continuing to work at a level that would let her keep it took almost all of her strength. When she got home, all her powers to *act* were exhausted. She sat in front of the TV, and did as little as possible. And, doing little, she felt even less. Everything that had been so bright and vivid – even after the forest, and maybe in a way *because* of the forest – slowly faded. Entropy set in, and the world tranformed to shades of gray.

Seeing Tina Louise's Diner had reminded her of Firsts, and that brought a few shades of color to her life. Holding Alex's hand had been hard, but she knew it was right. More of the gray disappeared – enough to see Tina Louise's horrific, laughable, and somehow *perfect* hair.

The colors were still faded, and much was still gray, still lost in mist. But it was a start.

And then the package Tina Louise held. The bright red thing that reminded Tricia of Sam's backpack.

Was he wearing it the last time I saw him? Or had he lost it?

But that wasn't all it reminded her of. It also brought to mind the boy they had named for the lost friend, and the toy they had bought their child. It was red, just like the backpack, so of course they had to get Sammy the little plush unicorn when they saw it.

It had been lost, too. The same day they lost Sammy, the same place they lost their friend. The red was gone, the color washed away, lost to a forest where everything was –

(Silver. Glowing. Like mist.)

– done up in shades of black.

Tricia shivered. Alex's hand tightened on hers, and she knew he was thinking of the same reds she remembered, the color that matched the thing Tina Louise now held.

The diner's owner moved some plates to the side and placed the parcel on the table. It was about two feet long, about eight inches high and eight inches deep. Two lengths of black webbing were affixed to it, sewn to the red nylon fabric in inverted *u* shapes that served as handles.

On the top, on the end of the thing nearest Tricia and Alex, a laminated image had been glued. It showed a family – father, mother, son, daughter – smiling as they grilled hot dogs on a barbecue, the object in the parcel standing upright behind them.

"Tent's mine," said Tina Louise. "One of my kids gave it to me. Maybe my brother. Hard to remember sometimes." A strange look came over her, and Tricia felt suddenly like she was in danger.

(I'm seeing the man in the tree.

But he had no expression. He had no face.*)*

"It's… nice," said Alex. Kind Alex, dear Alex, who was always looking for a way to be nicer than he felt like being. Tricia looked at him. He was flushed: confused, embarrassed, scared. Just like her.

Tina Louise looked down at the red nylon package that held a four-person dome tent. She played absently with the handles, looking for a moment as though she might grab them and take the thing back into the kitchen.

"It was a present," she said again. A moment later she seemed to come to a decision. She slid it a bit farther onto the table. The message was clear: *"Here. Take it. It's yours now."*

Alex shook his head. "We're not the camping types," he said.

"Oh, I know that," said Tina Louise. "It's just..." She searched for the words, looking from Tricia to Alex. "I don't know. You're here. You've got things you're celebrating, and things you're mourning. I don't know how long you plan to stay in Sundown, but there are some nice places to camp just inside the forest. And I have a friend who decided to go on a trip and *didn't* go with a tent, and wished he'd had one after that. It's always good to –"

"We're not staying there," said Tricia. The words came out sharper than intended, and Tina Louise shied away as though worried she was going to be hit.

"We... we were just visiting," said Alex. "Just planning on driving around for a bit. Just passing through."

Tina Louise nodded, "Oh, I know that. But in case you decided to stay –"

"Then we'd stay in a motel," Tricia cut in. She did her best not to speak angrily, but wanted to sound firm. She wanted this conversation to end. It was too strange – and not just the oddness of getting a tent from a woman they barely knew. It was the little things. The way she said her brother was new in Sundown. The way she kept saying, "Oh, I know that," as though she was best friends with Tricia and Alex, or at least a nosy neighbor who watched them through a crack in the curtains around her kitchen window.

The way Tricia for some reason *wanted* the tent. Almost needed it.

Tina Louise shook her head sadly. "No motel in Sundown," she said. "And the one in Sunrise is closed. Remodeling." She laughed a bit and said, "Putting in wifi, too, I hear." Another strange, strangled laugh. "Technology, ain't it a hoot?"

"We're not planning on staying," said Tricia, one more time, hoping that this time –

"Oh, I know that," said Tina Louise. "Still, the tent's yours."

She walked away. Tricia watched her walk away. The old woman's shoulders slumped a bit as she walked, and by the time she reached the kitchen she looked like she had just finished a marathon.

She turned around at the last moment, and said, "Just in case." She shrugged, looking like the movement cost the last of her strength. "You never know."

She turned and pushed open the swinging door that led to the kitchen. The door, like kitchen doors in restaurants everywhere, sported double action hinges, so when Tina Louise passed through and then let go, the door followed her into the kitchen, then swung into the dining area, then back into the kitchen.

The first swing into the kitchen revealed Tina Louise, leaning against a counter, wiping her forehead.

Then a swing into the diner.

Then another slice of the kitchen: no Tina Louise this time. She had moved out of view.

Another swing.

A final pass into the kitchen, though this time the swing was so small that Tricia just barely glimpsed the man who was looking back at her. Just enough to see the same hair that Tina Louise sported. Her brother. The one who was "new," whatever that meant.

Then the door between the two worlds settled into place, making no noise at all, not even a whisper to mark the finality of the split.

Alex stood abruptly. "Nice of her to comp the meal," he said in a strange, gray voice.

"Nice," agreed Tricia.

He looked at the red pack on the table. "It reminds me…"

He didn't finish the sentence. He didn't have to.

Alex grabbed the handles. Lifted the pack. "We're not –" began Tricia.

"Oh, I know that," he said. Tricia wondered if he was aware that he had just mirrored Tina Louise's repeated statement.

Whether he did or not, he took the pack just the same. They left the diner, and he tossed the tent into the trunk of their car, then stood still. "Where to?" he asked.

Before Tricia could answer, she heard a shout: "*YOU!*"

She turned toward the voice and saw a man erupt from the shadows of an alley across the street. He looked like any other homeless person who would stay in an alley, though Tricia had to wonder how a "Pop. 1985" kind of place could spare even a single person for the role of Homeless Guy No. 1 in their day-to-day operations.

It struck her, then, that she had never seen anyone in Sundown. Just Tina Louise, a few people in the diner the times they came. No one else.

She had stayed within a few miles of this town for most of her life. She had passed through some of her most important experiences here; had the deepest roots here, in a way. But the place was deserted-seeming, and she was just now realizing that fact.

All this passed through her mind as the homeless person ran toward her and Alex. The shocked, sideways spin of thoughts was her only defense against the oddness of the experience at Tina Louise's place, and now the sight of an indigent rushing at her in a town that seemed empty, maybe dead.

Then she had no time to think of anything else. The man who screamed had run across Sundown's two-lane Main Street, into the tiny parking lot of Tina Louise's Diner.

"Hey!" shouted Alex. The guy glanced in Alex's direction, then turned his gaze back on Tricia.

It was a terrifying gaze. His eyes moved spastically, jerking in every direction but straight ahead. He was seeing many things, but Tricia suspected that reality wasn't one of them.

Before her body figured out what to do about this newest oddity, the guy was on her. He slammed into her, driving her to the ground. Alex was running as it happened, but couldn't reach her before she was falling, her head bouncing painfully off the pavement as the bum started screaming, "How many times? *When has it happened and when will it happen?"*

The bum grabbed her head, hands clamped tightly on either side. He lifted her head up, and she had a moment where she saw – with strange clarity – his beard. It was scraggly, but not long. A beard badly started, and what little there was of it was matted with dirt and food and perhaps a bit of blood.

The man pulled her head up higher. She saw his clothes. Less ratty than she would expect; indeed, they looked like they might have been very nice in the not-too-distant past. A button-up shirt, filthy and stained but with an expensive-looking cut. A suit jacket, the filth and the tear that spread along one side of the front panel doing its best to hide the original tailoring.

Something glinted on the pocket of his jacket. She didn't see what, though, because the bum/not-bum slammed her down on the pavement. Her head thudded against it, and everything went dark, though not before she heard the bum scream it again: *"How many TIMES?"*

12
(When Alex Had Grown)

It unfolded strangely for Alex:

The man, across the street. Shouting something that Alex barely heard because he was still trying to wrap his head around the weird turn things had taken in the diner.

The man, now on this side of the street. Now screaming incomprehensibly.

The man, heading toward Trish.

The man, tackling her.

Alex, who stood stunned for the first seconds of it, finally moved. He ran around the front of the car, screaming, "Get off her!" and then, "Help!" and then, "Trish!" as he saw the guy slamming her head against the pavement and screaming, *"How many TIMES?"*

Trish's eyes rolled back. A gauzy curtain of bright red – as red as the tent pack, as red as Sam's bag or Sammy's unicorn – dropped over Alex's vision. He screamed again, wordlessly this time, then tackled Trish's attacker. He drove his shoulder into the man's side and shoulder, pitching the stranger away from his wife, then riding the man down to the pavement beside her, ending up half-straddled over him, not sure whether he should try and pin the guy or start hitting him.

The guy squirmed, writhing like a fish, flopping around and trying to get free of Alex. He couldn't, though he did manage to roll over onto his back. He looked up at Alex as though seeing him for the first time, then said, "You, too?"

Then he did what somehow struck Alex as the strangest thing of all: he started to cry.

All the fight had dropped out of him as soon as he saw Alex. Now he was as limp as Trish, the only movement that of his body as it shook with shuddering sobs.

"Help!" Alex shouted. "Help me!" He hoped he was shouting loudly enough for someone to hear – maybe Tina Louise or her brother. He didn't know what to do until someone else came – he wanted to check on Trish, but didn't want to let the guy up.

"Help!"

A third time, and now Alex looked around. A quick glance to see if anyone was coming. There were several businesses nearby. A mom-and-pop corner store. A Postal Annex. A storefront with a window that proclaimed its willingness to handle taxes, *"Se habla español."*

A man who looked to be in his fifties or sixties was peeking out of this last. Alex, not wanting to take his hands away from the shoulders of the crazy man weeping below him, moved his head in tight circles that he hoped conveyed his need for the man to come out.

The man didn't. He frowned, then shook his head in an almost weary way, then leaned away and disappeared from view.

Alex looked back down at the man who was no longer struggling below him. He glanced at Trish, who was moaning softly and blinking. She rolled her head to the side, and mouthed something. At the same time, the guy beneath Alex jerked his hips up, suddenly trying to buck him off. Alex flew forward, posting his hands on the pavement by the crazy guy's ears to keep from eating asphalt.

The man was rolling toward Trish now.

He had a knife.

He reared back – not much, he was still mostly pinned under Alex – but more than enough to ram the knife right through Alex's wife.

Alex reacted automatically, wrestling with the guy's knife arm, pulling him into a roll that ended with them both several feet away from Trish – good! – but now with the madman on top, pushing the knife downward toward Alex's shoulder – not good at all.

"It's going to happen," said the madman, spittle flying from his lips, spattering Alex's cheeks. "Now or later, it'll happen. Some things don't but other things do. Things stay the same, even when things don't stay the same."

Alex clamped his hands around the guy's wrist, pushing up for all he was worth. The madman grunted and leaned into the knife. Alex couldn't stop its descent. All he managed to do was keep the blade descending toward his shoulder rather than aimed directly at his throat or heart.

Beside them, Trish rolled to hands and knees. She swayed, then steadied, and Alex could see her about to throw herself into the crazy man still trying to stab Alex.

"Don't do it!" Alex tried to say. But he only managed the first word before he heard a hornet buzzing.

A hornet?

The lunatic's weight suddenly shifted, and Alex suddenly gained control of the knife as the attacker rolled off him. The hornet sound kept up for a moment, then a pair of workbooted feet entered his field of vision. Alex followed them up to beige pants, to a thick black utility belt with a gun on it, to a greenish-beige button-up shirt that had a star pinned to it.

"Sorry," said the woman who had just saved him. She was holding a Taser in her hand, twin lines trailing from it to the back of the madman who had attacked Alex and Trish. The officer – a sheriff, according to her badge – grimaced and jerked her head at the man twitching on the ground. "I tried to stop him before he got to you, but…" Another grimace.

The madman was still twitching, but the violence of his seizures was lessening. The sheriff leaned over and, in a smooth motion, cuffed the attacker.

Crazily, Alex wondered why he himself hadn't been shocked when the guy got hit with the Taser. Even more crazily, the sheriff answered his unspoken question. "The design of the

Taser makes current just flow between the points of contact. No danger to anyone a bad guy is holding onto." Then, apparently correctly deciphering Alex's look of surprise, she shrugged and said, "People are curious about that."

Alex almost asked *what* people, and how often the sheriff had to do something like this, when he remembered: "Trish!"

He rolled toward her, scrambling to hands and knees, then just knees as he scrabbled his way to his wife. She was on her knees as well, bracing one hand against the car for support. "I'm okay," she said.

"Let me see." Alex felt the back of her head. A knot was forming there, but miraculously, he couldn't feel any blood. "We should get you to a doctor," he said.

Trish shook her head. "No," she said. "Not here. They can't –"

Alex nodded. There wasn't a hospital nearby – they were an hour from the nearest town big enough to have so much as a multi-doctor private practice, so they would have to go to the little general practitioner's office in Sundown if they wanted fast help. If it was even still there.

That was where they had been taken after what happened to Sammy. And Trish was right: the doctor hadn't been able to help a thing.

"You sure?" said the sheriff. "We have a good GP here, he can take a look at –"

"*No,*" Trish snapped. Softening her voice, she added, "No, thank you."

The sheriff shrugged. "Suit yourself."

Alex heard the electronic tone of the door to Tina Louise's Diner, and looked over to see her running toward them. No brother, though.

He's probably still in the back, being "new."

Alex almost started laughing at that. It would have been an ugly laugh, empty of humor and full of hysteria. He gritted his teeth and bit it back, then felt the back of Trish's head again.

"I'll be okay," she murmured.

Tina Louise stopped a few feet away, when the sheriff said, "It's over."

That, like so much of the day, struck Alex as odd. So did the fact that Tina Louise didn't ask any questions. No, "What happened?" or "Where did that guy come from?" or even, "Did you know my brother's *new*?" (and Alex had to grit his teeth again, harder this time, to keep that ugly laugh from coming).

"Okay," Tina Louise said. She looked at Trish. "You need an ice pack, sweetie?"

"I've got one at the station," said the sheriff.

"Station?" said Alex. A strange panic had set in, like the sheriff had just told him he was being taken away to be questioned and perhaps waterboarded. "We don't –"

"Julie," said Tina Louise. "There's time to give the girl –"

"It's *Sheriff Azakh,*" said the sheriff. Alex looked at her for the first time. She was about Alex's height, with brown eyes and light brown hair beginning to gray, cut so short it looked more like the haircut of a man than that of a woman. She had pale skin with a sprinkling of freckles visible on her nose. She looked like she was about fifty, maybe a bit younger. She didn't look like an "Azakh." Not that Alex knew what an Azakh should look like, but the name still struck him as strange; ill-fitting.

Curiouser and curiouser, thought Alice as she fell down the rabbit hole.

Tina Louise pursed her lips. "You want to fight or something?" she said to the sheriff.

Sheriff Azakh sighed. Alex wondered if that was the sheriff's primary expression. "No, Tina Louise. I just want to do my job and keep things moving the way they should, same as you do every day."

Tina Louise's eyes flicked toward Alex. Toward Trish. She nodded, then went back inside the diner.

The sheriff watched her go, then started pulling the crazy man who had started all this to his feet. "Up you go, sir." The guy tried to get his feet under him, failed, and fell flat on his face, which elicited yet another sigh from the sheriff. She pulled harder, and slowly the guy got to his feet.

Alex stood as well, then helped Trish up. She grimaced, and for a moment he thought she might fall again. "No, I'm okay," she said.

Sheriff Azakh jerked her chin down the road. "My office is just a block away. You can put up your feet there 'til you get settled." Yet one more sigh. "I have to take your statement, so you might as well relax while I process this guy."

The guy in question looked like he wanted to say something, but the sheriff shook him and said, "You're in enough trouble, wouldn't you say? Your little part in this story is over, so I'd say it's time to shut your mouth and do right by yourself unless you want me to zap you again." A spark of coherence entered the other man's eyes for the first time, and he nodded. "Good man," said Sheriff Azakh.

She sighed again.

"Come on," she said, and began to walk down the road, half-pushing, half-leading the man who had just tried to kill Trish, and then Alex as well. She didn't wait for them, just headed down the road, pushing the guy every once in a while.

Déjà vu suddenly gripped Alex. He was *sure* he had been here before; done all of it over and over again.

Of course. You keep losing things here.

He looked at Trish. *Not her, though. Saved her, at least.*

From what?

He knew he wasn't asking the question about this moment only. He was asking about the day they had lost.

The ghosts. The whispers and whisperers and the monsters behind the curtain.

The thoughts meant nothing; nonsense words pushing unbidden into his mind. Still, they almost staggered Alex. He clung to Trish now, half supporting her, half being supported *by* her.

Sheriff Azakh was halfway down the street, still shoving her prisoner along. Alex wondered why she wasn't driving the guy to wherever she was going, then realized he hadn't seen a police car anywhere.

Or any car, for that matter. Other than the man in the accounting place (*"Se habla español!"*) and Tina Louise, there was no one.

"It's empty," whispered Trish.

"Yeah," he said. He looked around. They hadn't taken the car, just started along behind the sheriff, going wherever she was taking them.

Following again. Not knowing where we're going – again.

Curioser and curioser.

The sheriff turned, heading toward a small, one-story building that looked like it might have been a bank at one time but now said "SHERIFF" in big letters on the front window.

Alex looked at Trish, though they both kept walking. She wasn't looking forward, apparently trusting him to lead her in the right direction. Instead, she was staring at a shop window. A sign above the shop proclaimed "TOOLS!" in almost exactly the same lettering as the sheriff's station used. Below that: "We buy lawnmowers and fix shovel handles" on a handwritten sign in the window, which struck Alex as immensely funny for some reason.

In the window, an old woman stood, only her head visible above the sign. She was in her seventies, probably, with the hard eyes and weathered skin of someone used to struggling. Tough as jerky, cunning as a fox – that was the impression Alex got of her. Other than that, he couldn't see much: she was standing mostly behind the lawnmower/shovel handles sign, and her hair was obscured by a large straw hat.

Again, that seemed funny for some reason. Alex giggled. Tried to stop it, but it came again.

Trish laughed as well – louder than him. "So people *do* live here," she said.

"Yes. A sheriff, a diner owner, a few folks who like to stare at strangers, and – don't forget! –"

"The new guy," Trish finished.

Both of them dissolved into laughter.

It wasn't really that funny, Alex knew. Nothing about today had been particularly funny. But sometimes you had to laugh because if you didn't you'd cry and if you started crying you might just keep crying until the day you died.

He and Trish were holding their stomachs, hiccuping and coughing they were laughing so hard. They only stopped when Trish weaved a bit. Alex grabbed her shoulders, worried she'd fall.

"I'm okay," she said. "Just a bit dizzy."

"Let's get you sitting down," said Alex.

"Good idea."

He put her arm over his shoulder. The rest of the short walk to the sheriff's station she leaned on him. Her weight on his shoulders and back was comforting, in a way. She was leaning on him again, and she hadn't done *that* in a long time, either.

Maybe Coleman had been right about them coming here.

Still haven't actually gone there, *though. Not to where we have to go if we really want to look at the spot where we lost a day, then lost* everything.

They arrived at the doors to the sheriff's station. They entered the place, and an electronic bell – the same one as at Tina Louise's Diner – buzzed its dry tone.

They entered, and Alex looked around for some kind of seating. He could have found a single grain of sand in this place, given how small and clean everything was, so finding the pale blue plastic chairs that lined one wall was easy.

He sat Trish down. "You –"

She waved him off. "I'm fine. Not even dizzy anymore."

"Let me check."

She leaned forward a bit. He felt her head. "Goose egg back there."

"That's all?" She winced. "Feels more like an elephant egg."

"Elephants don't lay eggs."

"Then one sat on my head. Close enough."

He chuckled. So did she. Like her leaning on him, it felt good. Shades of better yesterdays. Perhaps the hopes of better tomorrows.

He looked around. The front office was bisected by a railing with a gate in the middle, the kind you would see in black-and-white TV shows from a time where every cop was good, every crime solved, and everyone who went to jail was truly guilty.

Behind the gate sat a single desk. A cowboy hat with an honest-to-goodness star on it rested on the desk, beside a rotary phone that was probably installed by Ma Bell herself, back before she got swallowed by cell towers and roaming charges.

"It's like the sheriff's station that time forgot."

"Clean, though," said Trish.

"Sparkling," he said, consciously one-upping her.

She rose to the bait: "Like it's cleaned every five minutes."

"Like it's never been *used*."

"You could eat off the floor."

"You could do surgery on the floor."

"You could…" She shook her head. "You win." Then she said, in a tone that said she wasn't hopeful of winning this impromptu contest, "Make love on the floor?"

"Maybe we should try it. For science."

He was worried his response would fall flat. Intimacy had been a problem in the last months, as well. He wanted to sometimes, and could tell she did, too. But it was more a physical release than the act of closeness and caring it had always been. And that knowledge stopped anything from happening. He didn't just want her body, he wanted *her*, and wasn't going to be satisfied with just the shell of his wife.

Trish laughed delightfully. She waggled her eyes. "Maybe after the elephant gets off my head."

"It's a date."

Her voice grew soft and strangely plaintive. "Is it?"

Alex was saved from having to figure out how to answer that by the sheriff, who came through a door in the back of the tiny room. "You here? Good. Come on."

She waved and then disappeared back through the door.

Alex looked at Trish, who shrugged. *This is the weirdest day ever,* said the motion.

He nodded. He shrugged back. His said, *Weird is okay. We can handle weird.*

She reached out her hand.

He took it.

He didn't need to support her as they walked into the back of the office, but she kept holding his hand. He squeezed it. She squeezed his back, then switched her grip so her fingers twined through his.

That made Alex smile, and he was still grinning as he stepped through the back door and into what he saw was a tiny holding area. Two cells, each with a cot and a metal toilet. Two iron doors. Two keyholes.

Two people trying to kill each other.

The sheriff and the homeless man who had attacked them – still handcuffed, but looking decidedly more lively than he had when walking to the station – were struggling over the gun they both tried to control.

Alex took a lurching step toward them, something in the back of his mind screaming that he should help. He took an equally jerky step back, something in the *front* of his mind screaming that he had to get Trish out of here, get her away from this, get her safe and –

BOOM!

The gun went off.

Trish shouted in pain.

"Trish!" Alex shouted, though he heard nothing more than an echoing explosion followed by a high-pitched ringing. The gunshot had been deafening in the small space with nothing but hard surfaces that ricocheted sound so intensely the blast of the gun was amplified over and over.

Alex shouted again, and the word came out similarly muffled. Trish must have heard it, even so. She waved to show she was all right, the other hand clapped to one of her ears. But though she heard him shout, she wasn't seeing him. She was looking past him.

Alex turned and saw where the bullet had gone. The homeless man who attacked them had stiffened, but only for a moment. He slid to the floor, which was really the only option when a person's brains had been blown out.

Sheriff Azakh stood over the body, the gun still smoking in her hand. The body on the floor twitched once, violently and with a suddenness that made everyone watching it flinch almost as violently. Then it was still.

The sheriff put her gun back in its holster. Alex noted through vision that had collapsed into a tunnel that her hand didn't shake. She leaned down and put two fingers against the dead man's throat, but it was a cursory movement. She sighed, straightened, and said, to no one in particular, "He just went for my gun out of nowhere."

Then she turned and walked toward Trish and Alex. They glanced at one another, then parted to let the sheriff pass, through the door and into the reception area/lounge/waiting room in the sterile chamber beyond.

The sheriff picked up the old rotary phone. Dialed a number. The wheel spun after each number – *z-z-z-z, click-tic-tic, z-z-z-z-z-z, click-tic-tic-tic* – with agonizing slowness.

"Why doesn't she have a real phone?" asked Trish. Alex was relieved that he could hear her better than he expected. Both the dull roar and the high-pitched whistle had started to fade, though he suspected the next time either of them had their ears checked would reveal some hearing loss.

Alex knew Trish's question was as much one of shock and avoidance as curiosity. They were both focused on Sheriff Azakh –

(z-z, click-tic)

– in order to avoid focusing on what had just happened. Turned away from the partially-headless corpse behind them, staring at what passed for the image of authority and the sense of normalcy it pretended to provide.

But that meant they had their backs to the dead man, and thinking of what lay on the floor behind them made Alex's neck prickle. The hairs on his neck and arms stood at attention, and a cold sweat burst from his pores. For a moment he was convinced the man behind them was not dead. Or, if dead, was still moving just the same. Alex could picture the body hoisting itself up, leaning against the blood-and-brain-spattered wall behind it for support. Steadying itself, then lurching forward with hands outstretched, blanched and bloodless fingers clutching.

Alex almost looked back. Forced himself not to.

It's not real. Don't look back or –

(or you'll make *it real just like the whispers just like the man in the tree they're not real either unless you look unless you try to* see*)*

The sheriff spoke on the phone. "Doc, it's Julie. Better get down here." She glanced at Trish and Alex, evidently listening to whatever "Doc" was saying before responding with a, "Yeah." Her voice was absolutely calm, and Alex had the mad impulse to ask her how many people she shot on a daily basis.

Sheriff Azakh hung up and turned to Trish and Alex. "I'll need to take your statements. Better take a seat."

Alex felt suddenly numb. He and Trish walked to the seats in the front of the room. He felt like he was in a hospital – or, no, that was wrong. He felt like he was back in the room where they had brought him and Trish after the accident. The place where he finally woke, and found out his son was gone.

He didn't know how long he sat there. How long it was before "Doc" arrived. Not long. Sundown was a small place – even smaller than Sunrise., Pop. 1985 – so getting someplace quickly wouldn't be a problem.

"Where you find yourself at home," he murmured as the man Sheriff Azakh had phoned entered the station.

Beside him, Trish gasped and shook her head. He didn't look right away, but he knew what she was seeing – what they had both been dreading seeing since Sheriff Azakh made her call: a ghost. A thing from the past, long-dead but still moving. The hair on Alex's neck lifted again, and gooseflesh rolled over his arms in waves.

The doctor didn't glance around, didn't even seem to notice Trish and Alex. He just asked the question he had to ask, the *obvious* question – and the same one he had asked nine years ago:

"Where's the body?"

13
(When Tricia Had Grown)

Tricia didn't want to cry, but couldn't help it. It wasn't the pain in her head, or the nausea that kept twisting her stomach. It was the man who walked through the door.

For a moment she saw his face – nearly a decade younger, but already deeply lined, with gray hair so light it was approaching white. Still a full head of hair, though, and that made it look like he was an angel when she first saw him leaning over her.

"Alex?" she had murmured almost a decade ago. "Sammy?"

The doctor – Brown, he had called himself, Doc Brown like the character from the *Back to the Future* series that Alex liked – leaned over her and looked like an angel and then whispered words that clearly demonstrated that if he was an angel, he was the fallen variety. The kind that always made trouble in Heaven, just like he had made trouble then.

Would he bring trouble again, walking through the doors to the sheriff's station as though no time had passed and nothing had changed in his life?

He's even wearing the same shirt. *How can it be him? Shouldn't he be dead by now?*

Almost ten years ago she woke to his face and he told her: "Alex is fine. He'll be okay." Then he told her about Sammy. Not fine. Not okay.

And now here he was again. His hair was now pure white, and his scalp was showing through in a few places, the livid pink skin that some people develop there as they age.

He barely glanced at Alex. His eyes caught Tricia's, though, and she could tell he recognized her, too. But he said nothing.

Doc Brown was dressed in blue jeans and cowboy boots. A beige button-up shirt made him look oddly like the sheriff, like he was an undercover cop who had skipped out on Basic Costuming

101. He even wore a thick black belt – though where Sheriff Azakh's belt had a gun and pouches for ammo, mace, cuffs, and whatever else she carted around, Doc Brown's belt was empty save a knife sheath big enough to hold a Bowie knife with enough room left over to hide the Hope Diamond.

He stared at Tricia for a moment, then put down a large black bag he held and pulled out a white packet. He wrung it between his hands, then put it on the back of her head. The packet grew cold as he held it there. "It'll help the swelling," he said, then turned to the sheriff. "In the back?"

"How'd you know?" said the sheriff. Both of them spoke in the tones of friendly acquaintances making obligatory small talk when they ran into each other at the grocery store.

"Place is too small for it to be anywhere else," said the doctor.

Doc Brown and Sheriff Azakh disappeared into the back room. A moment later the sheriff returned. She went to her desk and opened one of the drawers. Tricia saw her leaf through file folders until she came to the right one. She pulled out a pad, then a pen from another drawer.

She walked through the gate that separated the front room of the station, then sat on the last chair that remained in the waiting area. She clicked the top of her pen, a sound that in that moment made Tricia think of someone snapping the neck of a small animal.

Sheriff Azakh flipped over the top page of the pad, and Tricia saw that it wasn't just lined paper, it was some kind of form. "Now," said the sheriff. "What happened?"

Tricia felt her mouth drop open. Beside her, Alex said, "Are you kidding?"

The sheriff shook her head. "Nope."

"You were *there,*" said Alex. "You saw it all."

Sheriff Azakh nodded. "Which is why I'll be filling out my own form later on."

Alex touched the back of Tricia's head. He adjusted the ice pack. "Better?" he said.

She nodded. And it was. Alex knew her so well, even with the walls of grief and guilt that had wedged between them. "Yeah." She turned to the sheriff. "Shouldn't someone else be taking our statements? Someone not... *involved*?"

Oddly, the sheriff looked as though Tricia had said something genuinely funny. Stifling a laugh, she said, "Well, there's my husband, who has the same job I do, but we don't get along and generally try to avoid being in the same room with one another. So for the time being, you're stuck with me, and I with you."

Alex shook his head in obvious confusion, as Tricia thought, What is wrong with this woman?

Not just the woman, though: the whole thing was wrong. Everything seemed like it was happening in a play, to someone else. Tricia knew that was probably a dissociative effect of shock, but knowing the truth didn't necessarily alter its power over you.

She needed to step back. She needed to have *Alex* step back so they could breathe and so they could figure out exactly what was happening here.

"Look, my wife's injured," said Alex. "We just saw a man get his head shot off –"

The sheriff finally showed some emotion. She blanched and said, "I know. I was there, remember? And I bet I liked it just as much as you – maybe less, since I've had to do it before."

"*Before?*" demanded Alex. "This has happened be –"

"No, not like that," said the sheriff. "We don't have crazies come in and assault people left and right. But I'm the sheriff, and when something bad happens, for some reason I'm usually the one who gets to deal with it." She shrugged. "And in this job, one bad thing sometimes leads to other, much worse things happening."

"And what happened back there?" asked Tricia, nodding toward the holding area. "What happened with that man?"

Sheriff Azakh sighed. "He grabbed my gun. I tried to get it away from him. It went off." She looked slowly from Alex to Tricia, then let her eyes rove over each of them once more before saying, "I'm just grateful it didn't hit either of you."

Her eyes lingered on Tricia for a moment.

The sheriff clicked her pen again – *ch-click,* one more tiny creature dead – then said, "Okay, let's start with the beginning."

She asked them questions. She wrote down their answers, flipping over the paper every so often. One of the times, Alex leaned forward and asked, "What's that?"

"What?" asked the sheriff. Following Alex's gaze, she showed him the page she'd been writing on, and now Tricia could see that it wasn't covered with words, but with strange sweeps and dots. "This? It's shorthand." She grimaced and said, "Not much in the way of stenographers around here, so I had to learn to do it this way."

Before Tricia could ask the obvious – why not just record statements and then have them sent out for transcription if necessary? – the sheriff continued her questions.

The sheriff flipped the page over to a blank one, and started asking questions again. But not before a thought flickered into Tricia's mind:

She's just drawing random shapes. She doesn't really care. She's just… doodling.

("It's a doodle.")

She wondered where she had heard that last bit, which was more an echo of a thought than anything else. She didn't remember… which meant it had to be related to the lost time of the forest, but how? What did that word mean?

The sheriff stood, went to her desk, and rummaged around in one of its drawers. She produced three Snicker bars and three bottled waters, which she passed out to all of them. "Thanks," said

Alex. He tore open the candy bar and took a bite, and Tricia followed suit.

It had been hours already, and Doc Brown had come and gone and come again more than once. No sirens, no hubbub. He just left the back, then came back shortly after, then left again.

The interview went on for a long time, but it still felt odd to Tricia. She was in shock, she was tired, she was emotionally overwrought. She knew all that, but even through those filters she thought something about all this was just… *off.*

What could possibly be off about it? Just an attack, a homicide, a doctor I remember from the day I lost my boy, and the weirdest interview experience of my life.

Doc Brown had finally gone an hour or so earlier, dropping a few pages on the sheriff's desk, then nodding at Tricia and Alex and saying, "Sorry about all this," which struck her as odd, before leaving.

More odd: he didn't take the body, or even indicate when he would do so.

It was just her and Alex. The sheriff. And – not to be forgotten – the dead body in the back room.

Sheriff Azakh inhaled deeply, then exhaled slowly. She read over the "writing" on the last page of her pad, then said, "I think that's about it." She glanced at a wall clock. "It's time I let you go."

"What now?" asked Alex. "Isn't there going to be, I don't know, someone from the medical examiner's office or your boss or something?"

Sheriff Azakh smiled tightly. "Probably the latter. I had Doc Brown phone the state police, and I'll call myself as soon as I get done with you two, so we can coordinate in figuring out who that nutjob was and what happened. As for the medical examiner, Doc Brown is the closest we've ever needed in Sundown, *or* Sunrise, for that matter." She frowned. "People mostly get along here."

"'*Where you find yourself at home,*'" said Alex, quoting the sign at the city limits.

Sheriff Azakh smiled tightly. "More or less. Hard to fight with yourself, right?"

"People do it every day," said Alex. He wasn't challenging her, Tricia could tell. He was just tired and, like her, trying to make sense of everything that was happening.

"Well, we try not to do it here. Leads to too much stress down the road, as it were." The sheriff sighed, then rubbed her eyes as she said, "You two can go. I'll need to see you tomorrow, though, so do you have someplace to stay in town?" Without waiting for an answer Sheriff Azakh looked at Tricia. "How's the head?"

"I'll live," said Tricia.

The sheriff nodded. "Well, I certainly am glad to hear it." She looked at the clock again. "Best get a move on," she said. She moved back to her desk, sat down, and started writing on another pad without another look at them.

Tricia looked at Alex, who shrugged. Apparently that was what passed for a goodbye in Sundown.

Alex stood first, a hand held out toward Tricia in case she needed it. "I'm okay," she said. His hand stayed out, though. She wondered if he was doing that in case he needed to steady her, or just waiting for her to hold his hand.

She had held his hand earlier, and it had felt good. More color came into the world when she did it, banishing a few more of those shadows and grays that had taken over in her mind. But the interviews with the sheriff had stripped that good feeling away, leaving her once more in a world painted in shades of gray, a universe of shadows and bleached bones.

Mist. Fog.

She shook her head and stood on her own. They left the sheriff's station. The tone the door made as they exited grated on Tricia's ears, and she wondered if there was permanent damage due to the explosive boom of the gunfire earlier. Probably.

It was dark outside. Only one lamp stood on the main street of Sundown. It glowed a weak yellow that created nothing but a pale halo around the bulb.

"What time is it?" asked Tricia.

Alex pulled his cell phone from his pocket. "Seven."

"Seems like ten or eleven."

"Yeah."

They walked together in the quasi-darkness. With every step they took, the feeling that they were alone grew in Tricia. The store fronts were all closed. No lights in any of them. When they arrived at Tina Louise's Diner…

"Well, *that's* weird."

"I think I'd like to get out of here," said Tricia.

Tina Louise's Diner was closed. The neon sign was dark. All Tricia could see through the diner's plate glass windows were dark shapes she knew were just the outlines of chairs, stools, the bar; but which her heart started screaming were monsters, ghosts, ghouls. They were just waiting for her to look away, then they would slink and slide toward her.

She felt Alex looking at the same thing, with the same dread visible on his features. "I think I'd like to get out of here, too," he said.

They turned to the car. It sat where they had left it before being attacked a million lifetimes ago. Alex took the key fob out of his pocket and clicked it. Tricia heard the blissful sound of the car unlocking – she wanted in the car, and fast – and she pulled the door open.

Even though she wanted to get in and get away, though, she paused. Something…

Alex muttered a curse at the same moment she realized what was bothering her.

The back passenger side tire was flat. Not just flat, but *flat*. The thing had so little air that there was only an inch of rubber between the rim and the ground. "I'll get the spare," Alex said. His voice quavered a bit.

"Should we call a tow truck?" Tricia asked.

Alex looked around. The town had grown darker, and as Tricia watched, the single lamp that had lit their way this far flickered and went out.

She looked back at Tina Louise's Diner. The shadowed stools and tables that had become monsters in her heart had not moved.

Then one of them did.

She gasped. Alex didn't hear her, though. He was bent over the popped trunk, grunting and muttering under his breath as he pulled out the spare. He didn't see the shadow detach itself from the others and move slowly closer.

Tricia wanted to shout. But inexplicable, irrational, unrelenting *terror* had wrapped cold fingers around her throat and squeezed the breath from her. She managed only a high-pitched whistling sound that barely carried to her own ears.

The shadow came closer. Closer. Resolving itself into a shape, though a shape without detail.

It was a person. Someone watching from inside the diner. Staring into the darkness, looking at the small circle of light cast around Tricia and Alex's car when she opened the door and the dome light triggered. And somehow she knew that if the lights went on in the diner she would see weirdly-colored red hair she knew on top of a face she didn't.

"He's new here," she heard someone say, and didn't realize she had said the words herself until Alex said, "What?"

She looked at him. "Someone's watch –"

She broke off. She had turned back to the diner when she spoke, only to find the shape was gone… if it had ever been there to start with.

An unseen man in the diner. An unremembered man seen in a tree.

Ghosts.

It was the first time the word had ever really entered her head as a descriptor of personal experience. It was also the only one that fit.

Alex leaned the spare tire he had pulled from the trunk against the back bumper of the car and joined her, squinting as he peered into the diner. He reached behind them and shut the door she had just opened. She yelped.

"Sorry," he said. "All I saw in the window was a reflection of the dome light, and I wanted to see what was in the diner." He squinted at the dark window. The shapes beyond.

Monsters in the darkness.

"I don't see anything."

Tricia didn't know how to respond to that. She could have yelled, "Don't you believe me?" But she didn't.

Alex opened the car door again. He opened the back door as well, as though having more doors open might coax the dome light into greater illumination.

He went back to changing the tire. It didn't take too long – he hated changing tires, so had bought a two-ton capacity car jack that popped their small car into the air in moments. She turned away from the diner with an effort, but still felt eyes on her back as she helped Alex, dragging the flat tire off the rotor so that he just had to turn and grab the spare while she put the flat in the trunk.

They worked well together. That hadn't changed. They were still on similar wavelengths, and she suspected that on some level that would never change. Even if the worst happened…

But that was foolish, wasn't it? Because the worst had *already* happened. Nothing worse than losing a child.

She had to move something out of the way to make enough room in the trunk for the tire to slide in. She wasn't sure what it was at first, then realized it was the bright red pack holding the tent Tina

Louise had given them. When the woman handed them the package, Tricia thought it was the weirdest thing that could happen today.

Got that one wrong.

She moved the pack to the side, hoisted the tire into the trunk, then rejoined Alex. He was already finishing with the spare. He tightened a final lug nut, then lowered the car, tightened the lugs again to make sure they were secure, and picked up the heavy-duty jack. He tossed it on the spare, beside the red tent, and Tricia slammed the trunk shut.

She glanced at the diner. The monsters were silent and still. The ghosts were nowhere to be seen.

She looked behind her. The town was dark. Even the sheriff's office was dark. The shops that lined the street stared into the center of town, shadowed windows like eyes of lonely skulls turning gray and then black in the night.

"We need to go," she said. "Now."

She realized Alex was doing the same thing she was. Looking around, left to right, at a town that no matter how small should have showed *some* sign of life.

Where you find yourself at home.

You won't find anyone else, *though. Just yourself.*

"I think you're right," said Alex quietly.

They both fairly ran to their sides of the car. Tricia was closest to the driver side, so she threw herself behind the wheel as Alex slammed the back passenger side door shut then rushed to get in the front. At the last second, he bent quickly and picked something up from the ground beside the car and shoved it in his pocket, drawing out the car keys at the same time and almost tossing them at her.

"Go, go!" he almost shouted.

Tricia was already turning the key in the ignition. The car was in good shape – no horror movie stalls, no banging on the wheel and screaming, "Not now, not *now*!" It just slipped from silence to its usual well-maintained purr, and Tricia put the car in gear and drove away. She passed the sign that welcomed them to Sundown. The sign to Sunrise was down the road.

They'd have to stay there. The sheriff had told them to stick around, but Tina Louise had said the motel in Sundown was closed. So Sunrise, with all its memories and all its emptiness, would have to be their destination.

And that meant they would have to pass by the forest. Tricia didn't want to drive past it right now, but going the other way would mean a much longer drive to the next town – a drive on a three-quarters-scale spare tire, hoping that it didn't pop or that some other emergency didn't happen. They had their phones, sure, but she didn't relish the idea of using them to call a tow truck out here. It'd be ridiculously expensive and, more importantly, it would take time to get a tow truck to visit them.

Tricia just wanted *away* from Sundown. She wanted to get into a bed and close her eyes and pretend nothing that had happened was real.

Even if it meant driving through the place where they lost Sammy.

14
Interlude
(When Sammy Was Young)

It's hot. It's dark.

Sammy hasn't been afraid of the dark in forever – that's baby stuff, and he's not a baby.

Well, mostly he's not. There are nights where it doesn't matter that he knows what causes lightning and he understands that the earth's rotation will bring the sun into view again. There are nights when he gets Daddy or Mommy, and they come and search his room for monsters.

He knows *there are no monsters. But knowing a thing is sometimes different than believing it. Belief is a thing outside knowledge, and at times exists beyond its power.*

So Mommy and Daddy come, and hunt monsters. Usually there are none. Sometimes Daddy finds a pillow under the bed. He holds it to his face and screams and spins around like he is in a life-or-death struggle against the pillow, then "pushes" it away and drop kicks it into the closet.

"Dead," says Daddy. And he is right. He killed the monster, because monsters can't exist when the lights are on and laughter is in the air.

But no lights are on now, no laughter sounds around him. There is only darkness, and heat. Sammy tries to scream. He inhales, but it feels like an oven rushes into his mouth and the hot of it kills the scream.

Darker and darker. He feels hands on him, jerking him left and right and back and forth.

Daddy? Mommy?

They don't answer, because he didn't speak. He hears screaming, though. Not his… he thinks. But he hurts enough to scream, yessiree. Everything is on fire, and he can feel a different kind of heat on his shoulder and neck and knows it is blood. That makes him want to scream even more.

Still, if you want to scream it doesn't mean you can. Sometimes you can't even breathe.

But he wants to breathe.

He has *to breathe.*

So Sammy does, no matter how it hurts. Sammy takes a single, quick gasp of air. Too hot, too painful.

He is still holding Silly Corny, his unicorn, and even as out of it as he is he cuddles it to his cheek.

Now hands are jerking him back and forth. Someone screams.

The hot of it all gets hotter, the screaming grows louder, and the darkness eats it all up and all gone.

15
(When Alex Was Young)

Friday.

For most kids, that meant a relief from school, a break from grown-ups demanding they do *this*, then *that*, then *this* again because *that* wasn't done right the first time.

For Alex – and, he knew, for Trish – Fridays meant dread. Fridays meant going home and spending a weekend avoiding a father and a mother who were more like ghosts, emerging for work and for food, than parents. Both Alex's mom and Trish's dad telecommuted, working for different companies, which allowed them to withdraw a bit further each day from their children and from the wider world beyond.

Alex's mother rarely spoke to him. Sometimes she talked in her sleep, and occasionally she screamed. Sometimes he heard her moaning in what sounded an awful lot like pleasure.

Both of those horrified him, though at the same time he suspected they were the best proofs he had that she was alive – because ghosts didn't have nightmares *or* sex dreams.

Trish reported similar doings: her father screamed, he moaned – though the latter didn't happen as often as Alex said it did in his house. He wasn't sure if that meant her father was less repressed than his mother, or if Trish was just better at hiding Severely Gross Things.

Whichever it was, both of them would be subjected to the possibility of such in higher concentrations during the weekend.

Though, he reflected, this weekend might be different. This weekend, there was Sam. Alex's and Trish's parents hated each other, but they couldn't possibly hate Sam's mom, right? Maybe Alex could pretend he was spending the weekend with Sam, and Trish could do the same, and the three of them could spend the whole weekend at the one-movie, always-deserted "cineplex" that

Sunrise boasted, or at the library where they could spend time at the surprisingly-well-stocked science section, or even at the all-night liquor store, where the owner had decided they were "good kids who deserved better" and so never enforced the no loitering sign tacked outside his front door.

Neither he nor Trish had broached the subject with Sam, though they both felt sure he would sign on. They hadn't met Sam's mom yet – a single parent, just like theirs, which pointed to their similarities just as strongly as everything else had – but from what they had garnered, he, too, would do just about anything to avoid that nightmare known as home life.

"She's crazy," he had told them the second day at school. The three of them were curled up in the shadow of one of the buildings, avoiding the sun and the other students during the forty-seven-minute "lunch hour" (which both Alex and Trish took as another revelation of the stupidity of this place). Sam was flipping through pages of some of the books he had brought – a book on string theory, one on ancient Israelite metaphysics, and another one analyzing the two of them in an attempt to validate higher revelation – and Alex and Trish were trying to keep up with the depth and breadth of their new friend's thoughts.

Sam sighed and said, "Get out Wells. It's the bottom text."

Alex pawed through Sam's cavernous red backpack. Again he saw the extra clothing.

"What is all that for?" he asked. He tried to make it casual, but knew it came out forced.

Sam put down the books. He looked at Alex, pursed his lips, and said, "For my mom. She's crazy,"

"They don't look big enough for her," said Alex. He attempted a joking tone, knowing it sounded just as forced and insecure as his previous question had.

Sam shrugged. He wasn't going to say anything more, Alex could tell. Then Trish put a hand on Sam's leg and said, "What's wrong?"

Sam answered with another shrug. Trish waited. Alex did, too, though he wanted to ask a follow-up. But he trusted Trish's instincts.

It was the right thing to do. Sam looked away and said, "We're… I guess you could say we're on the run, Mom and I."

"On the run?" Alex hated when people parroted part of a sentence as a question. But he suddenly felt what other kids must: slow and stupid. What Sam had said… how did *that* make sense?

"Like, from your dad?"

Again, Trish's woman's intuition –

(And she is definitely *a woman, isn't she, Alex?)*

– proved accurate. Sam nodded. "Yeah. I don't even remember him. But Mom says he's the most dangerous person in the world." He grimaced. "Of course, she says that about me, too, when she drinks too much. So I don't know how much to take it as true, but… I guess I believe her. Or at least, I believe her enough to keep a change of clothes in my bag, in case she says we have to go and we just *go*."

"Has that ever happened?" asked Alex.

Sam shrugged again, this time a "yes" shrug. "Twice. Once in second grade. Once… well, once two days ago. She said he almost caught us that time. We were in Minnesota."

"And now here?" said Trish. "Weird place to come."

Alex noted she didn't question Sam's story. Neither did Alex. The fear on Sam's face was too real, and his tones too strained for it to be anything but the truth.

Sam took a deep breath, then held it. "She owns a place here. Out in the forest."

"The old cabin?" said Trish, beating Alex to the punch. "The one near the stream?"

Sam started. "How did you know?"

"*Everyone* knows about the Haunted Cabin," said Alex with a guffaw. He waggled his eyes and said, in his best impression of a campfire storyteller, "And if you go to the stream and follow it down a ways, then turn into the woods, you'll find a path. You'll discover the cabin in the forest, and…" Suddenly it seemed too spooky for Alex to continue. Too real. He swallowed, then forced a smile to his face before he said, "Do ghosts really lurk in the mist?"

Surprisingly, Sam didn't join in the mocking. Alex thought he would have – indeed, the reason he brought it up wasn't curiosity, but to give his friend an out to change the subject for a moment. Instead, Sam shrugged and said, "I've only been there for two nights. Which is two too many nights, if you ask me."

A shiver ran through Alex, and he saw Trish shudder as well. They had both caught Sam's unusual wording. Anyone else would have said "days," but Sam said "nights." The look in his eyes said there was more to that story, too.

Alex loved to ask questions. He loved answers. But suddenly he wanted anything *but* answers. He didn't want to hear that there were things in the mist; that the forest came alive at night with strange lights and even stranger darknesses.

"Why here, though?" Trish asked nervously, obviously affected by Sam's story, too – or maybe just by the dark shadow that had seemed to fall over them when Sam mentioned where he lived. "I thought that cabin was just a derelict, and no one owned it."

Sam shook his head. "Not derelict. Mom said it was hers, and said it had actually been in her family forever."

"Wouldn't that mean your dad knew about it?" said Alex.

Sam shrugged and coughed, like this was a source of embarrassment. "She said he wouldn't come here. Because he knew better."

"What does *that* mean?" asked Trish; the same question Alex wanted to ask.

"I don't really know," admitted Sam. "She got drunk the first night we came here, though. She said…" He looked away, considering a point far beyond the horizon. "She said he knew he'd die there someday, so he wouldn't come." He shook his head. "Have you ever been to the cabin?"

"No," said Trish. "I don't know anyone who *has*. It's got quite the reputation. And the county sheriff's office has made it known a number of times that it's out of bounds for play. A kid tried to go there a few years back, and actually got hauled into a holding cell overnight. Everyone stays away."

"It's…" Sam's voice petered out, and he stared at nothing before finally concluding, "… *strange*."

"Strange how?" asked Alex.

"Nothing fits right. Nothing belongs to anything else," Sam answered. "So you've never been there?" he asked a moment later.

"No," said Alex.

"Not in a million years," agreed Trish. "Do you… I mean, have you… *seen* anything out there?"

"Only thing I've seen since I came here was you guys," said Sam, but he said it in a strange way, like he wasn't here at all, but somewhere else. He sounded *drugged.*

Silence stretched out. Not the comfortable kind. "Have you ever actually seen him? Your dad?" asked Alex quietly.

"You mean, do I think my mom's telling the truth?" He thought about it. "He's real enough that she keeps putting me in different schools under different last names." He sighed. "I caught a glimpse of something in her papers once. Had a picture of her and a man kissing her. I think he was my father."

"What papers?"

"I don't know. But it had my name on it, and what looked sorta like a family tree, only with my name on the top, and some of the names she's had me use below it. I was only four or five, I think. I was already reading, of course, but wasn't old enough to figure out a lot of things, just the same."

"Can you remember the rest of what was on the paper?" asked Trish. "Maybe if you –"

Sam interrupted with a shake of the head. "I can't remember it very well at all. I remember thinking it looked odd, and that there was this weird symbol all over it – like she'd been doodling, only it gave me the wigger-jiggers big time. Not just a doodle, it felt, like, *ominous* somehow." He laughed quietly, a self-deprecating sound. "I know I sound loony."

"Not at all," said Alex, and Trish nodded in total agreement. "The situation sounds loony, but you sound pretty sane. Which is scarier in a way."

"Tell me about it," whispered Sam.

"What was the... the doodle?" asked Trish.

Sam shook his head. "I can't remember."

"Get outta here," said Alex. "You're too smart to forget *anything*. You're smarter than me *or* Trish, and we both remember all the way to the good ol' fallopian tube days!"

Another self-deprecating laugh from Sam. Maybe more than that, maybe a self-*hating* one. "I don't have a lot of memories before five or six. I think that's because of my dad, too."

"Why?" Alex and Trish spoke as one.

"I don't know," answered Sam.

"Then why do you think it's because of him?" said Trish.

"I don't know."

Alex cleared his throat and said, "What were some of the other names on the paper?"

Sam laughed, but it sounded almost like a moan. "You'll get a kick outta this. "Some of them actually matched –"

The bell rang, and Sam shut his mouth. Like the resumption of classes meant the fairy land of learning and understanding they had carved out in this shadow of theirs had been overthrown.

"Go on?" said Trish.

Sam just started stuffing books back in his bag. Silly, since they were just going to end up on the bench again, talking about the same exact books

"Maybe some other time," he said.

Alex opened his mouth to keep asking questions, but Trish held his arm. Not romantically (though he would have taken it, even in the weirdness of the moment because Hormones), but to shut him up.

"We'll see you in a sec?" she said to Sam as he stood.

Sam looked at the two of them. He had to know that Trish wanted Alex to stay back so they could talk about him, but the smile that lit his face was both sincere and relieved. "Sure," he said. "We haven't even got to the Abrahamic astrological symbols yet today. That stuff's cool."

He left, heading in the direction of the bench the three of them were already referring to as The One True School.

As soon as he was out of earshot, Alex whispered, "Why'd you –"

"Dude, *cool it,*" said Trish.

Alex gaped. She had never said something like that to him before. There had never been a need to. They each knew what the other was thinking; when to talk and when to let silence do the talking (which he knew was a rare skill), and when to let silence just be silence (which he knew was even rarer).

Now he didn't know what she was thinking. That scared him in a way he couldn't easily define. "I just wanted to –"

Again Trish interrupted him. "I know what you wanted." She paused, and smiled as though to say, *It's okay. We're still the same as before. We're still* good *together.* "He'll tell us when he's ready."

Alex nodded. She was right. "Sorry," he said.

"Not me you have to apologize to."

"I'll tell Sam, then."

Trish shook her head. "Not him you *should* apologize to." She stood. "He'll tell us, though. I know he will."

But he never did. Not that day, not the day after or any time before now. But that didn't matter as much as Alex thought it might have. He and Trish didn't know much about Sam's past, but the three of them understood each other on such a deep level that it made life-facts seem almost irrelevant.

Sam was walking up now, and Alex was wondering whether to ask him if he wanted to help Alex and Trish ditch their parents so they could spend the whole weekend together, or if he should wait for Trish to show.

Even though he and Trish spent as much time together as possible, even though they hung out every day all day at school, still their parents insisted they go to school on a staggered schedule. It struck both Alex and Trish at times (they had discussed it) that this was a lot of organization; that their parents must be talking to – or more likely yelling at – each other when Alex and Trish weren't around, solely to keep their kids apart.

However it worked between Alex's mom and Trish's dad, the system worked like this: the person to leave for school earlier – school was just a mile away, and they mostly walked – left, then just waited a few blocks away for the other to catch up. Those walks were the best part of Alex's day, where he and Trish could talk to each other without parents, without teachers, without other students. Just them, alone in a world they made for each other.

But Trish hadn't been there when he passed by their spot today. He hoped she wasn't sick.

Just as he decided to ask Sam about going all-in on No Parents Weekend, Trish appeared. She walked into the school, entering the gates that delineated the boundaries between high school and reality only five or six seconds after Sam did. Alex had been waving Sam toward him, but his wave died almost immediately. Something was wrong with Trish; he could tell even before she walked head-first into the flagpole just inside the school entrance.

The hollow *bong* that sounded was enough to make Sam turn around, see what was wrong, and rush toward Trish, his backback bouncing up and down ridiculously as he pumped his legs.

Alex overtook him because of that, getting to Trish first. She had reeled back after hitting the pole, staggered a bit, then started walking again as though the impact never happened. It might not have, too, for all the difference it made. She had already looked dizzy and sick when she walked into the school. Hitting the pole made her look *less* loopy, if anything.

Alex grabbed her a moment before she fell. He would have fallen himself under the sudden weight of her sagging form, but Sam caught up and helped Alex ease Trish over to a nearby bench.

"You okay?" asked Sam. He was looking at her head. The beginning of a bright red welt was appearing on her forehead.

"What happened?" asked Alex. He wasn't talking about the pole, which he figured was of secondary – or tertiary, or hundred-and-fifty-seventh-ary – importance based on how she had walked in.

Trish blinked. She seemed to see him for the first time. "Oh, hey," she said in a vacant voice.

"What happened?" asked Alex.

She stared, uncomprehending for a moment. Then her mouth sagged open. She threw her arms around him, buried her face in his chest, and began sobbing.

Alex just waited. A few students walked by, sparing barely a glance for them before walking on. No doubt they would all be the topic of much discussion – *"Even Nerds Cry": a panel to be held at noon on the quad!* – but for now everyone avoided looking at them as she wept.

When she finally looked up, Alex realized he was so freaked out about her behavior that he hadn't even taken the opportunity to revel at the feel of her in his arms. Bad omen.

"My guppies," she finally said.

He blinked. "What?"

Her only answer was to start crying again.

16
(When Tricia Was Young)

Friday started off normally enough. Tricia woke up. Went to the bathroom, where she wondered if she was going to get bigger boobs and wondered if Alex was going to get bigger muscles. She hoped the first would happen, though she was loathe to admit it, and hoped the second would not. She liked Alex just the way he was. He was perfect.

It was hard to reconcile at first – growing to realize that she had started capital-L-Loving a guy she had lowercase-l-loved for her whole life. Or maybe not. The feelings of confusion had been intense to the point of painful, but it had actually only lasted a week or so. Then she decided to just roll with it.

Not that she would actually admit it *to* Alex, or dare act on her feelings. She had never been as smart with feelings as she was with more purely intellectual pursuits, but she knew that friendships were generally over when one person or the other wanted more than what they already had.

Plus, what if Alex didn't feel the same way? Sometimes she thought he might. Sometimes the way he looked at her made pleasant tingles run up and down her legs and spine and arms, and she almost said something.

But she held back. Confessing her feelings to him seemed like a bad idea. Wrong. She didn't want to try for more, because more would signal the death of what she already had with enough statistical certainty to make her shy away from any declaration of affection. She wouldn't take a chance on anything that might damage her best and only friendship, and that decision was final and permanent – even though she knew as she said it to herself that "final and permanent" meant "until I see Alex or hear his voice or think of him again."

Sigh.

Her daily Moment of Silent Confusion dealt with, she got dressed, had a piece of toast for breakfast, then re-thought her earlier conclusions about Alex before deciding she had been right and should never ever *ever* tell him of her feelings.

Final and permanent for real *this time… until I see him again.*

She was putting away the bread when her dad walked in, even quieter than usual if such a thing were possible. She asked how he slept, he grunted. He looked at the calendar on the wall, then fuzzed out for a long time. Just stood there holding a gallon of milk in one hand, a glass in the other.

"You okay?" she asked.

He seemed to come to himself. He shrugged, then put the unopened milk back in the fridge, the unused glass back in the cupboard. He stood at the sink and stared at nothing.

A muffled thud sounded outside: the sound of Alex slamming the door to let her know that he was leaving for school. She couldn't leave right away – Dad would stop her, just like he always did; like Alex's mom always stopped *him* from leaving at the same time Tricia did.

She waited the obligatory five minutes. She watched the clock on the wall, which clicked louder with each passing second, while seeming at the same time to go slower and slower. Time had ceased to have meaning, frozen in this moment: *See Exhibit A, the static figure of Dad, obviously in a stasis field between temporal intervals.*

Her dad whispered something. She didn't hear it. It sounded like, "Who are we?" which made no sense but what else was new?

"Dad?" she said. Partly out of genuine concern, but also because it was what she figured was expected of a daughter. She hadn't felt like much of a daughter recently. Dad had always held her at arm's length, as long as she could remember. He rarely hugged her, and when he did it was always a rigid embrace, like he wasn't really sure how hugging worked, or even why he was supposed to do it with her.

Things had gotten even stranger in the past few weeks. He came out of his bedroom, he drank a glass of milk for breakfast. He went into his office where he telecommuted, doing web design and maintenance for enough clients to keep the bills paid. He emerged at night to eat something, then went to bed. The only time he said anything was when she mentioned school or Alex.

Actually, he didn't speak a word even then. But the silence got frostier, which said a lot in its own way.

Now, Dad whispered something again. This time she heard it clearly. "We are who we are."

She wanted to ask what he was talking about – out of genuine curiosity this time, not any pretense at familial concern – but in that instant a look of revulsion came over his face. It looked like every bad smell, every bad taste, every bad noise ever created had all struck him at once.

The look scared her. She wanted to ask him what he had meant, but not if the price was understanding what had just happened in her father's head. Some things were better left unknown. Ignorance was never really bliss … but knowledge *could* sometimes be misery.

She stood to go to the door and head out to school – to Alex. She grabbed her bag, but before she left she realized that she had forgotten something important.

Gotta feed the fish before I go. Especially with the new fry in there.

Tricia had discovered guppy breeding in a book at the local library, and used some of her own money to buy a small tank and a dozen fish. Most of them died, but she bought a few more. Guppies were fairly cheap, even on the salary of a very-occasional babysitter for the Rolfes down the street.

And the fish were worth it, because guppies could be bred to be beautiful. The ones she bought originally were pretty plain, all things considered, but by pairing a few she thought had a desirable quality or two, by isolating them so they would mate, she started seeing some amazing changes. Their breeding cycle was fast, too, so she was already on her eighth generation. The seventh had some truly gorgeous specimens, with long, flowing tails and colors so bright they almost looked unreal. A few of them had bred, too, and she had the fry – the babies – in a specially-designed isolation tank that sat in the main tank but kept the babies apart from the sometimes cannibalistic parents.

No doubt some would be born mutants, hideous or sickly or both – that happened when you had a family tree that was mostly a single branch – and would have to be discarded from the breeding pool. But if the pattern held true, some would be even more beautiful than any that had gone before.

She was proud of her fish. She wanted them safe and well. But turning back she saw that her father still wore that same disgusted look on his face, only now he was staring at *her*.

She decided she would feed the fish tonight; that even losing the fry would be a low cost for avoiding that expression or even worse, finding out what lay behind it.

She turned back to the front door. Opened it. Took a step onto the porch.

I wonder what Alex will be wearing today?

Who cares?

You do. A lot. Don't lie to yourself.

She turned around to shut the door, trying to shut the door on the thoughts as well.

She grabbed the handle before she realized what she was looking at. The front of the door. The boring wood.

And her guppies.

Somehow, someone had stolen into her room in the night. The intruder had taken the guppies out of the tank and, with painstaking care, used clear packing tape to cover each one completely as the person taped each to the door. The dead things hung there, staring at her in glassy-eyed accusation, as though their ghosts were there with them, demanding how this could have happened, how she could have *let* it happen?

Under the guppies, a piece of paper hung on the door, affixed by yet another piece of tape. There was a light breeze, so the paper flapped up and down too much to see what was on it. Feeling like someone else was controlling her body, she pushed the paper flat. A single word was written there, in heavy black lettering:

DON'T

Something else caught at the corner of her eye and pulled her gaze to it.

The isolation tank, the one in which she had kept and protected the fry from the unwelcome attentions of their own parents. It sat on the ground beside the door. The fry were too small to be more than specks, really, but even at this distance she could tell they were dead: it was the only conclusion possible given what had happened to her other fish, and given the empty bottle of bleach that lay on its side next to the tank.

She still didn't scream. She wanted to, and deafening screams started ricocheting through her mind, but all she managed to vocalize was a strange, *"Uhn, uhn, uuuuhhhhnnnn."*

The last dissolved into a long, wordless moan.

A moment later, she felt arms around her. She thought it must be Alex. It must be him, it had to be him, Alex had known what she was thinking, what she felt, he was so in tune and he knew, he had to know, it had to be him and he would make everything be all right in the –

"I'm so sorry," Dad whispered.

For a brief, ecstatic instant, it was as though she *was* holding Alex. She could feel the same kind of love and attention Alex always gave her, but this time from the strangest of sources: her own father.

Of course, as soon as she thought that, and thought how much she would love a life with a normal home and a normal parent who loved her the way she had read about in books, her dad's arms went rigid. He shoved her away.

"School," he said.

"But –" Whatever she thought to say next disappeared, swallowed by the look on her father's face. The same look she had seen in the kitchen: disgust, revulsion… *hate*. And this time, she knew it wasn't directed at some memory or whatever he'd been thinking about before, it was directed at *her*.

Tricia stepped back, the force of his gaze a weight that drove her away and pushed on her so hard that for a moment she didn't think of her guppies, didn't think of the fact that someone had come in her *room* to do this thing. All she could think of was her father's look, and all she could do was concentrate on breathing in air that suddenly felt thick and wet. She was drowning.

"Dad," she choked.

Still wearing that expression, he turned away. "School," he said again.

"Someone… someone was in my –"

"I know." Even his voice sounded grotesque, whatever she had done to offend him coloring every aspect of his being. "Go to school."

"But I –"

He turned on her, and said, "What's done is done," in a calm, almost *relaxed* voice. He might have been passing pleasantries with someone he had known forever, making small talk with an old friend. But his eyes blazed, and in them she still saw disgust and anger.

The strange confluence of the two – the preternatural calm in his voice, the out-of-control rage in his eyes – pushed her back. She felt them like hands spinning her around, shoving her toward the school in steps that felt dizzy and out-of-sync with the rest of reality.

She didn't remember the walk. She didn't remember coming onto school grounds. She seemed to wake up in Alex's arms. She was confused, and her head hurt, and for a moment she thought Dad was holding her again. It felt like it had for that wonderful moment. Maybe it was all a dream, row row row your boat and wake up and start again and this time it would be *right*.

"What happened?" came a voice.

Who said that? Dad? He would say that, wouldn't he? He loves me, doesn't he?

Then the voice echoed. It wasn't a real echo, sure. But it sounded in her mind. It echoed, and distorted, and she recognized it for who it was, who *actually* loved her.

She held Alex tight, and knew that she would never do anything to risk losing him. He was the closest thing to family that she would ever have, and whether they ended up capital-T-Together or not, she would always be with him, captured by the powerful force of love and shared pain.

Other hands touched her shoulders: Sam. The other one who loved her, and the other one she loved. Not the same as she loved Alex – Sam was a wise brother, someone who knew much and would teach her all – but he was there, too, and strength flowed from him. Enough, at least, to get her talking.

She told them what had happened. Both Alex and Sam wore looks of astonishment that grew as she hitched out the words between choking sobs. The bell rang and one of the office staff came out – no doubt to tell them to get to class or at least to confine themselves to their normal bench – but saw what was happening and turned around and walked back into the office.

We're all freaks. No one understands how to take care of us, and no one even wants to.

But that was a lie. They were here for each other. That was what mattered. She loved Alex, Alex loved her, and they both loved Sam even though he was new.

She didn't love her father. Maybe she loved him before, even though he ignored or outright deterred her love with his actions every day, not anymore. The guppies were the final straw, and the reason that when Sam was taken she didn't even think about talking to the person she lived with.

Other than DNA and a place to sleep and eat, the only other thing that man ever gave her were empty expressions or, worse, looks of pure revulsion. She realized it on the day her guppies died, and that realization set her free to do what came next.

If her father had been taken that day, she would have gone to the police. She would have informed the authorities, then waited as one was supposed to wait in such a situation. Because she didn't love him, and could have let others find him or not as they saw fit.

But it was Sam who was taken, and she actually *loved* him, so she followed him herself; and Alex loved and followed them both.

That was just how it had to be.

17
(When Alex Was Young)

Alex didn't understand why someone would break into Trish's house and kill her guppies. Not just *kill,* either – but murder them and display their bodies by taping them to the front door. He didn't understand how something like that could happen in the house right next to his without him knowing about it. He didn't understand why her dad didn't call the police right away. It wasn't just vandalism, it wasn't even just a home invasion. It was straight-up-crazy, on a level that should have had cops crawling over it. Or at least *cop,* singular, since Sunrise had exactly one full-time police officer.

"Your dad's got to have some reason..." Alex began the sentence with no end in mind, and no end in sight when he reached the middle. What possible reason could there be for any of this?

"He does have a reason," Sam said. He hadn't left Trish's side for a moment, just as Alex hadn't. Alex was glad. He felt like he was out of his depth here, and would probably need to have Sam's help. Sam was so smart, maybe he could say the right thing that would make all this coalesce into some kind of sense.

And he did just that – though it was a horrible kind of sense. "He's crazy," said Sam decisively.

"No," said Alex. "He can't be. There *has* to be some reason that he..." Again, he couldn't finish the sentence. Sam was right, even though the idea that Trish's dad had finally boarded the train to Wackoville, USA, terrified Alex. It was one thing to have your house broken into by a madman; it was another to actually *live* with someone who had so completely broken from reality.

"He's a shit," said Trish.

The word startled Alex. He had never heard her curse before.

But thinking of what she had said, he finally nodded and said, "Yeah, he's a shit."

"Definitely a shit," said Sam. He grinned, obviously trying to jolly Trish out of her shock and terror. "Crazy, too."

"A crazy shit," Trish agreed.

"Don't you mean a crazy *poo*-head?" Sam corrected.

Trish laughed and sniffled at the same time. Alex felt a wet patch on his shirt where she'd been crying. "A *ca-ca* poo-head," she corrected.

"With a side of doody-face," said Sam. He laughed, too; and just as with Trish, the laugh sounded an awful lot like a cry.

"And a big heaping of wee-wee brain," added Alex helpfully.

Then they were all laughing. Laughing so hard that Trish kept crying, and soon Sam and Alex had tears streaming down their faces as well. Laughing so hard that a sharp pain stabbed Alex's side. He grabbed it, and saw Trish and Sam grabbing their sides, all of them in such hysterics that pain had come along to see what was so funny.

Alex vaguely heard a door open and then close, and a kid with buck teeth big enough to serve as industrial can openers said in a peevish voice, "Mr. Arkin wants you to quiet down. We're taking a test."

All three of them gasped, stopping the laughter. Then they looked at each other and started laughing again, even harder. The buck-toothed kid sighed and went back into his classroom and a moment later Mr. Arkin came out. He was older than God and rumor had it he was having an affair with the principal, who wasn't *quite* as old as God but had definitely seen the big bang first hand.

"You kids want to have detention over the weekend?"

Alex, Trish, and Sam looked at each other. Alex could tell they were all thinking the same thing: that wouldn't be a punishment, it would be a gift.

They all burst out laughing again. Mr. Arkin didn't give out detention assignments, though. He just went back to his classroom and tried very pointedly to slam the door – a gesture which was dampened by the hydraulics on the hinge that slowed his "slam" to a slow crawl.

That made them laugh harder still. They collapsed into each other, clutching hands and arms and bodies, hugging each other tightly and Alex couldn't remember ever being so scared, and so happy at the same time.

Three of them. They could fix whatever had happened to Trish. They could fix whatever was wrong with their lives. Three of them could do that, even if two had never stood a chance.

Three wasn't a crowd. It was *family.*

There was a screech. Alex barely noticed, only the tiniest sliver of his mind thinking of the fact that someone had pulled up and braked hard enough there would be skidmarks on the asphalt in the school parking lot. He barely noticed the quick steps of someone running toward the school gates. Then through them.

And then a third of him disappeared.

That was what it felt like when Sam was abruptly torn away from their knot of friendship and laughter and *safety.*

It all happened so fast, and yet seemed to dilate; instants pulled like taffy so they lasted far too long:

A shout.

A quick glimpse of a woman, long brown hair streaming out in unkempt knots behind her…

Sam, his face pale, his red backpack half-fallen from his shoulder, pulling it back up like that mattered…

Sam's mouth forming a perfect "o" of shock and bewilderment before screaming, "Mom, what are you –"

Time returned to something approaching normal as Sam's mother yanked his arm so hard that his teeth audibly clicked together. She dragged him through the school gates, toward a beat-up blue sedan that idled at the curb. She threw open the front passenger door, then shoved Sam in before running around the front of the car and getting in the other side.

Alex didn't really get a look at the woman. She was moving too fast, her hair streaming out in ragged waves as she pulled/pushed/shoved/ran. More than that, his gaze was arrested by Sam, whose fingers pressed against the inside window of the car. He was shaking his head, his eyes wide with terror. Mouthing something, over and over.

Help me.

Trish and Alex ran through the gates, running after the car, trying to follow it as best they could. It was stupid, bordering on insane. What were they going to do? Even if they had caught the car, did they just plan on holding onto the bumper until they got the situation figured out?

Sam was gone.

They ran back into the school, both of them heading for the same spot, no words spoken. They didn't just enter the school office, they *exploded* into it. Shouting at Mrs. Berkowitz, the secretary/receptionist/lunch monitor:

"Sam! He's gone! He –"

"Someone just dragged him away and –"

"– looked terrified and he –"

"– I think it was his mom who –"

Mrs. Berkowitz was in her thirties, and looked thin enough to blow away in a stiff breeze. But when she hollered – which she now did – Alex always felt like he was standing in front of an Army drill sergeant with an angry case of hemorrhoids.

"Shut *up*!" she shouted. She looked over the tops of her half-moon glasses, then said, "Is this about your friend?"

"*Yes*, it's about him!" shouted Trish. "Weren't you listen –"

Again, Mrs. Berkowitz silenced them, this time with a sharp glance at the principal's office. "Your friend was withdrawn from the school today, a few minutes ago."

"What?" Alex shook his head. "He just got here! And he didn't tell us –"

"Why would he?" asked Mrs. Berkowitz in a voice like honey laced with arsenic. "As you say, he just got here. Why would he bother telling you his plans?"

"Why would he take off?" demanded Alex. "Isn't it weird that he would just –"

Mrs. Berkowitz sighed, as though this was a situation she dealt with a thousand times a day. "Yes, it is weird. But it's also not against the law, and it's happened before."

"When?" demanded Trish. "When has *this* happened before?"

Another sigh, and Mrs. Berkowitz said, "There's nothing new under the sun, my dear. After you've been around a while longer, you'll understand that."

"Mrs. Berkowitz?" said Alex softly. The woman turned toward him, her own expression diminishing to something like sympathy when he said, "You didn't see him. He was scared."

She frowned. "What do you mean, he was scared?"

Alex thought about it, then shrugged. "Just that. He was scared. I don't know why."

As soon as he said it, he knew he'd made a mistake. Mrs. Berkowtiz's eyes narrowed, and she went back to filling out the form she had been working on when they burst in. "I doubt that very much," she said.

"You didn't –"

"And even if he *was* scared," she said, steamrolling Trish's concern, "what would you like me to do? Call the police? Say he was scared?"

"*YES!*" shouted Alex. "Do that! We'll talk to the cops if you're afraid to and –"

"That's about enough, mister!" Mrs. Berkowitz delivered the words quietly, but the intensity she packed in each syllable stapled Alex's mouth shut. She steepled her fingers, seemed to reconsider that – probably going through which hand-holding method would be most powerful in her mind – and then switched to clasping them on her desk. "We have – *had* – a student named Sam Jones. Mrs. Jones withdrew him from enrollment."

"But –"

"She is *moving*," said Mrs. Berkowitz. "She told us very clearly that that was the case when she called to inform us she'd be enrolling her son here, and also told us that she intended to stay here only a short while." Mrs. Berkowitz shrugged. "When she called this morning to let us know they'd be leaving, she said she had just gotten a job offer in Chicago and she was on her way to pick up her son. The offer came just after he left, and she was going to let him finish out the day until she realized they had to do a lot in order to get to her new job on time."

"But the way he looked," said Trish quietly.

The soft voice seemed to affect Mrs. Berkowitz more than their shouts. Her gaze grew gentle. "She told us he wouldn't want to go. She said he'd found friends for the first time, and moving away would break his heart," she added, and smiled sadly. "I know it's hard – more so for you three than for most – but people come and people go. It's not pretty, but it's life."

In other circumstances, Alex would have been amazed. That anyone had seen their relationship together as good – rather than a triumvirate of geeks and freaks – was a revelation. Even so, it was a revelation drowned out by fear.

"That wasn't it," said Alex, speaking softly as well. "He was afraid. We saw him."

Mrs. Berkowitz nodded. "I'm sure he was. How would you feel, to finally find someone who was able to keep up with you mentally, connect with you emotionally, and then have them ripped away?"

"That wasn't –"

This time it was Alex who cut Trish off. "Okay," he said, ignoring the angry glance Trish sent his way. It cost him to do that; felt like two years of his life fell away from him. But he soldiered on with, "We'll maybe write him a letter or something. Could you tell us if there's a forwarding address?"

Mrs. Berkowitz nodded. "None on file, but we usually get one when the new school asks for the records. If they do, I'll tuck your letter in with anything we send them."

"Thanks."

Alex pulled Trish outside. "What were you doing in there?" she demanded. "He wasn't scared of leaving *us*, he was scared of *his mother*." She softened. "What if he was right? What if she's truly crazy, and is going to hurt him? The way she looked…" Her voice slipped to silence, and then she frowned and Alex knew what she would say next – because he was feeling it himself. "What if she's going to kill him?"

"I think that's exactly what's going to happen," said Alex. He saw dismay in Trish's eyes. Partly for the threat to Sam, he knew, but he suspected that she had hoped he would disagree, would talk sense into her.

He couldn't. He believed in his gut, brain to balls, that Sam was in mortal danger.

"Then why aren't we making Mrs. Berkowitz call the police? Or doing it ourselves?"

Alex shook his head "What would happen then? Our one police officer – if he shows up, which isn't always a given – ambles over here, listens to us, then pats us on the head and that's that? Or even if he does go to the cabin, then what? He's met by a mother who's packing, and whose boy is away doing errands, or chores – or more likely, they're probably already gone to this 'new job.' He tips his cap and then corrals us and lectures us and our parents about false alarms and overreactions. And where does that get us?

Stuck in our houses? Maybe grounded – and for *sure* wasting hours dealing with all that? How does that help *Sam*?"

"So what do we do?" said Trish.

Alex could tell she knew already. But he said it just the same, because some things *had* to be said. Some plans could be spoken only inside your own mind. But sometimes you had to say the words aloud, or they didn't count. So he said, "We have to follow him," and Trish nodded and said, "Into the forest," and he nodded, and repeated the words: "Into the forest."

The words had been said. There was no turning back.

"How?" she asked. "Our parents won't help, because that…"

"… would mean helping us do something together. And they can't have that, can they?" Alex finished.

"Why?" she asked. It wasn't a question meant for an answer, which was good since he had no idea. Never had, and he suspected he never would.

Trish started walking. "Let's go," she said.

Alex followed her. It had been easy for Sam's mom to walk onto school property – the gate to the school was always open, small town hospitality and all that. That meant it was equally easy for them to walk *off* school property.

The school was at the west end of town. The forest was about four miles away, and the cabin maybe a mile farther, and half a mile in. Alex knew about it, the same as every kid and adult in town did. It was haunted, they said. Even some of the grown-ups said it, though most of them laughed… but he had noticed through the years that even those who laughed hardest tended to change the subject as fast as they could.

"We should stop by Merle's on the way out," said Alex as they began to walk.

Trish nodded. Merle's was a small gas station a mile down the road. Alex had no idea how the place stayed open; he couldn't imagine there was much call for gas on the small road that joined the equally small towns of Sunrise and Sundown. But open it stayed, and there was a small convenience shack attached to it where they could buy some food and water. The weather wasn't hot – it was fall, and the days had not yet morphed from "pleasantly cool" to "oh dear Lord why can't it snow and warm things up a little?" – but Alex knew they would need water and some energy. Maybe a lot of energy, depending on what they found at the cabin.

And what do *we think we'll find?*

In this situation, "best case," meaning they were right to go because Sam really was in danger, would mean a very bad case indeed. If his mom was nuts, wouldn't that mean they had to deal with her to save their friend?

Academic. They were going, and that was that.

Alex felt as though he was being pulled. He felt like Sunrise, the town he'd known his whole life, was really a small planet on the event horizon of a black hole. Not the forest, exactly, but something inside the forest. There was something dark there, and frightening, and yet it was also something he had to go and see.

They stopped at Merle's. Between him and Trish, they had six dollars and change, which was enough for a few bottled waters and some granola bars. They chucked them in their packs, and kept walking.

It was past noon when they got to the forest. The way seemed to stretch out in front of them, their destination growing farther away with every step they took. And with every step they took, Alex knew two things more certainly:

He wanted – *needed* – to do this.

And he was very afraid.

18
(When Alex Had Grown)

Alex didn't mind Trish driving. Some men did, he knew, but he was just as happy when she drove as when he did the driving himself. They usually decided who was driving by an uncomplicated formula: who has the keys ÷ who is closest to the driver's side.

It had always worked out fine, even after the accident that twisted their lives into a knot.

Tonight, though, he regretted not getting the driver's spot. He was freaked out by what had happened in Sundown – who wouldn't be? – and had thrown himself into the car without even thinking of whether letting the recently-concussed person drive was a good idea. Now, sitting in the car, with Sundown safely in the rearview mirror, he was noticing more and more how Trish was jittering so hard the car kept swerving. Maybe it was the concussion, maybe just adrenaline. Either way, the exaggerated motion of her hands communicated itself to the car. She hadn't spun off the road yet, but she kept getting closer and closer to that point.

Alex split his time between watching her and watching the road. He didn't say anything, just watched helplessly as she veered toward the yellow line on one side, corrected, then slid toward the white line that delineated the soft shoulder on his side.

And beyond his side… trees.

Not many. Not yet. This wasn't the *true* forest, just outlying trees. Scouts, ranging ahead of the dark army that waited just down the road.

Trish swerved. Corrected.

"You okay?" he said.

The set of her jaw was answer enough, even if she *hadn't* already been driving like someone who started the party a bit early.

Alex looked out his window. He didn't know if looking at her would disquiet or further distract her, but it wasn't helping *him* any.

Not that looking out the window was much better.

Tree…

Tree…

Tree…

The first ones he and Trish passed by were fairly small. Many were partially denuded, thrusting bony fingers upward, like the skeletal hands of giants buried in shallow graves. But they had awoken, found themselves hungry, and now rose to consume what they could.

Alex shivered. But he said nothing, and did not look away.

Tree…

Tree…

Tree…

It was terrifying. It was also hypnotic. A thin mist began to seep around the edges of some of the trees, shrouding their trunks in silvery light that refracted the car's headlights even at a distance. It created a fae world, a place where make-believe was real – and where people could find that make-believe was a very different place than they imagined as children.

All children, except one, grow up.

J.M. Barrie said that in his masterwork *Peter Pan.* But Alex didn't think the author could have known how true those words would be for some people, some parents.

Tree…

Tree…

Tree…

Red.

Alex jerked upright. He had almost been dozing, lulled into waking sleep by the metronomic passing of the reaching trees. Now he sat up, and peered behind him. "What the *hell*?" he shouted, his voice far too loud in the confines of the car.

Trish almost did veer off the road this time. The tires squealed, and she twisted the wheel hard, righting the car an instant before it surely would have spun out of control.

"What is it?" she shouted.

For a moment Alex couldn't speak. He pressed his face hard against the windshield, even though he knew that he wouldn't be able to see anything at this angle. It was a childish response, like craning his neck whenever Pac-Man traveled to the far side of the television in a video game, trying to see to the back of something that existed only in two dimensions.

But he couldn't help it. He was suddenly a child in make-believe, in Neverland, and the monsters became more real with every foot they traveled and every second that passed.

And at that, Alex realized the trees were no longer solitary things. Not scouts or isolated soldiers. He and Trish had passed beyond enemy lines.

This was the forest.

"What *did you see?"* Trish demanded again, her voice quavering as much as her hands.

Alex looked at her, but couldn't answer. His mouth opened and closed, but nothing came. Finally, Trish broke the silence, though not in any way he could have expected. She slowed the car and drew purposefully to the side of the road.

"Did you see it?" she asked. "I thought it was just me, but… Alex, *did you see it?"*

"I…" Grit packed his mouth. He swallowed with agonizing slowness, everything terror-parched and painful. "I don't know what I saw."

"But you saw *something*. What? What was it? *What did you see?"*

She was shouting at him. Her voice ricocheted off the windows of the car like gunshots in a holding cell, and Alex had the sudden impulse to fling open the door and run screaming from this place.

And in there? *Into the forest?*

(Yes. Yes, oh please, yes.)

"What did *you* see?" He asked the question quietly, and it was enough to coax his voice – his thoughts – to working again: "I saw something…"

"… red?"

She had completed his sentence, had completed his thought. But there was no comfort in that, no closeness as there had been. They weren't necessarily in sync, just trapped in the same nightmare.

He nodded. "I thought I saw, hanging in the trees –"

"His toy? Sammy's unicorn?"

Alex frowned. "No. Maybe." He pursed his lips, then decided, "No. *I* thought it was Sam's backpack."

They fell silent. The mist edged closer. It seemed to pool, like blood trickling from the trees of the forest.

The car coughed, and the electronics on the dash flickered. The clock display shifted in unsequenced bursts, and the radio turned on in a sudden shriek of static. Then the car hitched and everything returned to normal. The clock snapped back to normal. The dash lights brightened.

Trish looked at the dashboard.

She put the car in drive.

She pulled away from the shoulder, but didn't drive forward far before turning the car around. The road was technically a state highway, but still small enough that it took a three-point turn, then they went back the way they came.

Tree…

Tree…

Tree…

Trish pulled over again, the tires crunching over rock, loose gravel, and sun-dried insects as the car settled on the side of the road.

"Is this where you saw it?"

Alex didn't answer. He couldn't. He realized suddenly that one of the reasons he had always gravitated to math and science in his schooling and later his work was because they absolutely *had* to make sense. As soon as something didn't, you just scrapped it and worked out an alternate path that would. That was one of the defining qualities of true sciences and maths: the discovery of truth. Theories existed, sure, but only as possible pathways to that truth; as soon as they proved to be dead ends they were discarded.

There was no room for make-believe in math and science. Not when it got to the end of the road. And he found that he did not want to do something that would jeopardize that fundamental reality. He read of Neverlands and Wonderlands; of Dune and Omne, Commities and Corporations, framlings and Fix-Its. He existed in those places at times, and they had become part of his mental DNA. He would have passed these works and worlds to Sammy, and hoped to make him a child of his mind as well as his body.

But here, in the world where his body dwelt, he did not wish for Neverland *or* Wonderland. Both, at their core, were nightmares. He did not want the fantastic, and did not want to see such things peeking around the frayed edges of reality.

He did not want to go into make-believe...

.. into the darkness and the whisperers, the man in the tree and the ghosts.

Trish apparently understood that he wasn't going to answer her last question: *Is this where you saw it?* she had said, and Alex feared that answering would pull at that frayed edge, and reveal that reality wasn't a world, it was just a thin blanket over something dark and born of madness.

Trish switched topics. "What's in your hand?" she asked.

He looked down, realizing that he had been holding it since he got in the car. Realizing that he had seen it and snatched it off the ground before throwing himself in the car and getting out of Sundown.

"I don't know, really," he said. "I think it came from the –

(The dead guy the one who has his head splashed all over the wall in a town Pop. 1985 but is really a ghost town where nobody really lives at all.)

– guy who came at you."

"There was something on his pocket," she said. "It must have fallen off him, maybe when the sheriff tazed him."

"Probably."

"It's evidence then," Trish said.

Alex knew she was asking if they should take it back. But he suspected that going back would return them to a darkened, empty, *dead* place. So he didn't offer to return. He looked at what he held. The mist outside still reflected the splash of the car's headlights, and that illumination reached into the car. He turned on the dome light just the same: partly to better see what he held, partly because it transformed the car's windows from transparent glass into smoky mirrors. He sat in this car, and he also sat in the car within the glass. He could see himself in there, and it was comforting to think of his doppelganger rather than the forest.

The trees.

The red.

He turned the object over in his hand. It was a flat card, about the same size and shape as a credit card. It was cold, and heavier than he expected, and when he tapped it against the gold band of his wedding ring he heard the high *tink* of metal on metal.

One end of it had a small hole punched, and a metal clip was attached there. It looked like the kind of thing a government worker would wear; maybe an employee of some tech company. Only there was no company name, no employee photo or other writing. Just a simple design that he seemed to remember seeing before, though he couldn't be sure where.

But he remembered *everything*. So if he had seen this before, it could only be in one place, on one day.

He pushed away that thought by trying to analyze the card. It was real, it was something he could understand.

The card itself was a solid black, but the design on its front – a series of circles that wove into each other – was a stark white that made his eyes want to cross. They seemed elegant, deceptively simple the way some fractal designs seemed simple. It was only when you looked closer that you saw the eternal elegance built into them. Only where such constructs had always brought him a thrill of pleasure and a sense of discovery as he looked closer and closer –

(peering around the edges of the TV to whatever lay behind the game)

– this design made his heart sputter, forced sweat to burst from his skin. It seemed more arcane than anything. A portal to enter the dark mirror of reality. A place where the card was white, with black circles. Where up was down and down was up and *we're all mad here.*

He was suddenly not at all happy to sit beside his mirrored doppelganger.

Trish was craning to look at the card, and he suspected that she was using it the same way he was: as an avoidance of what they had seen. Because, like him, she was not a creature of make-believe.

Trish held out her hand and he passed the card to her. Their fingers touched, and hers were as cold as the metal card.

We should leave. This is a dumb time to look at the card. We should get out, and get away.

But they wouldn't. They were looking at the card, but he knew they would have to look out the window sooner or later. They would have to shut off all the lights and peer through the darkled glass.

What if he *had* seen Sam's backpack? What if she *had* seen Sammy's unicorn?

What if we hear the whispers? What if the whisperers come, and be*come.*

("They're coming. They're be*coming.")*

He didn't know where those thoughts came from. Another fragment of the lost day.

Trish turned the card over and over in her hand. "What's this design?" she asked, in a tone that indicated she didn't expect him to know the answer. "I feel like I've seen it before."

"Me, too," he said.

"Where did you see it?" Trish said.

"I don't remember."

She was silent a long time. "Do you remember other things? Like… the whispers?"

"Just tiny pieces. Dreams. Dreams of dreams."

"The whisperers. The man in the tree," she murmured. She looked from the card to him. "Did you believe it? *Do* you believe it? I hear whispers, and I dream bits and pieces, but I don't *know*. Was it make-believe, or real?"

His mouth dropped open a bit as she said the very words he himself had been pondering: make-believe or real? Forget *to be or not to be…* "make-believe or real" was really the question.

"I…" He shook his head. "I don't know. I don't want to believe it's real."

She looked at him searchingly. "The tent. Sammy's toy. Sam's backpack. Even Tina Louise's hair."

Alex knew she was talking about the coloration they all shared. She was also talking about what she – they – might have seen among sentinel trees.

He pocketed the card, as though to turn away from the entire subject. But even as he did, Alex noted that he hadn't tossed the card in the small recess in the dash made to hold pennies or trash or things of little value. He hadn't put it in the compartment under the armrests of the center console. He hadn't just discarded it.

He had put it in his pocket.

He wanted to keep it close.

And he was, he knew, going to get out of the car and follow what memories he could.

Before Alex really processed that, he pulled his own door handle. He opened the door. He slid out of the car and closed the door behind him. He heard the sound of Trish's door opening and closing.

Trish began walking toward the thing they had both seen. The flash of color in a mist-silvered night.

Ten steps off the shoulder and trees began to obscure the road from view. He could still see the car, but only in slices between the lone guards at the edges of the forest's domain.

A few more steps and the car was just a hint of color if he squinted and moved from left to right and back again.

The fog was pouring around them. The trees loomed, and bled silver mist.

The car was gone.

Alex reached for Trish's hand and clung to it.

"This is where it happened," she whispered.

At first he thought she was saying, *this is where I saw the red.*

Then Alex saw something that brought back a thousand moments from the lost day. The memories were still faraway, hinted at more than seen, but they were real – and clamoring to be let out of the dark recesses of his mind to which he had confined them.

This was where they entered the forest when they came the first time. The very place where they had come to find and then lose a friend.

"It's where we came looking for Sam," he said. At the same time, Trish murmured, "It's where Sammy… where it happened."

That was too much. When Trish said that, Alex backed away, shaking his head. "No. It's not. It can't be. And you were out when it happened. You couldn't know and couldn –"

"I was unconscious, but I came out of it a bit a few times. Just once or twice, for quick seconds. I felt heat, I felt myself get dragged out of the car and I saw a bit of the forest. Not much, but I don't forget things. I could never forget *that* place."

"You couldn't see enough to know," he insisted, his voice growing frantic. This couldn't be *both* places. Lightning didn't strike twice in the same spot like that.

Only that was a myth. Lightning struck twice in the same spot all the time. In fact, it was inevitable. Given enough time it would happen again and again, and some places had lightning rods that made it strike over and over again by design.

Trish pointed to the left and slightly behind him.

Alex turned, and felt like shrieking. He hadn't seen it before – the trees were so thick they blocked much of his view, even without the further-blinding effect of the fog – but at this angle he did.

A dead tree stump lay up on the ground. A single branch jabbed out of its side, into the air. It extended about six or eight inches, ending in a sharp point.

But it wasn't like that before. It was upright before. It was straight and tall and that branch stuck out and she bled so much and…

No. *It didn't happen here. It couldn't have.*

"I remember falling," whispered Trish. "I remember losing him." Alex didn't know whether the "him" was Sam or Sammy, whether it was friend or child. He didn't want to know. He didn't want to go to Neverland, and hoped Oz would never find him.

Trish muttered something under her breath. Alex wasn't sure exactly what she said, but he thought it mirrored what he was himself thinking:

We're in the forest now.

What will we find this time?

19
Revelation
(When All Has Become)

Some of you reading this may be wondering at this point, "Who is this person? Who is *telling* this story?"

The answer is simple: I am.

Of course, *that* just begs another question: who am *I*?

Some days I know. Others, not so much.

We're all in the forest, you know. All of us. I certainly am, *you* may even have been without knowing it. The forest reaches farther than its boundaries. It has long shadows, you see. And in those shadows hide all manner of ghosts, who tell us all manner of lies.

Because sometimes lies are the shortest path from truth to truth.

THREE:
AND INTO THE FOREST WE GO

20
(When Tricia Was Young)

"How long have we been walking?"

"How long *haven't* we?"

Tricia would have laughed, normally. But "normally" had packed its bags and bid farewell all of ten minutes after she and Alex entered the shade below the trees. So she had no laughter for Alex, no laughter for herself.

And, most especially, no laughter for the forest.

"Maybe we should have brought a tent," said Alex. "We could make camp and have s'mores and tell ghost stories."

He was trying to lighten the mood, she knew. But it wasn't working. She didn't think anything could have.

Soon after they passed through the line of trees that demarked the boundary between forest and road, a mist rolled in from nowhere. It seemed like it came from the trees themselves, like they had switched from exhaling oxygen to sighing great clouds.

Poison.

She didn't want to think that way, but she couldn't help it. The fog certainly seemed to have a noxious quality. She couldn't put her finger on why, exactly, but every time she felt the cool mist on her face or her skin she held her breath for a moment.

Alex was staring into the sky, as though trying to gauge what time it was by what he saw there.

She knew what he would see: fog. Silver mist above, and around, and soon it would be through them and would *be* them.

"No sun," Alex murmured.

Because it's gone. *The fog, the mist, whatever this strange thing is, has eaten it. Sun and moon and stars, like Genesis in reverse.*

Alex looked at her. "Do you think that's weird?"

"What *isn't* weird in here?"

Like her, she saw that Alex had no desire to laugh at the pitiful sally. Humor seemed like something they had left behind.

"Are you hungry?" asked Alex.

She shook her head and frowned. "What is that?" she said. She took a few steps forward. The mist shifted, and for a moment she could barely see Alex behind her. He whispered something she didn't hear. "What'd you say?" she asked.

She turned, and a shape loomed behind her. She almost screamed, but the mist shifted again and she saw it was just a tree…

Tree…

Tree…

Not a tree. I know that. I saw –

"What?" said Alex, stepping into full view. He shrugged. "I didn't say anything." He frowned at her. "You okay?"

She gave a small laugh at that. "Are you?"

He didn't answer, other than to look beyond her. He had a quizzical look on his face: *What did you see?*

At least *that's* still normal, she thought. At least I still know Alex as well as I know myself.

That was what she held onto. That was what gave her the strength to point at one of the –

(Shadows. Ghosts.)

– trees that kept turning insubstantial in the fog.

"What *is* that?" she said.

Alex stepped ahead of her, looking at the tree she indicated. He frowned and took another step. She matched it, because she didn't want to drift away from him. She didn't want to become a ghost in the mist.

She looked away, glancing behind them. The trees shuddered and shimmered, now close, now far. The shifting mist imparted an odd sense of movement to the trees, making them disappear, reappear; making them slink from side to side at the edges of her sight.

"I don't know what it is. You think Sam did it?"

She shrugged. "Doesn't seem like his style, does it?"

One of the trees had a carving – the kind of thing you would expect to be formed into a heart, with two letters and a plus inside. Maybe a crude arrow.

A + T. That's what you wish was there. Alex plus Tricia. Alex and Tricia, sitting in a tree, K-I-S-S-I-N-G.

And if not that… anything would be better than what's actually there.

Not a heart, not a crude arrow. The carving was a series of circles that blended into themselves, each one hard to see at the edges. Tricia had the sudden feeling that if she could look at them, smaller and smaller, they would continue on forever, down to microscopic and beyond. It chilled her, and made her think of movies with Satan worshippers, where they drew mysterious symbols and tried to bring about the End of Days.

Alex whispered, "Not carved."

She moved closer to the tree. Her skin crawled as she did so. She forced herself forward, though. Alex had moved closer to the tree, so that meant she could as well. She looked harder at the strange symbol.

He was right. It *wasn't* carved. The edges were too perfect, the curves far too smooth. Nothing had hacked this design into the tree. "Was it burned in?" she asked.

Alex shrugged, then shook his head, then shrugged again as he reached forward. He meant to touch it, she could tell, and it was all she could do not to grab him and yank him away from the thing, screaming her head off all the while.

He touched it.

There was no flash of light, no moment of pain like the dark outlines on the walls around Hiroshima and Nagasaki must have felt. Alex touched the circles. Nothing happened. He ran his fingers along the circles.

Nothing happened. Just mist and the shadows of trees.

"It feels like…" Alex exhaled in frustration, searching for what he wanted to say.

Tricia reached forward as well, touching the lines he had touched. She half expected them to be warm, as though he would have left behind a bit of his heat. Or maybe a bit of hellfire warmed the symbols from within.

Stop it. There's no such thing as demons or monsters or ghosts or –

(Whisperers?)

She hissed as she touched the symbol. The circles weren't warm. In fact, they were *cold.*

"They feel like ice."

Alex nodded. "Weird."

"Weird," she agreed, if only because she couldn't think of a word that went past "weird." Alex had showed her a book once, one of the fantasies he liked so much. There had been a word in there that she didn't like: *eldritch.*

That was what this moment felt like. An *eldritch* thing. She frowned, and leaned in closer to the tree. "It looks like it *grew* that way."

Alex nodded. "That's it. I couldn't figure out why the circles felt so weird. But the way they are, you'd expect them to be smooth. Perfectly carved or burned or whatever, but instead –"

"– they feel rough –" she continued.

"– like it's just *part* of the tree. The bark is there, same as everywhere else. And the carvings are cold."

They had finished each other's thoughts, as happened so often, and Tricia was glad of that. She clung to it. Some things remained constant, and that made her suddenly long to go back to a time before Sam, and live again in a place that was only she and Alex and nothing more.

"Should we turn back?"

The words burst from her without thinking, and she immediately felt ashamed. They had come in here terrified for their friend, for what might be happening to Sam even now. And she was thinking of ditching him – for what? Because of some fog and a weird carving in a tree?

But Alex looked like he was considering it. More than that, like he was *glad* she had said it. Only macho pride had made him hold out this long, she realized. One of their few differences: the cultural stupidity that he, as a man-in-training, had to be braver than anyone else.

Bravery, she had realized long ago, was overrated. Fear was a biological reality, and if you felt it there was probably a good reason for that fear. Men couldn't figure out the reasons, because they were so busy thinking of ways to prove they *weren't* afraid that they had time for nothing else.

Like figuring out where the danger actually was.

But now that Tricia had said something, Alex's masculine pride would allow him to consider what lay beneath their fear. The *thing* hiding in the mist of their hearts.

Tree…

Tree…

Tr –

Tricia flinched as she saw something move. She peered into the mist. In that moment, she thought she heard something. Thought there was something…

Whispering.

She couldn't make it out. And as she strained, she realized something else was drowning out whatever she heard in the forest. "Shut up," she hissed.

Beside her, Alex – who had been saying something, though she had no idea what – fell silent. "What?" he whispered.

She searched for the movement she had sensed. The flash of –

(Red.)

– color she thought she had seen.

Nothing. Just trees, unmoving; and mist, gray and unending.

"What were you saying?" she finally said.

"I was saying we could stay or leave." Alex swallowed loudly. "Up to you."

More macho stupidity. He wanted to leave, but was letting her make the decision – which, if you really thought of it, was a kind of cowardice.

She hated him. For the first time ever, she felt something other than friendship or affection or anything else that was good or bright. The feeling passed in an instant, but it shook her as much as anything. That was probably why she said what she said. Not what she wanted, which was, "Let's get out of here," but what she sensed he *didn't* want: "Let's keep going."

She coughed, cleared her throat. She looked away from the terrible flash of anger she saw on Alex's face. She wondered if he hated her in that moment, as well.

She pointed at the stream. They had found it easily, a few minutes before the fog came. It was, she knew, the only thing they really needed to guide them to the cabin where Sam was. They could find the cabin, find their friend, and then follow it right back out of the forest. "We follow this, we find Sam, and we leave."

He nodded and stepped forward, turning slowly and deliberately away from the tree and the strange design it held. He walked toward the stream, finding the point where the dirt softened and then became mud.

Alex turned to look at her. She joined him. As she did, his eyes flicked over her shoulder, looking again at the tree. He murmured something.

"What was that?" she said, lifting her foot high to avoid tripping over one of the serpentine roots that crawled everywhere in this place.

"Just something Sam said," responded Alex.

"What?"

"Not just a doodle."

Tricia froze, her foot still in the air.

(Sam: "I wasn't even sure what it was, really. I was only four or five, I think. I already was reading, of course, but wasn't old enough to figure out a lot of things, just the same."

Tricia: "Can you remember what it looked like? Maybe if you –"

Sam: "I can't remember it very well at all. I remember thinking it looked odd, and that there was this weird symbol all over it – like she'd been doodling, *only it gave me the wigger-jiggers big time. Not just a* doodle, *it felt, like, ominous somehow.")*

Out loud, Alex spoke Sam's next words: the words his friend had ended that conversation with: "I know I sound loony."

He seemed to flicker in her eyes, and for a moment Tricia wasn't sure if she was talking to Sam or to Alex.

What's happening?

She looked at Alex, and the sense of talking to two people disappeared. It was just Alex; had always *been* Alex.

Alex shook his head as though shaking off sleep, then reached out his hand.

She stepped toward him. She didn't take his hand, though. Yesterday she would have, and probably would have squealed internally in girlish excitement. But not here.

"The forest is waiting," she said.

Alex jerked, just like she had a moment ago. "What did you say?"

"I said Sam is waiting."

He shook his head, the color draining from his face. "You didn't, though. You said *the forest* is waiting."

She replayed the memory. He was right. She shrugged and a whistling, strained laugh lurched from her. "Isn't that funny?" she said.

Alex looked at her for a long moment. Then he stepped forward. Following the stream that cut through the forest. Toward Sam.

We hope.

She followed him for a few steps, then hurried her pace until she had drawn abreast of Alex.

"Don't get too close," he said.

"Nice," she snorted.

"Not to *me,*" he said, embarrassed. "I meant, the stream. I mean –"

He reddened, and she thought that was beyond cute. Maybe when he reached out his hand, he wasn't just trying to help her over the root.

Maybe it had been more.

Maybe maybe maybe.

Tree tree tree.

"This forest is a confusing place," she said.

"Definitely confusing," Alex agreed, then took a half step back and swept his hand in front of him in a ridiculous parody of a chivalrous bow. "After you, milady."

Again, at any other time she would have laughed. Now she shrank back. "No, after *you,* m'lord."

He held out his arm. "Together, then?"

She curtsied. They were play-acting, trying to pretend this was a normal place where they could joke and clown and be together and be happy.

But it isn't. It's the forest.

She took his arm. The play was better than the reality. That was what play *was*. An escape.

So she would escape, even as she went farther into the reality.

Together, they stepped forward. The stream burbled beside them, winding them deeper into the mist and farther into the trees.

The shadows kept shifting, though it was growing harder to see them. "Is it getting darker?" she said.

"I imagine so. That's what happens when the day goes on."

"How long have we been walking? It doesn't seem like we've been going long enough for it to get dark."

He snorted. "It's been *forever*, don't you know?"

"Seems like it, I guess. Still..." She looked up. No sky. Just a gray *nothing*. "The earth was without form, and void; and darkness was on the face of the deep," she intoned.

"And fartness was on the doodles of the trees," Alex said. Making light of the dark words, forcing them away with the potty humor he retreated to sometimes: another thoroughly *manly* thing to do.

She usually called him on it. Not this time.

"And blartness was on the mace of the meep," she said.

He made a face. "Shmand shmartness shmuz shmon shmuh shmace –"

"Okay, you win the dumb contest."

"I always do," he said smugly.

And the play continues. The Forest: Act One. In which our heroes travel into places they shouldn't.

For the first time it occurred to her that, though there was a cabin in the forest, she had never heard of a road leading to it. Sam had never mentioned one, either. His mother had driven up to the school in a car, but other than that she had only seen him walking into the school alone.

Tricia suspected that there was no road to the cabin. With that suspicion came the image of Sam's mother stopping outside the forest, then dragging him bodily through the trees. Perhaps worse.

The image heightened the oppressive feeling that this had all been written out; that she was doing something someone else wanted her to do, and that her free will had less substance and less reality than the mist around her. She looked around, half expecting to see an audience watching them sullenly: the worst opening night crowd in history.

She saw no audience; but something *was* watching.

She screamed and threw herself sideways. Her foot came down on a patch of loose soil and went out from under her. She screamed as she plunged toward the mumbling stream, and it was only the fact that she still held to Alex's arm that kept her from tumbling into the water.

Alex gave a strange grunt/cough as he went from being held by her to holding her up. He planted his feet, clapped his free hand over hers, which had clenched against his bicep as she –

(Saw the thing. The ghost.)

– fell. He pulled, leaning away from her to stop her from falling. She wished he hadn't. The stream wasn't that big here. It would have wet her up to the knees, maybe less. But in "saving" her from that, he was pulling her back in the direction she didn't want to go.

She had looked away. Just for a moment, when falling, her gaze had left the place she saw… *it*. Now, looking back, she saw that the thing was gone.

"What?" Alex was shouting. "What is it? What did you –"

"Shhh!" She hissed him to silence, so hard that spittle flew from her mouth. It disappeared in the mist, like the fog wanted to eat every single part of her.

"What did you –" Alex began, whispering the words.

She put a finger to her lips, shaking her head, and his mouth slammed shut. His eyes were moving, though, wildly bucking from side to side – from her to the forest and back again. She looked only at the forest, trying to peel through the fog, trying to find what she had seen.

She shook her head. Nothing.

"What was it?" Alex tried again.

"Someone's out there," she whispered.

Now Alex went stiff. "Sam? His mom?" he whispered back.

She thought about it. She had no desire to meet a crazy woman under these circumstances. So it could have been wishful thinking, but… "I don't think so. I think it was a man."

Alex's face curled into itself. Worry, fear, confusion. He shook his head, and she knew that the combined weight of what he was feeling would soon drive him to do something without thinking.

"Alex, don't –"

"HEY!" he shouted. "Who's out there? You hear me? Who the *hell is out there?"*

They waited. No answer came from the forest, but something about the lack of response bothered her just as much. Something –

Her hand, which still held to Alex's arm, spasmed. His gaze flew to hers. "Do you hear that?" she whispered.

He squinted and cocked his head. "Hear what?" he asked.

"Nothing," she said.

He smiled. "That's a good thing, ri –" His face, already pale, now blanched of all color. He had understood what she meant. "Where are the birds? The sounds?"

Any forest was alive. Birds sang, small animals walked over branches, wind soughed and stirred up the dead leaves and detritus that fed the earth.

But here… none of that. Not even –

She looked sharply at the stream. It had burbled and bubbled beside them, but now even it was soundless. All noise had fallen away from the world, and the void had drawn a bit closer.

She peered at the stream, leaning toward it. She couldn't even see it moving. She was sure it *was,* if only a little, but the streambed here must be so flat that it made the flow from one side to another nearly invisible. A current, yes, but a weak one.

"I don't see anything," said Alex.

"No," she agreed. "Nothing. Just like we're hearing nothing."

They stood like that a long time, and she knew they were both considering, again, whether to turn back or keep going.

The forest waited, silent.

A sound began. Finally, a sound.

Tricia felt herself relax a bit. The weird moment was passing. Sound was coming back. Soon the fog would blow away or turn to dew or whatever fog did when it was done being fog in this place.

But Alex was quivering. Still looking around wildly. She realized then that the sounds they heard weren't just forest sounds. No cracks of branches, no wind rustling leaves. This was too regular, too low and consistent.

"Something's whispering," said Alex.

Tricia nodded. Not just to agree with the "whispering" part, but to show he was right: it wasn't some*one*. It was some*thing*.

"... here... children..."

The whispers were disjointed, words elongated and then separated by odd pauses. They lengthened into a wheedling call that sounded like echoes bouncing through the world's longest and darkest tunnel:

"... heeeere... childrennnnnnnnnnnnnnnn..."

Then nothing, followed by a single shriek, like feedback when a microphone and speaker were placed too close together. The whine grew, and intensified, then coalesced into a single shouted word.

"RUN!"

Tricia ran. Alex ran.

Neither of them noticed that, in running *away* from the whispers, they were running *toward* the center – the heart, if you will – of the forest.

21
(When Alex Had Grown)

Doodle doodle.

("Like, ominous *somehow.")*

The words bounced around in Alex's mind, though he couldn't for the life of him figure out why, or where they had come from.

They came from the forest. Everything *comes from the forest. We came here in a car, but that car was part of the forest, too, and so was the road that led here, because the forest is the whole world.*

He looked at the tree they had found, with its jutting spike of a branch. It seemed to writhe in the mist, and for a moment he thought he saw it glistening wetly, a dark liquid dripping from it. Blood.

His mind spun. Like a car flipping, the dizziness of losing a child, the way Trish spun her ring around in a circle… like a…

(Like a doodle.

Like, ominous *somehow.)*

"I…" Trish fell silent. She was staring at the fallen tree and its spike-like limb, and he wondered if she had seen the blood. If it was memory or real.

"What?" he asked.

"Do I remember something about this place?"

He didn't know how to answer that.

"It's like –

*("*ominous *somehow")*

– like I've done this before."

"All this has happened before, and it will all happen again," he said. It was a line from a story that had terrified him as a young boy: a story about another boy who flew to children's windows looking for his lost shadow – and then stole them away to a place where they would never be found again. But he kept reading it, for some reason, and it had become something of an obsession – a story he returned to over and over again, even though he could remember and recite every word of it.

"We're not in a fairy tale," said Trish.

"Let's hope not," Alex replied. "Fairy tales were never really meant to have happy endings."

"Hansel and Gretel never should have gone into the forest in the first place," she agreed.

"Do you remember..." He couldn't finish. He didn't want to know, and in that moment would have given anything to forget what little he *did* know.

Trish shook her head. "Shadows." Her eyes focused, moving away from the trees, finding his gaze. "Do we stay?"

He looked toward where the car still sat. Out of sight, but close enough. Even with the thickening mist around them, there was no chance they could get lost unless they ventured in much farther.

"I think we should stay for a bit," he finally said. He bit his lip, then added, "I think we *have* to."

Trish nodded, but she had gone white. "But not overnight."

"No, not overnight. We just go in and –"

"If we're not going in overnight, then why do you have *that*?"

Alex looked down, where she was gesturing.

The tent – the bright red tent, like a bright red bag bouncing in a panic-run through the green and the gray of the forest – was in his hands.

"How did that –"

"You got it. You went back to the car. I followed you, and you opened the trunk and grabbed the tent, and said, 'Maybe we should have brought a tent,' then came right back here."

He didn't remember doing any of that, and he supposed that should scare him – should *terrify* him. But it didn't. He felt like he was being led. He didn't believe in predestination, or in fate, but the feeling was so real that he was hard-pressed to convince himself of those things in that moment. "We're not staying overnight," he said firmly. "Not in the forest."

But he was walking further into the treeline. She was following. He held the tent, and for the strange thought that they could make camp and have s'mores and tell ghost stories passed through his mind.

Then they were inside. Finger-branches interlocked over them, tree trunks rose behind them. They had left the car, the road, the world.

Something touched his skin, and he jumped. "Just me," said Trish. Her hand traveled down his arm, and he felt an electric thrill, so like the time before. The time they entered the trees and held hands and kissed for the first time.

What? We didn't kiss here. We kissed – we had that First – at Tina Louise's Diner.

Didn't we?

Everything seemed jumbled in his mind.

Trish squeezed his hand, just as hard as he was holding the tent.

He looked around.

"Do you know where we are?"

Trish nodded. "Heading toward the stream."

He remembered in that instant: mist. Seeing things, hearing things.

Whispers.

*Whisper*ers.

("They're coming. They're be*coming.")*

Things had been in that fog, that strange mist. Shadows had danced, and now…

Now the fog was coming again. He realized that, even though he couldn't see the sky above, even though it was *night* somewhere out there, he could still see clearly.

"The fog is glowing," he said.

"I know," answered Trish. "I just noticed it, too."

The fog brightened. A flash that Alex realized had happened a few times. Maybe it was brighter now, or maybe his mind just hadn't been able to process or accept it.

Another flash.

The fog had surrounded them, creeping in as slow and silent as a murderer in his bedroom. It clung to the trunks all around, and blanketed the world, so thick that he and Trish seemed to disappear at the waist. The world, in that moment, had no substance.

"We should go," he said.

Trish nodded, let go of his hand, and turned around. She took a step, then frowned and took a step in a different direction. "*Where* do we go?"

Alex turned around as well. He thought he turned a perfect one-eighty, but realized there was no way to know if he had been facing directly away from the road in the first place. People tended to drift to one side or another when they walked, he knew, so he could have been facing at a right angle to the road, or parallel, or anything in between.

And then he had turned "around." And after just that one half-turn – maybe a bit more, maybe a bit less – he had no idea where he was, or which way led to the road and safety and which led deeper into the forest and this strange, glowing mist.

The trees all looked the same here.

Tree…

Tree…

("A doodle."

"Mom says he's the most dangerous person in the world.")

"I don't know where we are," he whispered. He looked at Trish, and saw naked terror in her eyes.

In his peripheral vision he saw the mist wrap creeper vines around trees. It grew outward and inward at once, and might have come from the trees themselves for all Alex knew.

The gray was complete only a moment later. There were shapes in the mist, but they seemed to wax and wane, to draw close and then farther away.

The fog flashed. It was hardly blinding, but it was undeniable.

"This is impossible," said Trish.

"Totally," Alex whispered.

The fog flashed again. It felt like the mist was laughing at them.

A sighing sounded. Trish walked back to him and held tight to his arm. "Just the wind," said Alex.

He was lying.

"No. Something's here," Trish said.

Another line from that book flitted through his mind:

("Can anything harm us, mother, after the night-lights are lit?"

Nothing, precious," she said; "they are the eyes a mother leaves behind her to guard –")

"– her children," he finished.

"What?" whispered Trish. "What are you –"

The whispers came again. Louder. The hint of something unseen, the promise of something all too real. They grew, and solidified.

The fog flashed. The mist-light pulsed.

Alex began walking. He didn't care where he was going in that moment, just that they get away from *here*. He pulled Trish along with him. She came haltingly, her feet dragging as panic sapped her ability to move.

Then he *heard* the whispers, and as he did, he remembered hearing them years ago. The words were different, but still spoken in the same faraway voices, the whispers of the dead or dead-to-be.

He felt like they were different voices, but each spoke part of a single thought:

"… see…"

"… hear…"

*"… **nothing**…"*

The mist thickened, flashed.

Alex realized suddenly the ludicrousness of holding a tent in a place like this. He threw it away, cursing whatever part of him had wanted to stay here, and whatever part of them both had allowed them to walk into this place at all.

He dragged Trish a few feet. She was almost dead weight behind him, her eyes wide and tears streaming down her eyes. "Run," he whispered. "We have to run!"

She shook her head.

But she ran with him all the same.

It was a nightmare flight, down a path unseen to a destination unknown. He hoped they would find their way back to the road, but knew even as he ran that it would never happen. The trees were too thick, and seeing and hearing the things around them had resulted in both him and Trish spinning in a panic. More important than either of those factors, though, was a simple fact that kept slamming its way through Alex's skull:

The forest had them. It had caught them like flies in a web, and would let them go, or not, when it wished. And not a moment – or an eternity – before.

The mist flashed.

The forest laughed.

22
(When Alex Had Grown)

The trees of this place were far enough apart that a part of Alex understood that he wasn't likely to run into one, even hurtling forward in panic. But what if he stumbled on a root, or tripped over the bushes or slipped on the moss that coated so much of the ground?

And besides, Trish wasn't as fast as him. She was fast enough, but to run as hard as he could would mean leaving her behind. But they had to run, from some unseen threat, and had to run as fast as they could, so he reached back for her and found her arm and jerked her forward with him. He tried to grab her hand but couldn't find it. He wrapped his fingers as tight as he could around her forearm, but was afraid to let go after that. What if he lost her?

The whispers followed, keeping pace. He kept hearing breathing in his ears, like someone was panting right behind him, but he never looked back. He didn't know if it would be worse to see some spectral creature, or something born of nightmare and now made into flesh… or nothing at all.

Madness, either way. Madness behind, and madness all around as he and Trish ran, ran, ran through fog and flashing lights.

The trees started closing in, and Alex had to duck constantly as thin blades of wood slashed through the thickening fog. Sometimes, if the branches were large enough to make out through the mist, he managed to duck, and he would yank Trish's arm so she did the same. But just as often the branches were no bigger around than his finger, and the fog obscured them until the last second. They felt like whips, slapping him so hard he could feel welts rising on his face and neck and arms. Sweat got in his eyes and he wiped it away, realizing only when he saw the back of his hand that it wasn't sweat after all; that one of the branches had opened up a gash on his forehead.

Still he ran. Still the whispers bounced and echoed:

"See… hear… nothing… othing… othing… othing…"

He heard breathing, louder, with a strangely high-pitched tinge to it, as though the things in the mist were tired as well.

He heard something under the sound, too. He couldn't place it at first, but then his foot splashed down into water and he realized that he and Trish had found the stream that cut through the forest.

He was going so fast that the transition from brush and dirt to mud and moss-slicked rock took him utterly off guard. He tumbled forward, his ankle rolling under him, the smallest shout escaping before he was underwater.

Alex realized he was holding something. He tried to let go, but too late: he had dragged Trish into the water, too.

There couldn't be much of a current, but he still felt like he was being dragged by a giant hand. He felt himself tossed up and dragged down, then tossed up again. He reached out blindly, hoping to catch hold of something that would save him. His hands beat down on water, the liquid offering no hope. Then his knuckles slapped painfully against a hard, rough, cold surface. He kicked hard, looking for purchase, for some way to drive himself back to what he had felt.

There!

He felt it again, this time under his palm, grabbed at what he felt with the other hand as well. Both his hands reached around the rock and linked together on the backside of it.

He pulled himself up, taking a breath, gagging as he got a mouthful of water for his trouble. He almost went under again as something grabbed his belt and yanked. He reacted automatically, one hand unlinking for a moment, his body wanting to slap away the thing holding him. Pulling him. Trying to *drown* him.

He knew it was one of the *things*. One of the whisperers that taunted him, telling him he would hear nothing, see nothing, as though telling him he had no escape but the oblivion of death.

That thought drove him to full panic, but as soon as his grip loosened, he immediately dropped back under water and had to scrabble madly to get himself above the level of the rushing stream.

Something reached out of the water. The thing holding him down reached up, clawing at his face. He screamed – gagging again, more water trying to force its way in and kill him – and then realized what was pulling him down.

Trish.

She must have fallen on him when he tumbled into the current. Then she either got hooked on his belt, or had grabbed it and held on for dear life just the way he now was hanging onto the rock.

For a moment everything but his wife faded from his consciousness. He wanted so badly to reach for her, to help her climb up to safety. But if he did that, he knew he would relinquish his tenuous hold on the rock and would tumble back into the *impossible* current – and then where would they be?

He held tight, even though inside he was screaming in pain and terror, the image of his dead wife surfacing in the dark waters of his mind.

He heard breathing in his ears again, raw and ragged. This time the sound filled him with delight rather than dread, because it meant Trish was there, holding his belt with one hand, his arm with another. The breathing was hers, great gasps that turned into hitching grunts as she yanked herself out of the water, using Alex's body as support.

Her weight left him, so suddenly he was sure that she must have fallen back in. He looked behind him, braced to see her disappearing from sight below the water. It was only when he heard her scream, "Come *on*!" that he saw through what he feared to what actually was: Trish was laying on a long, flat stone nearby. It was large enough and gave enough purchase that she had stretched out on her stomach and now reached for him.

He let go and lunged in the same motion. The current tried to grab him, but Trish had a firmer grip on his arm than the water did. She pulled, a sound caught somewhere between exhaustion and pain tumbling from her lips.

Alex pulled, too. He clasped arms with his wife, then she pulled and got him moving – not much, an inch or two. But it was enough for him to finally get purchase with his feet on the rock that had saved him. He kicked off it and the force sent him flying. He hit the rock that Trish was on and almost slid right past her and into the water again.

Then he was laying on the rock beside his wife, both of them panting, both of them trying desperately not to let go of their purchase on the rock.

Alex rolled a bit, nudging closer to Trish. The water roared nearby, far faster and louder than it should have been.

Was it this loud before?

Was I here *before?*

He had been. He knew it in his guts, brain to balls, the same way he had always loved his wife.

But what *happened* here? That was the ten-billion-dollar question, wasn't it?

Another small roll/wiggle brought him close enough to Trish that he could shout at her, "Can you see a way out of this?"

In answer she shimmied a bit. Enough that she was able to get better purchase and lift her head a bit. "We're in the middle!" she shouted. "It's too fast! I can't – *oh*!"

Her sentence turned to a surprised shout, which Alex heard clearly as the sound of the rushing water – the impossible torrent that had done its best to drown their words as well as their bodies – suddenly disappeared. The wall of white noise was gone, replaced by a silence so absolute that even without looking Alex knew they must still be in the middle of the flashing mist.

"It's gone," Trish said.

"The fog?"

"No."

She didn't elaborate, but she was sitting upright now, so Alex figured that, whatever was going on, at least it didn't involve the danger of being swept away and drowned.

He sat up as well, and saw what she was talking about. His mouth worked up and down, trying to say something that would make sense of the situation. Nothing came.

The fog still surrounded them; he had been right about that, at least. But the stream had changed. Or rather, it *hadn't.* The stream was no longer a wall of current, but a thin, shallow line of water that glinted like a mercury thread in the mist, stitching its way through the green coat of the forest. A moment ago it had felt like category-five rapids. Now it was only shin-deep.

"What happened?" said Trish.

Alex had no answer. He was bedraggled and exhausted. He felt like he had been fighting heavy rapids.

I was *fighting heavy rapids. There was no way anything else could have happened.*

But then where had all the water gone? A glance at his wife told him that she had just gone through the same thing he had: she was utterly soaked, and still coughing quietly as her lungs emptied of water.

He looked up and down the stream. There was no sign of rapids. He saw small eddies as the shallow waters rolled over stones buried in the stream's bed, but that was all.

Just a stream, no matter what I felt.

He frowned.

A stream, and also rapids, and…

… rocks.

He and Trish were laying on the rock she had found, and had pulled herself onto. There were other rocks that he saw and remembered at least a bit from the moment he had tumbled into the river or stream or whatever it was.

But the rock he had caught at the last moment of his strength – the one that had saved them – was gone. The spot where Alex remembered the stone being was empty. Just slowly-moving water, less than two feet deep.

Am I remembering wrong? Did I just grab this rock we're on? Or did I grab Trish?

No. He distinctly remembered getting his shoes positioned against that other rock, the water still rushing over his knees and his side as he stretched between it and the rock where he now found himself.

Small. But big enough to anchor and help *save* them.

"What's happening?" he said, not really expecting an answer.

Trish coughed again, then said, "I don't think this was what Dr. Coleman had in mind when he told us to come here."

Alex almost laughed. He probably would have, but the fog was still all around them, smothering any levity. Instead of laughing, he said, "We have to get back to the road."

Trish nodded. She stood, wobbling a bit, almost slipping on the rock where they had taken sanctuary from water that apparently did not even exist. Alex leaped to his feet as she did, his mind shrieking that if she fell in the rapids would reappear as fast as they had gone. She would fall and be lost to him.

But she righted herself, then stepped purposefully into the water. In only a few short steps she was on the bank, then turning and gesturing for him to follow, to hurry.

She needn't have bothered. Alex was already moving, sloshing across the water and then slogging onto the mud that marked the line between wet and dry. He looked at the forest, or tried to. The fog was still thick, and blanketed everything with an impenetrable gray.

"I don't want to go in there again," he said.

"Me either." Trish pointed at the stream behind them. "I vote we stick by the stream. Follow it until it dumps out at the road."

"That's miles past where we stopped the car."

She shrugged, though she didn't look at him. Like Alex, Trish had her gaze glued to the fog that hid the trees – and anything else that might be there. "I'd rather hit the road and backtrack along asphalt for a few miles than go in there again."

He didn't have to ask what she meant by *there*. And he agreed completely. He turned to follow the stream. Took a step. Stopped.

Trish must have seen his frown, because she asked, "What is it?"

"I don't know what side of the stream we're on."

"What?"

"I got all turned around in the…" He didn't know how to finish the sentence. "The stream" didn't seem to cover it, but "the rapids" was just as jarring, given that they were not there at all. Finally he shrugged and finished, lamely, "The water."

Trish nodded. She looked around and he could see that she had gotten thoroughly spun around as well. The fog blanketed everything, and between that and the permanent, starless night created by the canopy of tree branches, there was no way of knowing north from south, east from west. Then she chuckled. "We're so smart, you and I."

"What is it?"

"Both of us have PhDs and have been doing advanced physics in our sleep since we were kids."

"So?"

"So we apparently forgot that water flows downhill."

He understood what she meant now. The stream was fed at one end by a spring in some of the mountains far past the forest, and ended at a reservoir southwest of where they had stopped the car.

They just had to follow the current until it got them out of here.

"My brilliant wife," he said.

She flashed him a grin, and even wet and bedraggled he was struck by how beautiful she was when she smiled. It felt like he was looking at the best version of his own potential. Like the world might turn out all right if he just kept staring at that smile.

He held out his hand. She took it. He looked at the stream. There wasn't much water, and there wasn't much light, either. But he could make out a few branches sliding in one direction as the current carried them toward the reservoir, toward the place where the forest ended and real life could begin again.

Alex meant to start walking, but his feet remained rooted for some reason. He finally realized that he was listening for the whispers. Looking for the shapes that had accompanied them in the mist. So, for that matter, was Trish, turning slowly in a complete circle that ended with her facing the same way he was: downstream.

"Hear anything?" she said.

"No. You?"

"No."

"See anything?"

"No. You?"

"Just fog," said Alex. "Let's go."

They walked along, and every so often he glanced to his right, as though they might have wandered away from the quietly burbling stream without noticing it. It stayed where it was supposed to be. The water level remained the same, too – no more phantom rapids or disappearing rocks.

He glanced over. He walked. He looked again.

He stopped walking.

"No," he whispered.

Trish froze, too. "What?" she asked. She turned her head side to side, staring at the fog and the shadows it hid. "What do you see?"

Alex couldn't answer her. He could barely speak at all, and the words he managed were almost a whistle through a throat clenched in fear.

"That's not possible."

23
(When Tricia Had Grown)

Tricia understood the world.

Oh, not in the details, not in the smallest areas – though she worked to do just that in her daily grind as a researcher – but the world in general, that was her *thing*. That was why she liked science. There were absolutes. There were things you could count on. Sometimes the absolutes seemed to shift or change – gravity was a different thing once you got big enough or small enough or added in different forces. But even those shifts and changes were themselves the product of absolute rules. Even when the rules had yet to be completely discovered or figured out, they were *there*.

Truth was truth, irrespective of whether you believed it or not. That was the point of science: to peel back what *appeared to be* and find out what *actually was*.

That was why she felt like she was being punched. Not just once, either, but over and over.

She had forgotten so much of the forest. Whether it was swallowed up by the pain of what happened here so long ago – and then what happened again, when she lost her son – or whether her mind had just hidden from things that seemed to countermand everything she thought she knew, she could not say. No matter why, the forest existed for years as a black hole in her mind. A few things, mostly seen in dream, existed in a tenuous hold between remembered and forgotten, in the event horizon of memory and whatever lay in the total darkness. Now, that event horizon was contracting.

She was starting to *remember*, and so also starting to realize how much danger she was in. Not just the physical kind, but the kind that threatened Self. The kind that could strip away sanity easier than she could peel an apple.

That was what she felt now, when she looked at the stream. Alex had pulled her with him as he ran away from –

(Memory. The thing in the dark. The monster. The man in the tree.

The forest.)

– the things that had hunted them from the mist. He had done the right thing, the *only* thing... but it was also the most dangerous thing. He had fled the shadow, and in so doing brought them deeper into the place where madness ruled not at the fringes, but at the heart. A place where science didn't work. Where they could walk forever without getting to their destination. Where she and Alex could fall into a stream that *wasn't* a stream, but a raging river.

Tricia honestly thought she was going to die twice. Once from being drowned in rapids, or dashed to pieces against the rocks that thrust out of white water to pummel and bruise them as they were buffeted to and fro.

The second time – the worst of the two by far – was the death that came when she crawled onto the rock in the middle of the rapids, and realized that there *were* no rapids. Just a stream, cloaked in creepers of mist that reached forth from the mist all around them.

The thing that had almost killed them wasn't even real.

But Alex saw it, too. He felt it. He's still dripping wet.

Alex stopped walking. "No," he said. His hand remained curled around hers, but his flesh chilled. It was like holding the hand of a corpse.

"What?" she said. He was staring at the stream, so she looked *away*. She didn't want to know. She didn't want more madness. She looked into the forest. The mist swirled, and its light brightened for an instant. The flash illuminated lazy circles of vapor that funneled in and out, allowing almost-glimpses of shapes and shadows.

"This is *not possible,*" Alex said.

And Tricia finally looked. She cursed herself, but it was impossible *not* to look.

Alex was staring at the stream. The water flowed, nearly silent against the rocks that made up its bed, fist-sized things smoothed by eons of friction. A whisper, nothing more. No loud noises, no rapids.

But it was flowing the wrong way. They had been following it down stream, the stream at their right as they walked. But now, when she turned so it was on her right side, she was facing *up*stream, against the current.

A small noise escaped her. It was girlish, almost the sound of a child finding an unexpected present. Not in keeping at all with the fear she felt as she said, "Did we cross over without realizing?"

Alex shook his head. "We've been walking with it on our right."

"Then we must have started off in the wrong direction." She sounded almost petulant, and hated it. But that was the only explanation, wasn't it? They must have been confused, and actually started going upstream in the first place. That was all. Just confusion because of panic, and they misread the subtle current.

It would be an easy fix: they just had to turn around, put the stream on their left, and do it right this time. Follow it downstream, get back to the road, then drive to Dr. Coleman's office and beat him to death for suggesting they come here in the first place.

Apparently Alex was thinking along the same lines, because he said, "I have never wanted to murder a health professional before."

She squeezed his hand, and felt some life come back into it. He squeezed hers back. Not too tightly, but tightly enough that she knew he was alive. That she wasn't holding the hand of someone who had died some time ago, and was only walking around because he hadn't quite realized it yet.

They turned around and started back the way they had come.

Downstream. Keep the stream on the left. We'll get out of here.

Soon they returned to the spot where they started. Tricia saw the rock she had clung to and then lain on to "save" herself from the rapids that had never existed anywhere but her own panic-duped mind. She clung to it again, this time mentally. It was a tangible thing, a piece of evidence that showed this was all real. Reproduction of a result was proof of its veracity. They had walked, and there was the rock. Now they would keep walking in their current direction. Downstream, to the road, and out of this place.

They walked. The stream at their left. The current sliding ahead of them. Alex kept looking down as though to verify they hadn't somehow wandered across the stream again. She would have laughed anywhere else, to see him doubting the obvious like that. Alex loved and revered science as much as she did, but he'd always been willing to follow rabbit holes that she deemed irrational. Sometimes he found truth at the bottom of them, but the fact remained he was much more prone to inspiration than she. If science had art to it, then she was a paint-by-numbers person, and Alex was more willing to be a Picasso: able to see not only what was there, but to imagine what it would be if the rules weren't followed.

She mocked him – lovingly – for that. Made fun of his need to follow flights of fancy, like he was the hero of one of the science fiction or fantasy books he loved.

But she would not mock him in the forest. He could look down all he wanted, and she would, too. Keep the water at their left, follow it downstream and –

This time it was Tricia who stopped. This time it was she who said, "Impossible." This time it was Alex who made a sound similar to the one she had made a moment before: a sound of surprise, doing its best to cloak terror.

"We must have turned around again," said Alex.

She shook her head. "We didn't," she said. "You know we didn't." Then she contradicted herself: "But we *must* have. We must have crossed over, and turned around so that walking with the stream on our left meant we were going upstream again."

It sounded ridiculous when she said it aloud. How could that have happened without them noticing it? And now Alex was playing devil's advocate, switching sides just as she had: "But we didn't. You know we didn't."

They were echoing each other. The words were repeated, but warped a bit each time. And that made sense, given what they were seeing.

They turned around. That was what you did when you were going the wrong way: you turned around. Now the stream was on their right side, and now it was flowing the direction they wanted it to flow. They walked again, and Tricia tried to convince herself that they had just started out wrong, or gotten turned around, or any of a million other possibilities that made more sense than a stream whose current shifted directions over and over again.

The stream behaved now. Tricia allowed herself to relax as the water ran before them, moving faster than she and Alex walked, as though the water itself was also excited to get out of this place.

She looked at the stream. On her right side. Water flowing ahead.

She looked at the forest. The mist flashed.

She looked at the stream. Right side. Water flowing *the wrong way.*

"We didn't turn around. We *didn't.*"

She wasn't sure if she said it, or Alex did. The forest was stripping away reality, and maybe it would strip away the differences between them until they were just one person.

It is just one person. Just me, moaning in a straitjacket in a padded cell and wondering when someone is going to change my diaper.

"We didn't turn around," said Alex. "Not this time."

Tricia gave a small laugh, the giggle of someone asking for a drink while drowning. "Then we must have gotten it wrong again. We started out right the first time. We just have to turn around and…"

She didn't know what to say after that. She turned around –

(Stream on the left, *dear girl, just like you have to get it* right *this time, or you'll be* left *behind, so get it* right *until the people in white come with your meds.)*

– and started walking. The stream was on her left. She was following the current.

She took two steps. Alex let his hand, fingers still intertwined with hers, let his arm extend as she took those steps. But he didn't follow, forcing her to either stop or let go. She didn't want to do either.

"Come *on,*" she said. "We know what we have to –"

"It'll just change again," he said dully.

"No, it won't." She jerked his hand with each word, as though trying to physically shock him into agreeing with her.

"It will."

Maddening, his insistence on the impossible. He was following a rabbit hole again, that was it and that was all. Things had seemed to stop making sense, but that was just an effect of their exhaustion and fear. They were going in the correct direction –

(Stream on our left, *which is the* right *way to follow it downstream.)*

– and there was no room for denial. They weren't in a lab this time, where he could follow flights of inspiration/fancy with nothing worse than a wasted day resulting. They were in the *forest,* in the most dangerous place she had ever been. They had to cling to truth, to the real.

They had to follow the stream out of here.

Tricia looked around, trying to find some way to convince Alex. She saw a patch of dying rushes near the stream and plucked some of the dried leaves. They had sharp edges that cut her palm.

Not deep enough to bleed, but deep enough to sting. She didn't care. She was getting out of this place, and science, as always, would show the way.

She tossed the bits of plant into the stream. Or tried to – the sun-dried leaves were so light that the slight breeze here just tossed them back at her. No matter. She plucked a few more dessicated leaves, unclenched her hand from Alex's, and waded out a few feet into the stream.

"Don't!" Alex shouted. He looked like he might say more, but then his jaw clenched and she knew he was trying to maintain his own fragile grip on sanity.

She put the leaves in the stream, shaking her hand a bit so the ones that stuck to her palm as soon as they got wet would let go and do what she wanted them to.

In the instant she let go, she was suddenly afraid. What if it didn't work?

But it *did* work. "We follow the leaves," she said. "They'll be easy to follow visually, and we can trail them right out of this rotten place."

She didn't add, *And that'll prove that the stream's current isn't switching. We keep it on our* left, *and get* right *out of here.*

She waded back out of the stream, backing toward Alex so she could keep the leaves in sight. They were moving fairly quickly, so by the time she rejoined Alex, she and Alex had to hurry to follow them before they slid into the mist and disappeared.

She and Alex slid in mud, tripped over roots and bushes, but neither suggested they slow. For her at least, the dead leaves had become her last grasp at reality. At things that truly *were,* instead of things that lied; things that merely *appeared* to be.

Even so, the leaves started drawing away from them.

Fine, she decided. She'd just grab some more. She'd toss them into the stream (still at her left!), then they'd follow *those* leaves and it would be impossible to get lost because they would never lose sight of the thing that would lead them out of here.

The leaves sped up suddenly, caught by a swifter current and on the verge of disappearing from sight. Tricia felt panic clawing at her and leaned down so she could find more leaves and toss them in before the first batch were lost to sight. No way to get lost if she followed a guide at every second, right?

She scrabbled quickly at the ground nearby. She found a few rocks. Too heavy. She grabbed some leaves that were so old they fell apart as she touched them.

The remains of the rushes were almost gone from sight.

She started to panic. She knew it was stupid, they were fine now. The stream was on their left, and they'd been following it long enough she was confident they wouldn't get turned around again.

But still, part of her screamed, what if they *weren't* fine? What if they lost sight of sticks and leaves that floated along the stream and showed them the way and somehow got turned around again and it would be that much harder to figure out what was happening if that happened and the world would seem that much darker and stranger and she would have that much more pain as she fell into the rabbit hole herself and lost herself just like Alice just like –

A nonstop mental monologue of panic cut off as her fingers found a small pile of sticks. Barely more than twigs, really, but big enough to follow. She tossed them the instant before the rush leaves that had been her and Alex's original guide disappeared from view.

Beside her, Alex breathed a sigh of audible relief. He'd been thinking along the same lines as her. "We're fine," he murmured, walking again as the sticks began to move in the same direction as the others had – which meant they could follow the stream on their *left*, to find the *right* way out. "We're fine."

She and Alex followed the floating sticks. The mist curled around them, like it wanted to hold them fast. She forced a smile to her face, and forced rational thought to her mind.

The mist is just vapor. Nothing to it, just like there's nothing to the forest. Just bad memories and worse not-memories that hide in those black holes. Trauma explains it all, but even pain that causes lost memories can't stop the power of science. Water flows one way – high to low. We follow it, and we're fine.

They kept following the sticks she had tossed in. The current was slower here so they didn't have to walk very fast to keep up with their improvised compass of sorts. She even had time to stop and find some more sticks, anticipating that the current might speed up at some point, and not wanting to relive that moment of panic as she worried about losing sight of the thing upon which she had hung her hope of returning to normality.

"I'm not built for this anymore," said Alex.

"What?" she asked.

"All this walking and running." He chuckled – a bit forced-sounding, true, but she could hear relief in his voice.

A bit of dead plant and we're fine and dandy again. Because Science!

"Me either," she agreed.

"But really, nothing has happened. We're just out for a stroll that turned out to be longer than expected," he said.

"Nice night for it," she said. "What with the moon being so… whatever it is."

She meant it as a joke. It came out as a reminder of how little they could see. Nothing above, nothing to the sides. Just water and mist and branches clasped in a death-grip above their heads.

They followed the sticks. The bits of wood had slowed still further, twisting and turning lazily. Tricia wanted to run ahead of them, but forced herself not to. She was not going to give this place any chance to fool her. She would follow the sticks, which followed the current, which followed its course to the reservoir.

The sticks slowed more. More.

More.

And they stopped.

Alex sighed, not in relief this time but exasperation. "I thought we'd be back at the road by now."

"No," she said, searching for a way to explain his concern away. "We're just following the sticks, and the current's moving slowly."

"Isn't time supposed to fly when you're having fun?" he said dryly.

"Like I said: the current's moving slowly."

Alex laughed again. It sounded a bit more forced this time. "Should we just start walking ahead of the sticks? Keep the stream at our left and all good?"

She didn't answer. He didn't repeat the question, and she was relieved that he didn't. She didn't want to move ahead of the sticks that had led them so well to this point.

They watched the sticks, which floated a few more inches – it took forever! – and then halted and began turning in place. They must have been caught in one of those minute whirlpools that were invisible to the eye but brought small things to a momentary halt.

They'll start moving again. We just have to be patient.

The sticks spun, lazily, mockingly.

They spun.

Then they stopped.

Then they started moving again. A concrete direction. The *wrong* direction. Tricia moaned as she followed them as they floated back to her, then past her. She turned to face them as the current dragged them away.

If she followed them now, she would have the stream on her right.

Tricia moaned.

"How are they doing that?" Alex all but shouted. Something like rage rippled his features. He made strange, animal sounds as he bent over and ripped a knot of weeds out of the ground. The plants came up, trailing roots that curled like dirty intestines. Alex stomped down/upstream, the water at his left as the twigs in the stream disappeared into the mist behind him and Tricia.

"Where are you going?" she shouted. Terror wrapped a cold hand around her own intestines and squeezed. "Where are you –"

"To get to where the current is stronger. Past whatever weird made the other sticks…" He didn't finish, just tossed the handful of leaves and roots into the stream.

They floated the wrong way, too. They were heavier, and should have been able to escape whatever small eddy had made the individual leaves Tricia tossed in act so strangely. But they went the same way. Downstream would be on her right.

Something broke inside her as she watched the weeds float past, and Tricia found herself in the stream, no memory of running into the water. It was deeper here – up to her knees – and the weeds disappeared behind her as she splashed to the center of the stream.

The current was strong. And even though it had dragged the weeds away behind her, she felt it pushing her *forward.*

Somehow, the current was flowing one way at one point, and a few yards farther was moving the other way. Tricia knew that waterways could change course over time, but that time was measured in terms of *miles* and *eons* or, at the very fastest, if humans intervened by digging canals or putting in dams, in terms of miles and *years*.

Waterways did not and *could not* shift directions in the course of *yards* and *moments*.

Splashing. She looked ahead of her and saw Alex doing what she had just done: running into the stream. He leaned over, thrusting both his arms into the water up to his elbows. He looked at her, and she could see the question in his eyes: *Which way is the water going?*

She pointed toward him. "The water's going that way."

His hand slowly lifted. He pointed at *her.* "That way," he said.

She closed her eyes. Something could explain this. Something *had* to.

She started moving toward Alex.

"Start walking toward me," she said. "There's got to be a sinkhole or something between us. Something causing it."

And what caused it before, *Trishy-baby? Any answer to* that *little mind-bender?*

Shut up. There's a rational explanation.

Alex started toward her. The sound of his movement carried easily and well, and she wondered what else might be hearing them. She hadn't heard anything in the trees or mist since Alex and she ran from the whispers.

There weren't any whispers. Just wind.

It was words.

No. It wasn't. Couldn't be.

Still, no sense taking chances. She quieted her splashes as best she could, moving slowly but steadily toward Alex as he moved slowly but steadily in her direction.

When he was ten feet away, Tricia whisper-shouted, "Still going the same direction?"

"Current's pushing me toward you," he answered in the same tone. "What about where you are?"

They were eight feet away now.

"It's pushing *me* toward *you,*" she answered. Six feet.

"So it has to be something between us." five feet.

"Yeah. Has to be."

The current swept against her. Pushing Tricia toward her husband. Four feet.

Alex stared at her, obviously waiting for her to tell him she could feel a change. She stared back, just as obviously waiting for *him* to say something.

The current pushed her toward Alex.

He kept walking toward her.

"Which way?" she whispered. Two feet.

"Toward you," he answered hoarsely. He took another step. "Toward you," he repeated. One foot away. She could reach out and squeeze his shoulder.

She stepped forward again. She stood *beside* Alex now. Both faced in opposite directions. The current pushed against the backs of her calves. She took another step forward. She had passed Alex. He was still looking straight ahead, which meant he was looking away from her.

Another step. Two feet past him. Three. Four. Five.

She glanced over her shoulder. "Which way?" she said quietly.

Alex slowly raised his hand. It was visibly trembling. He pointed… straight ahead of him. The opposite direction of the current she still felt, and which had led her to and right past him.

Her world spun again. Science was supposed to help this. It was supposed to provide answers, or at least the sense that answers were out there, somewhere.

But science had, apparently, left the area.

Tricia could think of no way to fool herself. A sinkhole draining the water to an underground river was a poor enough explanation for a current going in one way in the stream, while going the opposite way a few dozen feet later. But if that were the case, she and Alex would have seen something to indicate the drainage. A hole or –

Or be honest. *A hole big enough to explain the shift in the current's direction on a stream this size would be easily visible, and likely would have knocked us off our feet and sucked us down into it before Alex and I ever got close to each other.*

And even if that had been a possibility, she knew of nothing – no physical force at all – that would explain how she could stand right beside her husband, each facing opposite directions, and they could both feel currents pushing the backs of their legs. Like they were standing on opposite sides of some invisible forcefield that separated what appeared to be a single body of water into two parallel lanes with the water being driven in opposite directions on each side.

On impulse, she sidestepped. She was standing directly in Alex's "lane" now, though still facing away from him. A moment later, she heard similar motion and knew he was doing the same as she had: sidestepping to get into her "lane."

She looked over her shoulder. Alex was looking over his.

"Which way?" she said.

He pointed at her. "Toward you."

She pointed at him, echoing his words. "Toward you."

Alex frowned. His finger, extended toward her, now bobbled. "What is it?" Tricia said.

"I don't feel anything," he answered. "No current, it just…" Then he froze. And Tricia knew in that instant what he was feeling, because she was feeling the same thing.

The current *shifted*.

It was pushing against her shins one moment, then against her calves the next.

"Which way now?" Alex whispered behind her.

"Away from you," she answered in the same whisper. "You?"

"Away from you."

She sidestepped again. One foot in each lane.

On her left side, the current pressed against her shins again.

On her right, it pressed against her calves.

Then it switched. Just like that, it pressed against her calves on both sides. Then against her shins. Then one of each current going against her left calf, and pushing equally hard against her right shin.

The current divided directly below her.

She heard a strange sound coming from Alex. She had never heard it before, a dry sob that sounded like his soul was being ripped out of him.

She turned to face him. He did the same.

The current swirled. Now one direction, now another.

"It's impossible," he whispered.

She agreed.

But it seemed, at least here in the forest, that *impossible* was just like *truth* in the rest of the world: it existed regardless of whether you believed in it or not.

As they watched, one of the twigs she had thrown earlier floated into view, running between her legs and heading toward Alex. She remembered it, because unlike most of the dead things she had been tossing in the stream, this one had a single bright green stalk growing out of the side – a small bit of life struggling to be born.

The stick continued toward Alex. As it did, it drifted ever so slightly, moving left, moving right.

It passed under Alex's legs. He turned around, automatically moving to the side so Tricia could watch it with him.

The twig hypnotized them as it slowly... slowly... slowly moved to the center of the stream. It hung in place, then began slowly spinning on a center axis.

Tricia realized she couldn't feel the current on either leg. Then it returned, and before the stick finished a single revolution it shifted twice more. Backward to forward, forward to back.

The twig stopped spinning. It seemed to tremble, then started to shake as though suffering a grand mal seizure. The shaking grew more pronounced, and then an odd sound came from it. Louder than it should have been, and unmistakeable. It was the shredding, tearing sound of a green stick being twisted beyond its tolerance. The small branch separated, and now one half was on each side of the invisible place in the center of the water, torn apart by an impossible current in an impossible place.

Alex turned toward Tricia, terror in his eyes. She knew what had driven him to that terror – were they about to be torn apart, too?

She and Alex moved out of the water as one. They walked slowly, with odd deliberation, heading for the same side of the stream. They walked to each other on the bank and clasped hands. They looked at the silvery water sliding through the silvery mist.

On impulse, Tricia reached down and grabbed one more handful of leaves. She threw them into the river.

The leaves clumped together. A moment later, the mass split in two. Half went one way, the other half proceeded in the opposite direction.

A moment after *that,* the leaves stopped moving. They were still floating, but statically, no movement at all.

"Which way do we go?" she asked quietly.

"Does it matter?" Alex answered in an emotionless monotone.

"No. Not in this Hell."

And it didn't. They both turned and started walking. Impossible stream on their left, impossible forest on the right, but Tricia knew that, no matter which direction they had chosen to go in that moment, it wouldn't have made a difference.

Because no matter which direction they chose to go, they would only end up walking deeper into the dark heart of the forest.

"We're going to die in here," she whispered. Only to herself, so quietly it barely reached her ears. But the forest seemed to sigh around them. The forest had heard.

And the forest, she thought, agreed.

24
(When Alex Was Young)

"I have… to stop."

The words came out between gasps. Alex had been running so far and so hard that he worried the words themselves might push him over the edge. He and Trish had dropped their bags somewhere during the run, but instead of lightening his load it weighed him down. The bag had represented the mundane, banal world of high school – and right now "mundane" and "banal" sounded pretty good.

He wondered, between thunder-sounds of his heart beating far too fast, if a kid his age could just keel over of a heart attack.

"Me… too," panted Trish. She put her hands on her knees, then apparently lost the strength to do even that and instead she half fell into a squat, her arms crossing over her knees and her head resting on her arms.

Alex wanted to follow suit – how very much he did! – but something inside him was shrieking that one of them had to keep watch.

Though, to be honest, he didn't know what he was keeping watch *against*. Or, for that matter, what he would do if the thing out there in the mist decided to reveal itself.

He looked around. Searching for the whispers.

There was only the sound of the stream, which he and Trish had somehow managed to follow even in the midst of their mad flight.

Follow the stream. Follow it upstream, and get Sam, and get out.

It wasn't much, as far as plans went, but it was something. Enough to push the panic back to manageable levels. He no longer felt the urge to run blindly, though he knew that if the whispers came back, he likely would react just the same.

"What were those things?" asked Trish. She was still panting, but less heavily, and some color had returned to her face.

"I don't know."

"They had to be *something*."

He knew what she was saying: it had to be something that *made sense*. Something that science could account for. There was no room in Trish's life for the irrational. One plus one always equaled two.

Of course, that meant, numerically, that the infinite existed. Alex had teased her about that once, telling her that if infinity was real, then anything could happen. Infinite time, infinite possibilities.

Trish did *not* like that. And at this moment, neither did Alex.

"Ghosts," he whispered. He knew it was a mistake as soon as the word left him, but he couldn't catch it, couldn't shove it back in his mouth and bite down on it until it died.

Trish looked up at him, something like rage lighting her cheeks with fever spots. Unlike him, though, she managed to swallow whatever she wanted to say. It would have been something devastating, though, he could tell.

Not for the first time, Alex realized that he loved her – which meant she had the power to destroy him.

Alex looked around, as though checking once more for danger, though this time it was more to keep from looking at her.

"Should we keep on?" he asked.

"What do you think?" Trish said.

He shrugged. "We've been in here a long time. We ran a long time. We're probably close."

Trish nodded and stood. She closed her eyes as though fighting the urge to vomit. "Stupid to get so close and not help him."

"If he even needs our help," said Alex. Again, they were words he shouldn't have said. To his surprise, though, this time Trish didn't get mad. She looked tired, and sad, but not angry.

"He needs our help. I can..."

She didn't finish. Alex suspected that was because the words she would have had to say were "feel it."

He felt it, too. Something was out there. Not just the things that had whispered to them in the fog, but something worse. Something that had put Sam in danger.

Us, too.

There was nothing to be done about that. They could either turn back and abandon their friend, or they could continue. There were no half-measures here, not in the forest.

"Let's go," he said.

Trish nodded. She took point, drawing slightly ahead of him. It was weird not walking side by side, but he knew why she had done it. The forest pressed close to the stream in this place. She didn't want to go in there – a decision he heartily supported – but that meant they could either walk abreast with one of them in the stream, or they could string out along the narrow bank.

It also felt suddenly like a military operation. A scout in the lead, rear guard behind. Stringing themselves out so as to be less clumped; less of an easy target.

He shivered.

His heart had settled down a bit since their crazed run, but now it went back into overdrive. The rush-roar of his pulse returned for a moment, deafening in the hushed isolation of a mist-clad forest.

Trish stopped walking suddenly.

"Do you hear that?" she said, and Alex realized he wasn't hearing his pulse alone. Under it there was a strange sound, so out of place in this moment that he couldn't place it.

Rapids? Where are there rapids around here?

He and Trish turned toward the sound. As they did, the sound disappeared. Alex saw no rapids. Just the stream, whispering its way along a rock-strewn bed on its way through the trees. Beyond that, the other half of the forest. Around it all, the mist.

Whatever had made the sound was gone.

"Come on," he said. "I think we should keep going."

They started walking again, and this time he took the lead. No sense of chivalry or feeling that Trish needed looking after – she was tough and strong and could handle just as much as he could. But even though she didn't *need* looking after, any more than he did, he *wanted* to look after her. And he did need to follow that desire.

I'd die for her.

But I'd rather not do it just yet.

Maybe I should get her out of here.

That wouldn't happen, he knew. Tricia would never have allowed the one friend they made in their lives – other than each other – to face the danger of an unstable parent, or the danger of being in the forest itself. And, Alex knew, neither would he. They were in it together, and both of them would see this through to the end.

He could see Sam's face. Even in the one week that had passed since he showed up, he had grown noticeably more drawn. Not any thinner, really, but as though his skin had been stretched a bit tighter over a bit less. He was disappearing in stages, though he refused to address it.

Alex felt wetness on his feet. He'd been so involved in his thoughts that he had wandered into the stream. He felt the current pushing him back, trying to stop him from finding his friend. He imagined it as a living thing.

Go back, it whispered. *Go back, and never come here again. Go back… or die and fall into me and I will sweep you away and you will be lost forever – not just your life, but the very memory of your existence will be wiped clean by my current.*

It was such a deep, dark thought that he jumped right out of the water and onto land when he felt something touch his arm.

It was just Trish. "You okay?" she asked.

His only answer was a sickly laugh. "Sure. Aces. Great."

"You were talking," she said.

"I wasn't."

"You were," she insisted. "You were whispering."

He felt cold. "I wasn't. I know I wasn't."

Both of them looked into the fog.

Nothing. Then a flicker, far away. Another pulse of brightness, closer this time.

They looked to the other side of the stream.

A few sticks slipped idly by, twirling in the stream's unseen eddies.

And with them came the whispers.

"Turn around..."

Alex reached for Trish. Their fingers found each other.

"Turn around... Turn around... Turn around..."

The whispers echoed toward them. They started out in what Alex would have guessed was the other side of the stream, but with each repetition they sounded louder, closer. They were *in* the stream.

A thick patch of fog wriggled its way out of the mist, floating forward with the echo and obscuring the other side of the stream. It floated forward as a patch of white in the pervasive silver of the air. The fog had been mysterious and frightening before. Now it seemed *alive,* and full of malice.

The fog stopped. It roiled in the middle of the stream and as it did Alex saw something dark within it. A hunched form, unclear in the haze but undeniably there where nothing had existed only a moment before.

Just a trick of the light – or of the dark.

For a long moment, the shape didn't move. Then it shifted slightly, and there was no way that Alex could pretend it was a just a thicker patch of fog or a shadow cast by branches overhead. It was a *thing,* a nightmare that should not be.

Another shadow came into view. Dual wraiths that slid slowly forward, toward the stream's edge, where Alex waited with Trish.

"Die..."

The whisper was lower than the others had been, but the small sound still pierced Alex's heart.

"Die..."

"Come on," whispered Trish. Her voice didn't tremble; she might as well have been waiting for him to go with her to class after lunch ended. But he felt the slickness of her palm, the clamminess of the flesh beneath the sweat.

She pulled, and he came with her. They moved slowly, backing away carefully because to run, it seemed to Alex, would invite the things in the mist to consume them.

The trees and the mist closed ahead of them. For the first time, Alex was glad that the forest cloaked so much all around them.

They continued backing away until Trish stopped with a murmur of pain. He risked a glance back and saw that she had backed into a tree.

The lowest branch, a thing as thick as Alex's leg, jutted out of the trunk at just Trish's height, and from there grasped at the sky along a knobby, knuckly path that made Alex think of arms and legs that had been badly broken and had healed crooked.

"You okay?" he asked Trish. She was rubbing the back of her head, and when she pulled her hand away he saw darkness on her palm. Blood. He leaped forward, turning her around so he could look at the wound.

"Ow!" she shouted, albeit in a whisper. "How bad is it?"

Alex shook his head. "I can't see. Too dark."

"Dark?" she laughed. "Hardly."

"What do you mean?" Alex asked. He looked back into the trees, wondering if they should keep moving. But he heard no whispers, saw no dark patches.

"Haven't you noticed how light it is?"

Alex hadn't. It seemed pretty dark, in fact. There wasn't even a moon above them. The trees were everywhere, the canopy a continuous ceiling of darkness, and –

He froze, his fingers still in her hair where he had been feeling for her wound.

Trish was right, and Alex felt like a fool. The highest branches of the trees covered them completely, and the fog hid any glimpses of stars or sky that might have slashed through the canopy.

But they had been able to see. Not much, but far more than they should have.

He looked around. He was a product of modern civilization, which meant everywhere he typically found himself at night had lights. Main Street, stores, restaurant, his home. Even the gas station was lit brightly on the rare occasion when he and his mother were out and about past sundown.

But he didn't *notice* the lights. They were just there. One time he and Mom had even driven from the store to their place with the headlights off the whole way. Neither noticed until they pulled into the garage and realized they couldn't see the back of the garage, so were likely about to plow right through into their living room.

She had laughed. It was a faint, not-very-funny laugh, but even a thin laugh was more than she usually allowed herself. She had said something, as though to excuse the lapse, and Alex said the same words he remembered: "You hardly notice the light until it's completely gone."

Trish nodded. "But it never *was* gone, so we never noticed. I just barely did a second ago, when I turned around and saw the tree and got mad at myself for not seeing it. In the dark. With no moon, no stars."

"Where's the light coming from then?" he asked.

She waited. She knew the answer, but wanted him to figure it out for himself. Or just didn't want to speak the words.

"The fog," Alex said

She nodded. "It's glowing. Just a little, but…"

They peered into the woods. They turned around, trying to find the spot where the light was coming from. It had to have a source, didn't it? Fog didn't glow.

Alex remembered reading a story where there had been a glowing fog. The idea had made him laugh at the time, even though the book purported to be scary. He wasn't as bound to rationality and logic as Trish was, but for some reason that glowing fog seemed utterly ludicrous at the time.

Not now, though. Not *inside* such a thing.

"Where's the light coming from?" he asked. He hoped Trish would have an answer. Some scientific fact she had paid attention to while he was engaging in his flights of fancy, and which would explain the luminous mist.

"It's not coming from anything." she answered.

He shook his head. "No. It has to come from somewhere. Light follows a path, we know –"

He froze. Trish clenched her chest when she saw his face, as though trying to keep her heart from exploding. "What is it?"

"The path. The stream." Alex turned in a circle. "I don't know where it is from here."

"We just put the tree at our back and…"

"… and walk a straight line through the trees, through the mist," Alex finished, trying to keep his expression from revealing what he thought their chances were of doing that: somewhere between "not good at all" and "zilch."

Tricia forced a smile. "The stream is pretty long, and I know it meanders around a bit. We should bump into it if we even walk in a *sort* of straight line."

Alex shook his head. "And what if we end up back where we were a second ago?" he said.

There was one thing in the river. Then two. And what if they turned to four and then eight? What if we go back and see a thousand of the things, all whispering, "Die… die…"?

"We can't just go back," Alex said.

"And we can't just leave," Trish answered.

"No," said Alex. He thought. "Maybe we can go around in a circle. Maybe we can hit the stream closer to Sam's place and miss…"

Whatever is in the stream nearby.

He didn't say the words, but knew Trish was probably hearing them just the same. She shook her head. "Same problem as before," she said. "We don't know where we are, exactly, so how do we walk to a spot – *any* spot – with any kind of precision?"

Alex had no answer, so he went back to Trish and turned her around once more and felt at her head. She winced but didn't cry out, which he took as a good sign. "I can't see the cut," he finally said, "but from what I can feel it's pretty small."

Trish looked at the painted palm of her hand. "Lot of blood."

"Head wounds do that," said Alex. "I fell out of a tree once and whacked my head in about the same spot. Bled like crazy."

Trish looked like she might laugh. "I remember. I was there."

"Oh yeah. And weren't you the one who insisted that I climb higher and higher? And weren't you the one whose shoe fell on my face?"

Trish put on a look of fake innocence. "I have no idea what you're talking about. You just weren't good at climbing trees."

"Certainly not as good as you were at footwear-related arboreal attacks."

"I still think it's just because you weren't good at climbing."

He snorted. "Probably. But a size five Nike in my mouth didn't help much."

They were both talking, which they probably shouldn't have been doing, but Alex felt like the quiet would have been too much to bear, and could tell Trish agreed with the sentiment.

They hadn't been able to run from the whispers, or from the things that made them. But at least they had a tree at their back, and that was something.

Plus, the talk had given him an idea. He looked at the tree, then peered at the others nearby. The one that had attacked Trish in the darkness was substantially thicker – and so likely taller – than the others in the immediate vicinity. Perfect.

"I can climb it," he said.

"What?" said Trish. "What are you – oh. No."

"It's the best way. I climb to the top, look at where we have to go. Maybe I can even get above the fog and –"

"And fall right out of the tree," she said. "Or don't you remember the moral of the story you just shared?"

"Don't get shoes thrown at my face?"

She snorted and, without another word, grabbed hold of the tree branch that had just brained her. "Help me up."

"Sure you don't want me to –"

"I need help on the first branch because it's high up. But I can do it myself if you're worried about poor little me."

She pronounced the last, *poe widdow me,* which was what decided Alex. It was a trace of the old Trish, who was more than willing to give him grief when she thought he was being a pain. They were in the forest, and things were terrifying, but if she could be this strong, so could he.

It was a lie. He was not strong. He was terrified. He kept jerking his eyes around as though to catch something creeping up on him from the edges of his vision. And sometimes, he thought he did.

But Trish was grabbing the branch, hooking her hands around either side and not waiting for him. Her feet lifted off the ground and she did an awkward swim through the air with them until the soles planted against the trunk of the tree.

"Wait. I've got you."

Alex made a stirrup with his hands, right below her. She grunted gratefully and stepped into his grip, then he pushed up as she stepped higher and together they wrestled her into the tree.

He had helped her, but even at this height – so low a fall could not possibly hurt her – his fear hummed into overdrive. "Careful," he said. "Just go high enough to see where –"

She snorted. "Really?" she said, already pulling herself up to the next level of branches. "I was going to get to the tippy-toppiest and then pitch myself down. Do you think I could get to terminal velocity before I exploded all over the place?"

"Not funny," he said.

Trish stayed there a moment. He dared to hope she would chicken out and let him be the one to take the risk.

She hoisted herself up. Up again.

He tried not to stare at her butt. Apparently even in the face of death and ghosts and the madness that was worse than either of those things, the male teenager was just as worried about procreation as anything. Fight or flight? No, it was fight or flight – and how to stare at girls during both.

Alex loved Trish's smile and her eyes the very best. One was kind, the other intelligent, which he viewed as her two best qualities. But he had to admit the rest of her wasn't hard on the soul, either.

Just as with a moment ago, he knew he was hiding from terror in a sense of silliness. Terror could not exist in the same moment as laughter. Fear fled in the face of mirth.

And for a teenage boy, the thought of your best female friend's – *only* female friend's, he corrected – butt was more powerful even than laughter.

Hormones: the real *best medicine.*

But Trish was disappearing into the branches above. Worse, she was disappearing into the mist that shrouded the forest in general and this tree in particular.

The fog flashed, and as it did, shadows flitted past in the periphery of his vision, and Alex thought he heard them whisper:

"… never leave…"

"… you die…"

He squinted, then looked around. Tried to convince himself he hadn't heard anything; that his imagination had run amok.

"Find them."

"Find them."

"FIND THEM."

"… out of time…"

He closed his eyes. "It's not real," he murmured. "Not real, it can't be real."

He opened his eyes. The shadows were gone. But was the fog thickening around the tree, around where Trish had gone?

That was what had happened when the… *things* had appeared in the stream. What if they were up there now? Crackling noises came from above, but what if they weren't Trish? What if *they* were following her even now? Climbing a bit faster, or maybe just *appearing*. Maybe just below, where they could grab her and pull her down and she would slam into branch after branch and be dead before she hit the ground. Maybe just yanking her off the tree and *into* themselves, to become one more specter that would forever haunt the forest.

Alex felt his pulse start thrumming again. His pulse quickened as his heart pounded inside his ribcage, a beast that wanted so desperately to be free it would kill itself – and him – in its frantic attempts to escape.

"Tr –"

She fell.

Oh, dear God, no, don –

Thought dissolved as he heard the terrible sound of his friend, his *life*, slamming into a branch. She screamed a short, piercing shriek that sounded almost like the aborted wail of a loon.

Then she was silent and there was only the meat-wood *thud, thud, THUD* of a body slamming downward. Noisier than he would have thought, like she was falling from a hundred or a thousand feet rather than only thirty.

Another sound joined the cacophony of gravity at work. The *thud* turned to a sound that reminded him, insanely, of the last dregs of an ICEE at the gas station. Drinking with Trish, the two of them sneaking out for something that would have been, could have been, a date. A wet sucking, then more slaps of flesh against the tree, then more wet noises, then a final, horrible noise that was a mixture of both.

Then nothing.

Trish had not fallen. Not all the way. She was still in the tree.

Alex didn't want to look up. He had to look up.

He did look up.

Trish hung above him, her body pinned to the tree by some of the smaller boughs that jutted out of the trunk, and which now impaled her. Four branches protruded from her body at neck, shoulder, chest, and thigh.

That wasn't what caused Alex to start screaming, though. He barely saw that.

Her face.

Her beautiful face.

Where has her face gone?

A fifth bough looked like it had probably been snapped off by her body as it fell. The naked end of it jutted out and up at an angle, and the other part of the sheared off limb lay tangled in a knot of branches nearby. That branch was thicker around than Alex's arm. It shouldn't have been able to snap like that under the weight of a girl falling from maybe twenty feet who weighed all of a hundred and twenty pounds when soaking wet and wearing five pounds of clothes.

But it did snap. The ragged edge of it glistened red where it ended about a foot away from the trunk. Something dripped off it. Too thick to be blood.

Something fell on Alex. Wet and warm – and hard.

Her skull.

The branch had punched right through her head. Into the back of her skull, out the ruined remnants of what had until moments ago been his ideal of beauty in the world.

Alex screamed. He screamed, and didn't care if the things in the forest heard. If they came for him. If they made him a thing like them – a ghost, a wraith.

He was already dead. His life was gone, and so twisted and mangled he could barely see anything through the gore.

Another thing fell on his face.

He wiped it away. Something cool in his hand.

He looked.

His scream now was louder than any that had gone before.

Trish's face was gone. Exploded by the tree that went through her skull and brain and pushed her face apart to reach through.

And Alex held part of that face in his hands. He screamed. Because he was staring at her eye, cradled miraculously, magically, *obscenely* in the palm of his hand.

25
Interlude
(When Sammy Was Young)

He fell asleep to heat. Now he wakes to heat even worse. The worst heat of all, the worst heat he has ever felt. He feels like he is in an oven, and Sammy worries he is in Hell. He heard Callee Prescott talk about Hell once, and asked Mommy and Daddy if it was real.

They laughed, and said of course not, but there had been something in their eyes that said they were lying. They both believed in Hell. Maybe they had seen it, even.

The hot is so bad, and so terrible, and worst of all it's a dark *hot. It's a hot that makes Sammy float in and out of sleep and twisted dreams of flying glass and blood and trees reaching for him.*

Then brightness blinds him. Cool air breathes life into his lungs.

Sammy blinks. He sees a form. He thinks it is a person, but cannot be sure, because the light behind the person – strange, bright, pulsing light and wisps of fog that trickle in and out of it all – is blinding. "Are you an angel?" he asks/whimpers.

"No," says the person. "I wish I was."

Sammy can almost see. Almost, but not quite. He can just feel the hot and the hotter and the hottest of maybe-Hell. Only the feel of his unicorn still clutched in his little fingers gives him hope that maybe this isn't that place. Would Hell let him have his favorite toy?

He sobs. The brightness has come just like the dark, but it's all the same. It all hurts and makes him afraid.

The person – angel? Devil? – has been speaking in a whisper that does not tell Sammy whether the whisperer is man or woman, and the light around the person shines so bright he still can't see who or what looks at him. Now the voice speaks again, still a whisper, though this time the person/thing sounds like he/she/it is talking to herself/himself/itself. "The dead don't stay dead in the forest. Remember that."

26
(When Tricia Was Young)

In spite of her tough words and bantering tone, Tricia was terrified of going up the tree. It was the right thing to do – or at least, the only one they had thought of that sounded like it might help – but that didn't mean she had to like it. Still, she put on a brave face and concentrated on not letting her voice quaver or her hands shake. If she showed any reticence, she knew Alex would insist on going in her stead.

He really *wasn't* as good a climber as she was, and she was grateful that he had the good sense to admit it. She knew he wanted to protect her – he was a good guy, and wouldn't let others take risks that he could have taken in their place.

And maybe especially you, Tricia. Maybe he feels protective. More than a friend.

She almost tried to toss out that feeling, then realized it was better than thinking about the fog or the forest or what Sam might be going through or any of the other dangers that had become her world.

She went with her feelings. Thinking about how kind Alex was. How he worried about her. How he had held her that morning, when she was weeping about her guppies.

And had that been only a few hours ago? That had seemed like the worst thing that had ever happened – the worst thing that ever *would* happen – at the time. But now the cruel killing of her fish with the word "DON'T" hung on the door seemed almost trivial.

She wondered if *she* was the guppy. A small thing, totally at the mercy of its captor. She could be nurtured and cared for as a pet. She could be bred as an experiment. She could be killed as a thing of no worth.

Don't think like that.

She concentrated on climbing. She'd always enjoyed climbing trees – hence the event where Alex got a shoe in the face – but had to admit it got a bit harder each time. It was one thing to swing from branches as a third-grader, when you weighed next to nothing; another to pull yourself up an inch at a time as a high-schooler.

The branches of the tree were rough under her palms. It was a pleasant, familiar feeling at first. But as she ascended, the ridges of bark began to pull at her skin. She felt scratches form on her hands and arms.

She did as much with her feet as she could. Even that began to hurt, though. Ramming a tennis shoe into the point where branches met trunk was the best way to go, but the branches were at a steep angle. Her body weight pushed her feet deeper into the wedge between branch and trunk than was comfortable, and by the time she had climbed a few yards she felt like the pressure was warping the small bones in her foot.

And what would Alex think then*? Would he ever fall in love with a club-footed freak?*

No help for it. She'd rather have club feet than fall. So she wedged her feet tight, pushed up with her legs, and pulled with her scratched palms.

After climbing for a while, she looked around. She hoped she might be able to see above the trees nearby; to spot the stream and maybe even something that would point a clear path to Sam's place.

She saw only trees. She'd have to go higher.

The branches started to thin. She switched from sturdy limbs to slim ones that bent and creaked every time she put weight on one. She tried to make sure she always had at least one hand and one foot on different branches, so if one or the other broke she wouldn't fall. A fall from this height could kill her, and would definitely break some bones.

A branch cracked under her. She switched her weight to the hand above her, which was holding a limb that was also far too thin for comfort.

The branch her foot rested on crackled again, but didn't break.

She kept climbing.

She looked around every few feet. Finally she was above the other trees. The fog was still everywhere, but… was that a slit in the trees? A thinning, barely seen, that would mark the stream?

She turned a bit. Doing so made her perch shake. Not just the branches this time, but the trunk itself moved from side to side. It was the thickness of a sapling at this height, only five or six inches in diameter, if that.

But she needed to get a better look, and that meant moving. Another crack sounded as she turned. She froze.

The tree, it seemed, had a malicious sense of humor. Lots of crackling and crunching, but no actual breaks. Yet.

She turned a bit more. An inch at a time. The fog was thick, but she thought she could see something. Something…

Tricia smiled. She leaned over a bit, intending to call down to Alex. To tell him what she had seen.

Before she could, a giant shadow obscured her view. It seemed to come from above her, then plummeted into and out of her eyesight in an instant. She gave a shriek of startlement and fear, then peered down to see what had happened.

She saw something pounding its way downward, slamming into a branch, flipping off it, hitting another one below that, bouncing like a pinball down to the next level. Something big, though she could tell little else of it before it disappeared among the branches.

She started down almost instantly, moving faster than she should, almost flinging herself down the branches and limbs at a dangerous pace. All she could think of was that the thing she had seen was another *shadow*. She didn't know what they were, but she knew this: it was heading for Alex.

Halfway down, she heard him scream. She moved even faster, no longer climbing but in a strange kind of controlled fall. All but plummeting toward Alex, toward whatever had fallen to him and was *hurting* him.

He screamed again. Louder. Longer. A *wail* of anguish and pain so great that it tore her own heart in two. She wanted to call out, to ask what was happening. But what if it wasn't one of the whisperers? Maybe it was Sam's crazy mother. Wouldn't it be better to stay quiet; maybe take her (or *it*) by surprise?

She clambered, climbed, fell… and finally realized what it was that had passed by her like a dark rocket or a meteor falling to earth.

It wasn't a shadow, wasn't a whisperer, wasn't a *thing*. But she wished in that instant that it *was* such a mystery. The horror in the shadows couldn't be worse than the person who was pinned in the tree, skewered by a half dozen branches, one of them jutting right through the corpse's head.

Then she heard Alex sobbing. It jarred her enough to get her moving again. He was still alive. He needed help. Needed *her*.

She dropped past the corpse, doing her best not to look in its direction. That was almost as bad as looking at it. Even in the short time it took her to climb below it, she felt like it was moving, reaching for her. She imagined it yanking itself off the branches, a perfect circle missing from its head, blood and brain dripping into the tunnel that remained –

She dropped the last few feet. Just to the right of Alex, who was kneeling, almost bent double, on the forest floor. He was crying, sobbing in a way she had never heard before. Jagged, agonized wails that sounded like each one came up violently, painfully.

She ran to him, put a hand on his shoulder.

"Alex."

He screamed in terror, throwing himself to the side and landing hard on his bottom, his arms and legs already yanking him along the forest floor, crabwalking away from her. She took a step toward him, her hand still reaching out. "Alex?" she said again.

He stopped his mad dash away. He froze and stared, the look of someone who has seen a wish come suddenly true.

Tricia blinked, and sometime in the nothing-time of her eyes closing then opening again, Alex was upon her. Not just hugging her, not embracing, but *engulfing* her in himself. In the midst of fear and confusion, he was holding Tricia so completely, so without reservation – to an extent and with a closeness that she would never have dared even dream of feeling.

"You're alive," he whispered in her ear. She felt tears wash over her cheek, and wasn't sure if they were his or hers. "You're alive."

"You, too," she said. "I was so afraid that you'd –"

She couldn't bear even to finish the thought. She could only hold him, alone in the forest, awash in silvered mist.

Neither said more. They held each other for a time that felt to Tricia like a delicious eternity, yet ended painfully soon at the same time. Alex drew back. "I thought you were dead," he said.

It was only then that she realized that blood streaked his face and clothing; that some of the warmth on her cheek probably wasn't tears, but the blood that painted his flesh.

"Who was it?" Alex asked. His eyes darted over her shoulder, angled up. Looking at the corpse.

It suddenly hit her: what she had seen; what she had had to climb past. The horror of the maimed thing hit her all at once, and she turned to the side and vomited. She felt like she would puke herself into oblivion, and then Alex was there. One hand went to her forehead, holding her up, his hand pleasantly cool against the fevered nausea that squeezed her stomach. The other hand was on her back, rubbing it softly as he whispered, "It's okay, it's okay," over and over even though they both knew it was a lie.

When she had managed to spew her guts out all over the ground – hopefully she didn't get any on Alex – she took a shuddering breath. Waited. She thought of the man in the tree and hiccupped and thought she might vomit again.

"Easy," said Alex, his voice soft and calming. "I've got you, Trish. I've got you."

His words and touch gave her the strength to bite back the waves of nausea and stand. "Sorry," she said. She looked at the sodden mass in front of her. "Super attractive."

"Are you kidding?" he said. "All the cool kids are doing it."

She laughed, then thought better of it. "Don't be funny," she said. "I'll start again."

"No funny here," Alex said quietly.

He was still rubbing her back, still had his hand on her forehead. She straightened a bit more. "I'm okay."

"You sure?"

She nodded. She jerked a chin at the tree, indicating the dark shape that still hung in the branches, but careful not to look *at* the thing. "What was that?" she said.

"I don't know," said Alex. "I figured you would, since you had to be right by whoever it was when they fell or jumped or… or whatever."

She shook her head. "He fell from above me."

Alex frowned at that. He started to look in the direction of the body, but jerked his gaze back to hers without quite glancing at it. Surprise tugged his eyebrows together. "I thought you had to be near the top by the time it – he – fell. That's why I was so scared. I thought you fell all the way from the top."

"I…" Now she was the one confused. "I was."

Alex shook his head and let out a low whistle. "Someone took a dive from a different tree?"

"No."

"No?"

"No. There… there weren't any trees taller than the one I was climbing. Not for a couple hundred feet, at least."

Alex's confused look deepened. "You must be wrong."

Irritation took the place of nausea. "I know what I saw. Something big fell right in front of my nose. It came from somewhere above me, then bounced its way down and I freaked out because I thought it was coming after you. I thought it was one of the *things*," she said.

"The whisperers," said Alex quietly.

Tricia started at Alex's use of the same term she had coined in her mind. *Whisperers*.

She took a breath as a fresh wave of nausea washed over her. Alex moved as though to hold her. She waved him off. "I'm okay." She shook her head, telling herself she would *not* puke again. Once was embarrassing enough. "But Alex, I know what I saw. The bod –" Her mouth went suddenly dry. She swallowed, trying to work up enough spit to continue, "It fell from *above* me."

Alex shuddered. "That means he was trying to get *you*. Specifically. We have to –"

She held his arm. "No. No one was trying to get me – at least not that way."

"But they jumped right at you."

"No, they didn't."

"I don't understand." Alex's eyes were pleading. Begging her to make sense of what he was hearing.

She couldn't. All she could do was take a deep breath and say, "They couldn't have jumped from another tree. The closest other one is a good thirty or forty feet away. And even if someone could jump that far – they couldn't jump *up* that far."

It took a moment for Alex to get what she was saying. "That has to be wrong."

"I was up there, Alex. There were no taller trees close enough to jump from there to where I was. That was why I went up there in the first place: it was higher than the trees around it, so I could hopefully see where we need to go."

That reminded her of what she *had* seen while in the tree, and she would have told Alex, but he said, "Then what? He jumped from a plane?"

Tricia looked up automatically, as though she might spot such a plane above them. But she had descended to the forest's domain again. She saw no sky. Nothing but branches and glowing fog.

"I don't know."

That was the refrain. Verse and chorus of the strange song that pervaded all in the forest: *I don't know. I don't know, I. Don't. KNOW.*

She was sick of it. There had to be answers. Answers fueled life. Made it safe and comfortable – or at least better than it had been. Understanding meant power. Once you understood a virus, you were on the way to a vaccine. Once you understood why a plane crashed, that became the beginning of the end for that problem. Once *she* understood the forest, they could escape.

That was why she began walking toward the tree again: to find an answer, and with it to move closer to the end of this journey.

"What are you doing?" Alex all but shouted.

"Seeing," she said.

"No!" he shouted behind her. She felt his hand on her arm, pawing at her, pulling at her. "Don't look, Trish, it's too –"

She yanked her arm away. "We *have* to."

He was silent. He followed her.

Together, they looked up and saw the man in the tree.

Tricia steeled herself, knowing she would see horror. It surprised her, though, how bad it was. Terrible when she had climbed past the thing, close enough to touch it. But here, looking up, it was somehow worse. The thing that hung above them loomed larger for the distance between them, like some dark god from myth.

It hung with one arm oustretched, pinned into that position by the branch that had gone through its shoulder. The other hung loosely, but without ease. Its face was still gone. And now, replaying the scene when she dropped out of the tree, she realized that Alex had been holding something when she came upon him. Something soft and round, cupped in his hand as he wept.

She turned away from the thought. She wanted answers, but were the *details* really important?

Just as she thought that, she heard Alex gag and choke back retching. That almost sent her to vomiting again herself, and only the thought of barfing in front of the person she had loved her whole life and now was starting to love in different, deeper ways kept her from losing it again.

Alex's hand fell on her shoulder. "He's got a coat on," he said hoarsely.

"Yeah," she said. "Dark green? Heavy."

"Like he expected to be out here."

She shook her head. "It's not that cold."

"No," he agreed.

"So why wear a coat?"

A foolish question, given the circumstances. But a loose string could unravel an entire cloth, so maybe this one could unravel a mystery.

"There's something on the pocket," said Alex.

She squinted. He was right. Something was on the breast pocket of the coat. But the darkness and fog were too thick for her to make out details. "I can't see what it's – what *he's* – wearing."

"I can't make it out, either."

She spotted another detail: thick-soled shoes on the body's feet. Like the arms, one leg hung propped at an angle – caught against the lowest bough of the tree before halting on the broken branches that pinned it. The other hung lower, looser. She could have reached out and touched its foot.

Again, she was reminded of stories of deity. Washing the feet of gods with tears, touching their wounds with hands that ached for evidence of pain.

Not me.

She forced herself to focus on the body's footwear. This wasn't a god. Gods didn't wear heavy, dark boots with thick tread. Work boots, or hiking boots. Again, this was someone who expected rough terrain. It was a heckuva lot better than the mud-riddled sneakers she and Alex were wearing.

That was all she could stand to look at. Alex pointed, but she cut him off. "We have to go," she said.

He didn't question it. Just nodded and asked, "Did you find a way out?"

She nodded, then shook her head, then shrugged. "Maybe out by through." At his quizzical expression, she explained, "I saw the cabin."

"Sam," breathed Alex in a tone that mirrored the way she felt herself: relief that they had a bearing. Worry that it reminded them both they could not leave this place. Not without what they came in here for.

"Sam," she agreed.

Panic rippled Alex's features. "I hugged you," he said. He spun in place, panic driving him to near-madness. "We turned. We lost our bearings. You have to climb – you *can't* climb again. Not again, not after –"

"It's okay," she said. "I can figure out the direction we need to go." She jerked a thumb over her shoulder. "We have a marker. We go straight out from the body."

Before anyone could say anymore – before she could even think about the grim reality of her last words, Tricia took Alex's hand and they began walking. She tried not to think of the fact that she was angling away a bit. She had come down a bit to the side of where she went up, angling to avoid the body. She had come up behind Alex, so between the body's trajectory and Alex's position she knew they had to go at a near right angle to the body.

One of the corpse's arms hung slack. The other jutted out, partially crucified… and making it look like the faceless body was guiding them, pointing the direction they must take.

She shuddered to think where a bloody, mangled deity would want them to go. And at what they might find when they arrived.

She forced back the thoughts.

She walked.

Alex followed.

Sam waited.

The forest watched.

27
(When Alex Was Young)

For Alex, walking through the forest had never been a picnic. Just getting here had been an exercise in patience, as the road stretched out before them. Or maybe time was what stretched, the seconds lengthening so that a walk out of town that should have taken an hour turned into a three-hour ordeal. Then, even before the fog arrived and with it, the whisperers, the going had been rough. He and Trish hadn't exactly dressed for hiking.

Then the fog did come. The whisperers arrived.

("… heeeere… childrennnnnnnnnnnnnnn…"

"RUN!")

But this was the worst. Walking with the man in the tree at their backs, and though Trish hadn't said anything, Alex knew she had seen what he did. The corpse had not only marked the beginning of this last path, but actively pointed the way.

The forest had caught them in life, and now Alex wondered if, should something happen here – something worse; something *deadly* – it would also claim them in death. The man in the tree had fallen from a nowhere-place – the same place where all that extra time on the road between here and home had sprung from, perhaps. Then the forest reached out its branches, caught the body, and snared it in a place where it would forever molder and decay until finally the tree would grow up around it and swallow it and the man in the tree would become *part* of the tree. Part of this place where all time and space coexisted with endless night and a journey with no destination.

Alex remembered a book that Sam had brought. One of his endless supplies of books, this one dealing not with science or technology, but history. Alex had wanted to read through a book on graphene – something Alex knew almost nothing about but which Sam, of course, had a wealth of information on – but Sam told him to look at certain chapters of a history book instead.

"History is yesterday," Alex said. "I don't care about yesterday, I care about today and tomorrow."

"If I have seen further than others," Sam intoned, thrusting the history book into Alex's hands, "it is by standing upon the shoulders of giants."

"I'm not interested in pop psychology, either," Alex retorted. "I'm interested in math and physics."

"I can see that," Sam responded seriously. Trish began to giggle in the way she did when she knew something Alex didn't. Apparently Sam recognized the laugh's meaning, because he winked conspiratorially at her.

"What am I missing?" Alex demanded.

"It wasn't a pop psychologist who said it," Trish managed, then burst out laughing as she said, "It was Isaac fricking Newton, you dope."

Alex pursed his lips, trying to decide how irritated he should be, and about what. Finally, he decided to acknowledge his error and be humble – which, he had found, was always the hardest thing to do at first, but had the quickest resolution. So he bowed low to Sam and said, in his best Samurai voice, "You have science judoed me, *sensei*."

Sam grinned as he bowed back, and said in similar tones, "When you have understood Greek mythology, Grasshopper, only then will you be ready to leave the monastery and travel the world proclaiming peace, where you will inevitably be pushed into a corner and Kung Fu someone to death weekly on a major network channel."

Trish had snorted, said, "Well *there* was a stunning display of mixed metaphors, terrible misunderstanding of Asian cultures, and accents that bordered on outright racism," and tried – unsuccessfully – not to laugh.

"But we nailed network TV, right?" said Sam, and blew her a kiss.

Alex took the book from Sam, intending to read it for a half hour or so before pestering his friend to give up the graphene text. An hour later, he had forgotten physics as he read about Styx.

He had always thought Styx was just a river, and was fascinated to learn it was actually a goddess who had sided with Zeus during the Titan war, and upon whose name an oath was sworn to end the battles between Titans and gods. She was endless, her byways known only to Charon, who ferried souls across her to the underworld.

We're lost souls, lost in Styx until shown the way by Charon – no ferryman this time, but a man in a tree pointing the way to judgment.

Certainly the forest seemed as much river as anything. There was a flow to the place, the trees stretching out, the branches touching one another and allowing a constant, unbroken stretch from organism to organism. A stream of greenery bound together by the flow of energy that never ended, but could be crossed just the same.

So we have a ferryman. So he's a dead guy in a tree. At least we know where we're going.

He tried not to think of the fact that, even when crossed, the trip was always one-way. Charon did not return people to life after their crossing. They stayed in the underworld eternally, and though the world had progressed since then, and myth either replaced or at the very least informed by science, no one had invented a way back from death.

At least, not that he knew.

And no matter what, we're *not dead. We're –*

"– going to die here,"

The fog flashed, and Alex froze. He didn't look behind him, afraid he might see their faceless ferryman standing there, one arm pointing eternally to the center of the forest, the other slack and loose because there was no way out, so no way to point.

"... die here..."

"The whisperers," murmured Trish, and it was only then that Alex realized she had stopped walking, too. A minute part of him had held out a hope that he was only imagining the words; that they were the echo of his own thoughts and not an actual, audible experience.

But Trish had heard it, too. The whisperers had found them again.

"... diiiiieeeeee heeeeeeeeeeeeere..."

Alex forced himself to turn toward the sound. He didn't shift the orientation of his body – he didn't want to lose his way again; no way was he going to allow Trish to climb a tree to figure out where they were going. Not after what happened before.

So he kept his body fixed on the way Trish had indicated they go. Only his head turned. Looking for the shadowed things that dogged them.

What are they?

He saw something. Not the whisperers – not yet, at least – but something on one of the trees. A shape, carved into the wood at about eye level. Interlocking circles that wove into themselves – the same shape they had seen on another tree. And just as before, the cuts – or burns, or whatever had made the shapes – looked perfectly smooth, though he had no doubt they would be rough as the last one had been. The smooth look of finely crafted woodworking, with the feel and texture of unblemished bark.

The circles pulled him. He gritted his teeth, fighting the urge to go closer to the tree and its symbol. He shook with the effort of keeping his body oriented on the cabin somewhere ahead, and on Sam.

Trish groaned and he knew she felt it, too. A singularity had opened in their minds, the gravity pulling, pulling, pulling them into the dark hole at its center.

The symbol seemed to grow, to take over more and more of the tree trunk. Then, impossibly, it *changed*. Like an old movie, poorly cut together and flickering as mis-matched images superimposed, one instant the symbol showed against the tree as a rough old scar, barely visible through overgrown bark. The next, it was lighter, with dark liquid streaming from the edges of the symbol, dripping slowly down the bark of the tree.

The tree was *bleeding*, and Alex – who loved fantasy and sci-fi but didn't really believe it and knew the difference between real and make-believe as well as anyone – saw in it an omen. He saw the image of his own face in his mind, blood streaming from a dozen wounds and still more of his life pumping from ears, nose, and even eyes. He saw Trish, her own fate the same as his.

Flicker: dark, smooth-looking circles in the wood.

Flash: bright slashes, dark fluid leaking like blood in the glowing mist. The images of himself and Trish dead and dying in the forest.

Flicker: smooth circles.

Flash: gleaming gashes.

He felt like something snapped in his brain. A psychic break, and then the circles were gone. The trunk of the tree was suddenly unblemished.

"Are you seeing this?" asked Trish. From her tone, Alex knew she wasn't sure which answer would be worse.

"Yeah, I'm seeing –"

He froze. The tree had snapped back to itself, the vision dissipating from Alex's sight – or mind, or whatever had just caused him to see what he had seen. But that wasn't all that had changed.

"The whisperers," murmured Trish.

The shapes, as always, stood in the mist. Close enough to be seen as to general shape, general size, but too far for any details. Just dark, hunched things.

The mist flashed, and the things started to move. Slowly at first, then a bit quicker, and then closing in fast. Alex was quick, but could tell at a glance he wasn't nearly as fast as the shadows were.

Worse than that, though, for the first time something accompanied the wraiths. The shadows had never brought sound with them, other than their words. They slid silently through the mist, as though they were part of the fog.

Now, as Alex faced ahead and, with Trish, began to run, he heard cracks, crashes.

For the first time, the shadows were more than ghosts. They were *real*, and *present*. They were crashing through brush, snapping twigs and branches. They could touch and be touched – if only in this strange place where things that shouldn't exist came into being.

The crashes grew louder, closer. Now they weren't just behind, but above. Branches splintered above his head. Something was falling, but he didn't look. What if it was another man, falling from nowhere, plummeting to his death as the tree branches punched holes in his chest and arms and face and popped his eyes right out of their sockets?

Alex was screaming now. Or maybe it was Trish. Either way, the shadows took up a similar wail, as though to mock their prey by imitation.

Then the cries shifted. Changed. Became one – a single, shrieking tone that was so different from the whispers that Alex's run faltered. His steps stuttered, then he nearly tripped and fell as he turned his head to see.

Nearly in step with him, there was Trish. She had all but stopped as well. He caught her gaze for a split-second. Then they both turned their heads further – he noted that she, too, was still being careful to maintain her orientation toward the cabin – and saw the fog plume and twist. The shapes that had followed them this far twisted in on themselves. For a moment he only saw one of them, then the fog split apart. Alex saw a flash of bright metal.

A knife.

The blade shone brightly in the fog's inner light, but it was a dark and fearsome brightness, subsumed by the red fluid that dripped off the blade.

The knife cut through the fog, held by Sam's mother. She looked even crazier than she had that morning. Her eyes darted in wide circles, the panicked, fevered glances of a creature cornered by a predator. She looked right, left, right, terror on her features.

When her gaze lit upon Alex and Trish, those features hardened. The fear disappeared from her eyes. No, worse. The fear was still there, but a terrible determination overlaid it. She was acting in a strange, purposeful state of panic that Alex had no experience with, no real understanding of.

He knew only that he and Trish were in worse danger than ever. Even before she screamed, "You! You caused it! It's your fault! Your fault!" She sobbed, and choked out, "I thought we'd be safe. I thought we got here early enough, but it all changed. *Everything changed again!*" Then, without missing a beat, she aimed the blade straight at Trish and ran toward her.

Trish turned. Nearly fell. Alex caught her, yanked her upright, and they ran.

He was still trying to keep in a line, trying to maintain a heading that would bring them both to the cabin.

Just survive. Just get away from the crazy –

A bough exploded from the fog ahead of them, a tree that they had not seen in the roiling depths. Alex ducked, and pulled Trish downward a few inches, even as she tried to do the same for him. She missed the branch – barely – but Alex's thoughts dissolved for a moment as his forehead found the limb. Stars appeared in the fog, bright flashes in the stranger illumination of the mist.

Alex reeled. Trish pulled him. He would have fallen but for her. She had saved him. She pulled him forward, and he thought for a moment he was screaming. Then he realized it wasn't him, it wasn't Trish. It was… it was…

What?

His thoughts rattled about his skull, ricocheting through his brain, bumping into themselves and cutting apart all pretense at understanding. The screaming, whining wail all around him dissolved into a series of jagged cries that cut his ears, cut his mind.

Not me. Not me. It's… it's her. It's Sam's mom.

Trish was still pulling, yanking him along as she ran. Behind them, Sam's mother wailed and shrieked wordlessly. Occasionally she would scream, *"YOU!"* Every time she did, the word unreeled at the final sound, the word turning to a wolf-wail in this moonless place where the entire world consisted only of tree, fog, shadow.

Alex looked back. She was close. So close that when she slashed the knife at him and Trish, it missed them by only inches. They both put on speed, and began zigging and zagging between trees. Alex thought for sure they must be turned around again. They would never find the cabin; would never find *Sam*.

If he's even alive. If she hasn't killed him already.

There could be no doubt that that was the woman's endgame, either. She had gone insane – completely, utterly, simply. Her gaze, when Alex risked another look, contained only rage and fear in a mix that had overcome the woman's soul.

She slashed again. This time the blade bit into his back. The cut was shallow, no deeper-feeling than some of the cuts already opened by branches and brush during one of this night's –

(Day's? What time is it? What day, what month, what year *is it? We've been here forever.)*

– mad rushes from terror to terror. But the cut bled more than his other scratches, and he felt warmth trickling down, gluing his shirt to his back. He cried out, and Trish screamed at the same time. Not hurt herself, he saw. She was crying for him, for his pain. The knife had cut him, but it had *hurt* them both.

Trish slid sideways, skittering like water dancing on a hot iron. She pulled him with her, and the move probably saved his life, if not both of their lives. The knife Sam's mother held slashed through the air where their necks had been a fraction of a second before. The madwoman growled – an animal sound. No comprehension, no understanding. Only *need*. Need to run, to flee, to fight, to *kill*.

Alex risked one more look back. Sam's mother actually looked worse than she had that morning. She looked like she had been dragged through the forest by a team of wild horses. She was filthy, her clothing torn, her hair a jumble of snarls and knots, her body streaked with dirt and sweat.

Oddly, that made Alex feel a bit better, even as he pushed himself to run harder. If she'd been out in the forest, running around and howling at the moon or whatever she did when she went full-crazy, that meant she probably hadn't had time to kill Sam. Maybe he was fine – other than the fact that he sprang from such an obviously cursed genetic line.

The fog thickened around them once more. Alex's hairs stood on end as he heard Sam's mother shriek, and also heard the whisperers. No words, just hurried tones that echoed his own fear. Turned it back on itself and made it hideous.

They had to slow down. They couldn't afford to, but they could afford a fall even less. A fall would bring them into range of the knife that he sensed still slashing and flashing behind him.

"Alex," Trish panted. A word of warning – she felt it, too. Something was changing.

"I… know…"

He couldn't say any more. He had to run, he had to push himself through the pain in his legs, the stitch in his side, and the terror that made every motion seem far too slow. Trish was doing the same, too. They had to slow for the fog, and still more from exhaustion.

The only consolation was the heavy breathing and sharp shouts that arced into the air as Sam's mother tripped over roots and brush. She never fell completely, though. Alex could tell from the sounds she made – and from the fact that, though he could hear her crashing into things, her screams were always so close, *too* close.

Another tree loomed. Another low-hanging bough that Trish ducked under and which almost caught him in the head just like the last one had. He jerked back at the last second. He almost fell, but turned the fall into a semi-controlled slide that brought him sideways and down, barely avoiding the tree and its sweeping limb.

He ran again. Listening, hoping.

What he hoped for happened. He heard Sam's mother's scream cut off suddenly, jerked to a halt by the same branch Alex almost hit.

He risked another look over his shoulder. There she was: on the ground, moaning in pain, blood sluicing in a thick sheet down her head from the gash the tree branch had inflicted.

The fog billowed. It swallowed her, and as it did her cries rose in pitch and in volume. They moved from a mix of madness and fear to tones of pure panic. "No, no, *noooooooo!*" she screeched, and the last word dissolved to a siren-whine of terror and pain.

It cut off as the fog flashed around them, a quick brightness that was like the mist had opened its eyes for just a moment, seen what was happening, and then fallen asleep once more.

The silence was now broken only by the crash of his and Trish's steps. Dead brush snapped, dry leaves crackled and spit.

He looked back. There was nothing but fog. A few upright shadows – the trees big enough to be seen through the mist. But even they looked insubstantial. They waved and bent in the gloaming, as unreal and untouchable as the fog itself.

There was no other shadow. He could still see the tree with its branch that had tried to trip them up. Sam's mother should have been visible, if only as a dark shape huddled on the ground.

Nothing.

Just brush. Just the dead things that made up the forest floor. The crushed, crackling things that had made their home under the trees.

Baby bones, tiny and fragile. The bones of the forest, and we're breaking them.

How will the forest respond?

It was only in that moment that he realized that the forest had transformed in his mind. It was no longer a simple collection of trees and mud and dirt and growing things. It was a single entity, a hostile force that drove him and Trish to the center of itself.

The cabin. That's where it will eat us.

Where it has *led us.*

And with that, as though he had been hearing not his own thoughts but those of the dark entity within this place, Alex saw it. The forest thinned, and a moment later he and Trish stood at the edge of a clearing.

And in the center of that clearing: the cabin.

28
(When Tricia Had Grown)

Tricia remembered going to the store once, and seeing a child shrieking, "I want my mommy!" as a chagrined looking middle-aged man dragged the kid through the frozen food section. She remembered thinking, "Why bother wanting that, kid? Mommy is probably no better than daddy."

She was smart enough to know that a lot of the sentiment was bitterness. She barely had a father, so what was she going to create in her head as the ideal of a "good" mother? Certainly not Alex's mom – she had been every bit as bad as Tricia's own parent.

But now, walking through the forest as an adult, she understood what the child had said. Because there was a part of her that wanted to scream it. Even as a grown woman, she was hard-pressed not to stamp her foot and shout, "I want my mommy!" in the hope that someone would appear and rescue her from this place.

She hadn't remembered that moment until coming here. The forest was bringing the past to life. The memories had started to return, though they were mostly quick glimpses, instants as blurry and half-hidden as trees in the fog.

She kept remembering a word: *whisperers.* It sounded in her mind, echoed and repeated. Sometimes it distorted, sometimes she heard it turn into a wordless scream that was somehow both familiar and alien.

Beside her, Alex slowed. Stopped. "Do you hear that?" he said.

She stopped walking as well. All she heard was the stream beside them, sliding along in its impossible currents. This way, that way, no way at all. Then she heard what Alex was talking about – or thought she did. She cocked her head, turning slightly in an instinctive motion to bring the sound closer, make it clearer.

"There!" Alex shouted.

Tricia craned her neck. Stupid, she knew – the change in her stance was unlikely to change what she heard. Only… it did change. Here in this place where the rules did not apply, that minute shift made the sound leap into the top tiers of her consciousness.

"Is that… laughing?"

Alex nodded. "Yeah." His voice was strained, and she understood why, because she was feeling the same thing. The laughter brought no joy, no mirth. First of all, it was the wrong kind. Instead of a joyous sound it was hollow. It was the laugh of someone readying to do something terrifying.

Worse, though, was the way it came to them, wafting through the mist on a current that made it seem too far away. Not just distant, but *impossibly* distant.

The fog, she suddenly thought, is all that keeps that sound alive.

"We should keep going, keep walking," Tricia said.

"Yeah, we should. But *where*?"

They still walked beside the stream, but that only meant at best a fifty-fifty proposition. They could be headed closer to the road where –

(We lost Sammy.)

– they could find help. Some passing motorist willing to assist them. Though on second thought, she couldn't ever remember seeing other cars on the small highway between Sunrise and Sundown. So maybe they wouldn't find help even if they made it out.

But the other possibility was that they were headed deeper into the forest. She could tell from Alex's glum manner that he thought that the most likely scenario. She didn't want to, but there were the sticks. Floating back and forth, then stopping completely as the current of the stream shifted.

We're just sticks in the stream.

The laughter came again. Distant, hollow, but invasive nonetheless. She was breathing the fog that kept the sound alive, so did that mean the sound could go *inside* her?

Alex had moved ahead slightly as she lost herself in the gloomy thoughts. Now he slowed. Halted.

"Something's out there," he said.

The laughter came again. Floating through the fog. Breathing it in.

"Something's there," Alex said again.

The laughter trailed off. Not like the sound was losing steam, entering that spot all laughs do where the body is tired of laughing and quiets. This was the trailing tail of an echo. The laugh might still be continuing somewhere, but the echo of it faded and disappeared, the sound no longer reaching Tricia or Alex.

They waited a moment. A crackling came from nearby. They both swiveled toward it, putting the river at their backs, waiting expectantly as the sound was repeated.

Tricia was struck by déjà vu. This had happened before. Or maybe it was going to happen *again*, even though that thought didn't make any sense. Still, she couldn't shake the sudden familiarity. Not the good kind. This wasn't coming home to Alex's arms, or picking up Sammy at daycare. There was no sense of homecoming, only a return to some dread long suppressed.

The crackling continued, but now the whispers –

*(Whisper*ers. *I called them whisperers and so did Alex.)*

– renewed. Like the laugh, they were mostly echo. *"Run... -un... -un... -un..."*

She didn't run. Neither did Alex. Where would they run to? She didn't want to go into the river again. But the thing that had caused the crackling sounds was ahead of them. They could turn to the right or left, continue on the same track they had been taking, or turn around and try to get out in the other direction. If the forest let them.

Every way was a bad choice. A moment later, everything worsened as the fog that had been roiling among the trees now stopped moving, so completely that Tricia would have thought she was looking at the world's weirdest mural if she couldn't see some of the barely-glimpsed branches waving slightly in a breeze.

She grabbed Alex's arm so hard he winced. "What?" he whispered.

"There's a wind."

"So?" Then he realized what she was saying. "Why isn't the fog moving? It has to move if there's wind." The last sentence pleaded more than stated a fact. Like he was asking her to reassure him it was true, and he couldn't be seeing what he was seeing.

As in so many other moments, she was in sync with Alex. Only this was a horrible moment for it, both of them knowing what they saw was impossible, but neither of them able to explain it away.

The fog started moving again. This movement was no better than the stillness had been. The mist had been curling, rolling for the entire time they had been in the forest. It still was, only Tricia was pretty sure that every twist of vapor was now moving exactly opposite to what it had a moment ago. If what she had seen before was a still photo, this was a movie running backwards.

"Yeah, I see it," said Alex, answering the question she hadn't even voiced.

All stopped again. All but the whisper of the mad stream behind them, and the crack-crackle-crack of something coming toward them.

The fog halted. It twisted into itself. Somewhere far away, light flared – like an explosion, but one that was utterly silent. No heat, no shockwave, just a blinding flash and then the light was gone and the fog separated and she saw…

"Sam."

She didn't know who said it this time: her, or Alex, or maybe even the whisperers in the trees. But she knew what she saw, and knew Alex was seeing the same thing because now it was his turn to grab *her* arm so hard she had to grit her teeth to keep from wincing. She didn't want to blink. Didn't want to look away from the boy she remembered, just as she remembered – in a bright, sudden flash, just as bright as whatever had lit up the fog – that this was how he had been dressed in the last moments they saw him. Jeans. White shirt, buttoned up to the chin. Red backpack. Blood smeared on his clothes, matting his hair.

She blinked, and suddenly it wasn't Sam at all. The person she and Alex were looking at had the same clothing she remembered Sam wearing. But jeans and button-up shirts weren't exactly rare, were they? Backpacks would be normal, too – most hikers would bring something to carry water and food. Plus, now that Tricia looked closer, she could see that the backpack wasn't the insane shade of red Sam's bag had been. Red, yes, but more muted; darker: the color of blood fresh from an artery.

Real blood was splashed on the shirt. But different patterns, Tricia was sure.

And the most telling of all: the hair, though about the same color, wasn't the shaggy, short haircut Sam had sported. It was long, down past the shoulders.

This wasn't Sam.

"It's a girl," breathed Alex.

The girl looked at them. She was so like Sam in that moment it made Tricia want to cry. But the girl's head tilted as she saw them, and Tricia saw the features that were so much finer. Hair color, clothing, wearing a backpack. Looked to be a teen, just like Sam had been. But that was where the similarities ended.

And had Tricia ever heard Sam scream?

(Yes. He screamed so loud that day.)

She thought so, and knew that if she had, it wasn't the high-pitched, eardrum-piercing scream the girl now let out. She turned, and Tricia knew she was going to flee. She couldn't let that happen.

It was desperately important that she not let the girl go; that she stop her before the kid disappeared into the forest and the fog.

"Stop!" Tricia shouted. At the same time, Alex shouted, "Wait!"

The girl turned to them. Just a moment. A glimpse of a face that was chalky under the blood. "Run!" shouted the girl. She pointed at something beyond Tricia and Alex.

They both turned.

The creek still bubbled and burbled, and maybe that was why they didn't hear the newcomer arrive. More likely, though, she and Alex had just been too focused on the lights, and on the newcomer who was not Sam.

A man stood behind them. Middle-aged, she thought – maybe only ten or fifteen years older than she and Alex, not young, but not anywhere near the point of physical decline. But just as with Sam and the girl, the differences diverged sharply at that point. Neither she nor Alex had – she hoped – the wild, almost manic look this man sported. Neither of them were grungy, Alex had never worn a beard – he hated them intensely for some reason – and certainly neither of them held an axe.

The man did, though. A double-bladed thing that she could have told came to a deadly edge even if it weren't for the blood that stained most of it. The red ran rivulets down the metal, and some streamed down the angle of the wood handle, painting the man's left hand with it.

He saw them, and shrieked. No words, but Tricia could feel the hate, the rage, and something deeper and darker beneath them both. Madness, pure and incarnate.

"RUN!" shouted the girl again as the man started splashing his way across the stream. The water hit the axe and cleaned the blood away, but Tricia could still see it. Even after she turned with Alex and the two of them ran after the nameless girl in the forest, she still saw the blood, and knew in her heart that more would join it. She or Alex or this girl – one or all of them was going to die. She

felt it, the same way she had been gripped by déjà vu moments before, only more powerfully this time.

No more splashes. The madman had made it across the stream. Either that or…

She dared a glance back as she ran, surrendering for a moment to the irrational hope that the stream had grabbed the man. That it had pulled him in every way at once and then twisted and torn him apart the way it had done with the twigs.

No such luck. He had crossed the stream just fine.

Tricia turned forward again and saw the girl glancing back as well. She saw the man and started screaming.

"We'll be okay," said Alex. "We'll be okay." The words bounced as he ran, jouncing out almost violently. The sound itself gave lie to the intent, and Tricia wondered if he had felt the same sense of impending doom that she had. If he felt – knew – that one or all of them would die.

"We'll be okay," she answered.

She had never lied to Alex before. The forest made that happen, too.

Behind them, the madman grunted and puffed as he ran. Every few yards there would be a dull *thunk*, like he was slamming the axe into the trunks of some of the trees they passed. It chilled Tricia. Made her want to vomit as she wondered in spite of herself if that was what it would sound like if their pursuer buried his axe in flesh.

Again. Remember the blood.

Another solid *ca-chunk* sounded. At least the guy didn't sound like he was catching up, though he didn't sound like he was falling behind either.

She and Alex were catching up to the girl, though. They ran after her, trailing a shadow at first, then details – an elbow, streaming hair clumped with red – then the entirety of her body as she tried so hard to keep ahead of the threat. But she was a girl. She was young. She didn't have the strength to get away.

Alex reached her first. He looked back at Tricia and she saw the question in his eyes. She waved to him, gesturing for him to keep going and help her. He nodded, put on a burst of speed, and reached the girl. He reached out a hand. She shied away, then realized what he was doing. Her own hand reached out, locking with Alex's, and he added his strength to hers. The girl was skipping along now, each step lengthened out an extra foot or two as Alex pulled her higher and farther than she could have gone alone.

It slowed Alex. Not too much, but Tricia was able to draw even with them both. She took the girl's other hand, which was already reaching for her. They ran in a chain, trailing single-file when the trees pressed close, side by side when the forest permitted it.

She kept glancing back. *He* was there. Keeping to a pace exactly matched to their own. She looked at Alex. His face wore the blank expression he got sometimes, when total concentration on a problem pushed him to a place beyond the world.

Ku-thunk. The axe bit deep into wood. Wind whispered, leaves rattling their dry-bone sound underfoot as small whirlwinds rose around them. The fog billowed and flashed, and Tricia wondered what it would bring this time. The whisperers had come with the fog and the lights, as had the strangeness of the stream, and then the girl and the madman who pursued them all.

What now? What worse thing is the forest holding for us?

A light flashed ahead. Tricia cringed away from it, realizing at once that they had no idea where they were going, and no idea where they were. The two most basic points necessary to get somewhere, and they had neither.

She risked a look back.

The madman was falling behind. His insane attacks on passing trees grew muted.

Then he was gone.

And then he was *not* gone, but *ahead* of them. A running form, rushing toward them, lit from behind by the flashes that kept blinding Tricia.

She screamed. So did the girl. She tried to turn away, but couldn't. She and the others were moving too fast now – everything was moving too fast, a freight train running at terminal velocity toward something unseen but deadly.

The fog exploded outward as the madman punched through it like a bullet.

Only...

"Sheriff!" Alex shouted. "Help!"

Not a madman after all. It was *Sheriff Azakh*.

Tricia had never thought of herself as a guns kind of person, but now she felt nothing but relief at the fact that the sheriff had a gun in her hand. Sheriff Azakh brought the gun up, and for a moment Tricia thought she was going to shoot Alex. "Don't!" she screamed.

But the sheriff had no intention of shooting. No sooner did she raise the gun than she lowered it. "It's you," she said, the words barely more than a whisper.

She was staring at the girl that Alex and Tricia were still pulling along. The sheriff's mouth sagged in shock. Tricia looked at the girl automatically, and saw Alex doing the same. The girl showed no recognition of the sheriff. Her eyes were glassy and vacant. Whatever had happened to her before this moment, it had driven her deep inside herself.

"There's someone following us!" shouted Alex at last. "He –"

Alex broke off as he turned. Tricia turned as well, a part of her marveling that she hadn't already felt the bite of the axe at her back. A much larger part marveling at what she saw behind them:

Nothing.

"What was back there?" said Sheriff Azakh. Tricia turned back to the woman who still stared at the girl they had found in the woods.

"A man," said Alex. "He was holding –"

"A knife?" said Azakh.

"No," said Tricia. "Axe."

The sheriff looked surprised at that – she actually looked away from the girl who had been the object of her attention. "Axe?" she said with a frown.

At the same time, Alex said, "Knife?"

Tricia looked back and forth between them. "What's happening, Sheriff?"

The sheriff sighed. "You may as well call me Julie, what with us being such good old friends and all."

The lights flashed, and the fog thickened again. Tricia tensed, knowing that nothing good was coming with the light show or the glowing fog that swelled around them.

"We have to get out of here," said the sheriff.

Alex snorted. "Good luck with that."

The sheriff nodded as though this made perfect sense. "I know. But maybe, if it's here…" She turned around, a slow circle that allowed her to take in the surroundings. "I think I know where we are," she murmured. "I think… Come on." She nearly barked the order, loud enough that Tricia and Alex both jumped a bit. "Sorry," said Julie. "I'm a bit… surprised."

She stared at the girl again.

Then the sheriff beckoned for them to follow her. She spared a last glance at the girl, then seemed to gather herself and get a bearing. She stared at one of the trees for a moment, and Tricia heard her murmur, "Maybe we can get above it. Maybe…"

Then she was off, jogging quickly away. Alex and Tricia shared a look. He shrugged. They both looked at the girl. She appeared nearly catatonic, though her grip on Tricia's hand had not loosened, and when she and Alex started forward the girl followed.

They walked, moving quickly but no longer running – thank goodness; Tricia had been nearing a point where she would have had to stop or suffer a massive heart attack. And she realized, too, that they had had no food or water for a long time. Too long.

How many times have we run tonight? How many miles, and how long is the night going to last?

More importantly, will we last through it?

Tricia looked at Alex and saw he was struggling, too. But he put on half a smile and gave her a thumbs up. Putting on a brave face, and she loved him for that, just as she saw his love for her when she mimicked the action.

Something at the periphery of her vision drew her eye. It was, she realized, the tree Julie had stared at before starting away. She pointed at it.

Alex kept jogging, drawing himself and the girl between them along behind Julie. But he turned to look at what Tricia was pointing at. When he saw it, he stopped. Only for a moment, and then he was jogging again.

He looked at Tricia over the top of the head of the girl between them. His eyebrows raised.

She shook her head. "I don't know," she said. "Nothing makes sense."

Alex gritted his teeth and jutted out his chin, indicating the cloudy form of the sheriff ahead of them.

"She's got some questions to answer."

Tricia agreed.

She had wondered a bit what the sheriff saw, and how it allowed her to seem so sure of herself. It was just one more tree, wasn't it? The same as all the rest of the trees around them.

But now Tricia and Alex saw that the tree was different. It bore a distinguishing mark: a series of circles that turned in on themselves.

The sheriff turned and gestured for them to hurry. "Come *on,*" she shouted.

"We're hurrying," said Tricia. "We've been running all –"

Ka-thunk.

Axe on wood. Axe on flesh. The sound of both echoed all around. Tricia jerked at the noise and looked back.

Thuk.

The sound came again, louder now.

Alex had heard it, too. So had Sheriff Azakh, and both of them oriented on the noise. Not behind Tricia and Alex, but ahead of them all and to the left.

"He couldn't have gotten so far ahead," said Alex.

"Unless we've been going in circles," said Tricia. She thought it likely. The forest had them, the forest wouldn't let them go. Tricia had never used mice or rats in her experiments – she focused on theory, not practical uses – but she knew that some of the experiments involved mazes. Usually they measured cognitive functions and learning, i.e., figuring out how fast the rodent could get through the maze.

Occasionally, though, there were darker, crueler experiments. Stimulus-response measurements taken as the mouse was fed and then shocked. Electrical impulses monitored as the rat's pleasure centers were stimulated, then monitored again as electrodes urged the creature's brain to feel every possible pain at once.

She wondered which kind of experiment they were part of now. Perhaps something or someone was measuring them, watching what happened when the subjects – her and Alex, the strange girl between them and now the sheriff – were put in a maze whose walls switched every few seconds. A place where the way out was glimpsed, or at least the sensation that the end was within reach was conveyed, followed by a shifting that turned them back again.

Hypothesis: subjects, when given an impossible task, will continue trying to solve said task until death.

Method: injecting subjects into a situation where test parameters change constantly, allowing subjects momentary sensations of control followed by shifting parameters that yank the frigging rug out from under them.

Result: madness.

Was Sheriff Julie Azakh another subject of this cruel experiment? Or was she one of the experimenters?

Even as she asked herself the question, Tricia knew the answer. The sheriff wasn't doing all this to them. Maybe no one was, because at its core this didn't seem like an experiment. The scientific method wouldn't preside over anything that was happening here. This was…

Paranormal.

Supernatural.

Ahead of Tricia, Julie swerved around a particularly large tree, ducking to avoid a thick branch that jutted out of the trunk. Tricia and Alex followed suit.

The girl between them did not duck, so deep into whatever hidey hole she had found in her subconscious that she didn't even notice the branch that could have knocked her out at the speed they were now going. Tricia envied her for that. For her ability to withdraw into a place in her mind where no fog or light or forest existed.

Ka-THUD.

The noise of the axe blade biting deep came again, and with it the sound of something crashing through the trees high above them. It was a sound Tricia remembered abruptly. She had heard this before. She remembered…

Then the memory was gone.

Another flash of illumination. The fog brightened, and Tricia knew she would hear *them*. Something made it inevitable, a predestined moment when she was thinking of ghosts, and so the ghosts spoke.

"Whisperers..."

Something about that single word chilled Tricia more than anything they had said before. They were naming themselves, plucking the title from her own mind and lips.

Science was all about discovery. Discovery meant understanding, understanding meant power... and naming things was a part of both. But now, hearing the things in the fog name *themselves* just made them more horrible. It was as though they were telling her that, named or unnamed, they would always rule in this place.

"Whisperers..."

She looked at Alex, who put on a sudden burst of speed that told her he had heard the word, too, and that he felt the same adrenaline rush of fear flooding his own mind.

She looked ahead of her. Julie had stopped jogging. She turned in a slow circle.

"Come on," said the sheriff. "I think we're almost –"

"Whisperers..."

This time, the sound did not end. It trailed off instead to a shriek of terror and agony.

Alex started running even faster. Tricia had to bend all her attention to fleeing, to following the sheriff.

Thuck.

The sound shouldn't have come through the screams. An axe biting into the wood of the trees should have been a nothing-sound in the face of all that they were hearing. But it did penetrate, almost as though the sound were not a wall, but a wrapping. A gift the whisperers had put in a sonic box, and now handed to Tricia.

Death. They're giving us death.

"Come on!" shouted the sheriff.

Thuk.

Tricia didn't look where the sound was coming from. It had shifted again. Behind her now.

"HERE!" shouted the sheriff. She darted around the side of a tree. Tricia and Alex followed, still leading/pulling the girl between them.

The fog flashed. The whisperers' screams crescendoed.

Ka-thu –

Tricia and Alex and the girl rounded the tree. As they did, silence fell. The screams disappeared, the fog that had roiled and billowed all around seemed to pull back. Even the sound of the madman's axe seemed to cut off too soon. She had the image of the madman disappearing but his axe remaining behind. Embedded in the tree and the tree gradually growing around it, sheathing it in pulp and bark and claiming it for its own.

Then the image dissipated, and she saw why the sheriff had led them here.

29
(When Alex Had Grown)

"Thank heaven," breathed Julie, and for a moment Alex had no idea why the sheriff was so happy. He saw only a monstrosity in the clearing beyond the trees. A skeletal thing that stood on legs impossibly long, impossibly thin. A monster so tall that it disappeared into the fog above.

Then his vision of it shifted, and he understood why the sheriff was so happy. It was like looking at one of those optical illusions: an old crone when viewed one way, a beautiful young woman when other aspects were focused on; or one of the sculptures whose eyes seemed to follow you, until you moved around to the side and saw that it was just a portrait painted on cardboard or metal that had been folded a certain way.

Not a monster at all. The thing in the clearing was some kind of tower. A watchtower, Alex figured – an enclosed platform high enough that rangers could look for poachers or vandals, or perhaps built so surveyors could do their jobs more easily. Maybe even for scientists who would watch and measure the growth of the forest over time.

Whatever it was, it offered the possibility of contact with the outside world. Somehow he doubted that Julie's walkie-talkie was going to be sufficient.

Evidently following the same train of thought as Alex, Julie said, "My radio doesn't work. Can't reach anyone. But I hope if the tower is high enough, if it's above…"

The fog.

Trish eyed the structure skeptically. "We have to climb that ladder?" she said.

"Unless you'd rather wait down here," said the sheriff.

"No thanks," Alex said.

"But the girl," said Trish, indicating the blonde teen whose hand they still held, and who still wore the vacant expression of someone who has blown more than a few fuses. "I don't know if she'll be able to follow."

Julie shrugged. Not a mean shrug, just pragmatic. "We won't know until we try," she said. She was trying to sound nonchalant, in control of the situation. But Alex could hear the tremor at the edges of her voice, threatening to crack her calm into bits and pieces.

"We should try," Alex agreed, as much to keep the sheriff happy as anything. If the one thing they'd found in here that represented order and calm fell apart, where would they be? He looked into the mist that still hung in the air – that was starting to seem like it always *would*. It was becoming the beginning and end of their world.

Trish nodded, and he saw the same resolve on her face. She would keep it together – especially now, with another person to care for.

She was thinking of Sammy, he was certain. Of the loss, and of keeping any other parent from experiencing that same loss. Maybe she was going even farther back, and thinking of *Sam*, and wondering how to bring this girl to safety the way they had failed to do with their friend.

Trish brushed a bit of matted hair out of the girl's face. "Honey, we have to go up, okay?"

The girl stared at nothing.

The fog flashed. "Uh, folks," said the sheriff. "I really think –"

"I'm not leaving her down here alone," Trish said between clenched teeth.

"I wasn't suggesting it," said Julie. She shook her head. "Not in a million lifetimes. But maybe if we start climbing, she will, too." She paused, then added, "She'll surprise you how tough she is."

Trish looked like she wanted to ask what the sheriff meant, but before she could Alex drew the girl forward. "Come on," he said gently. "We're going somewhere safe."

The girl pulled back, resisting. She shook her head, though her eyes remained unfocused, glassy and nearly blind to the world.

In the distance, Alex thought he heard something. The hollow sound of an axe biting deep into a tree?

Or a body?

"We have to hurry," he said. He pulled the girl again. Again she resisted.

Alex was calculating his chances of success if he just tossed the girl over his shoulder, kicking and screaming if necessary, and hauled her bodily up the ladder. He judged the chances to be pretty slim. The platform was so high it disappeared into the fog, which meant it was at least forty or fifty feet. Maybe much more, if it really was a surveying station of some kind. He wasn't in terrible physical shape, but he was far from being an athlete. Writing equations and formulas all day gave you pretty sturdy typing muscles, but that was it.

"Please," he whispered.

Trish's face lit up. He knew that expression: an epiphany. His wife leaned in close to the girl they had found and said, "Honey, do you want to get out of the fog? Out of the forest?" The girl said nothing, but her eyes focused on Trish. Trish nodded as though the girl had responded. "Me too. But to do that, we have to figure out where we're going. And the best way to do that is to climb up the ladder and get out of –"

"The fog," whispered the girl. "Get out of the fog." Her eyes shone. "I've been here so long. So many nights."

She moved toward the ladder.

Alex moved to help her, but Trish motioned him away. He understood: the girl was on the verge of a mental collapse, obviously caused by the lunatic with the axe. She might respond badly to a man shadowing her, no matter how well-intentioned.

Julie was scanning the forest. No more sounds came from its depths, not even the whispers. The air felt less charged, somehow. Alex really believed he had heard the axe a few moments ago, but something inside him whispered that the threat was gone, if only for the moment.

The girl began climbing. Trish followed. Alex motioned for the sheriff to go up. She snorted. "This isn't the time for chivalry. *I'm* the one with the gun, so I go last. Rear guard."

"Not being chivalrous," said Alex. "You have the gun so I want you up there in case something else is waiting already."

His skin crawled as he spoke. Not just because of the situation, he realized. It was his wording. He had said that some*thing* else might be waiting. Not some*one*. Even a lunatic with a bloody axe wasn't as worrisome as the... the... *thing* behind all this.

And it *was* a thing. Something in the air told him that – *whispered* it to him. Perhaps he heard the fog itself. Maybe every time he breathed in the vapor, he heard its secrets.

Or perhaps he was becoming part of the fog.

The sheriff nodded. She began clambering up the ladder behind Trish, but only went a few rungs up before she bobbled and almost fell the short distance to the ground. Alex read the indecision on her face as she tried to decide whether to sacrifice the security the gun afforded in return for a better grip, or whether to keep the gun out and climb with one-and-a-half hands. She opted for the first, shoving the gun back in its holster and climbing as rapidly as she could until she had reached Trish. Even then, he could hear her chanting, "Go, go, go," in time with Trish's movements.

Alex almost yelled at her – not a good idea, so he managed to hold back. He was ashamed of himself a moment later, as he realized the sheriff wasn't urging Trish on, but the girl above her, who climbed with metronome movements. Alex suspected the girl would fall, and was ashamed again as he realized his major worry in that moment wasn't the girl's safety, but concern that she would hit Trish on the way down and *both* of them would die.

But the girl didn't fall. The three of them continued until the fog had swallowed them by degrees: they were dark shadows for a while, then dark blurs, then nothing.

Only then did Alex begin climbing. He had been alternating between watching them and swiveling in circles, scanning what he could see of the forest, watching for movement, for the bloody knife coming at them.

No, axe. *Why would I think it was a knife?*

Nothing appeared. The fog hung silent. It felt quiet for the first time, truly quiet, rather than the expectant silence that had greeted them at every moment save when things were actually happening.

Something flickered. Not brightly – there was no surge of fog, no increase in the mist's luminous properties that made this place into a twilight realm.

But something had happened.

The whispers came.

"You have to climb…"

"You can't climb…"

Alex felt something cold on his back. He knew it was the whisperers, come at last to reveal themselves, to wrap cold, bloodless fingers around his arms and legs and neck and drag him into the fog.

He reached back. Felt the things that were there and realized it wasn't the whisperers. He had just backed into the ladder of the watchtower. He turned and took hold of the rungs, hauling himself up so fast he was almost flying.

When he was ten feet up, the fog flashed, brighter this time.

"You!"

"You caused it! It's your fault…"

Any other words would have made him climb higher, climb faster. These stopped him. They were words he had heard so many times in the last few years. So many times he had spoken them in his mind, or whispered them in the darkness, laying awake beside Trish as she moaned and twisted the circle of her wedding band even in sleep.

The fog flashed. Tendrils reached out, caressing him with cool mist. Fingers of the fog floated in front of his eyes, darting out, darting back, almost beckoning him. He didn't want to turn. He *wouldn't* turn.

He turned.

And saw the worst thing. Worse by far than a shadow in the mist. Worse even than a man clutching a bloody axe and obviously hoping to bloody it further.

He saw Sammy.

He saw his little boy, standing in the mist. Holding his stuffed animal, his treasured unicorn. Bright red in the mist, only this time the red was not cute or happy. The plush animal looked bloody. Sammy himself looked bruised and bloody as well. The boy stared up at him with confusion, the eyes of someone looking at his daddy and wondering what had happened and how it had happened and why oh why had his daddy *let* it happen.

Hands reached out of the mist, reaching for his child.

"No!" Alex shrieked, and jumped off the ladder. Ten feet up, and he simply let go and knew that part of him hoped he would die. Would fall and not just hit the ground but continue below it, to die and fall forever until he found the darkest places, the deepest pits. To pull the entire earth over him, the entire *universe,* and then descend below it all until all was darkness and pain and whatever nothing that waited beyond.

He hungered for it. Darkness and pain were no more or less than he deserved. He had lost his child.

He fell, but too slow. Before he touched the earth, the hands clutched Sammy. The fog billowed. It flashed, and Alex saw the form of something behind his son, his little boy. Alex screamed, and heard the scream of his wife, high above him. Part of him knew she was screaming for him, screaming because she heard *him* scream, and feared that the forest had taken him.

But the rest of him, the greater part that was his world in that moment, thought she was screaming because she felt Sammy near; sensed him in the way that only mothers could.

For the first time, Alex knew his son was dead. *Really* knew. He had told others he knew, when they asked after him and told him he had to move on – it was ten years, couldn't he move on?

He moved on from those friends instead. Trish had been his only constant. She understood that it was impossible to move on. The way they had lost their child ensured that truly moving on was forever both dream and nightmare.

Now Trish was leaving him, too. Drawing away from him just like Sammy was drawing away from him. A shape in the mist of his mind, torn away from view.

The fog flashed. It seemed brighter, not just in the area of the flash, but everywhere.

Something is happening. It's all coming together here, in this place, in the forest.

The words were unspoken. The only sounds he made were screams as, with a final flash, his son disappeared.

He ran into the mist, heedless of what he might find other than his child, his baby.

He found the patch of ground where Sammy had been. He found the place where Sammy – gone so long – had stood. It was a dream, a nightmare, a vision. It had been ten long years of loss, and Sammy returned to him as Alex had seen him that last day. No aging, no changing. There was no way he was *real*.

But there was something else at Alex's feet. He reached for it. Sammy's unicorn. It had always been red. It continued red here in this place that time and reason had abandoned. Only now the red was mottled. Part of it was the original color, part of it was matted with blood that had the peculiar bright/dark qualities of new-spilt life.

Alex reached for it, and expected it to disappear. It remained, this piece of Sammy. He took it, feeling his sanity escape him, slipping out as he sighed. The touch of his child's lost toy, his lost child still warm in the blood that soaked it, was more than he could bear. It wasn't real. It couldn't be.

But it felt so real. Mourning clung to it, and terror. The feelings that had stunned him and Trish in the hours after it happened, then wounded them in the following weeks and months, then – finally, and worst of all – gradually numbed them with the passage of years.

Mourning. Terror.

A terrible nothingness.

But the toy wasn't nothing. It was real and because the toy was real he had to show it to Trish because it meant their *child* was real. He was more than memory.

Memory, Alex knew, was the biggest liar in existence. Memory chipped away at the imperfect sculpture of reality. It left only perfection –

(Smiles, hugs, the delicious joy of a belly laugh of the kind only toddlers can manage, the belly laughs that shake them from head to toe and press out every milliliter of oxygen until they're almost blue from laughing and you worry they'll just suffocate right there, but only for an instant and then they gasp in every bit of air in the room and laugh again and again, and oh, dear God, I would give my soul to hear that laugh again.)

– behind, and the perfection rested in the few features left after time, that terrible destroyer, did its work. The rest was smooth, featureless…

… forgotten – and that was so much worse than simply *gone*.

Now, Alex gasped as so much of memory returned. Of the nights rocking endlessly, trying to get the baby to stop screaming at decibel levels that would put a jet engine to shame. Of the days when it seemed the infant was trying to set a record for number of diapers used in a single day. Of the terror Alex felt when he saw his toddler holding a butter knife and pushing it toward a wall socket he had managed to pry the baby-proof cover off of, then the terror shifting to anger when he tore the knife away and screamed, *never again never never again!*, then that anger shifting to remorse and a crushing realization of how much he loved and *needed* this child and the child-smell that permeated him as he held the crying Sammy close and whispered, *never never never*.

And beyond that, deeper memories surged. His and Trish's first time in the forest. Their lost friend.

The whisperers.

(The monster that took Sam away. The thing with too many arms, too many legs, too many heads *and far too much blood.)*

The memories were almost there. He could reach out and touch them. But to do that, and to hold them to him he knew he would have to drop the toy he clutched to his chest.

He did not drop the unicorn. He held the toy tighter. The memories he had been so close to finding – and perhaps even understanding – fell away from him.

Alex found the ladder that climbed like a fleshless spine up the center of the watchtower's scaffolding. He grabbed it with his free hand. He would not let go of the toy. He would fall first, and join his baby in the thing that had taken him away and then held him in limbo here in the mist.

Sammy was dead.

Sammy was lost.

But Sammy was here.

Sammy was found.

Alex climbed. He didn't look up, he kept staring down. Not at the ground – it was already lost in the mist. He stared at the toy he held so tightly he could feel warmth seep out of its stuffing and fur.

Blood.

That should have disgusted him. But it didn't. He held it all the harder, clutched it all the closer. The blood was Sammy's and it was real.

Wasn't it?

He climbed fast, and barely noticed that he was high enough to die if he let go. He didn't notice at all that the fog still clung to everything. The fog went on *forever*. There was no rising above it.

But there was rising above the level of the ladder. He hadn't looked up, so he screamed and almost *did* let go when the hand fell into view.

"Grab on!"

Alex looked up. Julie leaned out of an open trapdoor that must lead into the room atop the tower. She was half out over the edge, so far that Alex wondered how she wasn't falling out. He saw one arm close to her side, the hand out of sight beyond the limits of the trapdoor opening. She must be holding onto something that anchored her to her spot.

"It's tricky," she said. "Even if you've done it before."

Alex didn't understand. Was she talking about losing a child? Did she know what that was like? And done it *before*? Had Julie lost a child of her own? Did she understand that loss not once but twice?

She waved her hand. Reality snapped back into focus, if only a bit.

She wasn't talking about Sammy. She was just asking him to give her his hand for the last few feet of the climb.

He didn't. He didn't want to let go of the toy. She didn't see it, he supposed: it was held so tightly that anyone looking probably saw only his bloody hand. Even if she had, she wouldn't have understood why he was holding a child's toy given all that was happening.

He held it tighter. He didn't *want* her to see. Julie must have seen the determination in his eyes and misinterpreted it as some macho need to make his own way up the ladder. She sighed and said, "Suit yourself," and moved out of the way.

Alex shook his head. He climbed the last few rungs one-handed, and realized abruptly how high he was, how far he had climbed. He risked a look down. The rungs of the ladder, the tower's struts and supports all disappeared into fog at least thirty feet below. But he knew he had climbed much higher than the fog allowed him to see; high enough that a fall would be fatal for sure.

He still didn't let go of the toy, even when he discovered Julie was right: it *was* a lot harder to negotiate his way up than he would have thought. He tried to continue in the same way he had come this far. He moved one foot up at a time, both on the same rung, both heels hanging out over empty space. The rung he stood on was close enough to his single hand's grip that his body bent into a "C" and his butt hung dangerously out into nothing. Then he let go with the hand holding the ladder and quickly grabbed the next rung up. It meant for a nanosecond he was weightless as the third necessary body support disappeared, for another nanosecond he fell backward before catching himself by grabbing the next rung up with his climbing hand.

Only this last bit didn't work that way. He lifted his feet, planted them. All good, all according to plan. He let go with his free hand. Weightlessness, a fall. He reached for the next rung up, and discovered what Julie had been talking about: there was no rung. There was just a smooth surface – what felt like a metal plate, perhaps even the trapdoor itself. Nothing to hang onto. He scrabbled for purchase.

He began to slide. The falling sensation continued beyond its allotted time.

Alex almost dropped the unicorn. The hand that held the toy reflexively opened so he could use it to help arrest his fall. He almost dropped it again as he jerked to grab it, the thing bobbing and bobbling as he fought with gravity for possession of the toy.

He grabbed it. Secure.

But he was still falling.

The hand holding the toy went upward, determined to help its fellow even if that meant that it had to do it while holding something.

He found purchase.

Around him, a dim flash lit the fog.

Oh no.

The flashes came with the whisperers, the attacks. The ghosts and the madman. This time, though, it came with a scream. A high-pitched, banshee wail of terror so intense and so shrill it hurt Alex's ears and heart in equal measure.

He flinched away from the unexpected sound, which seemed to be coming from the guard tower. The flinch released the tenuous grip he had managed to get, and he slid backward into space. He would have fallen this time, would have plummeted into space and fog and then splattered all over the ground fifty or a hundred feet below.

Julie saved him. She had reappeared with the sound, leaning over and grabbing his wrist with a surprisingly strong grip. He expected her to start sliding out, too, but she was still anchored to whatever she had been holding before. She gritted her teeth and grunted, but held him until he could get his hands back onto the smooth surface above and then inchworm his way up the last bit until he lay, panting, on the floor of the lookout room.

The scream kept up the whole time. It got louder, if that was possible, until it consumed every other sound. If Alex hadn't been so worried about not falling, he might have screamed himself.

He wondered where Trish was. Why hadn't she come to help him? But as he rolled over he saw that she was kneeling next to the girl they had found, cradling her as she screamed. The shrieks continued until her voice became raw, hoarse.

Alex realized that it was the girl he heard screaming when he saw Sammy below. He thought it was Trish, but that was just another distortion of the fog and the forest. The girl they had found was screaming, not his wife. Trish hadn't been calling out, because she hadn't seen what he saw. Of course not – she couldn't have seen through the fog at that distance, any more than he had seen the ground when he ascended, or the watchtower until he was only a few feet away.

So Trish didn't know that Sammy had been down there. Alex wasn't sure if that was a gift or a curse.

Alex watched his wife, and how she cradled the girl who was in pain. It reminded him of how she had held Sammy. She had already been a loving woman, but their child had nurtured that love, and grown it ever larger.

Alex waited for the girl's shouts to end, and that was when Trish finally looked at him.

Alex held out his hand. The hand that held the toy. The hand that held tight to a past long gone. The hand that held, in a way, the last vestiges of their son.

The hand that was empty.

30
(When Tricia Had Grown)

The climb up the ladder had been terrifying. Not as terrifying as what came next, but Tricia didn't know that as she climbed. She knew she was in danger, and had been since the fog rolled in.

Maybe since the first time we came here.

Memories surged. That had been one of the points in coming here, hadn't it? But in that moment where she *almost* saw what she sought, *almost* glimpsed the reality her mind had hidden, she wanted nothing more than for it to be gone again.

Some things might be better forgotten than remembered.

She turned her attention back to the climb. She found herself hoping for the first time that the fog would do what it had done so constantly in this place: steal away her sight. Maybe if she couldn't see the ground, then she wouldn't be so afraid of falling and hitting it with a velocity that would not just shatter her bones but pulp them and then splash them across the forest floor.

She looked down and saw Julie, following behind and saying, "Go, go, go," with a regularity that spoke of terror or shock or both. Beyond her, Alex stood on the ground. He looked up, then looked around, then looked up again.

He dwindled a bit with every rung she ascended. He faded, and disappeared. There was nothing below but fog, and when she looked up she saw no destination, either. Just rung after rung ascending through mist, into cloud.

Just above her, the girl they had found was climbing. Tricia finally realized that the sheriff wasn't in shock: she was speaking in sync with each time the girl above reached for a new rung or lifted her feet a step. Julie was keeping the girl going.

"Keep it up, sweetie," said Tricia. She didn't know if the girl could understand her, but she seemed to go a bit faster.

Just when the climb seemed like it would last forever, a shadow fell across her. Only it wasn't really a shadow after all, for there could be no such thing in a world where the only light came from a luminous mist that pervaded everything so evenly and completely that no shadows *could* be cast.

For a moment, Tricia wondered at that. No shadows. Were they being pursued by shadows and wraiths, or were she and Alex and those they met in the forest the real ghosts?

Am I dead? Am I alive? Neither? Both?

Then her attention shifted to the thing that was not shadow. A dark shape above, that spread out over them as they climbed and eventually became the bottom of whatever room they were climbing up to. Likely a tower for forest rangers, or the police like Sheriff Julie Azakh –

(What's she doing here, anyway?)

– or maybe even some kind of research station. Tricia had had friends in college – going into different fields eventually, but still facing some of the same math and science classes she herself had bested, if a few years earlier than the average – who went into the field during summers, and a few had reported stints in towers overlooking fields or mountains… or forests.

No matter which the thing above them turned out to be, though, it should have one thing for sure: communication with the rest of the world. A CB radio or maybe even a cellular setup with a repeater that would extend the range of any phones used up there.

Above Tricia, the girl stopped. "Keep going, sweetie," said Tricia. But the girl didn't, and after craning her neck a bit Tricia saw why: she couldn't. There was a trapdoor above them, closed securely and with what looked like an electronic lock.

"Keep going," said Julie.

Tricia looked down. "We can't."

The sheriff muttered something under her breath. "Sorry," she said. "I forgot about the lock." She laughed, a surprisingly normal sound. "Can't seem to think why." She let go of the ladder, pushed back her hat, and passed the back of her hand over her brow. She tucked the hat back down, re-covering her short, gray hair. "The code's 5153552."

Tricia's affinity for and enjoyment of mathematics meant she didn't have to ask for the number to be repeated. Indeed, if she came here again in ten years she would likely remember it. She also noted the code was an unusual one – most electronic locks had even-digit unlock codes: they opened with four digits, or six or eight or occasionally ten. This one was seven.

And all that was irrelevant. "I can't reach it." She looked back up, hoping that she would see the girl they had found, already tapping the numbers on the keypad. But she wasn't moving. She didn't look like she was going to fall anytime soon, and had a tight grip on the ladder. But that was all. No movement, no awareness. She was looking straight ahead, peering between the rungs at something no one else could likely see.

Julie sighed. "You can't reach it at all?"

"No," said Tricia.

"You'll have to climb over her."

"There's no way," said Tricia.

"I know you're scared, but –"

"It's not that. I don't think my arms are long enough to reach around her and hold on tight and still key in the code."

The sheriff cursed below her. Tricia looked down, worried the sheriff was going to fight her on it. "Me, either, probably," said Julie. "Didn't think of that." She squinted up. "I'll switch to the other side of the ladder and climb up past you, then –"

"No, that's stupid," said Tricia.

"It's the only way we –"

"I know, but I'm closer."

Julie opened her mouth, obviously to protest. Before she could, Tricia swung around the outer rail of the ladder. Nausea swept over her for a moment as she hung around the outside, her left hand and left foot swinging loosely for a moment before finding purchase on the ladder. The right side was worse, but once she had a firm grip on the other side of the ladder she felt better. Not *good,* but better.

She climbed. Again, a moment of sickening vertigo as she realized that the girl above her had wedged her feet on a single rung, both of them at an odd angle that did not permit Tricia to grab the rung at all. She had to stretch extra. Not a nice feeling.

Once past, though, she kept climbing. She drew even with the girl. Whoever it was, she was in a place where the forest did not exist; where maybe the entire world was nothing more than the memory of a dream.

Tricia could reach the keypad now. She keyed in the numbers, murmuring them as she did so, mostly to let Julie know that she remembered them. As soon as she did she heard the sound of a lock hasp sliding back, and there was a small pop as the seal around the trapdoor let go.

"Uh… new problem," she said.

"What?" said the sheriff.

"I'm at a bad angle to open the door."

Again, not waiting for Julie to take action, Tricia swung around the ladder. There was room between the girl and the trapdoor. Tricia *thought* she could squeeze in.

Another round of stomach-churning as she slid back to the side she had started on. She was bent almost double, her heels directly in front of the girl she and Alex had found, arms bent sharply, one shoulder against the trapdoor. She push/climbed, moving up as the trapdoor did.

After a foot or so some kind of spring activated, and the trapdoor opened the rest of the way with a thud.

"Should be a handle – it was on the outside of the trapdoor, and you can use it to brace yourself when you pull up," said Julie.

"Got it," said Tricia. The move from the ladder to the floor of the room atop the watchtower was surprisingly difficult, but after a moment she lay on the door, holding the handle that the sheriff mentioned to pull herself up. Then, still holding the handle, she motioned for the girl to follow.

The girl hesitated, and Tricia saw doubt flicker in her eyes. If her experience in the forest had been anything like Tricia's, she couldn't blame her for that reaction.

"It's all right," she said. "I'm a friend. I'll help you, cross my heart."

And I hope we don't die.

The girl nodded slowly, then slapped her hand into Tricia's outstretched one. Tricia pulled her up, and a moment later Julie had scrambled through the trapdoor.

Tricia took a quick look around. Four walls, mostly made of glass for observation; a pair of tables; two folding chairs; a few boxes on the floor; a map tacked to a bulletin board that leaned against a table; a small generator; and some kind of radio that looked like it was probably high tech stuff around World War II.

She didn't care if the radio was powered by mice on a wheel, though, so long as it worked. She had to resist the urge to run to it and start punching buttons until help came, but then she heard Alex. His voice slashed through the fog, and she automatically leaned out through the trapdoor, trying to see.

She had thought he would be closer, would be up the ladder. But of course, that was ridiculous. Alex would have stayed on the ground as long as possible. He would have guarded her from the rear, watching as long as he could to see if danger lurked nearby.

Which meant he stayed that much closer to danger himself.

Brave, wonderful, stupid *man. If you die, I'll kill you.*

In the middle of that insane, panicked thought, she shouted, "Alex! Alex, what's happening?"

He didn't answer. Just kept screaming. A moment later, his voice cut out. "Alex!" she shrieked. "Alex!"

No answer.

She kept staring into the fog. Nothing.

She leaped to her feet and ran to the windows, hoping that she was above the fog. She knew that even if she was, even if she spotted a police station with a national guard unit standing in front of it, it wouldn't help Alex. But she couldn't just lay on the floor staring down and hoping to see him. She had to do *something*.

The windows allowed a three-sixty view all around the tower. And through them: nothing but silvered, glowing fog.

Something flashed. Nearby, but slightly below her. She knew that was where Alex was; where he had to be.

Tricia called again. Of course she heard nothing from Alex. But there was another flash, and this time it was joined by the sound of whimpering.

The girl. She still wore her backpack, even though she had wedged it between one of the walls and herself. She had hugged her knees to her chest, trying to rock backward as she sat on the floor. But she couldn't; there was nowhere to go.

She whispered something, but Tricia couldn't make out what it was.

Alex was down there. Out there in the fog. What was happening to him?

She didn't know. She thought she might climb down, but realized that unless she found Alex waiting at the bottom of the ladder all she would probably accomplish would be to get *two* people out there, lost and in danger. Besides, she felt an odd responsibility for the girl they had found.

We lost two boys.

Don't lose someone else.

Tricia crossed to the girl. She put her arms around her. The girl stiffened, then sagged and almost melted into Tricia.

Tricia stiffened, too. This was how she had held Sammy on nights when he was afraid. This was how she had comforted her son when lightning flashed, when thunder rattled the windows in their frames.

"It's okay," said Tricia. "All okay. You're safe. You're safe."

She didn't know in that moment if she was speaking to the girl she held now, or the teen boy she had so long held in her heart, or the toddler she would never hold again.

Echoing Tricia's words, the sheriff said, "It's okay. All okay." Tricia jerked her head toward Julie, wondering for a split second if the forest not only brought nightmares came to life, but also laid bare anyone's thoughts to those around them – a nightmare of another kind. She didn't know if Alex would love her, or if *anyone* would love *anyone* if all thought was laid bare.

But the words weren't directed at her. Julie had shimmied out over the edge of the still-open trapdoor, one hand reaching down.

"Grab on!" she said. "It's tricky. Even if you've done it before."

"Is it Alex?" said Tricia.

Julie nodded tightly. She waved her hand, and even as relief lightened Tricia's heart she wondered why Alex wasn't letting the sheriff help him up.

Whatever the reason, Julie shimmied backward and one of Alex's hands appeared through the trapdoor. It slapped the floor of the room, and Tricia waited for the other hand to come through, then the rest of him.

The girl, still in Tricia's arms, shivered hard. Tricia looked at her. She sensed Julie moving suddenly, but didn't look away from the girl, who was shaking so fast and hard it seemed like she was having a seizure.

Something flashed in the fog, and the girl in Tricia's arms *screamed*. Tricia had been cradling her close, rocking her a bit without noticing, so she got the full force of the shrieking, so loud she wouldn't have believed that it came from such a young, small girl.

Tricia screamed, too. She couldn't hear her own voice. The girl was wailing now, the voice so high Tricia expected the windows all around to crack and rain glass down on them.

Tricia turned her head away from the sound. She didn't let go of the girl, but she couldn't help leaning away. Then her eyes widened as she realized that Alex's hands – visible only a moment before as he pulled himself up – were no longer in view.

He fell!

Julie lunged forward in an obvious attempt to help Alex, leaning out over the hole in the floor too far to be safe.

Tricia ached to do the same. But for some reason she couldn't let go of the girl she held. Tricia's muscles had locked in tandem with the girl's own tormented spasms. She couldn't let go. She couldn't let go of what she held, she couldn't let go of the past… and suddenly she understood that holding so tight to this one thing that represented every sorrow she had ever felt would lead to her losing the one thing she still possessed.

She started to let go. To go to her husband. Then Julie wiggled back, and Tricia could tell the sheriff had her husband. He was safe.

She held the girl closer to her. Alex didn't need her as much, did he? Not in this moment. Not now.

A moment later Alex's hand reappeared, holding tight to the sheriff's own. His other hand appeared a moment later, then his head and shoulders.

The girl in Tricia's arms kept screaming for what felt like forever even though it was probably only a few seconds before the scream became a hoarse, throaty whisper.

Alex got to his knees, then held out his hand, palm up. It looked like he was giving something to her, but Tricia saw nothing in his hand.

Alex looked at the open hand in horror. He started to slide backward, almost plummeting right back through the trapdoor he had just managed to get through. Only Julie's quick thinking stopped him. She planted her feet wide, grabbed Alex's still-outstretched arm with both hands, then pulled, pulled, *pulled*.

Tricia finally let go of the girl. She let go of Sam, she let go of Sammy, and she went to Alex.

She grabbed his forearm as well. Alex barely seemed to notice her or the sheriff or the girl or even the fact that he was on the verge of falling a hundred feet or more.

"It was here," he murmured. He kept staring at his open hand as they pulled him up. His feet kicked a bit, whatever block his body and mind suffered unable to completely rid him of his need to survive.

But he didn't look away. Not as Tricia and Julie pulled him through the hole in the floor, not as they tugged him away from the danger it represented, not even as they finally had him far enough away that they flopped, exhausted, backward themselves and all three of them lay panting on the floor.

"It was here," Alex said again. He sounded shell-shocked, and that strange emptiness beat back Tricia's weariness.

"What was there?" asked Tricia.

"Mine," whispered the girl. "Mine all mine all mine."

Tricia looked at her. She was still in another place, her legs now bent up so that her knees were under her chin, hugging herself tightly.

"What is, honey?" Tricia said gently.

The girl shuddered, but gave no other answer.

Julie just shook her head, then stood and looked around. She made a sound, so full of despair that Tricia knew what she was looking at, even if she hadn't already seen it herself.

"It's out there, isn't it?" said Alex. He still sounded odd, drained, but at least he was *here*. "We haven't gotten above the fog."

The sheriff shook her head. "No. It's…" She shook her head again, then went to the generator that Tricia saw was hooked to the ancient radio by a jury-rigged set of alligator clips and frayed cords. She tried flipping a few switches, then pulled a ripcord. The generator didn't make a sound. Not even the slightest cough in response to her efforts.

Tricia knew it wouldn't. And she could tell the sheriff hadn't expected it to, either. The fog was all around. It wasn't ready to let them go, so stay they would.

"Why are you here?" asked Alex.

"I fell into the stream," said the sheriff, her voice strangely wistful. "I thought I was far enough away, and that it was too weak to do anything, but…"

"It changed on us, too," said Alex.

The sheriff studied him. "How so?"

"It was this little thing, and then it was fast, and then –"

"It catches you," said the girl who sat in the corner. "It drags you away from the world. From everything."

Tricia looked at her. "What happened to you?" she said. "Why were you out there?"

The girl shook her head. "I was out there forever." She laughed, an ugly, pained sound. "Just running and running, but I never got anywhere." She let go of her knees and passed a shaky hand over her face, hiding from the people in the room and the world outside.

"She must have been swept away, too," said the sheriff. Her expression, wistful a moment ago, darkened to something like sorrow.

"What is this place?" asked Alex. "What's happening to us?"

The sheriff smiled sadly. "The same thing that always happens. The forest…"

Alex held something out. For a moment, Tricia thought he was expecting them to see something he no longer held, like he had a moment ago. But something glinted in the fog-light, and she saw it was the card from the man who had attacked her.

"You didn't spot this before," Alex said to Julie. "It was on the man who tried to kill Tricia earlier today."

Tricia shook her head, wondering what Alex was doing. Lost evidence wasn't the point of the moment, was it?

But Julie nodded, and Tricia realized that Alex must have put something together that she hadn't. The sheriff stared at the card in Alex's hand. "You got that today," she murmured, speaking to herself as much as to the people in the room. "Today." She sighed.

The fog flashed. It didn't seem as bright in here, high up and far from the forest floor, but that could have been wishful thinking.

Tricia stood. She took a step toward the girl who now rocked back and forth against the wall. The girl's gaze jumped to Tricia. "We're lost," said the girl.

"I know, honey –" Tricia took another step toward her, but the girl leaned away and a pitiful mewling spilled out of her.

Tricia froze, then leaned away. The girl's keening slid into silence.

Tricia felt Alex's hand in hers. She squeezed it. It gave her strength enough to look out the window.

The fog was thick out there – thicker than before. But there were no movements at least. No roiling vapor, no dark shapes. They were above the trees, if nothing else. Even though everything out here was wrong, even though reality itself appeared bent, at least they were farther away from the ground. Distance meant something here. Maybe only the up-and-down kind, but that was a rational thing, and she could *work* with rational things.

Alex destroyed that moment of illusion. "We're never leaving, are we?" he asked Julie.

"Not all of us," said the sheriff. "The forest has us."

"What is the forest?" asked Alex. He motioned at the card, with its arcane symbol, its eldritch circles. "What is that?"

"It's not supposed to be here," said Julie. "We've tried to –"

The fog flashed around them. The girl on the floor whimpered, and Julie turned to her. "It's okay, sweetheart," she said. "You're safe with us."

"How can you say that?" asked Tricia. "How can you say that we won't leave this place, then say that... that..."

She gestured at the girl on the floor. Julie glanced at Tricia for the most fleeting of moments then focused on the girl again. "Because she *has* to live. She's so young, and the young have to live their lives." She frowned. "I think. Memory is funny in the forest. It eats what's happened, it almost seems. Which makes sense, I guess. But it's hard to remember a lot of things here." She stared at the girl. "But not her. I remember her."

Julie noted the trapdoor, which still sat open. She went to it, grabbed the handle to the door that was flush against the floor, and lifted it. She pulled, guiding the door in its arc that would close it, leaning over as she said, "We've got to figure out how to get out of this, and maybe even –"

Alex's eyes widened. "Don't!"

Something flashed. Not the fog. The flash was streaked with red, then sheeted with it as the axe buried itself in the sheriff's forehead. She stiffened, and the madman – still holding the axe – climbed up the last few rungs of the ladder.

The girl started screaming. "Don't take me, don't take me, don't –"

The madman looked at her. Julie was still on her feet, doing an insane tapdance as her cleaved brain fired random impulses in its last moments. She sagged, and as she did the murderer jerked the axe free. It made a terrible grating sound that Tricia knew she would remember forever – or at least, for the rest of her life.

Julie slumped, her body done with its dance. The madman moved aside, an almost languid motion of surprising grace that let the sheriff slide past him and through the hole in the floor. A dull thud sounded and Tricia knew the body had bounced into the ladder. Another thud a half-second later as the body ricocheted into a strut. The impact shook the floor. So did the second and the third, the epicenter of each shock bouncing through a different part of the guard tower as Julie careened through the supports.

Then nothing.

The madman stared. He didn't look at Alex or Tricia. He had eyes only for the girl on the floor.

"You'll understand why this has to happen," he said. "Or maybe not." He giggled, and whipped the axe sideways, a motion that flung blood across the room. Tricia cried out as the still-warm blood of the sheriff splashed across her face and arms, and heard Alex do the same.

The madman turned to them. "I have to kill her," he said, a sadness in his voice that was so genuine and so *normal* that it terrified Tricia more than any insane rant could have done. "She's where the ghosts come from. She's where the nightmare begins."

He swung his axe again, and the blood splashed Tricia and Alex and the girl as well as the madman stepped toward her.

"Sorry, honey," he whispered. "I couldn't do it for so long. But all good things must come to an end, right? That's what I want: for it to end."

He took another step. "It has to end," he whispered as he raised the axe. "It ends *here.* It ends *now.*"

Alex leaped across the room, and Tricia wanted to cry out, to scream: *"Don't!"*

But there wasn't time. And he wouldn't have listened anyway. He would die for her, she knew that. And in that instant, there was a kind of wonderment in the air. She thought that losing Sammy had broken them. But here, in this place, she remembered – not much, just a little. Just flashes. There had been blood and pain before. There had been devastation.

And what had saved her then?

The same thing that tried to save her now.

Alex.

The moment brightened her soul, brighter by far than the fog or even the glints of light that appeared within it.

This was a blaze. The instant birth of a sun within her. The moment that was first and last and everything in between.

It wasn't Tina Louise's Diner where I first kissed Alex. It was here. It was the forest. Here *is where I knew he loved me.*

The birth of a universe of love had taken a forever-nothing of time. It was eternal, so it existed within all time, and within no time at all. Light flared within her, so bright and hot it should have burned, but somehow it only made her happy.

Then eternity ended. The brightness dimmed and died. The universe ceased as the madman finished the swing he had begun a billion years and a nanosecond before… and buried the axe in Alex's back.

31
(When Tricia Was Young)

Tricia started forward. They were here! Somehow they had made it to the cabin, and that meant Sam was there. Because he couldn't be anywhere else. He had to be in the cabin; had to be *alive*.

Alex grabbed her hand. "Stop," he said, and pulled her back to the trees.

"What?" Tricia demanded.

"We don't know where *she* is."

Tricia didn't ask who he meant. The woman with her knife, last seen curled around her ankle in pain, tripped up by the same forest that had trapped Tricia and Alex within it.

"She's behind us," said Tricia. "We know that much."

"Do we?" asked Alex.

"Of *course*." Tricia nearly snarled the words, immediately surprised by the ferocity of her response.

Alex blanched. "But everything keeps changing. It…"

"*It* doesn't change. The only thing that changes is us. We keep getting spun around, but we know where we are now. The stream is that way." She pointed in the direction the stream had to be. "We get there, turn south, and we're back on the highway and then home."

Alex hesitated. But when Tricia pulled him toward her, he didn't resist. He kept glancing back the way they had come, even though he had to be seeing only what Tricia did: fog, thicker than ever. In front of them, she *could* see the cabin through the mist, but only as a blurred rectangular block with smaller rectangles that could only be windows.

The lights aren't on, but is anybody home?

Was that thought about the possibility that Sam *wasn't* there? Or, worse, that they would find his body in there, hacked to pieces by his insane mother?

Tricia didn't know, so she put the thought away. Every step they crept toward the house, she shoved it deeper and deeper. She knew it was dangerous to do that – not only because a lack of understanding might bring danger as she tripped into traps she had made herself willfully blind to, but because once started, where might it end? What else would she lock inside her, what else might she force herself to forget?

They reached the cabin, and even without the nightmare that had preceded this moment she would have understood why the kids in town spoke of it only in whispers. Why they dared each other to go there as a rite of passage, and why the rite of passage was never accomplished. Whatever notoriety a kid could achieve coming here would not be worth the payment in nightmares that the cabin would require.

It was ramshackle, little more than rough boards nailed to the most basic frame. Some of the framing was visible through the rotted wood of the walls, and some of it…

Tricia squinted. Some of the framing she saw wasn't just visible through weather- and time-beaten wood. It had actually been built outside the wall. That was insane, because it meant that the frame had been built piece by piece, with the builder sometimes working inside the frame, other times outside it as the walls went on. A mad mismatch that would require at least ten times the work and result in a corrupt, weakened structure.

The roof hung above it all, and looked much the same: half-rotted shingles, some of it looking like it was covered by nothing more than plastic sheeting, struts and supports running in short lengths on the outside as well as – presumably – properly in place below the roof.

It was outside-in, inside-out. And when Tricia realized it, she felt like she was looking less at a cabin than at the living heart of the forest. The forest was body, the mist was breath, but the center, the force that pushed life through it all… that was here.

"It's… everything," said Alex. He felt it, too, then.

They were still holding hands. They didn't let go as they approached the cabin.

Tricia headed toward the side of the house, the angle of it allowing her to see a sliver of what she thought was the front door. The front door, it was rumored, faced the stream. She had thought to rush in, grab Sam wherever he was, and then run for dear life until they reached that stream and follow it out of here.

Then home. Home and everything would be fine.

But Alex was pulling her away now, drawing her off to the side. She almost resisted, then realized he was right: they shouldn't just walk blithely in. They had to look around; had to verify it was safe and, more importantly, that they could get Sam out of there.

If he is here.

He is.

She and Alex went to the first window. They bent over as they approached, both of them hunching automatically – though even with the fog Tricia knew there was no way anyone looking out a window could miss them.

Then again, maybe no one inside would want to look out in the first place. Not if they had seen anything like what she and Alex had seen.

"I've only been there for two nights. Which is two too many nights, if you ask me."

She heard Sam's words, talking about whether this was a haunted place or not. The answer was now clear, so hopefully in this moment it would work to their advantage.

They crept closer, and heard nothing. No sounds of alarm, no movement at all. They peeked into the first window and saw a bare room. Like the outside, it was built haphazardly. Some parts of the walls seemed brand new, others seemed like the kind of thing Tricia would see in an old west movie: warped, rough, and leached gray by the years.

It was an insane place.

They moved to the next window. A bedroom. They could see bunk beds, several suitcases open nearby them, clothes half-pulled from inside, more clothing on the floor.

One of the beds had a bundle on it, the size and shape of a person. Of Sam. It could be a bunch of blankets twisted during a sleepless night, but it could also be him.

Alex looked at Tricia. She shrugged, nodded, and then shook her head. She didn't know what to do. But to do nothing was to let everything they had passed through be in vain.

She pressed her fingers against the window until she felt the pads stick to the glass, then pushed up. She grimaced as the window rasped against the casing. It sounded preternaturally loud, a small sound that somehow blasted through her and made her wince. She saw Alex wince, too – and he winced again as the fog flashed.

Something's coming. Something always comes with the light.

They heard a crackling behind them. Far away, but close enough to worry. Sam's mother was on the move. She had to be. And that meant she was coming for them.

Tricia slid over the windowsill and into the room beyond. She rolled to the right as soon as she was in, giving Alex room as he hoisted himself up and over as well. He turned and slid the window shut, staring out into the silvered mist.

Tricia glanced out as well, then touched Alex's arm and gestured toward the bed. He nodded, and they crept forward together. Again, they hunched over as they walked, and Tricia knew it wasn't to avoid being seen. Fear weighed on them ever-heavier. She didn't know how much longer she could go on before she was bent double, then forced to hands and knees and then to her stomach. The forest wanted them dead, she thought. But it wanted them afraid first.

They had reached the bunk bed. The bundle on the bottom. Tricia reached forward, but stopped when her hand was only a few inches away. The room was illuminated only by the impossible glow of the fog, but it was dark enough inside the lunatic cabin that her eyes had taken a moment to adjust. Now she saw and, seeing, could tell it was nothing more than blankets on the bed.

She looked to Alex. He had seen it, too. No Sam. He grimaced, then pointed at the door that must lead to the cabin's main room. Tricia nodded, sighing quietly.

Like everything else, the floor was a hodgepodge. Tiles, wood, brick – all of it was in evidence; and seeing it this close up, Tricia was surprised to realize the chaos of it all had a weird flow. Nothing she could put a finger on, but up close it seemed a lot less like something put together over a series of years or even decades, a bit at a time. It seemed more like a single item united by some pattern she couldn't quite grasp. A calico pattern that seemed random at first, but eventually you could see scraps of cloth that hinted at the life of its maker, the thing that had bound them all together and somehow made them belong.

Tricia didn't belong, though. Neither did Alex, and neither did Sam. Whatever dark thing had made this place, it had nothing to do with her or any other good thing. This was a bad place, and she wanted only to get out of it, after finding Sam.

She and Alex made it to the door. She put her hand on the doorknob and again winced as she turned it. The knob apparatus wasn't well-oiled. A dry, raspy squeal accompanied the twisting of the knob and she looked sharply at Alex. He nodded, though, so apparently the sound wasn't as bad as she imagined it.

She turned the knob the rest of the way. When the knob could turn no more, she cracked the door. An inch. She waited. Another inch.

She looked into the room beyond the door. She saw little save hints of white and gray, strips of non-color that meant nothing.

Another inch.

She saw something: shoes. They wiggled slightly, and when she opened the door another inch she saw they, and the feet within, belonged to Sam. He was laying on his side, and with every inch she pushed the door she saw more of him. He was tied hand and foot, ropes binding his ankles, more around his wrists, and then those ties connected by a short length of rope that kept him bowed back in what must be near-excruciating pain.

As soon as she realized what she was seeing, she shoved the door open and, heedless of anything else that might be in the room, rushed out and toward Sam.

He had his back to her, but he must have heard her coming out of the room. He rolled over, his eyes wide open, terror shining brightly within them. Shock tempered the terror when he saw Tricia, then his eyes flitted over her shoulder to Alex.

Sam shook in place. He grunted, but couldn't make any more sound than that. Not with the dirty rag tied around his head, the gag biting deep into the corners of his mouth as he struggled.

Tricia knelt beside him and started fumbling with the gag, then moved to the rope knotting his hands and feet together. She couldn't make a dent in either, the knots were too thick and too tight.

"Help me," she whispered to Alex.

He didn't answer. She looked at him, and realized he was turning a slow circle. Looking at the walls, the ceiling, the floor.

She finally saw what he was seeing. She had been so fixated on Sam she hadn't comprehended it herself, but now she did. Or rather, she *noticed* it, because the thing was beyond comprehension.

This room sported the same twisted, inside-out, outside-in construction as the rest of the cabin. The same jumble of materials that seemed chaotic at first but looked more and more like a pattern *just* beyond her ability to understand, the longer she looked at it.

And all of it – walls, floor, even ceiling - was covered in what, a few days ago, Sam would have called *doodles*. Every square inch was covered in the symbols that Tricia had seen: interlocking circles, twisting and writhing over themselves, consuming one another and then birthing what they had eaten once again.

"What is this place?" she murmured.

The words seemed to shock Alex out of whatever dark fascination had kept him from helping until now. He turned, wordless, eyes haunted, and knelt by Sam. He tried his hand at the knots as well, but had no more luck loosening them than Tricia had.

Before he even finished trying, she was looking around for a knife or something sharp she could use to hack through Sam's bonds. The room, she could see now, was some kind of front room/kitchen mix. Two walls that had windows allowing views of the fog and the shadows beyond. One wall with two doors – one of which led to the room she and Alex had just come out of, the other of which led to some other place, as yet unseen and unknown.

The third wall of the room was on the side where the sink jutted out of the wall. Beside it, a short refrigerator sat, and all around it hung wall cabinets that, like the rest of the place, showed neither rhyme nor reason in their placement, style, or material. Some were old and warped, others looked like they were plastic covered in formica laminate, still others looked sleek and new. The sink was modern-looking stainless steel, but had a pump right out of Tombstone, and the counters that sat on either side were equally mismatched. The drawers under the counters, too: no two were the same style, size, or made of the same materials.

Tricia ran into the kitchen, and started throwing open cabinets and drawers. Half of them wouldn't open at all, and she wondered if they were real, or just boards that looked like cabinets glued or nailed to the sides of the counter.

The third one that opened yielded a few forks, spoons, and table knives. Nothing helpful. She slammed it shut, wincing at the noise.

"Quiet," hissed Alex. He looked at the still-closed door to the one room they hadn't checked, then returned to working on the knots that still held Sam tight.

Tricia opened another drawer, and this time found paydirt: an assortment of sharp knives. Again, it was all a mishmash, but at least it was a mishmash she could *use*.

She grabbed one of the newer-seeming knives, one not spotted with rust or bent and chipped along the tarnished blade. The heft of it felt reassuring in her hand, and she rushed to Sam.

Alex moved aside to give her room. The knife turned out to be razor sharp, parting the individual fibers of the ropes Sam's mother had tied him with. Tricia sliced through the rope that bound Sam's ankles and arms behind his back, and he groaned with relief. He didn't straighten, though: he must have been in that position so long that his body had tightened and grown rigid.

After that, the going slowed drastically. The ropes had been tied so tightly around Sam's ankles and wrists that she couldn't slide the knife under them with enough give to turn the blade upward and saw effectively. She was worried about cutting down toward Sam's flesh, though, because the knife was sharp enough that when the ropes *did* finally give way she could easily see herself plunging the knife into his wrist or ankle, severing a tendon and watching her friend bleed out in front of her eyes.

That left the knots themselves. They were so tight that they turned a tangle of medium-thick bits of rope into a single, compressed clump that felt like steel cable. Tricia didn't give up, though, and a bit at a time the knot around that tied his ankles together began to fray. Tricia kept looking at the windows as she hacked at the knots, expecting every time to see Sam's mother staring in at them, grinning, knowing her prey was trapped.

She didn't see Sam's mother, but the fog flashed, and that was perhaps even worse.

"Faster," whispered Alex.

Tricia's hands began to spasm with the effort of slashing at the tough ropes. She held the knife out to Alex. He took it and began sawing away at Sam's bindings, working faster than her because he was still fresh. But he slowed, too, and was moving at only half-speed by the time he got Sam's ankles loose.

Alex moved to Sam's wrists. These knots came apart faster. Sam was free, but he still didn't move. He groaned in pain each time a knot came apart. "Can you stand up?" asked Tricia.

In answer, Sam tried to move his legs. Rather than rocking them back and forth or, even better, getting to his hands and knees, all he managed was a jittery set of spasms.

"I'll massage his legs," said Tricia. "See if I can get the blood running again."

"Okay," said Alex. He bent back to work, this time on the gag that so effectively silenced their friend. Like Tricia, he kept glancing at the windows, then would flick his gaze toward the door to the cabin's last room.

Tricia massaged Sam's legs. She felt time ticking away, and felt the cabin's insanity more oppressively with every passing second.

Alex put the knife down and began trying to loosen the knot on Sam's gag.

"Don't you think –" began Tricia.

Alex shook his head. "He keeps trembling. Spasms, I think. They're not big, but I'm worried about cutting him if I keep going." Sweat beaded his brow, and worry creased his face, but in that moment, bending himself to save his friend with everything he had, Tricia thought he had never looked more beautiful.

Was it wrong of her to think that now? Probably.

But could she stop it? No.

And did she even want to? Not even a little. She had passed through confusion, terror, pain, and now she was working to get her injured friend to a point where he could flee with them from this house that was madness made flesh. She wouldn't steal the bit of brightness that Alex's face allowed her in this moment.

Sam's legs stopped thrashing as she worked on them, and finally she could feel the movements smooth as he regained control of his abused limbs. At almost the same moment, Alex gave a little grunt of triumph. She saw him loosen the gag enough that he could slide it out of Sam's mouth. There wasn't much give, and Tricia saw blood flow from the corner of Sam's mouth as Alex pulled the gag down and the rags tore at his lips and chin. Alex didn't even try to pull the gag over Sam's head – it was off his mouth, and that would have to do for now. Alex just pulled the circle of cloth down over Sam's chin and let it hang from Sam's neck.

Just like a noose.

We're going to die here. One of us, maybe all of us.

The premonition was so intense, so real, that for a moment Tricia couldn't move. She was overwhelmed by the sense that this wasn't a moment of liberation, just a false hope before doom.

"Thank you," croaked Sam. He was crying, tears streaming from his eyes, laying bright tracks down his cheeks. "Thank you for coming back for me."

"Of course," said Alex. "Always."

"Thank you," Sam said again, and Tricia worried that he would start gibbering. If he dissolved into hysteria it would be that much harder to get him – or her or Alex, for that matter – out of this situation.

"Come on," said Alex. "We gotta get you out of here."

He put one of Sam's arms around his shoulders, and Tricia did the same with the other. Together, they hoisted their friend up to a seated position, then got him standing. He took a few trembling steps, almost fell, then righted himself.

Outside, the fog flashed. Sam's already-terrified eyes grew even more frantic. But the adrenaline apparently brought on by the light show must have trumped the pain in his legs, because he stood a bit taller, and Tricia felt the weight lessen on her shoulders even as Sam whispered, "We have to go. We have to go *now.*"

The door opened. Not the front door, not the one Tricia and Alex hadn't had a chance to check out, either. It was the door they had just come through a few minutes ago. The one that led to a mostly-empty room with nothing but a bunk bed, some suitcases, and a few clothes piled up.

Sam's mother stood in the door frame. Her hair was wild, her eyes wilder still.

Tricia still couldn't tell exactly how old the woman was, but the lines in her face and around her eyes were craggier than she remembered from her quick glance outside the school. The proximity to the forest and the secrets hidden in the mist-lights had turned her old before her time, and had driven her mad.

"I knew you were here," Sam's mother said, her eyes roving from Alex to Tricia. "The whisperers said so. No matter where I go, no matter how far or how *long* I run, they follow me. They're always there. Around me, inside me. All of them, all of me." Her eyes went to Sam's. Her gaze softened, and somehow that made everything worse instead of better.

Tricia knew then that she stood in the presence of a truly dangerous person. This was a woman who Believed in something. The worst people in the world aren't simply insane, they are *zealous* – willing to do anything to "make the world a better place." To "help" you, even if that means killing you to do it.

"Mom," Sam whispered. "Mommy, please…"

"I'M NOT YOUR MOTHER!" shrieked the woman, slashing the air with the ridge of her hand, as though trying to cut the words to ribbons before they reached her. "I can't be. I'm *nothing,* you hear that? You made me *nothing,* your father made me *nothing,* and *I made* me nothing…" She blinked, and her eyes went blank, her expression sagged away and left only void behind. "Some things change in the forest," she whispered. "But other things stay the same because I won't let me change them. Or maybe the universe won't or maybe it will or maybe it won't or maybe it will, row, row,

your boat," she said, then sang, *"gently down the STREAM! Merrily merrily merrily merrily, LIFE IS BUT A –"*

The end of the children's song dissolved in a fit of panting giggles, the sound a person might make on their deathbed, and were told the funniest joke in the world in the moment they passed into darkness. Her hand went to her shoulder and scratched it, her nails tracing slow, lazy circles on her shirt. Like the softness of the woman's gaze when she looked at Sam, this motion terrified Tricia. Something about the loose, lazy flow of her fingers on the shirt, the way her eyes rolled back.

The woman moaned. It was a sound caught halfway between ecstacy and anguish.

Alex grabbed Tricia's hand. She was already reaching for him as well. Alex and Tricia held Sam, and they held each other with their free hands. It created a circuit, and a strange, humming power seemed to surge through her. She gasped, and heard Sam and Alex do the same.

Her pulse quickened, and her hand grew hot where she touched Alex, her arm was hot where she held Sam. The thrumming, rushing noise of her heartbeat felt too loud in that instant, as though all three of them had been fused into one single person.

"Don't!" screamed Sam's mother. "Don't do that, don't say that, don't *think that!"*

She put her hands over her ears and closed her eyes, looking like an infant trying to make the world disappear.

Alex squeezed Tricia's hand once more. They let go of one another. The circuit interrupted, and the crackling, humming sense of power she had felt dissipated. As it did, the fog flared outside. Sam's mother turned to the nearest window, staring at it in horror.

"It's here. We're here. We're all here and it's here and *it never stops*!"

She fell to the floor, one knee on tile and the other on rough-hewn wood. She still had her hands on her ears, and now she started screaming, trying to drown out the words that had come with the fog. The whisperers.

"Faster..."

"Faster..."

"Faster..."

"Blood..."

"Blood..."

"Blood..."

They sounded closer than ever, like the unseen whisperers were in this very room. Tricia was starting to hear distinctions; subtle differences that made her think she was hearing the voices of numerous shadows. Differences in tone signaled the presence of more than a single entity. Not just one, but *many* whisperers hid in the fog.

One of the whisperers spoke louder, clearer than any of them. *"Help me,"* it said/sighed/screamed. Tricia felt like someone had taken a hose to her, freezing every inch of skin and covering it in gooseflesh that rose so hard and fast it almost hurt.

Sam's mother must have heard it, too. She screamed even louder as she rocked forward so far her head touched the floor.

"Go. Go, go, go *gogogogo,*" whispered Sam, repeating the words in a panicked litany that dissolved into wordless sound.

Alex nodded, and so did Tricia. Still supporting Sam, the three of them hobble-walked toward the front door, while Sam's mother continued wailing.

Tricia was glad. Not just because the woman seemed to have forgotten them for the moment, but because she wanted out of this place, this madhouse where the whispers were so close.

"The center," said Sam, sounding suddenly as though he had been drugged. "We're at the center of it all. The center, the heart, the middle-the-beginning-the-end." His jaw sagged, his mouth flopping open. Alex shook him. "Wha...?" said Sam, blinking and looking around like he wasn't sure if he had just woken from a dream or was still locked inside that sleeping place.

"Come on, Sam," said Alex. "We gotta get moving."

"Yeah," said Sam. Then he shook himself and said, *"Hell* yeah." He looked around again, one last time, and Tricia saw him taking in the images on the walls. "Doodles," he whispered.

He started moving, half limping, half being supported by Tricia and Alex as the three of them moved in an awkward knot toward the front door.

Tricia kept looking back. Sam's mother was still on the floor, and one of the times Tricia looked, she saw the woman fall to the side, still bent double. Tricia felt a moment of hope as Alex reached for the front door. She wasn't at all surprised in that moment to realize that the knob itself was ornate, a gold shank topped by some kind of crystal that created a timeless look that would be at home in an old, old mansion, or an ultra-modern home in Beverly Hills. She was equally unsurprised to see that the plate into which the shank was embedded did not match the knob. The plate was a yellowed, cracked thing that could be plastic or maybe ivory. Years had turned the thing from a simple mismatch into a thing almost beautiful in its grotesquerie.

Alex's hand covered the crystal. He turned the knob.

Tricia looked at the still-screaming form of Sam's mother. She expected the woman to leap up, to grab them all. To pull out her knife and rush them.

She didn't.

Alex swung the door open. They hobbled out into the fog.

"Second star to the right and straight on 'til morning," Alex whispered, though Tricia could barely hear him over the still-wailing woman they were leaving behind.

"What was that?" said Sam.

"Peter Pan," said Alex.

Tricia thought the moment was bizarre. They were lost in a forest, a madwoman after them, supernatural forces spinning them around and taunting them – and, she finally admitted, they *were* supernatural; that was the only thing that made, not sense, but the best kind of *un*sense.

And yet, we're holding a book club meeting. Right here in the fog. Right here, listening to the screams of the woman trying to kill us.

But she said nothing. Something inside her screamed louder than Sam's mother. Something inside her shrieked that this moment must happen.

"I loved that story when I was little." said Sam. He smiled dreamily. "*Peter Pan, or The Boy Who Wouldn't Grow Up.*"

It didn't surprise Tricia that Sam knew the subtitle. He knew everything. He was smart. They all were.

So we'll get through this. We'll figure out a way to get home.

Sam's eyes shifted, from whatever memory had warmed him back to the moment in which they lived. As they did the sense of foreordination and predestination passed away. Tricia felt free to move again.

So did Sam, apparently, because he pushed himself forward, moving his arms from Tricia's and Alex's shoulders. He wobbled, and Alex's arms went out as though to catch his friend.

Sam held up a hand, warding him off. "I can do it."

Alex nodded. "Good. We –" His expression changed suddenly, contorting to terror so complete it made even his beautiful face into a nightmare. His words turned to a cough, and as Tricia realized he was looking over his shoulder when it happened, she knew what he was seeing. She looked, too.

Sam's mother had stopped screaming. While they talked of fairie tales and mischievous children who flew away to Neverland when they should have been sleeping, Sam's mother had torn herself from the panic that incapacitated her. She stood.

She was walking toward them and as she passed the knife Alex had put down to work on Sam's bindings with his fingers, she scooped the blade into her hand. She was grinning as she moved.

Not running, but moving with the lithe, easy, *deadly* grace of a cheetah that knows it has run its prey to exhaustion.

"I know how to end it," Sam's mother said. "I know it has to end here, now. It ends, and then it never happens, and never will happen, and never happened at all."

She slashed at the air with the knife.

Tricia turned to Alex. They both turned to Sam.

All three ran into the fog, into whatever waited in the forest.

Behind them, they heard the cracks and crackles and snaps of a woman rushing through that same forest, tracking them, thirsting for their blood.

And beside them, the whisperers. Tricia kept seeing them in the fog, shadows flitting through the trees, always keeping pace, but always just out of sight.

They whispered the same word over and over, sounding nearly out of breath, as though they were things of flesh and bone and breath and blood instead of nightmare shadows in a misty world. They whispered into the eternal gloaming of the forest, and into Tricia's soul.

"Run..."

"Run..."

"RUN..."

32
(When Alex Was Young)

"Run..."

"Run..."

"RUN..."

Alex heard the whispers all around, but worse than that he heard them *inside* himself. He, Trish, and Sam ran through the mist, and he felt more and more like that went both ways. He was dissolving into fear, terror, pain – not just for himself, which was bad, but for Sam, which was worse, and for Trish, which was unbearable. He was turning to a mist made of silvered pains and regrets – a featureless vapor destined to blow away.

Sam ran between him and Trish, and though he wobbled he never fell. A few times Alex reached for his friend, but Sam always righted himself first. The three of them ran, but even in the headlong flight Alex tried to keep himself oriented. He wanted out of here, and he wanted Trish out of here. Sam, too, but not nearly so much. He felt almost cruel admitting it, even to himself, but if it came down to it he knew he would leave Sam to save Trish.

He would do *anything* – live or die – to save Trish.

A branch rushed toward his face, slicing out of the fog. He ducked, rolled, came up running again. He had drawn slightly ahead of Trish and Sam, so they were able to take advantage of the warning his maneuver supplied and avoid getting clotheslined by the limb.

Behind them all, the crashes came hard and fast. Sam's mother was howling, the sound more like that of a beast than a woman. They were all changing in the mist, in the forest. Alex was becoming nothing, fading away into a thing of pure fear. Sam's mother was becoming an animal, rabid and unthinking.

What of Trish and Sam?

He didn't know. He could only run.

"How… far… to the… stream…?" panted Sam.

"Not… far," Alex panted in return.

He had no doubt that was the case, normally. But how could he tell Sam about what the forest did? About the way distances shifted and places seemed jumbled and nothing could be counted on.

Except Trish. I can count on her. I can count on Sam.

"Run…"

The whispers were still there, though they sounded farther away than they had a moment ago. The fog flashed.

"Are they gone?" asked Trish. She didn't stop running. None of them did.

"No," said Alex. "They're not."

He heard Sam's mother, her words echoing in his mind: *"No matter where I go, no matter how far or how long I run, they follow me. They're always there. Around me, inside me. All of them, all of me."*

The fog flashed. Alex looked toward the light. It always had a place, he realized. It wasn't like the fog was brightening uniformly – the light had a source.

He looked back toward Sam and Trish as he said, "What's nex –"

He looked at Trish.

She looked at him.

Neither looked at Sam, though. Because Sam was gone.

"Where is he?" Trish shouted.

"I don't know!"

They both spun in circles.

"Trish! Alex!"

Both of them turned toward the sound as the fog flashed. Sam's voice, Alex knew. But it was too far away. There was no way he could have run away without Alex or Trish seeing. No way, but it had happened.

"Do you hear that?" said Trish quietly.

"Of course I do," snapped Alex. "But how did he get so far –"

"Not that." She held up a hand. Cocked her head. "Where'd *she* go? Sam's mom?"

Alex mimicked her motion, tilting his head to the side. "I don't hear her."

The fog flashed. And then Alex *did* hear her. He heard Sam's mother shrieking, but again he heard it far away. The shrieks were just as insane as they had been before, but distance gave him a measure of comfort.

"Run…"

"Hear…"

Something flitted past him. Alex spun, trying to see it, but all he saw was another shadow in the fog. It was about his height, whatever it was; beyond that he couldn't tell a bit about it. Even the height might be wrong, too, given how the mist curled and curdled everything. The fog transformed trees to hunchbacked skeletons, the sky to a distant memory. It warped everything, so he knew any impression he got of what he saw could be wrong.

Something ran past again. Again Alex turned, sensing Trish mimic the movement. The shadow – or perhaps *another* shadow – ran past. Again, just out of sight. A dark blur, the crackle of branches: these signaled its presence more than anything Alex actually saw.

His eyes opened wide. "I'm hearing them," he said.

"We're both hearing them," Trish said, before calling out, *"Saaaaam!"*

"Here!"

Sam's voice sounded farther away than ever.

Alex shook his head. "No, you don't understand. I'm hearing *them*. The whisperers."

Crack-crack-crack-crack.

Alex tensed, and felt Trish do the same beside him. "They're coming," she whispered. "They're *be*coming."

Alex understood, because it was the same thing he was feeling. The whisperers had been wraiths, the quick glimpses of them that Alex and Trish had caught accompanied by no noise other than the words the things spoke.

But now –

(crackle-crack-crack)

– he and Trish were *hearing* them. Not just the words they spoke, but the movements they made. They were *be*coming, yes, that was the right word. They were becoming flesh – or something like it. They were becoming *real*. Stepping out of shadow and into the mist-lights, to be seen, and to be feared.

"RUN!"

One of the shadows flitted by, so close that Alex suspected that if he had turned a bit faster he would have seen the thing – and would have been driven mad by that sight.

Even so, and even with the sound of leaves and twigs breaking under the thing's feet, the voice of it still sounded strained, hollow, distant. It was the echo of words the owner had spoken, then had walked away from before they fully ended.

Alex ran. He saw his life pass before his eyes: not just the life he had led, but the life he had hoped *to* lead.

He saw himself, a child growing up in a cold house. No home, just a place to shelter and sustain basic survival. There was no life in the place. Certainly his mother was never kind to him, never held or cuddled or whispered the sweet lies and sweeter truths that Alex knew should be every child's birthright, but which had passed him by.

He saw himself at school, realizing quickly that he would be isolated by most of the students – and a good share of the teachers – for his brilliance.

He saw himself graduate. He saw himself working, devoting himself to the search for knowledge, to discovering more about the way things really were, every day.

He saw children. *His* children. A boy, a girl. He saw them grow up and find their own happiness, have their own children, and the cycle would repeat.

And, of course, Alex saw Trish. She was his world. She had been for longer than he could remember, and he knew she would always be the north star upon which he fixed his course. She was the only thing that had kept him from growing up completely dysfunctional, the love she shared and the ability she had to understand him on the deepest levels making up for the absence of parental kindness or concern.

He also realized that he did *not* see one thing: Sam. It was as though when the fog – or whatever hid within the fog – stole their friend away, it had stolen even the memory of his existence.

No. I *remember. And I will find him.*

The light flashed. He and Trish stopped running, because the light had flashed in front of them… and it had never heralded any comfort. Just death. Just shadows, and wraiths, and the man in the tree, and –

Sam's mother exploded out of the fog in front of them.

She looked somehow more *alive* out here, like the fog had strengthened her. Or perhaps it was the opportunity for violence that did it. Either way, she looked different, stronger, more ready and willing to do anything and everything.

The fog curled around her; ate her. She was there one moment, gone the next.

"Where's Sam?" shouted Trish.

"I don't know. I don't –"

Alex couldn't finish. He was exhausted, and his mind finally realized how out of breath he was. He looked at Trish. She was gasping, too. She seemed diminished. The time in here – the endless, impossible time in this endless, impossible forest – had taken its toll. Two thoughts struck Alex. The first was the idea that Trish's strength and soul were being stolen by Sam's mother. She was a vampire of the soul, and that was why she seemed so much more alive, almost younger in the moment he had glimpsed her. The second, worse by far, was the idea that if the fog had swallowed Sam's mother, and Sam… what if it did the same to Trish?

Something flashed through his mind. Like when he had seen his life flash before him. A glimpse of something important, something that would make him *understand.*

"We have to find him," Trish said.

Alex gritted his teeth as her words chased away the moment. He dug deep, trying to find the strength to run again, to find Sam and get out of here. He suddenly felt like he didn't have the strength to move at all –

(She's feeding off me, too.)

– but knew he *would* find the strength to get Trish out of here.

Trish turned, looking around. She stumbled as she twisted, as though the tree roots around them were coming alive and trying to trip her. She righted herself, then shouted, "Sam!" She turned toward Alex. "Alex, I see him!"

Alex nodded as he, too, saw Sam.

Their friend stood not twenty feet away, looking as he always had. Same pants, same shirt, same red backpack they had seen so many times. But he seemed smaller than he had. He was being sucked dry, too.

"Sam!" Trish shrieked. She started running toward their friend.

Sam's face twisted in relief. "You came for me," he said, his voice breaking as tears threatened, then came in full, running down his cheeks and neck and into the collar of his shirt.

Crackle-crack.

Alex twisted, looking at the shadows that were flitting around. Some seemed to run right at them, disappearing from view before anything could *really* be seen of them. And the whispers came with them.

One of the shadows stood in the mist right behind Sam.

"Sam, *run!*" Alex shouted.

Even as he shouted, the mist boiled around them, obscuring Sam for a moment. When it broke apart, Sam seemed to have gone from twenty *feet* away to twenty *yards.*

The forest wanted them.

And what the forest wanted, the forest kept.

Trish had turned to look at him, just a quick glance, but the pale, pinched look on her face told him that she was seeing things behind him.

Sam stood too far away from them. Too close to the shadow that wasn't a shadow at all, Alex now saw, but his *mother,* the madwoman with the knife so thirsty for her son's blood.

Even as Alex focused on Sam – and on the woman he saw behind his friend – he heard the whisperers, louder and clearer than ever. They sounded almost *alive,* almost *real,* and that frightened him so badly that it eclipsed everything else.

They were *becoming.*

"… get out of this place…"

"… hear anything…"

"… see anything…"

"… just fog…"

"… turn around…"

"… this rotting place…"

Sam reached out as he cried, "Where's my mom? *WHERE'S MY MOTHER*?" He sounded far too young, fear transforming him from a fifteen-year-old to a five-year-old. But not screaming *for* his mother; he wanted to know where she was so he could run *from* her.

Which meant he hadn't seen what was behind him.

She was there, still rushing at him, her bright blade flashing and slashing through the air.

"Where is she?" Sam shouted, and Alex felt like screaming himself, because every time he blinked it seemed like Sam was farther away. "Where is*aaaaugh*!"

His scream fell apart, turning to wordless, mindless panic. Then he shouted again: "Don't!"

Sam shouted it. Alex shouted it. Trish shouted it. All of them joined in that moment, the forest melding them into one creature, one mind that felt only terror as Sam's mother gritted her white teeth and slashed at her son. She was too far, though, and even though Sam hadn't moved, she missed.

Or maybe the forest just wants her away from him, too. Maybe it's playing its games with us all.

Whether that was happening or not, Sam's mother was definitely closing in. She slashed again, shrieking, "Just *die*. Just *die and let everything never begin again."*

The mist roiled, parting like the Red Sea before Moses, and the fog flashed. The light fell on Sam's mother, and her knife seemed to cut it apart, turning it to diamonds that Alex knew would soon become rubies as Sam's blood was spilled.

"You have to die!" Sam's mother shouted, and Alex felt something strange from her. She was running toward Sam, Trish was running toward Sam. The whisperers flitted all around. The fog flashed, again and again until it was a near-constant strobe that rendered everyone's movements jittery. It was too much to comprehend, the ultimate in sensory overload. Yet Alex *did* comprehend it. He saw everything, and felt everything, as though the understanding he had always shared with Trish had expanded to include Sam and even Sam's mother.

Sam's mother... who was crying. Screaming, yes. Enraged and insane, yes. But crying as well, real grief sounding in her sobs.

And then Alex saw one more thing: he saw Trish fall. A possibility at the best of times, in a place so overgrown with brush and roots – a near-certainty at a time like this.

Alex was already running for her, the paralysis that had stolen his strength pushed aside by his terror for his friend. She screamed, and he put on a burst of speed as she twisted, falling not forward but to the side. She hit a tree, and Alex thought for an instant that it was lucky she hadn't fallen to the ground. The mist billowed, and he worried that she would have been buried in that glowing, pulsing, strobing thing and then the thing that held them captive. The mist. The forest.

Whatever minor relief he felt disappeared, though, when she hit the tree. She screamed, and pain cleaved him as he heard her agony. He shouted her name, and for once the forest played no tricks, because he was able to reach her in only a few steps.

He saw what had caused her screams, a moment before he reached her. She had spun as she fell, her back slamming into the trunk of the tree – and the force of her running, spinning fall had ricocheted her onto a small, broken limb that jutted out of the tree at *just* the right height. She had impaled herself on the branch that now protruded from her shoulder, dripping with her blood.

Alex ran for her, screaming her name. For a moment she was *all* he saw. Then the pulsing fog drew his sight; forced his eyes away from her, and toward Sam.

Sam was reaching for them. Reaching for *Trish*, and Alex felt his care and appreciation for the guy blossom into full-blown love as he realized Sam had forgotten about his mother and the danger she posed when *he* saw Trish hurt. Alex loved Sam, in that moment, like he loved Trish, and like he loved himself.

And so, in a strange way, he was about to watch himself die. Because Sam's mother had caught up to him.

"It can't start!" she shouted, and slashed down again.

Sam twisted, a bizarre hybrid of panic and grace that Alex knew he would remember forever. He dodged, and his mother's swing – that would have slashed him to the bone, or maybe decapitated him completely – missed by millimeters.

Sam twisted as he dodged, coming around to face Alex and Trish. He ran toward them.

"Alex! Tricia!"

Alex didn't know what to do. He wanted to help Sam, but what would he do? Trish couldn't run if something happened to him – she couldn't run whether he won or not.

She can't run.

She has *to run.*

"Hold on," Alex whispered. He encircled her body with his arms. He had dreamed of hugging her, of embracing, of *holding* her. But he had never dreamed that it would be to yank her off a branch that had torn its way through her body.

Trish screamed in agony, and Alex did, too. His own shoulder pulsed sympathetically, and if he could have taken the actual wound, the actual *pain* in that moment, he would have.

Alex felt the forest watching her pain. Felt Sam, running toward him. Felt Sam's mother, wanting to kill them all.

Focus. Help Trish. Get her moving. Get her away.

Alex pulled, and Trish's body came free of the branch with a wet, sucking noise.

It punctured her lung. It must have. How will she run?

How can we get away now?

The light pulsed. The whispers surged.

"… Alex…"

"… get out of here…"

"… Tricia…"

"… get out…"

"… Sam…"

"… in this Hell…"

"… people don't stay dead…"

It *is* Hell, Alex thought. Because Hell is the place where we lose our minds, lose our lives, lose our*selves*.

He was wrong, though. Hell had not yet arrived. But it was coming. Soon.

33
(When Alex Had Grown)

Alex had seen it all happen. He screamed, "Don't!" Then the madman who had just buried his axe in Julie's skull pulled himself into the ranger's tower with them and the girl Trish held was screaming, "Don't take me, don't take me, don't –"

The madman yanked his axe loose, and Julie fell through the hole in the floor and thumped and thudded her way to earth. Gone.

"You'll understand why this has to happen," said the madman –

(and for a moment Alex remembered for a moment he remembered another killer, a woman who held not an axe but a knife *but so much of it was like this moment so much and then the moment was gone)*

– and then he added, "Or maybe not," and laughed, and flicked the axe in the air. The dead sheriff's still-warm blood splashed across Alex, and he heard Trish scream and knew the fluid had spattered her and the girl who cowered with her as well.

"I have to kill her," said the madman."She's where the ghosts come from. She's where the nightmare begins." He stepped forward, and Alex knew this was it, Trish was going to die.

"Sorry, sweetie," the man whispered. "I couldn't do it for so long. But all good things must come to an end, right? That's what I want: for it to end." He stepped toward them, raising the axe as he whispered, "It has to end. It ends *here*."

Everything drew into sharp relief. Alex saw the madman. He saw Trish and the girl they had found. He saw the blood that spattered their lovely faces and turned them to grotesque parodies of their beautiful selves. He saw the gore that spattered the rising axe blade, the blood splashed all around the still-open trapdoor.

"It ends *now*," said the madman

Like hell it does, thought Alex. And ran forward as the axe came down.

He had a moment to think what a stupid thing he'd done. Rushing a lunatic with a double-bladed axe, with only the barest of ideas what to do next.

The axe hit him. He had another instant to be thankful – he had run forward fast enough that he got fully inside the arc of the blade. Then his body realized that, though it had avoided the sharp blade, the butt of the handle and the killer's hands clenched around it had come down hard on Alex's back. His ribs felt like a red-hot steel belt had wrapped around them, burning everything they touched and tightening so much he couldn't breathe couldn't breathe couldn't *breathe.*

He almost fell. Almost went down and that would have been it. But Trish saved him. Even as darkness puckered the edges of his sight, even as he felt like letting the black take him and be done with it all, she saved him. Trish screamed, and the pain in her scream was so exquisite, so all-powerful, that he knew at once she had seen the axe hit him. That she thought the blade had bitten into him, rather than his back coming into contact with the handle and with the killer's arms as the blade slapped nothing but empty air an inch beyond the curve of Alex's buttocks.

The sound of her pain, brought on not by fear for herself but anguish at what had happened to *him*, energized Alex. He had no plan, just an idea. But that idea pushed him, too. He kept moving forward, throwing his arms wide and lowering his shoulder and hitting the guy as hard as he could.

He slammed into the killer's midsection, and thought he heard something crack. Maybe a rib? He hoped so. Whatever it was, the killer grunted in pain, and wheeled back. Three quick steps…

… and the last step ended in nothing. His backpedaling foot found the open trapdoor. He reeled backward, and now Alex *did* feel the blade of the axe as the killer tipped into space. The madman slammed down with his weapon, like a mountain climber using his climbing axe to arrest a fall, and the sharp edge drove into Alex's back just above the shoulder blade. Alex screamed in pain, and straightened automatically as his body tried to get away from the agony.

That was a mistake.

The axe, already deep in the muscle of Alex's back, dug a furrow over his trapezius, down his collarbone, and several inches down his chest before finally pulling away.

Alex wanted to vomit with the enormity of the agony that crashed over him. But he choked down the rising gorge and, instead, *smiled* as the killer wheeled back, placed another foot into eternity, and then plummeted through the trapdoor.

The smile felt like it was pulled right off his face an instant later – or maybe he was pulled away from the smile – as the killer's hand lanced forward and grabbed hold of the front of Alex's shirt. Suddenly Alex was falling, too. He screamed as the shirt pulled taut against him. The light cotton felt like steel wool scouring the flesh from his bones where he'd been wounded.

He pulled back in spite of the pain, trying to keep from falling forward while trying to peel the killer's fingers from his shirt. It didn't work. He lost his footing and tripped forward and would have fallen through the trapdoor if he hadn't managed to wedge his good hand against the far edge of the door frame. He was planking across the opening, the killer hanging off him with one hand, the other still clutching the axe.

The killer smiled. "Maybe you'll do. Maybe I can end it with *you*," he spat. He hefted the axe one-handed, but the sound of tearing rent the air, and in spite of his pain Alex enjoyed the sight of the man's eyes widening as he realized what must come next.

The seams of Alex's shirt ripped.

The killer, his handhold suddenly gone, fell.

But not far enough.

At the last second, he swung his legs forward, using the last traces of momentum to propel himself toward the ladder. For a moment, Alex thought he wasn't going to make it. Then the killer's right leg caught in the space between two rungs. His left leg jammed through the space below, and his downward fall turned into a short, fast arc that ended with his legs twisted around the ladder's rungs, his head smacking into another rung four feet below. He let go of the axe, and it clang-clattered its way downward, disappearing in the fog.

Alex almost followed him down. His shoulder was screaming, one arm hung loosely. The other was slick with sweat or blood or both, and rapidly losing its grip on the frame of the trapdoor. He gritted his teeth, unable even to call out for help as he bent every last muscle fiber to the task of keeping himself from plummeting. Only if he did it, there would be no hangup in the rungs. Just straight down, a quick trip, a quick flash of pain as the ground liquified him, then nothing.

He was slipping. Slipping.

Then he felt hands around his stomach. More hands pulled at the ragged remains of his shirt, pulling it the same way the killer had. Only where the killer had pulled him toward doom, these hands lifted him to safety.

He tried to help, but couldn't do much more than keep himself rigid so that he'd be easier to grab hold of.

Then he was falling again, twisting to the side this time as the hands gave one last, concerted yank. He fell back and down, landing only inches from the trapdoor, half atop Trish, his head in her lap.

She pushed the sweaty hair from his face. "I thought I'd lost you," she said, then she was hugging and kissing him all over his face. "I thought I'd lost you," she said, again and again.

"No such luck," he managed.

She laughed, a strange hiccup-chuckle that conveyed all the fear and relief and pain she had dealt with over the last few seconds. Alex wanted to laugh, too, but the motion of Trish's laughter felt like shards of glass carving through the flesh and bone of his shoulder.

"Oh, honey," she said. "I'm sorry."

"'Sokay," he managed. Then he braved more pain to look around. "Where's the girl?"

Trish gestured with her chin, and Alex followed the movement. The girl sat huddled into herself again, but he knew that she hadn't been there the whole time.

"She helped save you," said Trish quietly.

"I know." He turned his gaze to the girl. "Thank you," he said.

"I want to go back," she whispered.

"Where?" asked Trish.

"To the way it was before."

"Before?"

"Before he came. Before he killed everything. Before he took me away."

Trish looked like she was going to ask another question, but Alex reached up with his good hand and touched her arm. "Let her be," he said.

Trish nodded. Her eyes took on a peculiar cast. "What were you holding?" she asked.

It took a moment for Alex to even understand what she was saying. In all the insanity, he had forgotten what he saw below the tower, what he brought with him up here, what had been *gone* when he held it out.

Was it real?

"I thought… I thought I found Sammy's toy," he said. "But I must have dreamed –"

"My toy," whispered the girl. "Mine."

Alex looked at her. She was still glassy-eyed, but she had come out of herself to save him, and at least she seemed to be responding to things around her. It was an improvement.

"It wasn't, um, your toy," he said.

"I dropped him," she said. "I dropped my toy in the forest." For a moment her eyes came alive and she looked right at Alex. "You found him."

"I found…" Alex licked his lips, which were suddenly parched.

"What?" asked Trish, her voice choking with emotion, with hope. "Did you find Sammy's toy?"

"*My* toy," said the girl. "You found him. I dropped Dopey Monkey."

For a moment, Alex wasn't sure. He had thought he found Sammy's unicorn. The toy that was so dear to the kid, a gift from his parents that he took everywhere with him. They had lost the toy the same day they lost Sammy. Everyone figured it had been burnt in the fire. But what if…

Alex saw himself picking up the unicorn, below, in the mist. But at the same time, he saw something else. In one flickering image in his mind it was the bright red unicorn. In another it was a bright red monkey, so detailed a picture that he couldn't have imagined it from nothing. Some people believed that God had blinked the universe into existence, *creatio ex nihilo*. Alex didn't believe that, but he *knew* he couldn't conjure complete toys from his imagination.

The forest. It twists everything from what really is to… to whatever it *wants you to see.*

He saw it again. He wasn't picking up a unicorn. It was an ape. Dopey Monkey.

But even then…

He looked at his good hand. Splashed with blood – some his, some the sheriff's, some probably from other victims of the madman – but otherwise empty. "Where did it go?" he murmured. "Either way, where did it go?"

Again, the girl's gaze became more present. "The forest took it. It takes things, and it gives them back… different."

"What does that mean, sweetie?" asked Trish.

The girl didn't answer. Instead, a moan issued up from below them. The sound made Alex shiver. The killer was still there. Alive.

And waking up.

"Is that…" Trish didn't finish the question.

Alex nodded. "Yeah." He rolled over, pressing himself up with his good hand.

"What are you doing?" Trish asked, her hands darting back and forth as though determined to stop him one moment, then not wanting to touch his wounds and hurt him the next.

"I gotta get down there."

"*Down* there?" she said. "Why would you –"

"Because he's tangled in the bars, but what if he gets *un*tangled? What if he wakes up and comes back up here?"

"We fight him. He's got to be hurt. He –"

"What if he's not?" said Alex. "You think you could fight him off? Or her?" he added, gesturing at the girl, who whimpered and pulled a bit tighter into herself.

"I don't know," said Trish. "But what are you going to do?"

Alex just looked at her. He didn't want to say the words, but the look in his eyes must have communicated his plan. Trish put a hand to her mouth. "You can't," she whispered.

"I can," he said.

"You could kill a man?"

Alex thought about it. Thought about pushing the killer off the ladder. Not in the heat of a pitched battle, but as a premeditated act. He thought about peeling the man away, and watching him drop and knowing he was dead at Alex's own hands.

He looked at Trish. At the many small wounds she'd suffered running through the woods. At the fear in her eyes. He looked at the girl, curled up on the floor of a watchtower that only allowed a vista of mist. Her hands opened and closed, and he somehow knew that she was holding "Dopey Monkey" in her mind. Clutching a memory of comfort and love.

He looked back at Trish. "Absolutely," he said.

Trish shook her head, and Alex opened his mouth to argue why it was the right, the *only,* thing to do. But she wasn't shaking her head at that. She wasn't fighting him on the necessity of the act. Just on how it had to be accomplished. "You can't do it," she said. "I will."

"No," he said automatically.

"You going to play gallant knight?"

He didn't know what to say to that. Because the simple fact was he *didn't* want Trish to go through it. He didn't want her to have the burden of knowing she had killed someone that way. It would stain her.

It would stain him, too, if he did it. But that was all right. If someone had to *be* dirty, let it be him. He would become –

("They're coming. They're becoming.*")*

– what he had to become if it meant Trish's survival. But he couldn't ask her to bear that burden.

"You're not asking me to do it," she said. "You *can't* do it, and it has to be done."

He hadn't said what bothered him, but she knew what it was just the same. She always did, didn't she?

She's so close. So much of the best of me.

And she has to be the one to do this.

He looked at the girl one more time. He nodded at Trish.

She kissed his cheek, then slid toward the open trapdoor. "Careful," he said.

"It's tricky. Even if you've done it before." Isn't that what Sheriff Azakh said, before a deranged lunatic put an axe into her brain?

He wanted to stop Trish. What if that happened to her?

He dropped the axe. He can't use it.

But he knew that wasn't the entire list of disasters that could happen. It wasn't even a big part of it.

Below them, the killer moaned. He still sounded out of it, but the moan was louder. He *was* waking up.

"Wait, Trish," Alex began, but she ignored him and disappeared through the trapdoor.

Moving as quickly as he could through his pain, Alex crawled to the edge of the trapdoor. The pain was still there, but buried in fear for what was about to happen. Not just fear for the act itself, but fear of what it would do to Trish.

She stood on the rungs just above the killer by the time Alex got to the trapdoor. The guy was about ten feet down, and Alex wondered why Trish had stopped descending. Had she changed her mind?

Then Trish shifted her weight and swung out into empty space. She *wasn't* changing her mind; she just couldn't do anything without going onto the other side of the ladder.

Alex's heart leaped so high it felt like it bounced off the roof of his skull, then plummeted into his toes. He almost cried out, but gagged the noise down, worried that any sound might surprise Trish, might make her lose her grip and fall.

Behind him, the girl whispered, "I lost my toy. I want my toy." She sounded a decade or more younger than the teenager she must be.

Alex didn't look back to check on her. He couldn't. Not with Trish now descending so that she was even with the moaning form of the killer. She climbed down to the closest rung where one of his legs had wrapped itself. She threaded one arm around the side of the ladder, through the gap just above the killer's leg. She grabbed his foot with her free hand and pushed.

Nothing happened. She pushed again, grunting a bit. The killer moaned as though in response, and Alex saw his wife shy back. She was going to fall, he knew it. She'd fall and then what would be the point of… anything?

She didn't fall. She switched her grip slightly, then moved her attention to the killer's other leg and foot, twisted around the ladder rung and the side of the ladder.

"What's happening?" he asked.

Trish looked up at him. "I can't get him loose," she said. "He's wedged in too tight."

The killer moaned. "Kill… stop it…"

"Get back up here," said Alex.

"I can try again."

"Just get up here!" he shouted.

The killer started twitching. "Has to end… has… to…"

Trish started climbing, moving fast. But she stopped when the killer moaned out another set of words. "Have to kill… have to… end… Mandy." Trish looked up, then started climbing again. He saw her lips move, and the mist drew her words to Alex's ears: "We'll save you, Mandy. I promise."

Alex hoped she wasn't lying.

34
(When Tricia Had Grown)

Tricia felt like she was in two places at once. Then three, then four, then a dozen. First she was here, now, hanging above a killer on a ladder so high she couldn't see the ground. The next place she was: in the forest, looking for Sam. Then she was in a car, turning over and over, her husband's and child's screams following her into darkness. She was at home, with her father – always so angry, so despairing, and at the same time so *empty*. She was at Tina Louise's Diner, she was…

… everywhere.

Then the strange sense of *everywhere, everything* dissipated and she existed only in a place where a madman wanted to kill her, to kill her husband, to kill –

"It's… Mandy," muttered the killer, or at least, she *thought* he said that. He sounded oddly peaceful, more like someone caught in the throes of a vivid dream than an unconscious murderer wedged into place against a ladder, and the words came out more like, "Ssssmand…"

"Trish, come on!" shouted Alex.

She held to his voice. Climbed toward it, like it was a lifeline every bit as sturdy and substantial as the ladder under her feet and in her hands.

He reached for her. She took his hand automatically, not even thinking about what she was doing or how it must hurt his wounds to stabilize her. Alex didn't make a sound, though he gritted his teeth and his eyes glimmered with barely contained pain.

"Sorry," she said.

"It's… it's okay," he managed. He looked through the trapdoor. The killer was silent, motionless again.

"He dead?" Tricia asked, surprised and sad to realize how much she hoped the answer was yes.

"Your guess is better than mine," said Alex.

The killer moaned again.

"So much for that," said Tricia. She turned to Alex. "What now?"

Alex looked almost surprised. "I didn't think much, really. Just wanted you away…"

Even as he said it, she could see him casting around for something to use against the man who wanted them all dead.

Because he lost a toy, too. He lost his own Dopey Monkey.

The thought was insane – though given everything that had happened since they came to this place, it was pretty low on the crazy-o-meter.

Alex stood and went to the table that held the radio. He tried to move it, hooking his good hand under it and then pulling. It didn't budge.

"Heavy?" she asked.

"No," he breathed. He looked under it. "Bolted to the floor. And the radio looks like it's bolted to the table."

Even in the terror of the moment, the ridiculousness of *that* penetrated. "We're in the only earthquake-proof lookout tower in the world." She giggled, then clapped her hands over her mouth, afraid of letting the sound continue. If she kept laughing, she might not be able to stop.

Alex grabbed one of the room's two chairs, grimacing as he dragged it over to the trapdoor. Tricia realized what he was doing. She grabbed the chair out of his hand, then the other one as well, and pitched them both through the hole in the floor.

The angle was bad. One of the chairs missed the killer below them completely. The other glanced off his foot, but obviously didn't do any damage. Alex went to the generator.

"Let me," said Tricia. He nodded and she shoved it over the side of the trapdoor.

It did less than the chairs. The weight of it slammed it down *too* fast, and it arced into the first rung, slamming into it hard enough to ricochet outward and miss the killer by a good five or six feet before it was swallowed by the fog.

No flashes. Nothing coming.

Small comfort, that. And she knew, somehow, that the reprieve wouldn't last long.

Alex was nodding as though he had expected no more. "Should we bother with the cork board?" he asked, gesturing at the bulletin board that leaned against a wall.

Tricia shook her head. "No. I think we have to get out of here."

Alex looked at her, then at the girl who hugged herself into a knot on the floor. "What about her?"

"We take her."

"I know that. But… how? Will she go with us?"

Tricia didn't know. She went to the girl and knelt before her. "Sweetie?" she said. The girl didn't respond. "We have to go," said Tricia, then added, "Mandy."

She expected the girl to moan or cry or just stay hidden away in her mind. Instead, the teen nodded absently. She didn't look like she had heard – her expression didn't change a bit from the vacant, shell-shocked stare – but she stood and moved to the trapdoor. Waited.

"I'll go first," said Alex.

"No way," said Tricia. "You're hurt –"

"And that's why I go first. Because I'm hurt. I might have trouble holding on."

Tricia didn't want to think of that, or of the implication that if he fell as the first one, at least he wouldn't bring Tricia or the girl down with him.

He looked at Mandy. "I'll go first, then you, honey, okay?"

She nodded again, though her eyes were still glassy, unfocused.

Alex looked at Tricia, and she saw the concern in his eyes. "We'll be fine," she said. Then, turning her gaze to Mandy, she added, "Won't we?"

The girl didn't answer.

Alex levered himself out so his legs hung down. For a moment he started to slide, and Tricia leaped toward him.

"No, it's okay." He stopped sliding and grinned a sickly smile. "Just had to find the ladder."

His shoulder, where she could see it through the tattered remnants of his shirt, was still weeping blood. There were some dark patches that had started to clot, but most of the cut was a wide-open slit that looked like a wet maw, opening and closing as it blindly sought its next meal. The hand on that side was useless, and she had no idea how he could get down the ladder.

He'll do it. It's Alex. He does what he has to do. He'll be okay.

Alex gave her one last attempt at a smile, then lowered himself below the level of the trapdoor. Tricia leaned over, watching him for a few rungs. He seemed to be doing okay, but he had to work one-handed, which meant that he would step down, step down… then let go with his one hand and then quickly slap it down against the next rung. A three-point anchor, which became two points and a weightless fall every few seconds before the third point held fast again.

Tricia's stomach roiled. She didn't want to look away – something whispered that the minute she looked away, Alex would fall; that he had only been held aloft this long because she held him fast in her gaze. But she also couldn't bear to see him falling a few inches at a time. Controlled falling, yes… but for how long? How long until sweat or blood slicked his palm and he slipped and fell and left her alone in this place –

STOP IT. Get moving. Don't waste what he's doing.

Tricia shut her eyes for a second, gathering her strength. When she opened them, the teen was staring at her.

For some reason it spooked Tricia. "Mandy?" she said.

The teen didn't answer. Her gaze went to whatever safe place it had sought throughout the night. Moving like an automaton, she sat and then began sliding toward the hole. Tricia held onto her arm, trying to provide support for the girl as she swung out into nothing before catching hold of the first ladder rung with her feet. The girl's muscles clenched at Tricia's touch, but she didn't shout or scream at her to let go or get away, so Tricia maintained her grip until the girl had lowered herself far enough that Tricia couldn't reach her.

Tricia's turn.

She rolled onto her belly, scooting backward, feeling her legs drop slowly into empty space, trying not to think of Alex falling, of Mandy falling, of *her* falling.

Or of the killer.

He has to be past him, right? Alex has to be past him.

Then she remembered, with a sickening sinking feeling, that she had had to climb around the side of the ladder to get to a place where she was even with the killer. It had almost made her vomit, hanging out into nothing – for a moment, the height seemed every bit as terrifying as the man she was trying to dislodge.

How would *Alex* do that? How would he get past the killer? How would Mandy get past this man who wanted so badly to kill her?

One foot found the ladder. She shimmied backward a bit more. Her feet dropped to the next rung. She pushed herself back still more, hanging just that much farther into mist and empty space. Her feet were both on the rung now, and they stepped down the foot gap to the next one. Now she was far enough that she had to reach down and grab the topmost rung with her hand. The other hand joined it and she looked down.

Surprisingly, both Alex and the girl had already passed the killer. He was moaning and twitching, but both of them had swung around the ladder, passed the madman, and continued climbing down while Tricia eased herself out of the tower.

Alex was far enough down that she could barely see him in the fog.

She abruptly remembered something. There was no sense of the understanding or comprehension that usually accompanies actual memory, though. Tricia saw only a quick flash: Sam, running beside her and Alex, three teens running in terror.

Then she saw only Alex with her. Sam was gone.

And if I don't see Alex now, the forest will separate us. If my husband drops out of sight, I'll never see him again. Just like we lost Sam.

She hurried. She wanted to yell at Alex to slow down, but the madman who still hung between them was making more noises. His limbs were twitching, movements like someone coming out of a deep dream on a hot summer day. "End," he moaned. "Just be… *over…*"

She drew even with the killer's foot. It was still trapped in the rungs, trapping him upside down.

Hope it hurts. I hope you broke your legs all to pieces.

At any other time, in any other place, she would have had no doubt that his legs were indeed broken; *shattered.* But not here. The forest didn't grant that kind of favor.

Lower. Looking at his shirt, bloodstained and torn.

Lower. Staring at the back of his head. He was facing away, and she was thankful for that, though it meant she was looking at hair that had matted with blood from the head wound that marked where he had hit his head on the ladder.

But whether she could see his face or not, Tricia's mind kept casting up images: the killer's eyes snapping open, looking around, sensing the prey nearby.

She kept going.

She was past him. Still close though.

Another rung. A bit farther.

Something tugged at her hair.

She dropped automatically, allowing herself to fall, knowing even before she looked up what she would see. She dropped a few feet, then jerked to a halt as she grabbed a rung with both hands, both feet finding purchase as well. She looked up.

He was staring at her. Reaching for her. She saw a few of her hairs clutched between the clenched fingers of his hand.

"I have to end it," he whispered.

"No you don't."

He started crying. Tears ran down his face – which in this case meant they carved bright streams toward his hairline. For a moment, it seemed like gravity was playing games. The forest's tricks weren't confined just to time and space and everything in between: the very gravity of the universe could upend itself in here.

"I do," he whispered. "You understand. You *have* to."

Something about the way he said that, so quietly and yet fervently, chilled Tricia to the bone. She felt like she would see her fingernails turning blue if she looked; that if she blinked, tiny icicles would shear away from her eyelashes.

Tricia lowered her head. She could still see the girl below her, but Alex was little more than a hint in the fog.

Tricia started climbing down, afraid again that losing sight of Alex would allow the fog to steal him away.

Just like Sammy.

Just like Sam.

Above her, she heard grunts and groans. Something bounced off her shoulder and she yelped and almost lost her grip. She looked down and saw a shoe, falling into the always-hungry mist. She looked up.

The killer had one leg free. It was streaked with blood, but it was free.

She looked down. "Hurry!" she shouted.

No answer came. She couldn't see Alex. She could barely see the girl.

I've lost him. I'll lose her.

Tricia hurried down. Faster and faster – so fast it was dangerous, definitely fast enough that she should have caught up with a semi-catatonic teenager or a one-handed man, wounded and bleeding.

But she didn't. The forest played its tricks, and the world distorted to its twisted design. Now she couldn't see anything below her but mist. She looked up and saw nothing but the fog there, either. She was suspended in a nowhere-land. Purgatory.

She shook her head. *Keep moving.*

She climbed down. Down. Down. The descent took longer than forever. She remembered something she heard kids say back in grade school: *I hate you infinity.* Followed invariably by the object of their ire responding, *I hate you infinity* plus one!

The kids said that in third and fourth grade. She knew it was stupid – not because they were wrong, but because they were *right* without knowing it. An infinite line, for example, if viewed as the total set of all its infinite points, well that number would be larger than the number of integers that belonged on that line. There really *was* an "infinity plus one," but these kids weren't invoking it that way. They just wanted to one-up each other.

She and Alex had made fun of it, sitting alone around the side of the building during lunch, comparing the contents of their brown paper bags even though they both brought the same thing as each other each day – a PB&J and a few veggies packed in Saran wrap. "They don't even know about cardinality," said Alex, and laughed. "Dummies."

"I know!" She laughed, too. "Trade you carrots for celery?"

She thought she knew the truth of "infinity plus one." But she didn't. Not then, not later in college, not at work, with access to the most advanced knowledge that science could supply. No, it wasn't until now, hanging in the middle of a mist that went forever up, forever down. The ladder never ended, did it? It was infinite, and the number of steps she would have to take to reach the bottom was infinity plus one.

"I hate you infinity plus one," she whispered. It sounded like a prayer on her lips, albeit one she didn't understand, to a deity she couldn't begin to fathom.

The forest. That's the only god here. Just the forest.

Then she stepped down – she had moved mechanically, without realizing it, her body continuing even though her mind had all but given up hope – and her teeth clacked together as she came down painfully a good six inches before she expected to. Not on a metal rung, but on dirt.

She looked around and saw Alex. "Thank you, God," he said.

"I didn't think you believed in – *oof!*" she said as he engulfed her in an embrace that, though one-handed, managed to push the breath out of her lungs.

"I'll believe in anything if it means I can have you," he whispered into her ear. "Anything at all."

A voice floated down through the mist.

"I… seeeeee youuuuu…"

The words, elongated to the point they were nearly howls, morphed to shrieking laughter. The killer. She couldn't see him through the fog, but she could tell he was too close for comfort.

The fog brightened. It was, for the first time, right on top of them. The flashes came centered on a point about twenty feet up. She saw the light, and the perfectly dark shadow-lines of the ladder, a hunched shape rapidly moving down the structure toward them.

The lights flashed again. Again she saw the ladder, the dark spine of the watchtower. Again she saw the backlit shadow of the madman, a parasite wriggling down the spine.

One rung closer.

Two.

He faded into the silvery light of the fog.

The mist flashed again.

The skeletal ladder.

And nothing else. The madman was gone.

"Where did he go?" asked Alex.

"The forest has him," whispered the teenager beside them. Her voice sounded dreamy – or maybe just haunted. "But it has us, too. Both of us, and it never ends in here, because it never really begins." She laughed, a sound disturbingly like that of the killer's deranged cackling.

"Let's go," said Alex.

"Where?" said Tricia. She looked up the ladder. "He's not up there, so we're safe for a second, aren't we?"

"No," said Alex. "I don't know if anywhere *is* safe, but I do know I don't want to stay here. I don't want to be anywhere that lunatic knows we've been."

Tricia nodded. She took Alex's hand, and with the other she grasped Mandy's. The girl's hand was limp, unresponsive, but when Tricia pulled her she came along willingly enough.

They ran into the fog. As they did, Tricia felt something tickle the edges of her conscious thought. A string. A bit of information that, if she could just catch hold of it, would unravel all that had gone on here. That would let her remember all that had gone before –

("Doodles."

"You came for me!"

"Just die. Just die *and let everything never begin again.")*

– and so also understand all that was happening now.

She was running away. Running from the watchtower and… and…

It was gone. The thread pulled out of her fingers before she could grasp it, tug it, pull apart the veil over her memory.

The lights flashed.

Alex slowed. "What is it?" said Tricia.

"It's… something."

She felt it in that instant as well. *Something*.

Something was going to happen.

Something was going to come for them.

Something was going to kill them all.

And, because it was the forest, and none of the rules applied... maybe whoever it was would keep on killing them forever.

That was when the worst thought invaded her mind. The thing that shook her, and made her want to start screaming, and even – for just an instant – made her understand why she had forgotten what happened all those years ago.

What if it's already happened? What if the wraiths aren't the ghosts? What if we *are?*

35
Revelation
(When All Has Become)

I have been thinking a lot about revelation. About what happens when the curtain is torn aside and we see what really *is.* No biases, no ideologies. No false notions, no beliefs that color the facts. Just a pure definition of reality.

Definition: from the late fourteenth century word *diffinicioun* (or *definicion,* depending on who you ask; I always ask myself, for obvious reasons). Either way, it means a setting of *boundaries*. A determination of *limits*.

But what if reality is a thing eternal? That would mean it has no limits, cannot be defined. It is circles and spirals, turning into themselves over and over and never ending. You follow one revolution to its terminus and discover only one more circle beyond – or, worse, you find yourself back where you began. In that case, truly, J.M. Barrie was right: all of this *has* happened before, and it will all happen again.

So… reality. Eternal. Without boundary. Without definition.

But human beings require definitions. We need them to create a kind of power: knowing where something ends means knowing where its limits are; knowing, specifically, how badly it can hurt us before it ends. Whatever *it* is.

That is why, I think, so many of the prophets worked out their salvation in fear and trembling and all that. Assuming that they really saw Eternity (capital E-eternity!), they saw… everything. Which means they saw a thing of no definition. Ultimate power. Alpha and Omega – not meaning "the beginning and the end" in the sense of "once upon a time" leading to "and they all lived happily ever after" and then closing the book. No, Alpha and Omega meaning that if you reach Omega you find yourself at Alpha again. If you stand at point Alpha and turn around, you do not see Alpha-minus-one. Or rather, you do, and it is Omega.

Circles, circles, circles. I see them everywhere.

I have received revelation.

The curtain has been torn away, the veil lifted. I have seen the beginning from the end, and the end from the beginning. It has made me insane, it has made me sane. It has energized me, it has enervated me. It kills me and then makes me live again. It has given me all knowledge and none at all.

Because *I* am Alpha and *I* am Omega.

Two bodies, two *people*, cannot exist in the same place at the same time, no matter how brief the overlap.

And I do not simply *believe* this.

I *know* this.

I have *seen* the truth of this eternal, irrevocable fact.

Yet at the same time, I am the beginning and the end, and round and round the mulberry bush (or the misted trees) we go, followed by the ghosts and wraiths that never quite step out of the mist.

Yet those ghosts and specters they are real. They see us, just as we see them. That, too, is part of the eternal, endless madness that is the only reality.

I cannot believe what I have done. What I *will* do.

But no matter what, it will happen. It will happen over and over, and perhaps some of the details will change, but there will be constants. There will be scars borne by all, there will be wounds suffered at our own hands, and blood we save and blood we spill. Jesus suffered for us all, then asked us to take up his cross. Which meant he suffered for us, then asked us to suffer for him, which meant we suffered for ourselves. Round and round we go, merrily merrily merrily.

I used to laugh about the idea that Jesus was a god. But now, I'm not so sure. Maybe he was. Maybe *He* was. It's entirely possible, because what if… *He* was *Me*?

I am all.

I am none.

That, you see, is why this is *my* story. Because all stories in this world are mine. I am endless, without defining or bounding, either on the right hand or on the left.

I will do this thing. I will touch the stars with my works, and create them in me. For I am a god, and so I have become also Death, the *creator* of worlds.

I know I am insane.

But I know it with the perfect discernment that only a truly sane man or woman can possess.

I don't know if I am the first, or the last. But what I do now makes it all irrelevant.

FOUR:
IN THE BEGINNING

36
(When Tricia Was Young)

Tricia felt the branch hit her; felt the pain as it pierced her shoulder and the strange numbness that came with it. She wanted to sink into that numbness. She wanted to surrender to nothing and float in the mist and *become* –

(*"They're coming. They're* becoming.*"*)

– mist herself.

She heard whispers.

"… Alex…"

"… get out of here…"

"… Tricia…"

"… get out…"

"… Sam…"

"… in this Hell…"

"… people don't stay dead…"

They sounded so real, so close. And that meant she was dying. Because when the ghosts sounded this real, didn't that mean you must become one of them yourself?

She heard something, a cavalcade of dry *snaps*, and managed to turn her head toward it.

She saw Sam. Face shining with sweat and terror, running toward her and Alex. And behind him, there was Sam's mother, swinging the blade she held.

The light pulsed.

The whispers surged, but this time Tricia couldn't hear anything. It was just a mass of noise, like the biggest party in the biggest city in the world. So many whispers that they seemed eternal.

Sam's mother's bright, terrible knife plunged toward her son's back. She was too close. There was no way she could miss.

The mist swallowed them both. More than swallowed – *consumed* them. It happened in total silence, a silence so loud that she felt but did not hear Alex go crazy for a moment. She felt his strong body, his strong arms that had pulled her from the tree –

(I'm the man in the tree, Daddy!

Stop it. You're insane.

See my guppies?

DON'T.)

– go rigid as he realized what she did: that mist or not, fog or not, Sam was dead.

And in that instant of realization, of revelation, she heard him scream. It was a shriek of terror and pain so perfect, so exquisite, that there could be no lying. Only a death-scream could be heard in the silence of the forest.

Alex turned to her, and she wondered why. Then she felt her own body straining, and realized that she was screaming, too. She couldn't hear it through the twilight mist and the silence that blanketed her world, but Alex could. Alex could hear her shrieking in pain – pain for a punctured body, pain for a punctured heart.

He always knew what I felt better than I did.

I love him.

The last realization, firm and clear, did not make everything all better. That was the stuff of movies, of romance books. But it *did* make her stop screaming. She fell back into the silence of the forest. Then Alex spoke, and sound returned to the world. She heard her own labored breathing, the shifting of leaves and the soughing of the wind, the life-breath of the forest.

"I have to get you out of here," Alex was saying, panic running his words together so they came out in a single breath. "Can you run? She's out there, she's coming, I know it, but I don't know where or what she'll do."

He spun around, searching for the woman who had killed her son, had killed *Sam.*

("Thank you," he said when we found him. "Thank you for coming back for me." But it wasn't enough, was it?)

Alex went rigid. He had done that already – too many times, too many moments where shock stilled his body – but not like this. He felt like a statue to Tricia. A corpse, riddled with rigor.

We're both dead. We're the whisperers. We've... become.

Light flashed in the mist.

Then Alex did something strange. He put his hands over her eyes, like she was a child in a movie that had suddenly become a bit too scary for comfort.

And he started to scream.

He had fallen into an abyss of terror, so black and deep she didn't know if he would ever resurface. And because of that, he didn't cover her face completely. He wanted to shield her from what he had seen, she knew that, just as she knew that given the choice he *would* have protected her, fully and completely, from the monstrosity that walked from the parted mist.

It had the height of a human, but the resemblances with *H. sapiens* ended there. It was a jumble of jutting limbs, wobbling along on a trio of legs that protruded from its center in all the wrong angles, while another leg extended from its back like a misshapen tail that flopped about as the thing moved. Its spine twisted impossibly, and she saw ribs that extended out through the flesh of its torso, shards of bone that curved outside its skin, glinting almost metallically.

Two of its hands reached forward, and it *screamed*. Not from the contorted head that stuck out of a scarred shoulder joint – a head where the mouth and eyes and nose numbered too many, where the tongue waggled loosely from its perch outside the thing's head. No, it screamed through the mouth embedded in the palm of one of its outstretched hands.

White bits fell from that mouth.

Teeth. It's screaming out its own teeth.

The screams ceased. The monster continued vocalizing, but the noise had a cadence and rhythm that made her feel like it was *talking* to her. Its voice – if it could be called a voice – was as insane and sad and horrible as its screams had been, but they had an undeniable intelligence.

"Ih-hz-soond-Ih-nnnn-ear-ih-nnnn-aow..." it wailed. The tongue fell from its mouth, and the sounds dissolved into a terrible, meaty *"uhng-uhgn-ughn"* as it step-staggered toward her and Alex.

The mouth on the head that extended in a lopsided, ungainly sack from the creature's shoulder opened and began to scream as well. This sound was deeper than the other, the two of them singing a song that Tricia knew she would never forget, not even if she lived to be a thousand years old.

And yet, she had to see it. She had to hear it. She had to *witness* this –

(becoming)

– moment. She pulled at Alex's hand, still clapped ineffectually over her face. She yanked, pulled, but his hand stayed there, stayed there...

The forest's lights brightened and died.

The creature was there, but disappeared along with everything else in the dark.

The whisperers came again. Not whispering this time, but *screaming* – a single high-pitched, almost girlish scream, as though even the specters feared the monstrosity the forest had birthed.

But when the light came again...

It was closer...

Darkness fell. Light flared...

It was closer still...

The mouths shrieked...

Alex was no longer screaming, just going, *"Ah, uh, ah, uh,"* in an eerie mimicry of the monster's "words"...

Closer...

The thing's hands reached out...

The fog billowed…

Tricia knew this was the last moment. She tore Alex's hands away, and for a moment she felt no pain, no fear. This was the end, so what was there *to* fear?

Without fear, she knew, she would finally see.

The fog twisted, curled. Tendrils of mist writhed across the creature as it lurched toward them. The tendrils joined, tying themselves together, then thickening, becoming sheets of mist that fell over the creature. The thing howled, then the last tendril writhed across the gaping mouth in its still-outstretched hand. The thing became a dark blob in the fog, then a shadow, then a hint…

… and then nothing at all.

Silence again. Not the strange, *loud* silence of before. Just silence as she had always known it. Empty, calm.

The mist still surrounded them, but there were no more flashes of light. No more shadows darting in their periphery, following in their footsteps, hunting.

No more whispers, no more whisper*ers*.

Alex stared into the space that had held the abomination, and now held only dead leaves and broken sticks and the mangy patches of shrubs that covered the ground. A long time seemed to pass.

He looked down at her.

"Help me," she said, her voice tiny and quivering.

It was an odd thing to say, in a way. Shouldn't she ask what they had just seen? Shouldn't she be asking what they would do now?

But no… just a simple plea. That was enough.

Maybe it's ending.

Alex nodded. She felt like he was answering her thoughts. She hoped so. Hoped he felt what she did: that it was over. Or at least, *nearly* over.

Alex looked at her shoulder, grimaced, and then pulled her to her feet. The pain that had been absent now came back to her, centered in the red-hot spot at her shoulder, but it coursed through the rest of her body as well.

"We have to get out of here," said Alex.

A strange groan/laugh hybrid escaped her. "Really?" Then the vestige of humor withered and died. "Where's Sam?" she asked.

"I don't know where Sam is," said Alex. He looked like he was searching for something to say next, for some sentence or phrase that would make all this make sense. Finally he just said, "Gone."

For a moment, that wasn't enough. For a moment, she wanted to scream that they had to keep going, had to keep looking.

Then she remembered the way Sam had looked as his mother plunged the knife down.

She remembered the savage look in his mother's eyes.

She remembered the finality with which the mist closed over them.

And knew Alex was right: even if the two of them made it out of here, Sam wasn't coming out of the forest with them

Alex saw her face. He read her thoughts in the way only Alex and – to a shorter but not necessarily lesser extent – Sam had ever done. "How are we going to find our way out of here?" he asked.

"Pick a direction," she said.

He nodded and took a step, her arm over his shoulder, bearing her weight. Another. Another.

He looked at her. "Okay?" he said.

She nodded. He stepped forward again, but she planted her feet. He looked at her, an eyebrow cocked, wondering why she had stopped.

She kissed him.

It was a fast kiss, just a brush across his lips. But his eyes lit up even in the midst of the madness and – true to form – the forest took the small moment, the mist twisted it into an eternity. A sweet island in the middle of the stream of pain and loss.

They parted. She smiled. "I'm okay," she said.

Alex looked a bit confused – befuddled, maybe. She almost laughed at the expression. So cute, so endearing. She would remember this moment, she knew. She was hurt and afraid, and didn't know what was going to happen next. But for some reason those pains and flaws only heightened the perfection of this fleeting, forever moment.

Alex grinned. He turned forward again, then took a step. He had Tricia's good arm over his shoulder, bearing a lot of her weight – maybe most of it. What happened next shouldn't have surprised her, but it did: he tripped over a root.

They had tripped so many times in this long day/night/twilight, but for some reason this one felt like a particularly malicious move by the forest. Like it should have seen them, clutching each other, using one another for support, and should have respected that unity.

A small shout of surprise came from Alex as he fell. The world seemed once more to slow down – another warping of reality courtesy of the forest – and Tricia saw that Alex's trajectory would take him right into a fallen log. A branch poked out of the side of it, one that ended in a sharp point, and though she didn't think he noticed it in the instant of falling, she saw it clearly.

Images flashed through her sped-up mind: Alex impaling himself on the branch, piercing his shoulder just like she had; of Alex falling against it throat-first and tearing out his jugular and carotid; worst of all, an image of Alex twisting as he fell, tumbling into it and the sharp point spearing through the back of his skull, going through his brain, and then emerging through his face, pulverizing it.

Alex can be me, or Alex can be the new man in the tree.

NO!

Alex had been holding Tricia's good arm over his shoulder as they walked, but let go automatically when he started to fall, trying to stop her from tumbling down with him.

Her body didn't care what he was trying to do, though. Her body wanted to save *him*, so even as he loosened his grasp, she tightened hers in an attempt to stop him from falling – or at least guide the fall away from the tree.

Pain exploded in her shoulder. She moaned, but didn't let go. Alex tried to shake himself free – he didn't care about falling, he just didn't want to drag her down – but she clenched her teeth and pulled harder as her own wounds tore anew.

She had a moment to think, I don't think my lung's punctured after all. Lucky!

Then the pain in her shoulder increased by an order of magnitude as she hit the ground, followed swiftly by Alex's entire body weight falling on top of her.

She screamed now, finally. And just as before the forest had stretched time like taffy, taking a fraction of a second and pulling it into what seemed like hours, now it compressed the moment. Gray blobs exploded at the edges of her sight, then turned into black balls that danced across her vision and then melded into darkness that covered her eyes. An instant, a forever. She didn't know.

She felt Alex roll off her.

Darkness. She heard him saying something. Or did she?

A flash of light. Silvered fog. Shapes in the mist.

Whispers. Whisper*ers*.

She was hallucinating. She had to be, because Sam was dead, but she heard his voice nonetheless. "Alex?" said the dead boy.

Light flashed, darkness came, light returned. She felt/saw/heard Alex turn in place. Still nearby, but now looking away from her.

"How?" Alex managed, and then Sam's voice said, "Alex, I think I –" before a snapping noise interrupted him and Alex screamed, "Sam!" and then darkness fell one more time, and no light shone beyond it.

37
(When Alex Had Grown)

Alex ran forever. That was what it felt like. The mist-light had robbed him of any sense of time or place, so whether he passed through a millisecond or a millennium he couldn't say. Sometimes he ran in front, holding Mandy, dragging her along as she held onto Trish's hand and dragged *her*. Other times Trish ran in front, the order reversed. Sometimes he wasn't sure *who* ran in front – or if they were even there at all.

He felt that sensation of dissolving into the fog.

Becoming.

What did that mean? He thought Trish was talking about the whisperers when she said it, but now… he wasn't sure. What could the things out there *become*? Was there something worse they could be?

The light flashed. He sensed movement, turned, and heard Trish scream.

The killer was running toward them, the fog parting to allow a quick glimpse before cascading over him again. But Alex could still hear him shouting: *"Maaaannnnnddddyyyyyy!"*

The fog parted, and Alex blinked. The killer was still hurtling toward them, but now he was… different. He seemed smaller, farther away. And he wasn't holding an axe now, he was holding something else. Small, but –

The fog whispered over the madman.

Mandy screamed and tore away from Alex's grasp, wheeling around in fright. He tried to tighten his grip, but when she yanked at him the vibration of it ran through the long gash that ran over his shoulder from his back to his chest and his fingers loosened automatically.

"Wait!" Trish screamed.

Mandy didn't wait. She ran.

Alex and Trish started after her. They were both in pretty bad shape, he knew, but hopefully they could get to her; could help her the way they hadn't helped their friend or their son.

She was fast, though. She ran like she knew the forest, dodging around trees and under branches with an agility that Alex envied. Before, she had been as clumsy as either he or Trish, obviously as much a stranger to this place as they were. Now, though, she ran like a deer through its woods, like a person who knew every inch of this forest that had no end.

Alex realized then that he was running the same way. Leaping over branches and brushes that could have would-have-could-have-*should*-have tripped him up. So was Trish. She didn't run, she *danced*. She flitted over the bushes and roots, dodged around trees as though she were a creature of fae, a thing born to the mists and the nightmares.

The end was coming. The end of… whatever this was. He was being led to something, drawn by some force he couldn't see and catapulting him from his world of science and facts and truth into a world where all was mutable.

Nothing was real here.

Which meant everything had the potential to exist.

The flashes came faster, faster. Shadows flitted everywhere, so thick that at times he could see nothing but darkness, covered only by a thin scrim of silvered light.

He lost sight of Trish. He found her again.

She was dancing, leaping over branches like someone who has spent her existence doing that –

(the darkness closed around her…

… opened again…)

– she was tripping now, the darkness had caught her and she was falling, beautiful, graceful, terrible –

(the darkness closed…

… opened …)

– now it wasn't Trish he followed but Mandy, looking back at him and screaming like he was trying to kill her but he wasn't he was trying to save her save them all and –

(darkness…

… light…)

– the light flared, so bright it became his world. The darkness was gone but he was blind, all the same. Pure darkness was the complete absence of light, the photons bouncing in and not bouncing out. Nothing to reflect to the eye and give it something to interpret.

But there was too much light, now. Too much light, too much to see and nothing to understand and –

(darkness…)

– something hit him. For a moment he didn't know where he was, or even *what* he was. He was not Alex, he was only the light and the mist and the eternity they contained.

Then he hit the ground. Rolled. Something gripped him as he tried to rise. Threw him down. He tried to get up again, but felt a knee slam down on top of his chest. Still he writhed and twisted, but a fist slammed down on the wound that wrapped around him, front to back. He felt a finger or thumb press the wound, then press *into* it.

He screamed. The scream finally drew back the brightness, and let him look away from the undefinable, unending lunacy of the forest. He saw a face.

"Trish?" he said. It was her. Why was she –

The face flickered. Madness withdrew a bit more. He saw who was really over him.

The killer. He had lost his axe, but now he held a knife, held in one hand high over his head while the other burrowed into Alex's flesh and kept him paralyzed with pain.

"I have to do it. Have to kill you all, then I die, too. It's fair. I'll kill myself, it's fair."

Alex struggled. He twisted in spite of the inferno that raged in his chest and back. Or maybe it was *because* of that fire. He bucked in rage and pain and the killer's fingers popped out of his wound as the killer fell forward.

The madman posted, his bloody hand driven to the ground beside Alex's head. The knife came down, too, driving into the earth beside him. It was bloody, and seeing it, the fight went out of Alex. Because the blood was either Trish's, in which case she was dead, or it was Mandy's; and Trisha was *still* dead, because there was no way she would have let the killer get to the teen without dying first.

"I'll make it quick," said the killer. "I deserve that much, at least, don't you think?"

And Alex saw, as his brain began to misfire with grief and terror, that there was something tucked into the waistband of the killer's pants.

A red, tufted thing.

An ape, staring with one eye. The other was gone, the place where the button had been a ragged mass. Dirt matted the little toy.

Trish is gone.

Mandy is gone.

The forest took them all.

The knife fell toward him and…

38
(When Tricia Had Grown)

... Tricia, who was so like Alex in so many ways, had been running away from him. Away, because she was chasing Mandy, who ran away from her as though she was the thing that wanted to hurt her.

She's going to lose me.

Tricia couldn't let that happen. The mist-flares and the darkness that ruled between them had become a constant. A blinding flash, a blinding darkness, and she could see only bits and snatches of the world around her in the picosecond of twilight between those extremes.

Yet she continued to run. To chase Mandy as though, if she caught the girl, she might also be able to catch the others who had left her.

Her friend.

Her child.

Her husband?

She stopped, suddenly and completely.

Mandy was gone. Whether to the darkness or to the light, Tricia could not say. But there was no following her. And why had she tried? Really? There was a girl out here, but her *husband* was here, too.

The light flashed, darkened. Blinding brightness, impenetrable darkness. The beginning and the end, with her caught in the middle.

But isn't that where I'm supposed to be? Isn't that what life is? We're all caught in an instant between before *and* after, *and so all we have is* now.

With that realization, she understood. The forest might take all from her, might steal it away and make her lose her life and –

(Become.)

– maybe worse. But it had given her this at least, this moment where she saw what she had lost, and what she might still lose before it all came together and night fell in the forest. Or maybe before dawn began.

She had to find Alex. She had left him alone long before she left him to run after Mandy. Because she'd been running after Sammy before that; and, to a lesser extent, she'd been running after Sammy's namesake. She'd run after Sammy, she'd run after Sam, and she'd lost her husband as she did.

Tricia turned a slow, silent circle. The flashes kept coming, though it wasn't the brightness that coaxed tears to life and make them run down her cheeks in an unbroken stream. It wasn't the light, it wasn't the dark – just how fast they came, one after another.

She turned, turned, turned.

And she saw Alex, running. He was passing her, unseeing as he ran. She had gotten turned around – though she couldn't say when it happened – and was now following him. She ran after *him*, and saw him performing almost balletic maneuvers as he followed/fled his way through the forest.

Then he stopped, and spun in place. His mouth was wide open with surprise, delight, terror, understanding, confusion. Every expression she had ever seen on his face was there now, all at once. She wondered if he was experiencing the same realizations and sensations she had undergone. She wondered if he had been running from her as she ran from him. Maybe he had been as broken by loss as she.

The killer burst out of the forest.

One moment he was nowhere to be seen, and it was just Alex standing between the tall, unblemished trunks of what looked like the hugest trees in the forest.

The heart *of the forest.*

(Remember?

You were here once before.)

The killer ran for Alex, who was spinning in circles, not seeming to see through the dark-light-dark of the place. Tricia tried to shout for him, to cry out. She wasn't fast enough. She felt that feeling usually peculiar to the ever-never-time of night terrors: her tongue bound itself, rendering her speechless; her legs pumped as hard and as fast as they could, but she was moving slowly, so slowly, *too* slowly.

The killer hit Alex. Drove him down to the forest floor. Alex struggled, then shrieked as the madman jammed his thumb into the gaping wound on his shoulder.

She was still running, but slower and slower. Each time the light snuffed out was like a barricade she had to blast through. Each time the darkness disappeared became a wall she had to climb.

"I have to do it," said the madman to her husband. "Have to kill you all, then I die, too. It's fair. I'll kill myself, it's fair."

Alex bucked his hips up with a cry. The killer, atop his chest, was thrown forward. His free hands planted on either side of Alex, but not for long before he posted up and Tricia realized for the first time he was holding a knife high above his head.

He seemed even farther away. Even smaller. Alex, though, seemed bigger somehow: her terror for him pulled him close, made every detail of his face and body stand out in ultra-high def down to the very pores. He writhed, and shook, the killer atop him in a grotesque mockery of lovemaking.

She thought she saw something at the killer's side. A tuft of red.

In the madness of it all, she thought for a moment it was Sammy's toy. Then she saw another bit of red and realized that the knife the killer held over his head, about to slam into Alex, dripped with crimson.

Alex is here.

I'm here.

And that means he found Mandy. It's her toy tucked into his waistband, her blood on his blade.

Tricia's heart, already aching from the strain of her run, now seemed to stop.

The fight went out of Alex, too. Every muscle in his body seemed to slacken.

"I'll make it quick this time," said the madman, the killer, the *murderer*. "Don't I deserve that much, at least?"

The lights made everything surreal. The forest's strobing lights, its *pulse,* sped up more and more here at the heart of it all. The killer raised his knife a bit higher.

Blink – higher.

Blink – higher.

Blink – the killer stabbed down.

Blink – something *hit* the killer.

A body hurtled out of the forest, and just as Tricia had thought the toy the killer held was Sammy's before realizing it was Mandy's, so now she thought Sammy bolted out of the forest. A Sammy as he should have been: not the bright little boy he had been, but the teen he should have *become,* and just as she had imagined.

Only this person's clothes were torn. Bloody.

His hair was matted.

He was beautiful more than handsome. His features finer than she would have thought. Because it wasn't her son. She had lost her son – he had been *stolen* from her – long ago. No, this was Mandy.

And that, now, was enough.

Mandy slammed into the killer with a snarl. She was small, but young and strong and the force of the blow was more than enough to knock the killer aside.

They both rolled, bodies twisted together so closely they seemed bonded at an atomic level; it was hard to tell where one ended and the other began. Then the bond loosed, a strange fission producing two smaller objects where only one had existed before.

And just as with any fission, a burst of energy seemed to push back the dark-light-dark, the mist that waxed and waned. Tricia felt her body return to normal speed, her mind regained control of her tongue.

"Alex!" she shouted. "Mandy!"

The run to this point had been a flight through forever. But time contracted as well as expanded in the forest, so in only two steps Tricia was at Alex's side, helping him up. He shouted, but pushed up with her help, the two of them hurrying because there was Mandy, struggling to her feet; and there was the killer, already on his feet, already slamming the knife in the girl's direction.

The light flared again.

One great –

(Final?)

– beat of the forest's heart. And with it, Tricia *remembered.*

This is where it happened before.

Sam's mother.

The heart of the forest.

The monster.

She looked at Alex. Saw understanding come over him, too.

Both of them knew what had happened before, here, in this exact spot in the forest; they remembered a monster, and finally understood where it had come from.

She knew her husband stood beside her. Physically, yes, but also in a way that he hadn't been – or that she hadn't *let* him be, or some mix of the two – for a long time.

She ran.

Alex ran.

They ran *together*, and as they did, Tricia remembered Alex's phrase:

All this has happened before…

… and it will all happen again.

39
Interlude
(When Sammy Was Young)

Sammy is hurt.

He is afraid.

He has blood on him, all over his neck and chest and his shoulder. He thinks it is his blood.

And then the devil-angel who pulled him from the dark and the heat after the car crashed said a bunch of things Sammy didn't understand.

Now, the angel-devil jostles him. Sammy's shoulder explodes in pain, and he screams so hard and loud he thinks he'll never stop.

But eventually, he does.

Eventually, he forgets.

He enters a place that, like the angel-devil, is both dark and light. It is a strange place, and the pain that made him scream drifts away. He actually forgets it.

It happens to everyone: people forget. People are *forgotten.*

But for one brief moment before that last forgetting comes, he opens his eyes and sees where he is.

The forest.

40
(When Alex and Tricia Begin to Become)

Alex ran with Tricia,

Tricia ran with Alex,

both of them
ran
toward the man
and
toward Mandy.

Alex threw himself
forward and up,

Tricia pitched herself
at the killer,
aiming low,

just as Trish flew at
the killer's feet,

at the same time as
Alex went high,

and together they
collided
with the killer
and drove him
into the spot
they had seen
a monster,
so many years,
so many eternities,
before.

Alex gasped, his mouth

opening into a wide "o"
of shock,

Trish gaped, one hand
covering her mouth
in disbelief,

even though they both
guessed
the next of
the forest's tricks.

But even guessing what
would happen,
he flinched and
gave a yell as

Because even guessing what
would happen,
she flinched and
shouted as

the mist
closed
over the killer.

Alex didn't
look away, though.
He watched

Tricia didn't
let herself
look away, though, from

the fog,
the *mist*,

as it
separated,

letting him see
the past,
the present,
and the future,
all of them
combined at

allowing her to view
what was,
what is,
what will be,
all of them linked at

this moment,
which happened,
and happens now,
and will happen again.
Forever.
In the forest.

41
(When Alex and Tricia Begin to Become)

Together, Alex and Tricia both saw the killer, stumbling back.

They both saw the mist flicker, and in that instant they could see something else. A flashing, overlapping image.

A madman with a knife.

A madwoman with a knife.

Both raised their weapons.

Both stumbled as they flickered.

They were apart in the light.

They fell back in the dark.

Alex and Tricia heard a loud, horrific scream. In a night of screams and terror, this one shriek stood above and below them all. It was the beginning and the end of horror, the alpha and omega of pain.

Two bodies cannot exist in the same place, at the same time. Not even, it turned out, in the forest.

So the forest took them.

It took the woman.

It took the man.

It bound them together as a monster.

Tricia and Alex fell back. Not with fear for their lives, this time, but in disgust at what had been done – at what *they* had done.

The thing – with too many heads, too many limbs, too many bodies – fell more than stepped toward them. The flickering light of the forest fell over it, and it disappeared in the darkness –

(disappearing to a past where they had seen the monster before)

– then reappeared again, in this place, in this *now,* a bit closer.

Mandy was screaming in terror.

Both Alex and Tricia wanted to comfort her, but couldn't find the words.

The monster was screaming, too. Two screams, one from the mouth on its misshapen "head," the other out of the mouth like an angry slit in its outstretched palm.

White things tumbled from one of its mouths. Teeth.

It reached forward and its screams shifted.

"Ih-hz-soond-Ih-nnnn-ear-ih-nnnn-aow…" it screeched in its high/low voice, before that sound, too, fell away and shifted to nothing but the grunts of a dying animal.

Its back arched, twisted impossibly far. Like a stick, twisted in a stream. Ribs jutted from its skin. Some of them broken in pieces, some of them glinting like the blade of a knife or an axe.

The mist-lights brightened, and the monster was there.

Darkened, and it was gone.

Bright, dark, bright, dark, there, gone, there, gone, closer, closer, closer…

The thing's gait faltered a bit more with every step. Even in the forest, two things – at least, two *living* things –could not occupy the same space in the same time, because to let it happen would be a twisting of nature beyond what that branch could stand, and so the bodies of the madman and the madwoman had been twisted together, tips of toes to temporal lobe, brain to balls. The ribs Alex had broken when he kicked the madman were there, clinging to the outside of its chest rather than the inside, broken even further by the twisting of two moments and two people into one, melded with the metal of the knife and axe the madman had carried, had lost, and which now still shone in the mist-lights.

It was an impossibility made flesh, though that flesh was corrupt and, Alex and Tricia could see, quickly dying.

More shadows appeared in the mist. Several stood near to Tricia and Alex, so close that either could have reached out and touched them if they dared. The shadows said no words, but seemed to chant in time with the monster. Nonsense sounds, that a young Alex had made so long before, watching this moment from the other side of the mist: *"Ah, uh, ah, uh."*

Closer…

The thing's hands reached out…

The fog billowed, seeming to reach for the monster, tendrils of vapor like the curling vines that climbed some of the forest's trees. Where the mist touched the monster, its skin blackened and sloughed away, its muscle melted like hot wax.

The creature broke free of the grasping mist. It took one last, awkward, ungainly step.

It fell.

It hit the ground hard, its grotesque mass driving it to the earth with a dull but substantial *thud.* It took a last gasping, rattling breath through the mouth on its head, then the mouth on its hand breathed that air out.

And then it did not move at all.

The strobing stopped. The mist hung motionless and silent.

Then the monster moved again. Before either Tricia or Alex could run or scream or both, they realized that its movement was different this time. It wasn't lumbering to its feet or coming after them. It seemed to collapse into itself, like a balloon slowly deflating.

A moment later it looked less like a balloon than a puddle. It became a gelatinous, mottled mass of darks and lights, almost translucent at times. The mass settled still further. It burst along the sides, and ichorous fluid oozed out. The fluid settled into a pool on the ground, then the pool flashed and became something like glowing dust.

The mist surged forward and swallowed it whole. The dust flew into the mist, hovering as bright sparkles for a moment, then the sparkles diminished and disappeared, one with the vapor where they had finally come to rest.

The fog hovered there a moment. It flashed, then withdrew again, leaving only empty earth behind.

Tricia and Alex looked at each other. "Is it over?" said one. The other began, "I –" but then the mist flashed.

The forest had one game yet to play.

The whisperers were back. Only a few, but the mist curled and danced and in that moment both Tricia and Alex saw their old friend, Sam.

He was just as they remembered: wearing the same shirt buttoned to the collar, the same red backpack with its books that had delighted them all and pushed them to learn new things.

Alex and Tricia ran toward their lost friend, both aware as they did that the whisperers beyond Sam also rushed toward him. A race between the living and whatever *things* lived only beyond the curtain of mist.

They ran, and the shadows flowed. Converging on a single point, and somehow both Tricia and Alex were aware that whoever reached Sam first would possess him, truly and completely, forever.

Sam turned toward the shadows. He was going to them. Going *away*.

Someone ran out of the mist. Not a shadow this time, but someone *real*. A figure with a dark green jacket and khaki pants, a broad-brimmed hat perched atop the head. The person had appeared in a spot closer to Sam than Alex and Tricia, closer even than the shadows beyond.

The mist curled around Sam. He began to fade behind the mercury wall.

"No!" shouted Tricia, while Alex screamed, "Stop!"

Sam turned toward them, and they reeled. It *wasn't* Sam. They had both seen their old friend, they *knew* they had. But how could they have seen him, when it was Mandy who now stood before them?

The figure that had appeared out of the mist leaped forward so fast he was a blur. A hand grabbed Mandy's shoulders and yanked her away from the shadows that had sought to take her.

As everyone watched, those shadows coalesced into a single form. The person who still held Mandy whispered something into the mist, toward the *thing* that sought to take her.

The wind blew.

The mist drifted away.

The shadows drifted away with it.

For the first time since the strange, otherworldly fog had come into the forest, bright, *natural* light pierced the gloomy gloaming of the mist-lights.

The person who had pulled Mandy away from shadow turned and faced Alex and Tricia.

And they stared into the eyes of Sheriff Julie Azakh.

"You fell," said Alex, and Tricia said, "You died."

They had seen Julie's head nearly chopped in two by the killer in the watchtower. They had seen her keel over and slip through the trapdoor. They had heard her fall, ricocheting off the ladder and the tower's supports.

But, they now realized: they hadn't heard her hit the ground.

And when they climbed down, they had been pursued by a madman. No time to look around. No time to investigate. Even so, one more thought ran through both Tricia's and Alex's minds (and though the wording was slightly different for each, the substance was exactly the same):

We didn't see a body, did we?

"Damn," said Julie. "What a day this is turning out to be." The words were quiet, meant only for her, but both Tricia and Alex heard.

"He's dead," said Mandy dully. "The man who chased us – my dad – he's dead, isn't he?" Then, with hope: "Isn't he?"

"Yes," said the sheriff. She looked at Alex and Tricia, taking both of them in in a heartbeat. "But things don't always stay dead in the forest, do they?"

The words electrified the air. Alex and Tricia felt them – this was real truth, and one more piece of what was happening, what they were starting now to remember, fell into place.

Cracks and crackles sounded nearby, the sounds of something making its way through the forest, and Alex and Tricia realized that they had already turned to face the place the sounds were coming from – and that they had done so *before* the sounds came.

Alex and Tricia could remember papers they had written and read years before. They could write pi to a thousand places and recite entire books verbatim. But that kind of memory was nothing compared to what they felt now.

They were starting to truly *remember* what had happened in the forest when they were young, and to understand what was happening now that they had grown, and what *would* happen as they continued to…

… become.

Mandy let out a small moan as she turned to look toward the source of the cracks and crackles, obviously terrified at what might be coming from the trees *this* time. But Alex put up a hand and said in a calm voice, "Don't worry," and Tricia finished his sentence, knowing what he would say just as *he* had known she would finish his words: "It's one of *us*."

Julie looked at them. "Your eyes have been opened," she said.

"And they're beginning to see," said Doc Brown as he stepped out of the woods, followed by two people with heads of hair that were peculiar shades of red: Tina Louise and the unseen man she called her brother. "They're becoming," Doc Brown said, then he looked at Alex and Tricia and continued, "Aren't you?"

42
Revelation
(When All Has Become)

I thought I was God, I thought I was Alpha and Omega.

But I look upon what I have wrought and I cannot say, *"it is good."*

It is a horror.

I have tried to stop it. I have tried to take it back. Billions of ways, with millions of faces, in quadrillions of times and quintillions of places.

Everyone, parents and children, lovers and friends, said it could never be done.

They were wrong, though. And now they are gone. The others are gone, and there is nothing beyond this moment, because they all said it *could* never be done rather than the only thing that mattered: that it *should* never be done.

But I did it. I didn't tell anyone else, not even the person I love most in the world. I just *did* it.

And it went so… very… *wrong*.

So many things ended, so many lives and loves truly *lost* – which is so much worse than simply ending.

But I can fix it. I can do it again, and do it right. Because I am all, and all is me. I am Alpha and Omega, the first and the last. I am God, and…

… and oh, God, what have I done?

FIVE:
CIRCLES

43
(When Alex and Tricia Begin to Become)

For a moment, Alex and Tricia *knew*. The forest could do that. In this place, you could remember what you had forgotten and, sometimes, could remember even things you never knew.

But that was fleeting. It came and went like mist.

For a moment they knew everything.

Then the wave of memory, the unforgetting of things unknown, receded. The fog came in again, both in their minds and in the forest itself.

Doc Brown looked at the fog that curled and thickened. Shadows appeared beyond it, but he seemed unconcerned – about them, at least.

"You have to move," he said. "Or the timing won't be right…"

(And memory flows again: Tina Louise in the back of her diner, arguing with her brother, snapping, "No you won't… Because the timing has to be just right or it'll happen too early or too late, and then what happens, huh?"

And then, Sheriff Azakh, who is dead and yet not dead, keeps them for long hours, interviewing them and taking "notes" that, Alex and Tricia realize, are not notes at all. She just needs them to stay; needs them to be there until she looks at the clock and says, "I think that's about it." She glances at a wall clock and says, "It's time I let you go." Then she looks again and says, "Best get a move on," not because she needs to do a report that will never be filed, but because the timing has to be right.

She had known they would be there. Just like Doc Brown did, with his black bag that held the ice pack he knew Tricia would need. No reason to bring such a thing to examine a corpse, but he knew she had been hurt. Perhaps he had somehow seen or even lived *through that moment before.*

It was all for them, all so Tricia and Alex would enter the forest at the right moment and then –

The memory fades. The fog curls in.)

Julie nodded. She turned and began running into the forest. Tricia and Alex followed, knowing somehow that they should.

They ran only a few steps, though, before Mandy shouted in terror, "Don't leave me!" The shout became a shriek as Tricia and Alex turned back to see Doc Brown and Tina Louise's brother wrestle her to the ground. Doc Brown had a hypodermic ready, just like he had had the ice pack ready. He plunged it into Mandy's neck and she went limp.

Alex and Tricia knew they had to follow Julie. But they knew, too, that they must protect Mandy. They stepped toward Doc Brown.

He looked at them. "It's just something to help her sleep, and to forget." He shook his head. "Ignorance can be bliss, and sometimes it can be survival." Something approaching fear flashed over his expression. "Now go! Go or we all die."

Julie ran. Tricia and Alex followed. The fog curled around them without ever quite touching them.

"Stay close," said Julie. "We're in a pretty stable corridor, but you don't want to wander far or you end up in the stream and it's hard to find your way back to the right place at the right time."

("I fell into the stream," says the sheriff in the watchtower, when they ask how she came to be in this place.

Then memory – or perhaps the forest itself – takes Alex and Tricia into the cabin, where Sam's mother is babbling, "Some things change in the forest. But other things stay the same because I won't let me change them. Or maybe the universe won't or maybe it will or maybe it won't or maybe it will, row, row, row your boat," then singing, "gently down the STREAM*!"*

And now Tricia and Alex know that neither the sheriff nor the madwoman speak of the water that bisects the forest. They speak of the stronger and, in the forest, much more erratic stream of time.*)*

Julie sped up suddenly. Alex and Tricia, forgetting once more, wondered why Julie had put on the sudden burst of speed.

"Why… so…" panted Alex.

"… fast?" finished Tricia.

Julie shook her head. "Because *you* have to see it. But *I* don't want to."

Before Alex or Tricia could ask what Julie meant by that, they saw a tree they knew well.

"This was where…" began Tricia.

"… we saw the man in the tree," said Alex.

Julie said nothing. But the fog spoke, in its way. The mist curled around the tree, and Alex and Tricia saw shadows at the base of the tree. Two shapes in the mist. One began climbing.

(The shadow – Tricia, when she was a child, watched by the older Tricia, the Tricia who is becoming – climbs carefully but quickly, worried she will fall but knowing this is her and Alex's best chance to find a way out of here.)

The shadow-Tricia climbed, the shadow-Alex watched from below. And the now-Tricia, now-Alex understood that just as they saw the children as shadows, so the children would see *them* as the same terrifying wraith-creatures.

The now-selves realized as one: *The ghosts we saw were – are, will be –* us. *Every word we heard the whisperers speak as children, we said as adults when we returned to the forest. Every word we heard as adults is something we said as children.*

We haunted ourselves.

We *were the whisperers.*

Now-Alex, now-Tricia watched as the shadow climbed, higher and higher. Then the shadow disappeared. The *tree* disappeared. In its place – the same place in space, though later in time – a watchtower appeared. The now-selves watched as a madman climbed up. A moment later, a body came plummeting down.

Julie.

She fell into the fog, and the time-stream swept her away, even as she continued to fall. The tree that *had* been grew to meet her as she fell *down* through space, and fell *back* through time.

Julie fell, and died in the tree. A boy and a girl saw a man in a tree – but how could they know it was not a man at all, but a woman wearing a thick jacket that seemed to add to her bulk, her axe-split head hidden by the mangled skull and face shredded by the branches of the tree.

Alex and Tricia looked at Julie. She was hunched over.

(Their eyes open further.

They see Julie's close-cut hair in the town, the night they meet her. It is brown, beginning to gray, just as it is now, as they follow her through the forest. Their sight flickers, and now they both remember her under the watchtower, even though Alex was not there when it happened. "Sorry," she says to Tricia. "I forgot about the lock." She laughs and says, "Can't seem to think why." She lets go of the ladder and pushes back her hat, revealing her short gray hair.

Not graying. Just gray.)

Alex and Tricia stared, now in shock. "You know when you die," said Alex.

"You've seen it," said Tricia.

Julie nodded.

"Why would you go in there?" said Alex. "Why would you –"

"Because it has to be done," said Julie. "Because some things matter more than what we want. Some things *have to happen*."

"Why?" asked both Alex and Tricia as one.

Julie's only answer was to begin running again.

Tricia and Alex ran after her.

They ran, and saw shadows running toward them, they saw themselves young, running from the wraiths that were them grown older. They saw themselves only hours before, running from the shadows that seemed to hunt and track them. Both times, as teens and as adults, Alex and Tricia had followed similar paths, so at each time, the shadows seemed to dog their steps.

Some of the shadows that now-Tricia and now-Alex saw came closer than the others. They resolved into faces that were familiar, though it took them a moment to recognize them: the man who had watched from the window of the business that offered to do taxes, *"Se habla español"*; and the old woman from the place that sold "TOOLS." She was wearing the same straw hat she had worn then.

The sheriff hailed them. "You found them," said the tax man.

"Have they –" began the TOOLS woman.

"No, not yet," said Julie, looking at Alex and Tricia. "What time is it?"

The old man looked at his watch. "A bit after one in the morning. You?"

Julie looked at a watch on her own wrist. Alex and Tricia realized that both were exactly the same, with a strange, octagonal design they had never seen before. "It's almost three for me," said the sheriff.

"Do you want us to keep looking for Alex and Tricia until you find them?" said the TOOLS woman.

Julie shook her head. "No, you already know me and my group will find Alex and Trish, so you can head on back to

Sundown. But if you run into my group, don't tell us – me especially – you found me later in the forest, or what time we're going to find Alex and Tricia."

"Of course not," scowled the old woman. "You think we don't know the rules?"

The tax man peered at Julie. "Are you okay, my dear?" he asked.

Julie smiled tightly. "I just saw…"

"Your fall," said the old man. "I'm sorry. I know that's always hard on you." He looked like he would have said more, but instead he drew back. "Come on, Heather," he said to the TOOLS woman.

They walked away and disappeared into the trees. It wasn't that they walked far enough away for Alex and Tricia to lose sight of them, but rather the fog reached out and took them away to another, earlier *when.*

Alex and Tricia felt conflicting emotions. They reeled under all that was happening. They felt relief at finally –

(Becoming.)

– understanding what had happened to them as children.

And yet, as it turned out, they understood very little. They made the mistake of thinking they were smart, and were about to find out how very stupid they were, and how painful it could be to have the comfort of ignorance torn away.

44
(When Alex and Tricia Begin to Become)

Julie kept running, but not so fast. She glanced at her strange watch, and slowed still further. A few minutes later, Alex and Tricia heard the burbling bubble of water. The sheriff led them toward it, and soon they saw the small stream that had been one of their only reference points – not that it did much good.

The sheriff jumped over it. Alex and Tricia moved to follow, but something made them stop. A wisp of fog curled along the stream, following its course, then reversing and going back.

Julie nodded. "It should be safe now."

Alex and Tricia jumped the stream. "Why is this place different?" asked Tricia.

"Who says it is?" said Julie, almost chuckling. "This is where the center of the gate is. The center, the beginning, the end – those are the points with the most crossover."

(Memory waxes strong. Understanding flows.

Alex and Tricia see the stream as it appears to be, and more importantly as it is. *A raging body of water one moment, a near-silent trickle the next. Flowing one way, then the other. Changes that would take eons take, in this place, the time between the opening and closing of an eye. Rapids come, rapids go. Rocks that have stood there for millennia remain, others are there and then gone in an eyeblink.*

The river shifts. The things inside it shift. And things that come from outside it can be caught up in the changes. They can feel the shifting currents, they can be caught in the rapids. In the worst cases, they can be twisted to pieces like a twig.

Alex and Tricia see their shadow-selves, confused in that time at what they have seen. Their now-selves also see something else. A flickering, glowing thing, another shadow, this time of what will be crafted here, that is so massive it defies description. Neither Alex nor Tricia can make it out fully. It is just a hint, a trace. Not even *a shadow, but a shadow of a shadow.*

Understanding wanes, though less than before. The becoming is anchoring to them. The understanding remains stronger each time…)

"A gate," said Alex.

"Through time," said Tricia.

"Yes," said Julie. "Three points where it's strongest. The point of entry will be –"

"At the spot where the watchtower now is, where the tree once was," said Tricia. It wasn't a guess.

Julie nodded. "And the exit will be –"

"Where the cabin stands," said Alex.

(There are two places where time has been more than shadow. Where things have not just hinted to each other, but torn each other apart. One is the watchtower, where Julie had fallen/now falls/will fall and been torn by a tree that overlapped in space but not in time. The other is the cabin, which was a patchwork of cabins that overlapped so tightly that they had compressed and melded together.)

"But why us?" said Alex.

"What do we have to do with this?" asked Tricia.

"Everything," said Julie. "Everything, and every*one.*"

"That doesn't make sense," said Alex.

Julie smiled tightly. She stopped jogging. "It will." She looked around. "We're here. We're then."

They had reached the road that stretched between Sunrise and Sundown.

The fog began to thicken.

"Get ready," said Julie.

45
(When Alex and Tricia Begin to Become)

As teens and then as adults, Alex and Tricia had spent hours walking through the forest. They had walked countless miles to find the stream, and more to find the cabin. But that was when they walked alone, and walked not only through space but through time. They had fallen "into the stream," and now walked with a guide who led them around the fogs and mists of time, and that made all the difference.

The fog thickened, and shadows flitted into and out of sight. Tricia and Alex could see themselves at different times in the forest when they focused on the mist.

"Listen up," said Julie. "Because what I'm about to tell you is the most important thing you'll ever hear, and maybe the most important thing *anyone* will ever hear."

Alex and Tricia reached for each other. They squeezed their hands tightly together, drawing strength from the person they loved.

Julie saw it. Her eyes grew sad.

"A few years from now, you two are going to be part of a team that discovers time travel. You'll determine that going back is dangerous – too many paradoxes, too much chance of wiping yourselves out, or changing history in some way that makes what you've just done impossible."

"We don't even do that kind of thing –" began Alex.

"You will," said Julie. "Trust me." She looked at the road, appearing to listen for a moment. She looked at her watch. "You and your team, the four of you, will make a jump. Five minutes forward on the first try. You anticipate no problems going a few minutes forward like that – you figure you'll just disappear from the space-time stream for a few moments, and reappear five minutes later. So you program the machine, you go in the entrance."

Something came to Tricia. "The circles. On the trees."

Julie nodded. "They're the logo of the company you and your team own. Fractal Circles."

"Who was the man who tried to hurt Tricia?" said Alex. "Back in –"

"Later," said Julie, her voice suddenly harsh. She took a deep breath, and checked her watch again. "You go through the gate, the four of you. When you come out, you discover something's very wrong. Your teammates come out just when they should – five minutes later. But you two," said Julie, gesturing first at Tricia, then at Alex, "don't come out at all."

"We die?" said Alex. He squeezed Tricia's hand. She squeezed his back.

"No," said Julie. "You're alive, the other two manage to confirm that. But they can't narrow down *when* you ended up."

"What do they do?" asked Tricia. Her voice was hushed, almost reverent.

"They do the stupidest thing possible," said Julie. She sighed and closed her eyes. "They try to *fix* it."

"How can that –" began Alex, then his eyes widened.

Tricia realized what the problem was at the same time. "They go back to before they traveled the first time. They try to stop it from happening – to save me and Alex *before* we're lost."

Julie nodded. "And the trouble begins. It doesn't work. You two still end up going. You still get lost." She shrugged. "Some things can be changed. Some can't."

(Again, that sense of understanding. Memories of the past, leading to understanding of the future. A madwoman, whispering in a cabin in the forest, "Some things change in the forest. But other things stay the same..."

And the man who attacks Tricia in Sundown, then tries to stab Alex in the same shoulder that the killer will gash with his axe, the same shoulder that Trisha wounded so many years before, the lunatic screaming, "It's going to happen. Now or later, it'll happen. Some things don't but other things do. Things stay the same, even when things don't stay the same.")

Alex touched his shoulder. Shouldn't he have bled more? His fingers probed beneath the tatters of his shirt and found, instead of blood and a gaping wound, an old scar long-healed.

Julie nodded. "The forest does some strange things. Especially to you and Tricia and… your team. You're like temporal lightning rods."

(And they remember the times that events have stretched, or compressed, or seemed to do both at once. The forever-times that they walked to school together, the mile to school seeming much shorter and much longer. They thought about the minutes in classes that ticked on far too long. They thought of all the love and the closeness they had developed over the course of only a few days with a new friend.

But a few days could be one thing for someone normal, and quite another thing for someone who had ventured/does venture/will someday venture into the forest.)

"Why?" said Tricia. "*Why* are we lightning rods?"

Julie looked at the road again. The fog was thickening still further. It flashed. Tricia's and Alex's hearts quickened. They could almost hear each other's thoughts:

We are becoming, and something is coming.

"The other two on your team keep trying. They keep going back, then going back again. There are dozens of them, hundreds. They overlap, they go backward and forward. Sometimes they come through the gate *different.* Little changes sometimes – blue eyes become brown, curly hair becomes straight. Sometimes the changes are bigger. The other members of your team are a man and a woman, but –"

"You keep talking about this team," said Alex. "But who –"

"But sometimes," said Julie, ignoring him, "they come out of the gate as two men. Sometimes two women. Still *them,* essentially. But also changed. They remember always being the way they are when they come out. A man comes out a woman, but the woman *knows* she has always been a woman."

"How is that possible?" asked Tricia, dumbfounded.

Julie shrugged. "We think that some of it is just an effect of folding space-time. You fold up a piece of paper, you unfold it, you fold it up again, you unfold it. The paper can start to get torn, the integrity weakened. If you've written something on it – a history of your life, for instance – the ink might smudge."

"That's some of it?" said Alex. "And the rest?"

Again, Julie hesitated. "We think sometimes… sometimes we think it's something some of the iterations your team members do on *purpose.*"

Alex's jaw dropped open. "Why would they do *that*?"

Julie's look grew exquisitely mournful. "For love, at least at first. They don't find you, and don't find you, and don't find you. So the other two members of your team, the iterations of them that are obsessed with finding you two, think, 'Maybe it's not *Alex and Tricia* that are lost so much as *me* that can't find them.' Then the answer is obvious: if it's me that's the problem, if it's me that's not smart enough, or the right me to find Alex and Tricia, then I'll change me."

"People can't *change* their own gender," said Tricia. "I mean, they can, but not eye color or hair or –"

"It can be done *in utero,*" said Julie.

"But that's imposs –" said Alex.

"People can't travel through time, either," said Julie. "But a great many things once thought by the knowledgeable to be impossible have *always* existed, and are being discovered anew every day." She laughed. "It's pretty easy, actually, if you know how to do it. Just a powder stirred into a drink, and an X-chromosome becomes a Y, simple as that. You can even give it to someone without them noticing, if you want to change the pregnancy and they don't."

The fog had reached its thickest.

Alex and Tricia started hearing a rasping hum. They could tell Julie heard it, too, because she cocked her head.

The hum grew, and with it Alex's and Tricia's understanding grew also. "The other members of the team," said Alex. "Who are they?"

"One is Mandy," said Julie.

"And the other?" whispered Tricia.

The fog flashed.

The hum grew, *surged*. A shadow raced down the road.

Julie stepped into the road, right in front of it, just as the shadow solidified and turned into a car that Alex and Tricia knew well.

The car turned to avoid the woman that had appeared in front of them. It skidded, and flipped over once, twice, three times, before ending up on its roof.

Something *popped*, something inside the overturned car crackled, and flame flickered to life.

Alex and Tricia could not believe what they were seeing. They stood still as Julie ran into the road and yanked the door open. She reached into the car and dragged out a form, then another.

Alex. Tricia.

She reached in again, and this time pulled Sammy out.

Alex and Tricia – *now*-Alex, *now*-Tricia – watched it happen. They couldn't move. Not even when they heard screams, not even when one of the *then*-people rushed at Julie. Not even when the car exploded and, as it did, the car and the fire and everything else disappeared.

Only not quite everything.

Julie was still here with them.

She was whispering to the little boy she held in her arms. He was asleep or unconscious. But even insensate, he still clung tightly to his red unicorn.

"Meet the other member of your team," said Julie, and held out Sammy to his mother and his father.

46
(When Alex and Tricia Begin to Become)

It was a dream, far sweeter and more lovely than any dream had ever been. Alex and Tricia kissed their child, smothered him with love even as he slept. "Will he be okay?" Tricia asked Julie, somehow knowing the answer even before Julie nodded and said, "He's just asleep. And it's best he stay that way right now."

"Why?" asked Alex. "We should wake him and –"

"No," said Julie. "Let him sleep. Let him dream good dreams even though the nightmare is beginning around him."

"Nightmare?" said Alex.

Julie closed her eyes as she spoke. "I'm going to tell you a story. Then I'll tell you why it has to happen, why it has to come true." She looked from Tricia to Alex. Neither of them spoke.

Julie nodded. "You'll take Mandy into your home. You'll never mention any of this again. She won't remember much, either. The forest…"

"… can make you forget things," said Tricia.

"Yes," said Julie. "She'll forget most of what's gone before, and she'll love you as her parents. You won't be her parents in actuality, though – which you *will* make clear to her. That's why she'll end up falling in love with Sammy, and he'll fall in love with her."

Alex frowned. "They're too far apart in age."

Julie shook her head. "Sammy's a genius. So, as you'll discover, is Mandy. The age difference will matter less and less."

"Okay," said Tricia. "So they fall in love. That's not a nightmare, though, right? Sounds like a good thing."

Julie gazed at her like you might look at a precocious, but naïve, child.

"Mandy and Sammy will study physics. Time. They'll ask you to join them. You'll found Fractal Circles, and build the gate. You'll go through. Sammy and Mandy will come out. You two –"

"Won't," finished Alex. "You already told us that. But if our children are fine, then…" He looked at Tricia who nodded. "Then we don't care what happens to us."

"You should," said Julie. She smiled tightly. "They try to find you. They try and try, and sometimes things change. On one of the tries, they bounce back farther than they intended, farther than anyone has yet gone, and for some reason they can't come back. They're stuck. Marooned in a version of the world where they can't seem to find any more of the selves they have created with their endless jaunts through time."

"How far back?" asked Tricia. "What would –"

"Marooned," said Julie. "But that's all right. They are in love. They have each other. They move to Sunrise – it's the place they know best. They struggle for a few years, but eventually they're happy. They hack into government computers – easy for super-geniuses from the future – and give themselves new names and identities. They have children, whom they name after their parents. Tricia and Alex."

As their names were said, Tricia and Alex felt a chill sweep them. Tricia held Sammy so tightly he groaned.

"Don't hurt him," said Julie quietly. She reached out and, with infinite tenderness, stroked Sammy's cheek, though she didn't look away from Tricia and Alex as she did so. Continuing, she said, "Eventually, Sammy and Mandy realize that their children aren't just named after their parents…"

The chill Alex and Tricia had been feeling intensified.

"… not just named after them," said Julie. "Their children, little Alexander, little Patricia… they *are* their parents."

47
(And Once Become, Become Undone)

"No," said Alex hoarsely. "We won't. We –"

"Why would we do any of that?" said Trish. "We won't let it happen, we –"

"You *will let it happen!*" Julie thundered.

"Why?" asked Alex and Tricia at the same time.

"Because of that first jump," said Julie. "That first trip where you two go in but don't come out."

(Alex and Tricia remember the monster. The broken ribs that curve around the outside of the thing's body, grasping both the male and the female of it, binding them together as it staggers and falls and turns to ooze and then to dust and sparkling embers, then to nothing as the fog takes it away.)

"Ashes. Dust," said Alex. He looked at Tricia. Sam was asleep still, clinging tightly to his mother. There was blood on his shoulder. Because in the forest, some things are destined to happen over and over.

Tricia said, "Dust," and looked at her son as well. She looked at Julie. "His shoulder is hurt," she said, and touched her own shoulder. Her own scar.

Alex touched his scar, too.

"Who is Mandy?" Tricia said. Or maybe it was Alex. Did it matter anymore?

"Sometimes things change," said Julie. "Sometimes they stay the same." She began to shrug out of her coat. "Sometimes they tweak things, and instead of Sam, there's a Samantha, though she prefers to be called Mandy." She unbuttoned her own shirt, too, enough to bare her shoulder. "We're all scarred," she said. "It's one of the things that happens every time, to every iteration. Something hurts us, pierces us in the shoulder. Red things show up a lot, too, and none of us – none of the iterations of Sammy, none of the iterations of Mandy – know why. The universe has a sense of humor, perhaps."

"You're…" Alex couldn't finish the sentence.

"I'm Samantha, all growed up," said Julie. "One of her, anyway. Every time one of me goes through the gate, it changes something. But the old versions of me don't disappear. Some of us keep looking for you – not *you,* but the versions we lose that first time. Some of us stop, and have their own lives. One of me founded Sunrise, actually. One of Sammy founded Sundown. One of Sammy grows up to be Doc Brown, one of Samantha grows up to be an old woman who sells tools – though mostly they're really watching, making sure that this moment can happen. That Sammy and Samantha can find each other in this place, at this time."

"Why would anyone want this to happen?" Alex asked again.

"Some of us – some of our iterations – ask that same thing. Some of us go crazy. They might try to kill you –"

(The madman in Sundown, who bore the Fractal Circles tag. He was/is/will someday be Sammy. He was/is/will be their son, in one form or another, after one or two or three or ten thousand walks through the gate. He will change, like a copy of a copy changes. The temporal flux will alter his eyes, his hair. They will drive him mad, and he will try to kill his mother so that he will never, can *never be born.)*

"Even your own parents," said Julie –

(Our own children, *think Alex and Tricia.)*

– and, after licking her lips, Julie continued, "will have their doubts from time to time."

(Guppies taped to a door. A genetic experiment that forces a family tree to branch less and less, creating beautiful freaks, too much for Tricia's father, who will someday be born as her son, who sneaks into her room and stops the experiment, then relents and repents the next day while the pets are still hanging from the door, because he knows that all this has happened before, and it must *all happen again...)*

Julie shook her head, anguish in her eyes so full and deep that Alex and Tricia realized she was feeling every bit of the pain they were.

("Shouldn't someone else be taking our statements?" says Tricia. "Someone not... involved?"

The sheriff tries not to laugh, because everyone *is involved. Julie is Samantha, iteration number 8,162, as near as any of her other selves can figure out. Her husband is Sammy, of the same iteration. "Well, there's my husband, who has the same job I do, but we don't get along and generally try to avoid being in the same room with one another." It is true, but also a lie. She and her husband get along well. They struggle with their reality. Brother-sister, husband-wife, grandmother-grandfather. The family line turns into itself, tighter and tighter. It is disgusting, an incest of the like never known. Most of the time Julie can stay away from that man who is so closely related to her.*

But sometimes she can't. Sometimes her husband comes to her in the night, and though she knows it is her grandfather, her brother, herself with but a single chromosome shifted, she takes comfort in him. She loves her husband like Alex loves Tricia. She loves him, temporal lobe to tips of toes, brain to balls.

She loves him, physically and mentally, because he is and always will be, like Alex is to Tricia, like Tricia is to Alex, the thing that is easiest to love and easiest to hate: he is herself.)

"We won't," whispered Tricia.

But Alex knew she would. He knew her so *well*. She was his sister, after all. Sister, lover, friend. She was his grandmother, and one more thing…

"The monster broke its rib," said Alex.

"Yes," said Julie, peering intently at him.

"And it was Sammy and Samantha. The crazy man with the axe, the insane woman with the knife."

"Iterations," agreed Julie. "They stole other iterations of themselves, thinking to end it all. One stole her husband away when he was five. One stole his wife away when she was five. They followed such similar paths."

("Some things change. Some things stay the same.")

"And because they were lightning rods, time and space bent and brought them here, to this forest. To us."

Tricia looked at Alex.

Brother, grandfather. Lover. Father of my child – my children.

She loved him. He loved her.

She hated him. He hated her.

"Why will we do this?" she asked.

Alex was always the one – the iteration – more prone to flights of fancy. That was why he made the connection first. But Tricia would have as well, sooner or later. They were so much the same.

"Because a rib was broken. A man was created from a woman, or a woman from a man. They were brother and sister and father to infinite iterations," said Alex. He looked at Julie. "Right?"

She nodded. "You've figured it out. Your eyes are opened."

Tricia got it. She looked at Julie. "When we go into the gate, when we're catapulted backward and don't come out…" she gulped. "How far back do we go?"

"To the beginning," said Julie. "You are brother and sister. You are father and mother. You have been all these things for so many iterations."

"Are we the first ones?" said Tricia.

Julie shook her head. "When you have broken infinity, there are no firsts, no lasts. There are only points on the circle. One is here, now. Another is later, at the gate. Another is farther around the circle, so far in time that it becomes *earlier* again. You land at that point – later for you, but *before* anything any of us have seen."

Julie touched Sammy again. Softly. Lovingly. She looked at Tricia, then at Alex. "You are the mother and father of all of us. Not just the iterations, but *everyone*. You slingshot back through time to a place where there is no human alive. You are the first, just as in this place, you are the last. You are Alexander and Patricia, but someday, far in your future, far in this world's past, you will be known as Adam and Eve."

Tricia knew what Alex was thinking. Alex knew what Tricia was thinking.

They both spoke the words. "Why?"

"Because all human life has sprung from us, in one way or another. All human life belongs to us, and so we must care for it and protect it. My lot is to protect you, over and over, as many times as I can; and one day, my lot is to die here, protecting you. Yours is to walk this path with eyes wide open, and know that one day you will be the beginning again, because you chose not to let yourselves be the end."

No one said anything further. Tricia held Sammy as long as she could. She smelled his hair, and it was just as she remembered it being. The smell she loved hadn't changed.

Alex reached for his child. Tricia passed him over, and Alex held his son, his grandfather, his descendent and his progenitor.

"What did you say when you saved Sam all those years ago?" said Alex, remembering his friend jerked out of harm's way before his mother could kill him.

"*Was* that you who saved him?" asked Tricia.

Julie shook her head. "No, I saved *Samantha.* I saved myself, in iteration. Just as my husband saved your son in another iteration." She smiled. "But we both would have said the same thing. We're so very alike, you know."

"I know," said Tricia.

"I know," said Alex. "But what..." he began.

"... *did* you say?" finished Tricia.

Julie smiled. "I said the words I hoped would be true. The ones that give me hope this is all worth it: *it will all be all right in the end.*"

Trisha nodded.

Alex nodded.

In his sleep, little Sammy nodded.

A few minutes later, Doc Brown and Tina Louise and her own brother/lover/husband/father or whatever iteration he was came from the forest. Mandy – Samantha – walked unsteadily between them.

She saw Alex and Patricia, and her gaze lit on little Sammy. "He's hurt," she said, her voice still slurred. "What happened?"

"Everything," said Alex.

"Nothing," said Tricia.

No one asked any more questions.

They stood at the edge of the forest for a long time. Which, in the forest, was a very long time indeed.

And which, in the forest, was no time at all.

A REQUEST FROM THE AUTHOR:

If you loved this book, **I would really appreciate a short review on Amazon (or anywhere else you'd like to post it).** Just click the book's product page, then go to where it says, "Write a review" and let others know what you thought of the book.

Ebook retailers factor reviews into account when deciding which books to push, so a review by you will ABSOLUTELY make a difference to this book, and help other people find it.

And that matters, since that's how I keep writing and (more important) take care of my family. So please drop a quick review – even "Book good. Me like words in book. More words!" is fine and dandy, if that's what's in your heart.

And thanks again!

HOW TO GET YOUR FREE BOOK:

As promised, here's a goodie for you: sign up for Michaelbrent's newsletter and you'll get a free book (or maybe more!) with nothing ever to do or buy. Just go to http://writteninsomnia.com/michaelbrents-minions to sign up for your freebie, and you're good to go!

*

FOR WRITERS:

Michaelbrent has helped hundreds of people write, publish, and market their books through articles, audio, video, and online courses. For his online courses, check out http://michaelbrentcollings.thinkific.com

*

ABOUT THE AUTHOR

Michaelbrent is an internationally-bestselling author, produced screenwriter, and member of the Writers Guild of America, but his greatest jobs are being a husband and father. See a complete list of Michaelbrent's books at writteninsomnia.com.

*

FOLLOW MICHAELBRENT

Twitter: twitter.com/mbcollings
Facebook: facebook.com/MichaelbrentCollings
YouTube: youtube.com/MichaelbrentCollingsAuthor

ACKNOWLEDGMENTS

I usually do the acknowledgments with a thank you to various people. A few who are always there: the members of the Collings Cult (my street team and some of the coolest people in the universe); and my wife.

They are both named in this one, as always. But I have to especially thank my wife on this one. In many ways *The Forest* was my most ambitious project to date, and my sweetheart made it possible. Her suggestions on every book are welcome, helpful, and kind without sparing me honesty. On this one, they were *beyond* important. If it weren't for Laura, this book would be a red-hot mess. Maybe it still *is*, but that one's on me. So anyone who enjoyed the book, please give a bit of a hat tip to my wife, who kept me from looking stupid. If you hated the book and think I *did* look stupid, then it's my fault. Laura did her best, but you can't blame Michelangelo for failing to build perfect sculptures using a mix of Silly Putty and used chewing gum.

This may sound like false modesty, but, to reference something I heard once: at least I'm smart enough to know how stupid I am.

A big thanks, too (on the subject of my stupidity) to the following people, who keep me from looking dumb. Too dumb. Too much dumbly. Ack! Okay, here they are (and please note they didn't help me on the Acknowledgments, so that's why I look much more dumberesque here):

A special, enormous, Big Gulp-level thank you to Julie Castle-Smith, who has helped me time and again, and did a yeoman's work in catching mistakes in *The Forest*, even if she can't spell "dilate" correctly.

Another enormous thank you goes to Julie Balla, who went above and beyond the call of duty by sending a bunch of notes about things that didn't work, and who helped polish the final product until it shone. Or is it shined? I'll have to check with her.

Logan Kearsley also deserves special notice, for getting this one done early (finally!) and, more importantly, for being a huge help and a great cheerleader.

Christine Morgan and Malina Roos: you are both Ladies of Amazing. Not only for putting up with (liking?) my early work, but for being some of the greatest examples of grace under fire and dealing with the extraordinary in ways that humble me.

A big (huge huger hustest) thanks to my Collings Cult, my friends and street team, who work so tirelessly to find mistakes and to spread the word about my books. Indie authors have no marketing team, no public relations group. Or, at least *I* don't. But I do have the very best street team in the world. They are a part of my success that I cannot understate or overthank.

And even among them, I have to call out some who gave extra help with that whole "stupider" thing, namely: Cat B., Clinton Cluchey, Shannon Coleman, Solana Cragun, Stephanie Edrington, Hjordis Eythorsdottir, Doreen Fernandes, Sean Flanagan, Chris Forbes, Carol Ford, Linda Grindstaff, Debra Hartman, Emily Haynes, Patricia Klos, Victoria Morton, Kim Napolitano, Dale Porter, Jen Potcher, Kel Purcill, Mary Jude Schmitz, Christina Smith, Frank Spinney, Cher Spradlin, Barb Stoner, Nicole Toscano, Cyndi Wannamaker, Jenny White, and Kathy Zisek.

That list is in alphabetical order, so no getting uppity, people, or I'll turn this book around and go home – and no, we're not stopping at McDonald's again because you just ask for too much sweet & sour sauce and then we end up spilling it and –

Sorry. That last bit might have been a flashback. Definitely more about me than the folks on the team who helped so much, and who deserve to have pools full of sweet & sour sauce if that's what flips their switches (I try not to judge).

And to my fans and readers: I am blessed beyond measure to have you in my life and for the infinitely appreciated gift of your time.

- Michaelbrent Collings

NOVELS BY MICHAELBRENT COLLINGS

STRANGER STILL
SCAVENGER HUNT
TERMINAL
DARKLING SMILES
PREDATORS
THE DARKLIGHTS
THE LONGEST CON
THE HOUSE THAT DEATH BUILT
THE DEEP
TWISTED
THIS DARKNESS LIGHT
CRIME SEEN
STRANGERS
DARKBOUND
BLOOD RELATIONS:
A GOOD MORMON GIRL MYSTERY
THE HAUNTED
APPARITION
THE LOON
MR. GRAY (aka THE MERIDIANS)
RUN
RISING FEARS

THE COLONY SAGA:
THE COLONY: GENESIS (THE COLONY, Vol. 1)
THE COLONY: RENEGADES (THE COLONY, Vol. 2)
THE COLONY: DESCENT (THE COLONY, VOL. 3)
THE COLONY: VELOCITY (THE COLONY, VOL. 4)
THE COLONY: SHIFT (THE COLONY, VOL. 5)
THE COLONY: BURIED (THE COLONY, VOL. 6)
THE COLONY: RECKONING (THE COLONY, VOL. 7)
THE COLONY OMNIBUS
THE COLONY OMNIBUS II

THE COMPLETE COLONY SAGA BOX SET

YOUNG ADULT AND MIDDLE GRADE FICTION:

THE SWORD CHRONICLES

THE SWORD CHRONICLES: CHILD OF THE EMPIRE
THE SWORD CHRONICLES: CHILD OF SORROWS
THE SWORD CHRONICLES: CHILD OF ASH

THE RIDEALONG
PETER & WENDY: A TALE OF THE LOST
(aka HOOKED: A TRUE FAERIE TALE)
KILLING TIME

THE BILLY SAGA:

BILLY: MESSENGER OF POWERS (BOOK 1)
BILLY: SEEKER OF POWERS (BOOK 2)
BILLY: DESTROYER OF POWERS (BOOK 3)
THE COMPLETE BILLY SAGA (BOOKS 1-3)

Cover image elements by Jorge Casais from Shutterstock.com.
Original map design elements by Ryan Simmons.
Cover design by Michaelbrent Collings.

website: http://writteninsomnia.com
email: info@writteninsomnia.com

For more information on Michaelbrent's books, including specials and sales; and for info about
signings, appearances, and media,
check out his webpage,
Like his Facebook fanpage,
follow him on Twitter,
or
subscribe to his YouTube channel.

Printed in Poland
by Amazon Fulfillment
Poland Sp. z o.o., Wrocław

52478948R00222